From *The New Yorker* to *The Los Angeles Times,* critics raved about Tr[...] novel, *Platitudes.* Now, her[...] new display of what Ishma[...] "humongous talent."

In *Home Repairs,* we come to know Austin McMillan through the pages of his journal, a frank, funny, often overheated self-portrait of a privileged young black man who is obsessed with women. We first meet him at an elite prep school, secretly mortified because at the ripe age of sixteen he has yet to kiss a girl. Wondering where he's gone wrong, he sits down to chronicle his passions, from his first kindergarten crush to the teenage sirens who now overwhelm his dreams.

Though his list grows as he moves on to the Ivy League, the lessons of experience prove all too elusive: a smile still rockets him to manic bliss and a cross word drives him to despair, but his vivid imagination is never matched by the reality of his life. Austin's musings are hilarious and poignant, his pain always masked by humor as he ricochets his way to manhood.

Also by Trey Ellis
Platitudes

Trey Ellis

SIMON
&
SCHUSTER

Home Repairs

New York
London
Toronto
Sydney
Tokyo
Singapore

SIMON & SCHUSTER
Simon & Schuster Building
Rockefeller Center
1230 Avenue of the Americas
New York, New York 10020

SIMON & SCHUSTER and colophon are registered
trademarks of Simon & Schuster Inc.

Designed by Deirdre C. Amthor

Manufactured in the United States of America

10   9   8   7   6   5   4   3   2   1

Library of Congress Cataloging in Publication Data

Ellis, Trey.
   Home repairs : a novel / Trey Ellis.
      p.   cm.
   I. Title.
  PS3555.L617H6   1993
  813'.54—dc20   92-43868
                                    CIP

ISBN: 0-671-76924-3

A special thank you to
Eric,
my agent and my friend.

PART ONE

"To All the Girls I've Loved"

Unbelievable. We danced a few fast songs together and I wasn't too spastic, so I thought maybe I had a shot. A few other guys were swarmed around her as usual (her stretch pants look just like leather until you get in the light, so she is real popular).

1979, wow. The eighties are almost here, I'll be in college for them. You'd think there'd be levitating cars and people living three hundred years, but I bet not. You'd think by then I'd have been laid, but I bet not either.

Anyway, three fast songs in a row ("Brick House," "I Will Survive," and some other disco song), and I'm sure Marshall's going to play a slow song. He almost got kicked out of school for having LaTasha in his room, so I know he's romantic. I sideways between two supertall basketball players standing in front of where she's dancing with Lenny and get ready. I forgot gum again so try to clean and freshen my teeth with my tongue. The disco song sinks and there's a long silence where the mumbles of everybody rise. Joie is so brown she almost disappears under the dim lights until she pulls her pressed wings of black hair out of her face and turns to the light. Her dimples stop me from breathing. She scans her squadron of groupies because *nobody*'d want to slow dance with Lenny and his lard. She looks me right in the eye and freezes my heart. I step back. The speakers softly spit out "Da-da da-da da-

da-dah," the opening trumpet notes to Earth, Wind and Fire's "Reasons." I step forward, but Kofi shoves past me and takes her hand. Kofi's father's like the chief justice of the Supreme Court of Ghana; no wonder he's not shy. Somebody once said we look alike (especially after I've been in the sun and my skin's cleared up a bit).

Anyway, he practically sticks it in her on the dance floor. I don't know what Mr. Mertens was doing, some chaperon. Phillips Academy Saturday dance number 168, still not even a slow dance with a girl. It's too late. I've waited too long. Sixteen and not even a slow dance, forget about a kiss. After college I'll need one of those sexual surrogates just so I can hold down a steady job.

Where was I . . . I just leave the dance, don't hear the music anymore or pseudofriends probably saying good night. Outside I breathe again, gulp the winter blowing mean from New Hampshire. I let its wind, cold and thick like ice water, wrestle my sweater, my chest. The path from the gym to Taylor West, my dorm, is not really lit but bejeweled by tall street lamps. Around each lamp swirls a white Afro of icy wind like the halo on painted candles on Christmas cards. I don't zip my coat and hope for someone even sexier than Joie to see me and realize how sensitive I am and save me before I die. I hate the sound of a party, the feel of a warm room full of people when you're just outside it crunching and slipping over ridges of frozen slush. Main Street is empty, and its black is washed white with dried salt. I say "Hey" to a couple coming toward me on the path as if all systems were go. As Taylor West gets bigger before me, the sound of the TV becomes louder, louder even than the sound of ice exploding beneath my creaking running shoes. A war is going on on "Battlestar Galactica," and Jason, Kip, and the rest of the dorm even nerdier than I (yes) are off on some other planetary system. Inside, I'm the only black kid, so a stranger here, too, and sneak past them and upstairs. I want a Coke, but not the loud rumble of it being slammed down to the slot.

That brings me back up here to my half of our dorm room. I don't know how I'll explain to Kurt what I'm doing here in the dark, alone and clothed. But today, no, Monday, I'm going to change my life. I'm going to lift weights and look at what the cool guys wear and wear those clothes. I'm going to stop eating in Upper Right with Ben, Guy, Jason, and Kip and the rest of those guys right off the "Are You a Nerd?" poster. They are so brainy in their black glasses and too tight pants, they look retarded. How can you blame Joie for not wanting your little wiener schnitzel poking a pinhole in her fake leather pants?

Where did I go wrong? It seems that every weekend of my life since puberty has been this depressing. When I look back on it I see just a string of girls and women I've run after who've run away from me. I've got to figure out what I've been doing wrong before I waste the next sixteen years of my life and I'm *thirty-two years old!*

I'm going to dredge up all the bad memories I've had in my love life and see if hindsight will show me what I've been doing wrong. I need to get better soon—at least before college the year after next. I probably should turn on a light, but I like the glow of the streetlight on my walls, eyesight be damned. So here goes:

R u t h i e

Marquita, my mother, was doing her residency at the University of Michigan, and Fletcher, my dad, was finishing his Ph.D. thesis in sociology. I attended the university's experimental kindergarten and immediately fell in love with Ruthie, the "Kissing Cootie." She was very cute, blond, and used to chase the boys around the playroom, corner and kiss them regardless of race, creed, or coloring. I zigzagged away like the rest of the boys, but never so fast. I never really went through that "Girls are greasy, grimy gopher guts, mutilated monkey meat" stage. I think I was always stupid for them. By now Ruthie must be a superfantastic kisser. When I think that I haven't been kissed again in eleven years I could puke.

Though one day she came in and didn't kiss anyone anymore. She said her parents were getting a divorce (the first I'd known). She said it was because they liked each other too much and didn't want to wreck it. A few days later somebody ran over my fingernail with a scooter and the nail turned black and fell off. It was worth it just to see the wrinkled, scary, and vulnerable skin under my nail.

Lynn Bronson

She must have been in at least sixth or seventh grade, maybe even tenth (it seemed so grown back then). I was in fourth or fifth. Her brother Bobby, a year ahead of me and two feet taller, was my best friend even though they were from Alabama and white. He used to scream he was Stonewall Jackson and chase me and beat me up. But one day walking by the river in back of the A&P, a bunch of black kids from downtown Ypsilanti beat the shit out of him. Anyway, I loved his sister and cut her picture out of the elementary school yearbook and kissed it a thousand times before going to sleep. Then Leslie found it. If I were rich, I swear I'd get her a sex-change operation so I'd have a brother instead. Here's why: Leslie shows the picture to Lynn, lip stains and all. Even now my heart gets a little too big and cramps my lungs when I think about it. My sister, Bobby, Lynn, my parents, could talk of nothing but my perversion for weeks. Shortly afterward I felt a lump in my ten-year-old chest and became convinced I was dying of breast cancer. I told my sister that I loved her.

Weed Whacking

I wish I could remember exactly what day it was, that night in fifth grade. I don't know how it even occurred to me. Clogs had just come into style, and some of the older girls at Spring Glenn were wearing them with their sundresses. Brenda O'Donnel and

Elise Grassa were best friends, sixth-graders, and were crouched over a stray dog in the playground, petting it. Forget about their new boobs in the stretchy tops of their dresses. It was their bare heels and the clean, vulnerable soles of their feet rising out of the sheath of blue-and-red velour clogs that made it hard for me to keep standing. Infrared photography would have revealed all the heat in my body transferred to my crotch. I could hear the blood surging out of my brain, past my ears, and down. I wouldn't have been surprised if the energy then bursting my Sears Toughskins jeans zipper had levitated me three feet in the air, suspended me from my center of gravity. Brenda and Elise stood up, clapping closed the arch of their feet on the smooth wood of their Dutch-inspired shoes, and the spell was broken. I fell back to earth.

That night in bed, after Mary Tyler Moore, Bob Newhart, and Carol Burnett, a flashback of their feet visited me there on the top bunk. Leslie was asleep in her room, my parents were watching TV in theirs. The masking tape holding my *MAD* magazine mini-posters to the wall in front of me was going hard and stale, and the torn pages were peeling down my wall. With the sound of passing cars came their headlights projecting the shadow of my windowsill on the far wall of my room, sliding it over, up to the ceiling, and out. I thought it might snap in my underwear, so I took them off. I didn't really know what was happening down there, so I checked it out. It didn't hurt to touch it. At all. In fact . . . Checking and double-checking to make sure my dick was fine, the world closed in on me and I felt purely self-sufficient. I felt a pleasant humming. I felt the blood in my veins. I felt . . . Holy shit! What the hell was that! I stared at my dick as it twitched alone like a dying man being fibrillated with those cool electric paddles. It no longer wanted to play. You know how in shows like "My Favorite Martian" Bill Bixby, in the first episode, discovers that the truly extraordinary and unexplainable exists in his own backyard? Well, that's how I felt. If I could lift a hundred times my weight or read minds after that night, I wouldn't have been surprised.

I had my secret for a school year before I learned its name.

Then one night I pulled away my hand and some sort of gross glue webbed my fingers. I knew it was cancer. Something worse than blood. "All right. All right," I remember telling myself. "Enough of that. It was fun while it lasted, but that's it. The end."

Teachers and Halter Tops

I've fallen in love with every lady teacher I've ever had, even mustachioed Mrs. Raspy.

Halter tops and sunglasses have always been my favorites. I remember riding my bike back from the Hamden Plaza shopping mart when this lady in a convertible VW drove past me. "My God, a topless lady's driving around in a convertible bug just like Lady Godiva!" She was halfway up the hill, but the light was just turning red. I blasted up the hill as fast as I could on my little banana-seated Stingray (remember, that was way back in the days before bicycles had gears). I was almost there, I was, when the light went green. She tried to put her orange bug in gear but rolled back three feet and crumpled my front wheel.

"My God, little boy, are you all right?"

She ratcheted up her emergency brake stick and flew back to me. From the front, her halter was relatively modest. Her hair had been covering the strap behind her neck, leaving her back naked to the waist. Out of her straw purse with little yellow straw flowers sewn on it she pulled out the first fifty-dollar bill I'd ever seen.

Shawniqua

Sixth-grade summer, Dayton, Ohio. I spent a few weeks each summer with my mother's parents and they always rolled out the red carpet, so it wasn't bad. Shawniqua lived next door to them, and Leslie, Shawniqua, and I would play in the dirt and shoot

BB guns together. Grandma took us to Cedar Point one day. On the Screamin' Eagle roller coaster Leslie sits in the car in front of us, poking her arms in the air on the way to the top of the big hill. Shawniqua had been leaning into me all day, and I was beginning to feel something even though she was overweight and not so good-looking. I wait until we're at the very top of the clank-clankety chain pull to the top of the first rail hill, the scariest place in the world, and lay my arm over her shoulder. On the way down, fast, she cuddles into my side, screaming. I felt like a man. After that I sort of stayed away from her. I spent the last weeks hunting my grandpa's front yard with an old broomstick with a nail on one end, gigging wastepaper in the grass. I probably broke her heart, and that's why the rest of my life has been one cruddy dry spell.

Cynthia

Back in regular, nonboarding private school, Cynthia Brown was one of the few other black kids there. I made the mistake of telling my mom I liked her. All excited, she tells me to ask her to the talent show, tells me even what to say. Leslie had never been happier, dancing on the grave of my dignity. On the kitchen phone I dialed and tried to ask her out, but I couldn't get air past the top of my chest. I just wanted to instantaneously vaporize. She said she was doing something like donating a kidney the night of the talent show, then of course shows up with her girlfriends, who huff and wobble their eyes in their heads when they see me.

Columbus, Ohio

I still don't really remember what happened that night. I would ask Leslie if she wasn't such a jerk. My aunt Rita, who looks like Lena Horne and is about the same age, has a rich friend, a guy she jerked around and didn't marry who became a millionaire. He's got kids my age. He's got a big boat on a lake and a Kawasaki jet ski and a Porsche 911 Carrera. The son was weird. He and his best friend would go around all the time and not include me in anything. But the daughter (I wish I could remember her name, it was only two years ago), her folks had carted her off to a military academy to calm her down. It wasn't working. She was flirting up a storm with me even though she was older and pretty cute. So there we are, jet skiing and playing on the boat until late. I don't remember how we ate, but before you know it it's bedtime. The son and his friend lock themselves in the main bedroom and make noises like they're having sex for hours. They were really stupid. The girl, Leslie, their baby eight-year-old sister, and I were forced to all share the pull-out sofabed. I'm grossed out about sleeping in the same bed as my sister, especially with this flirtatious sexy girl in the same bed. What if I popped a boner over the girl and accidentally rolled onto Leslie? I'd start hanging the neighbor's cats and conducting black masses in the basement.

So I go to sleep in the construction site of steel struts and sharp springs that is the land below a sofabed. I hug the pillow and think of this girl, when I hear her above me. "It *is* too crowded up here." Movements above me threaten to squash my head, my knee. Then I see bare feet and legs to the side of the bed. She was sleeping in a man's football jersey like sexy Susan St. James in "McMillan and Wife." I had all my clothes on. I turned away and pretended to sleep when I felt her climb under with me. Oh, Lord, I remember praying, I know I prayed to get laid, but I'm too young and my sister's right above me. So there she is right next to me, warm like a radiator, and I scoot my butt back, now full in the wash of her heat (note: use "wash of her heat" in a creative-writing assignment someday). My heart's twitches batter my chest, raise me off the floor. I millimeter a heel behind me—more and more— until it finds her bare shin and surges energy into me. A milestone, my first bare shin. Count, Austin, count, I say to myself. On ten just turn and kiss, on ten. "One . . . two . . ." Not so slow, stupid, she'll have fallen asleep. But she's got to want it; why else would she have come down here? But what about Leslie? I'll be nervous enough about getting it up without bashing my sister from below on every upswing.

Turn! I scream inside my head, and I do and maybe I try and kiss her, maybe I try and touch, but all I remember is screaming and confusion and then nothing. I swear to God I don't know if I dreamed it all or not. But if she really had screamed, Leslie would be teasing me about it to this day. Maybe it's like one of those "psychological thrillers"? Maybe something really awful happened that night and when I remember it I'll finally be cured.

Heather Nallabuona

She had the finest butt in all of my old high school. I know I'm supposed to be more romantic than that, but it was the truth. When she walked past me I couldn't think. Asking her out was out of the question. She was in and I was out. This was two years ago. I had already been accepted as a transfer to good ol' Phillips Academy, Andover, so this spring trimester of ninth grade I couldn't have cared less about the jerks I was leaving behind.

We had assigned seating in school assembly at the old school. It was a waste of time, cops coming in lighting fake marijuana incense or the headmaster reading off yesterday's always losing scores. But behind my row of L and M last names (Lanovic, Lilto, Lode, McMillan—Amy, McMillan—Austin, that's me, and the Matto twins) sat the row of Ns, Ps and Qs. Heather Nannabuona almost always ended up right behind me during the exiting shuffle. And each morning I'd be happy.

With five days left of school the idea came to me. Maybe (I thought back then when I was even stupider), maybe if I could just touch her butt, then my at that time fourteen-year losing streak would break. As soon as the idea crawled into my sick brainpan I knew it was a good one. I grinned for days just thinking about it. In my fantasy under the covers of my bunk bed she'd catch me in the act and realize the demented depths of my love for her and invite me to partake of her family's swimming pool that I was sure she, as a rich Woodbridge kid, would have had. (Maybe I'm getting a little better now that I'm a junior. These thoughts seem crazy even to me now.)

So every day throughout that week I timed my paces with hers, practiced the sweep of my hand to her butt, then the scoot around to her side. What could go wrong?

This, perhaps: "Hey, did you see that? Austin just pinched Heather's ass!" A commotion would arise and I'd soon be surrounded by hundreds of laughing, snarling shithead students. She'd glower at me, and I'd tremble. She'd be fighting back obscenities, then poke me in the breastbone and exhale a "Ha!" so overfilled with pitying derision that I would swoon on the spot and awaken hours later in the nurse's office to the scowl of Assistant Headmaster Collins.

I carried on with the plan anyway. I knew that if I didn't go through with it, I'd feel even more the failure.

Thursday, the day before the end of this crappy school, and I'm ready. As the cop tells us not to accept stamps from strangers this summer because the glue on the back is probably really LSD, I keep turning around to the empty chair behind mine. Somebody must have tipped her off. I was sure the authorities were waiting for me outside.

Friday. Chris, Morgan, and the rest of my friends still don't know what's up. I'm wearing a brand-new striped, short-sleeved button-down for the occasion. I even splashed on a drop of Dad's Aramis but washed it off with soap. She'd tell the cops he smelled like Aramis and their German shepherds would hunt me down in Bio. Anyway, I don't hear a word of the assembly. I guess he wished us a safe and productive summer. My ears are tuned only to her breathing, her heartbeat, to the bell at 9:05 signaling dismiss.

BINGbingBING

Folks cheer, crowd to the aisle. Jeans, she's wearing jeans, and the sight of her butt almost paralyzes me with joy. I step past those between us and shadow her. The sharp light of outside is coming fast, and the safety of the crowd will soon dissipate. I swing low my hand and do pinch her butt, as firm as honeydew. I want to stop, look at my hand that has just had communion with paradise, but I do slide past her, as she, startled, turns away from me and behind herself. I suppress a sprint but speed outside and down the stairs to the Drama Department bathroom. Inside a stall I scribble in pen on the gray-painted steel, "I Pinched Heather Nallabuona's Ass!!!!" Then I cackled like a nut, uncontrollably, for minutes and minutes. If the school assembly cop had been within earshot, he'd have been sure I'd licked a whole book of stamps. I was so happy. The Bio exam was just starting, but I didn't really care. I wasn't a coward anymore (until tonight).

J e n n y

I met her last summer on the Vineyard, and we're long-distance boyfriend and girlfriend, though we haven't kissed yet. We used to rent my dad's boss's house in Truro, on Cape Cod, but last summer they decided to try Martha's Vineyard because there are other black people there. I imagined a cottage on the beach, but instead we were in a prefabricated housing development on sand landfill far from the water. Our house was Amazon tree frog green or maybe pistachio. As I wrestled the cooler from between my legs, then, outside, wrestled the bikes off the roof, I sensed the body of a next-door neighbor but couldn't see them through their screen door in the bright light.

That night I was killing Leslie at Jarts in the back when next door's back door opened. Cute, I thought, but nothing to bark at the moon about. Then she walked right up to me, not Leslie. "You have any gum?" She was already chewing a steak-size clump. The heat she caused in me would have dried my clothes—if they'd been wet. I vowed to carry a pack of Bubble Yum with me (even though I don't chew it) for just such occasions, the way grown-up guys who don't even smoke carry elegant lighters.

A week later she—

"Austin?" Kurt stiffens in the doorway and pushes in the old-fashioned button that turns on the light. I'll hide you among the dust bunnies behind the radiator.

> *He's finally asleep, or jerking his chain in his room. I told
> him I was fine, plenty of people sit in dark rooms alone, he
> just never knew because he never lived with one. It's mid-
> night. I'd like to stay up all night getting my life together, or
> at least down in this journal, so by dawn I'd finish and step
> outside into the cold, pink light of dawn in my robe, cured.
> But I haven't lived enough. I'll be done by one.*

A week later Jenny and I are best friends. She's tiny, as brown
as wood, but has bright green eyes. We went with her mom and
brother and sister and Leslie to South Beach one day, and of course
I got to see her in a bathing suit. Still, I've seen *Playboy* women
and *Penthouse* women, too. My feelings for Jenny aren't "wham,
bam, thank you, ma'am," at all. We shared our own loaf of Portuguese sweet bread and lay on a big towel by ourselves. She asked
me if I was a good kisser, and I told her I hadn't gotten any
complaints. I'm still proud of this line because it was (is) the truth.
My pillow and thousands of pictures in porn mags haven't yet
complained about the way I kiss. Of course she said she's this
Olympic kisser, and as she was talking she was smacking away at
the Bubble Yum or maybe Bubblicious by now, but grape, anyway, and her lips put like a tractor beam on my brain, and if
her mom and Leslie hadn't been around I swear I'd have tried
something.

A few days later just the two of us were sitting around the housing
development's pool in the middle of the night (at least ten o'clock),
listening to the bugs being zapped by the people in the real house
across the street.

"Austin, do you know what the bases are?"

"Of course. We have girls down in Hamden, Connecticut, you
know."

"So how far have you been?"

"Let's just say I'm one of the league's most valuable players."
I said this, I really did. It's the single greatest line I've ever
uttered.

"Yeah, right." Then she laughed. "So what's first base?"

....

"Kissing, all right? Making out. Everybody knows that."

"Second?"

"Touching, a breast."

"Through a shirt or bare?"

"Uh . . ."

"Most valuable player, I'm *sure*."

"Look, maybe you don't know, but when you're in medias res— that's Latin for 'in the middle of things,' in case you didn't know— you don't have time to keep score." I can't believe I talked to her like that. Maybe I'm not such a spaz after all. Jenny brings out the best in me. I'm suave and electrified every time we talk about sex and stuff.

"I want to give you a psychological test."

"I hate tests. My dad's a sociologist, and my sister and I spent our childhood playing with army men in white rooms or looking at pictures of animals chewing each other up for three dollars an hour for all his friends. I made enough money to buy a gas-powered model dragster, but I'm sick of them already."

"What's your favorite color?"

"I don't know . . . blue."

"What's your second favorite color?"

"Yellow, I guess."

"What's your favorite body of water?"

"What? I don't know. A pond."

"You wake up suddenly and you're in an all white room. Where are you?"

"I hate these things."

"C'mon. If you don't answer, it's worse."

"I don't know . . . a hospital. . . . Why are you frowning? What? How'd I do?"

"Well, your favorite color is how you see yourself—blue. And your second favorite is how others see you—yellow—"

"That's a bunch of crap, let me take it aga—"

"Your favorite body of water is how you make love. You said a pond. I said crashing waves."

"That's what I meant to say, wait—"

"And if you're a happy person, the white room is heaven. If you're unhappy, it's a hospital."

"Fuck."

Her little sister, Gail, came over even though it was late.

"Hi, Austin, would you like a Nutter-Butter?" Gail was always offering me stuff like I could be her elementary school friend or something. "Jenny, Mom says are you packed yet because Dad says we're going to try for standby for the six o'clock ferry."

"You don't have our address, do you? Gail, go get some paper and a pencil." Gail twirled around and raced two paces in her flip-flops, then tripped, kicked them into the dark, and skittered to her house like a little animal in the woods. (This all happened last summer, and next summer's only a few months away. I can't believe I'm so depressed over Joie when Jenny's up there in Spring-field, Mass., waiting for me.) They left that morning. I set my alarm for six and watched her go, through my screen.

That next day I mailed her a shoebox full of Bubble Yum. By the time I got back to Hamden I still hadn't heard from her and was a little jittery, but four weeks and three days later I received my very first love letter:

Hey Austin Big Mac Attack!

You don't mind me calling you that do you, Austin? Even though we just met this summer I think we'll be around each other for a long time. It was a gas talking to you about the bases and kissing and stuff. A lot of guys get so shy and clam up when the talk gets sexy. Oh, THANKS FOR THE BUB-BLE YUM!!!! I'm chewing on it right now. The 'rents are p.o.'d at you because they were trying to get me to cut down. I stick the used blobs all over the house under things I'm sure Moms will never find but she does and goes schizo. "You look like a cow, young lady," bla-dy, bla-dy, bla. I'm chewing three squares at one time now and my jaw is like on fire it's so sore, but it should make me an even better kisser.

*School is already started and it might just be a good year.
The PSATs are coming up but I'm not too worried about
them. I'm also probably going to be a yell leader for football.
Mr. Lilly, my homeroom teacher, is the coach and says I've
got such a big mouth it's a shame to waste it in classes. He's
a jerk and I think a pervert too but it might be fun anyway.*

                                                    See ya next summer,

                                                  Love, JENNY

I wrote her another letter and am waiting for her reply. She's
so wild, so alive, she makes me less gloomy and uptight.

That's it. That was my life—at least the sexy bits. Writing it
down helped, I think. Sure I'm a loser, but I've had some fun as
well. Thinking about Jenny and her craziness and her smile makes
me think there's hope for me yet. I'm sure she's one of the most
popular girls in her school, but she likes me. I didn't realize that
having a girlfriend like Jenny would be like me going out with
Virginia Pena or Marie Fanzinger or one of the other ultrababes
on the gymnastics team. Here at school you couldn't pay them to
even hold my hand (unless we were in a play or something. That's
actually a good idea. There's often a make-out scene in a play).
Maybe I'm different in the summer. Maybe that's what I'm going
to grow up to be.

Anyway, from this night forward I'll write down everything that
happens between me and girls. In History 35 last week we learned
that the Puritans kept diaries and would read them only after many
years, hoping to notice the hand of God shaping the long run of
their lives. Maybe I too will notice a pattern and stop screwing
up. Maybe ten years from now (when I'm twenty-six!), Miss September and I will laugh over this pathetically cute adolescent angst
on our Hawaiian honeymoon.

J o i e

Yahoo! Last week's all-school dance I didn't hover around her waiting for a dance, and maybe she missed me or something because this weekend, at the "Af-Lat-Am" (Afro-Latino-American Society) dance, while everyone else was bouncing with so much rhythm that the 115-year-old Peabody House's second floor rose and fell like the deck of a ship, Joie kept staring at me. She was dancing with Akbar, who's really big and good-looking for girls who like humongous guys, but she kept looking my way and smiling. This was all during "Play That Funky Music, White Boy." I look to Marshall, and he holds up the next record and smiles at it like he loves it, so I guess it's going to be a great slow song. I march out on the dance floor even though "White Boy" isn't over yet, just repeating and going softer and softer. Joie looks under Akbar's shoulder to me and smiles. I cough to lubricate the old vocal cords—now would be no time for a voice crack. But I don't even have to say anything, she just steps past him and we stand at each other, waiting for the next song. I can't believe it's "Just to Be Close to You, Girl" by the Commodores. It's the most romantic song in the world and of course now my favorite ("No one to love, and no one to love me but me. Aw, girl, then you came into my life, you made my jaged edges straight . . ."). She holds her hands out like she's going to catch me, and I *did* feel like falling, but we shuffle into each other's arms. I sense her heat a foot before I touch her. Her smell of sweat and Lauren perfume intoxicate. Then I become aware of my boner and stick my butt out a bit to hide it in the nest of my crotch. I try not to flinch when we touch and open my eyes wide to record everything to report back to you, Mr. Journal.

Slowly, slowly, we sway back and forth, barely moving, almost imperceptibly turning in a small, small circle. She is so warm. I am so content. She moves her thigh and bumps my sharp dick but doesn't scream. I feel some part of her face on my neck, I think her lips, but I'm not sure. My whole body is humming like an electric transformer, humming so loudly inside of me that she must have heard it.

And I didn't want to do anything else with her, either. I didn't want to throw her down on the dance floor and go apeshit. Slow dancing alone was more wonderful than I'd imagined. I could keep doing this for years before I needed to move on to actual in and out naked stuff. Besides, I couldn't really control myself just *dancing*. If I tried anything more, I'd probably come before my pants dropped to the ground.

March 16, 1979

Joie

I never thought we were boyfriend and girlfriend or anything, but I didn't think she was so easy. I asked her to the Friday flicks, but she said she was busy. I found out from Marshall that Akbar's parents were in town, and he invited her with them for dinner at the posh Andover Inn. I guess that's why she slow danced with him tonight. But for the next slow dance there I was, but she said she'd promised Kofi. I asked Anita to dance and she said yes, but it wasn't the same. I kept wanting to look over to Kofi and see if she was nibbling his neck. In Africa they probably lose their virginity at eleven in some sort of wild ritual with beautiful and experienced topless women.

April 4, 1979

Weight Lifting

As I wrote in the first entry, I was going to try to change myself even though I live in the nerd dorm and have geek friends. I've been going to the weight room for the last two months, and I think it's helping. At first I tried to go late, when the jocks wouldn't be there, but I didn't have time to study and AP Calc was (is) kicking my butt. After Search & Rescue (which, during the week, is pretty low key, just climbing small boulders in the quarry or practicing map orienteering in the sanctuary), I'd rush to the gym, but the lacrosse jocks (wearing T-shirts that say "Chicks Love Our Sticks") would already be there. I was about as tall as most of them, but they could fly up the pegboard/climb the rope/bench press twice as fast/as fast/as much as me. The PG football players, gigantor Medford and Lowell Red Sox fans, funny-talking townies usually more racist than southerners, are nice to me in the gym for some reason. Or not nice, actually, but helpful.

"Come on, ya wimp. One more"—pronounced *mo-ah*—"or I throw you out of here"—*he-ah*—"on your asshole." I bench 165 now, when two months ago I was lucky to lift 135. I'm just a *Playboy* magazine width away from six feet, and with luck I still might grow. I wish I knew how tall my birth parents were (are?), so I'd have a clue how I'll turn out.

April 10, 1979

Paul Revere House

So maybe it was a little stupid and 1950s-ish, but it was scary and fun and the closest any of us in Taylor West will probably ever come to girls' panties. I don't know who thought it up first, but Guy, Jason, Kip, and I guess me myself—all of us uppers— were the actual planners. All the seniors except Simon DePetris thought they were too cool to come, even though most of them had never touched one, either.

It was exciting to go to bed at ten and get up at two. At first Kurt didn't want to come because his History 35 term paper was behind schedule, but we all shamed him into going. Everybody but Marty was in, but we're all sure he's queer. We asked Jason, his roommate, but he just gets all quiet. I don't know if he made a move on him or what.

We met in the common room because it's semidetached from the dorm so Mr. Geddes won't hear anybody giggle. We all brought ski masks or bandannas and flashlights. I headed Alpha company. Kurt and four lowers were in my squad. One of them, Danny, was wearing a bright yellow "Smith College, a century of women on top" T-shirt, and I made him change to something dark like we'd said. We were the first out the door.

I wish we had known when the campus police made their rounds. Instead we just scampered down the bright path to Main Street, doubled over, waddling. Across the street we could hide among the school buildings on our way to our objective, Paul Revere, the biggest girls' dorm. We waited in the bushes, teeth chattering. I didn't think the spring could be so cold, but I'd never known it at 2:30 A.M.

Finally Bravo and then Charlie companies showed up without too many hitches. A couple of guys wimped out, but they'll be sorry later. Guy and Kip and two lowers were getting the ladder from the West Quad South toolshed and were going to meet us at Sam Phil Hall afterward. They wanted it that way. They said they didn't mind not being in on the actual raid.

I look to everybody, who're looking to me for the signal. I must admit it felt great. I mouthed the countdown and nodded my head with each number ("three, two, one . . ."), then I said, *"Go!"* and the sound in all that silence shot us all. But they sprinted past me and into the girls' dorm *shouting*, Alpha company to the third floor, Bravo second, and Charlie first. I ran in last to meet Alpha company up top; craziness was everywhere, twenty-five unlaid adolescents *screaming* in the girls' dorm. The lawlessness of it all fired me. A few girls came out of their room just as I jumped the last stair to the third floor. They were pissed. The guys suddenly got real quiet and studied their sneakers.

"What the fuck do you nerds think you're doing?"

This we hadn't planned on. Then Danny comes out of nowhere and shrieks, "Your panties or your life, Miss Curler-head!" See, the girl had been sleeping with curlers in her head. This unlocks us, and we all *shout* and run past her into the open rooms and steal panties from their top dresser drawers.

The problem was, we only had about three panties, and that wouldn't be enough if the other floors didn't do much better. The ten other doors on the floor were still closed and you can't very well knock during a panty raid, so I grabbed the doorknob of a closed door near me—quickly but not so sure, as if it might have been hot—and turned it and entered. Maybe I'd have seen the girl masturbating with a vibrator or two girls in a lesbian love nest on the single bed, or God knows what else. Instead, a not-so-pretty girl from Kurt's calc class has slept through all the noise, and I whip open her panty drawer and leave without disturbing her. Then behind me I run into Mrs. Stableton, Paul Revere's house counselor, and, more important, my Latin teacher.

"Austin! Get you and these boys out of here this instant!"

I question my planning skills. This moment, which seems so logical now at four o'clock in the morning, I had failed to foresee. Alpha company fell all over itself in a rush down the narrow steps. I don't know why nobody died.

Outside, Bravo and Charlie companies awaited us. Everybody's giggling. I'm the only one pissed. But the other guys scored fifteen panties in all, and that would be more than enough. But most of the guys hobbled back to Taylor West while Kurt and Danny and I rush to Sam Phil with the loot to meet Guy and his crew. They'd already set up the ladder and hung the sign that read "Taylor West Presents." We all rushed to write a letter on each panty, and we screwed up so there were too many r's and not enough e's, but luckily panties have two sides. I don't know what the campus police were doing, but they never came. We strung up "P.A.U.L. R.E.V.E.R.E.," a letter on each panty, and ran back home.

Mr. Geddes stood in his doorway in his ratty bathrobe as we got in. He was trying to scowl, but you could tell he wanted to smile. He just shook his head.

"I don't want Mrs. Stableton to ever have to wake me up again, okay, boys?"

"Yes, Mr. G."

Upstairs, everybody else went right to sleep. I had to write this all down. I've never seen four o'clock before. I like it. It's like you moved to a different planet that looks just like this one but empty and dark. I feel like I'm the only one awake sometimes during the day, but at four in the morning you *know* it's pretty much true.

Maybe we'll be famous tomorrow. Certainly *The Phillipian* will take a picture. Maybe some girls will think we're charming.

April 22, 1979

Jenny

Here's a copy of the letter I wrote her today:

Dear Jenny,

School is great, but I can't wait until this summer to be back on the beach. The only bad part will be that I will be away from the gym for a whole month. Did I tell you I've taken up weight lifting? It's not boring like people say at all. Only thing is, I'm not used to being treated like a piece of meat. Everybody's commenting on the "new me," guys and girls, now that spring is here and I'm wearing T-shirts. The girls just come up sometimes and grab my biceps and say, "Austin! What happened?" Some of their boobs have grown this year a lot, but you don't see me coming up and grabbing them.

Besides that, I've been studying hard. I guess you'll take the SATs next year. They're the same as the PSATs but scarier because they're real. It's weird thinking about college in the eleventh grade (they call us "uppers" here, no relation to the drugs). Do you still want to go to Wellesley? Stanford's still my first choice because I'd kill to live in California, but Yale would be sort of fun because I grew up there. If I don't get into either, I'll hitchhike across America or become a soldier

*of fortune in Africa or go to Cornell or Duke or someplace
like that.*
I can't wait to see you this summer.

Very truly yours,
Austin

M a y 1 0 , 1 9 7 9

M s. R o d

She's been my Lit B teacher all spring trimester. I had seen her
around campus and had thought she was cute, but after two months
of boring Jane Austen with her, I'm falling desperately in love.
She's really young, maybe even under thirty, and has these huge
black eyes and eyelashes that shoot out from her huge eyes like
parts of an explosion, frozen in midburst. She's very smart too
and suggests all these wonderful books to read. She thinks I'm
funny. I make her laugh at least once every class. There's this
picture from *Playboy* this guy in the dorm showed me for Viva
lingerie entitled "Dress the Night Fantastic." In it, this sexy lady
is wearing this pink negligée with this pink boa while sexily in-
trospecting herself in a full-length mirror. One leg is bent up on
a counter to show off a creamy thigh and this supersexy high-
heeled sandal with poufy pink fur over the strap over her red
toenails. It's just about the sexiest image I've ever seen. And Hugh
Hefner—Hef—can just summon her to his office and have his
way with her. (When I think about how lucky this guy is, I just
scream.) Anyway, the lady in the picture has big eyes like Ms.
Rod, so for about two months now I think about her dressed like
that while I whack off into my sock in bed. I read somewhere
about postcoital depression. That's true. I always feel like shit right
after I do it. It must be something in our genes to keep the pop-
ulation down or at least to spread out the time between babies.
    Ms. Rod has an incredible body, but I didn't notice it until
Pete, my friend in class, said so. That's how in love I am. But

now I notice the clasp of her bra that pokes out of the back of her blouse. I pray she's coming to my side of the class to erase something. Her whole body wiggles and her butt dances in my face. I strain a look between the buttons of her blouse when she leans over a desk to explain to a stupid PG (postgraduate) jock the function of lightning in *Wuthering Heights*. I notice the eight inches of calf visible between her skirt and her shoes. Her calves actually are pretty weighty, but, hey, nobody's perfect.

About ten days ago she leaned over me, and for long moments I was actually living on her perfume vapor instead of oxygen, like the first prehistoric fish that flopped up on shore and didn't die. I thought my hard-on was going to knock over my desk. Then just today something so great happened, I wish I had my camera.

She was handing back these papers we wrote on "wealth as metaphor" in *Pride and Prejudice,* and as she handed me mine she bent over, and I guess an extra blouse button was open or something, but I saw this mountain of cleavage and just about fainted. I got a bad grade on the paper (to me the book's a boring soap opera) but didn't care. I wonder if she did it on purpose just to see me sitting there with my mouth dropped low. I think I actually made this sighing noise, low, like coming, when I saw it. Maybe she gets off knowing that every night dozens of horny boys are humping their pillows and whispering her name. But no. She's too sweet for that. She's only been here one year, but she's leaving in June to teach at MIT. She promises she'll keep in touch. I hope so. Next year, with a letter of recommendation from an assistant prof. at MIT, Stanford wouldn't dare turn me down.

M a y 1 2, 1 9 7 9

J o i e

Yahoooo! I've slow danced with her a few times, but tonight I decided to go for more. I was feeling depressed and needed something good in my life. The Af-Lat-Am had its elections today. I was running for treasurer since I knew no one would elect me president. But I got killed anyway, by Janine, a lower who isn't even good at math. So maybe my best friends at school aren't black kids, that doesn't mean I can't keep track of how much we spend at dances on Hawaiian Punch.

So after dinner I went back to the Af-Lat-Am, pissed and determined to zero in on Joie. There we were on the dance floor, and the heat and sweet funk was just rising from her hot neck like the smell of good food cooking on a stove. Like Dracula I dug into her neck and kissed it, and I could feel her stiffen, then get back in the beat and knead my boner with her thigh (sheathed in the flimsiest Danskin wraparound skirt). It was then that I felt it. Wet on my neck. My whole body was sweetly electrocuted. When she raised her lips her spit on my neck felt so cool, though the rest of me glowed so hot. I'm on the road to being normal, I remember thinking.

We danced some more fast songs, just the two of us, then Donna Summer's "Last Dance" came on and she danced with Akbar. Still, when the lights went up (and I realized what an ugly place for the sexiest moment of my life), Joie came back to me and asked me if I'd walk her home. When perfect words are said you don't believe them.

I sort of laid my hand on her hip, high and away from her butt. Okay, actually I held it there near her hip and only once in a while touched her. We didn't say anything all the way home, I just kept licking my lips to try to instantly remoisturize them before the first kiss. Underneath the ivy-covered doorway of her dorm I turned toward her and slowly, painfully slowly, tilted my head to kiss her. My mouth was open just wide enough, I thought, halfway between prudish and lewd. In my head I started to count. On twenty I'd dive in. Around twelve she said, "Thanks and goodbye," and bounced inside. Walking home, I touched the side of my neck and I swear to God it was still a little wet.

M a y 1 4 , 1 9 7 9

J o i e

I just came back from Latin. Walking through the quad, I saw her with her friends and, after practicing to myself a few times, barked a chipper "Hi!" She smiled a crinkly, flabby smile and guided her friends away from me. She asked me to walk her home, then I didn't try and kiss her. She hates me now. . . . I'm late for AP Calc.

Shit!! I searched her out in the dining hall and found her in lower left. Two of her friends were just leaving, so I took one of their seats without even asking. She looked around me and behind her for relief from this tiresome bore—me. I was on the verge of swallowing my fork and ending it all. I looked her dead in her beautiful, vast, sensuous brown pools called eyes and forgot my question. Like a witch, she has an invisible power over me. I can't believe how long we were silent. Then she spoke: "Look, Austin, last night was fun, but let's end it there." When death-carrying words are said I don't believe them, either. How can the same language you use to order extra jimmies on butter pecan twirl at Brigham's be used to snatch out your insides? As soon as I've convinced myself that Joie, the goddess of beauty, really liked me, she left. I wasn't in love with her, by any means, but you never know. I guess I had been silent again for I don't even know how long when I whined, "But why? What did I do wrong?" She said nothing, just squashed her rice pudding against the side of its bowl.

"Joie, did you hear me?"

"Yes."

She breathed loudly a few times, hinting for me not to press it, but I wasn't going anywhere. "It's just that I don't like anyone around me *all* the time, you know? Just not all the time."

"*All* right."

....

M a y   3 0 ,   1 9 7 9

J e n n y

She just sent me this postcard:

Dear Austin,
  I can't wait to check out your new hot bod on the beach!
I bet all the chicks are warm for your form.
                                   Love, Jenny

P.S. Write back! I love getting letters!

M a y   3 0 ,   1 9 7 9

Dear Jenny,
  I should be studying for exams, but your lovely postcard
clouds my thoughts and I can think of nothing but you, but
us. I ache for this summer; the fresh wind on the ferry as
the seagulls surf the wind we spill begging for french fries;
us lying on the beach hand in hand, heart in heart, as the
surf rises to tickle our feet.
  Our first kiss shall be magnificent.
                                   Love, Austin

Those are the best sentences I've ever written. I'd like to fit them
in somehow to a paper so Ms. Rod can see how I can really write
when I feel the assignment.

I've just copied over this letter to a nice piece of paper, but you'll
never believe it, *I've lost her address!!* She didn't leave it on the
postcard and I can't find her last letter, though I've looked everywhere. She's going to think I hate her and bring some jock goon
with her to the Vineyard. I'll have no choice but to challenge
him. After my lip is split and my eyes swollen shut, maybe then

she'll realize how much I care for her and send him away and nurse me back to health.

June 9, 1979

Joie

I'll try to remain calm and write legibly and tell this story in chronological order.

I had my last exam this morning, History 35, and it was hard but not terrible. I'm pretty sure I clinched a spot on this term's honor roll. If I concentrate and grade grub enough to get on the honor roll fall term of next year as well, I'll be a shoo-in for cum laude come spring.

Anyway, I was feeling great and everybody is hugging and saying "See you next year," except the seniors, who get to leave for good. Almost everybody not a senior is leaving this afternoon, but Mom and Dad aren't coming to pick me up until tomorrow morning, so tonight I felt sort of out of it in the dining hall with all the seniors excited and already distant and me just feeling more of the same. This year was okay, better than last year at my old school, but boarding school didn't turn me into a suave non-virgin as I'd hoped. So I'm up in the room, alone, since Kurt left, and that's nice. I thought maybe I'd weed whack like six times in a row to celebrate or something, but I was still shell-shocked from the physics exam (though I'm now sure I aced it) and fell asleep at nine.

Suddenly the door was alive with movement and noise. I watched it in half sleep and only eventually understood the pounding. I arranged my underwear, stood behind the door, opened it a crack, and bent around it.

"A girl's downstairs to see you, believe it or not," said some senior.

It didn't matter who it was. I pulled on three pairs of pants before deciding on my burgundy corduroys and slid into my Qiana shirt with the cowboys and wagons on it. Even though it's a little stained, it's the only cool thing I own. I ran to the bathroom, but as quietly as possible, and I leaned into the wall so she wouldn't be able to see me from the stairwell. Splashing cold water from the sink, I rubbed the gunk from the edges of my eyes, combed out my Afro as best I could. It's too long and the back was hopelessly matted from sleeping on it, but the pain of trying to inflate it woke me up even more. I reached inside my shirt, rubbed a damp washcloth under each arm, and scratched a gland (I'm sure I'll never sweat on my left side again).

I watched myself in the mirror and didn't hate what I saw. I unbuttoned the shirt an extra step and flexed my new pecs and relaxed them, over and over to try to pump them up before the meeting.

Okay. I stepped down the stairs, one at a time for the first time ever, like a prince.

"Dad, I'll be right there. I don't know what's keeping him."

Joie stared upward, her neck so long, from the mouth of the stairs. I saw her and smiled, and she smiled back.

"I was on my way out when I remembered we hadn't said good-bye."

She looked like an angel: her hair, a swirling black mass, like a nightcloud, dared not venture 'neath her shoulders; instead, when it reached that barrier, it swirled back against itself, desperately avoiding that abyss. Her eyes, rich with the color brown, and full with life, energy, sensuality, would, if I looked into them for more than a moment, drown me in their bottomless waters. Her lips, puffy and pressed forward, stared at their victim, demanding, not asking, to be kissed.

She closed her eyes and opened her lips just slightly. I loved this sight and wanted to run and get my camera. I kept her waiting not because I had the nerve to play hard to get, but because I did not want the single greatest event of my sixteen years to be over so soon. But I did lick my lips, then blot them, lean down to her, and press my lips against hers. I felt inflated by her energy and held my lips to hers longer than I had thought I would have dared. We stepped back from the spot and opened our eyes simultaneously. She winked and left.

The corners of my lips threatened to levitate me grin first high above the ground. I jumped up the stairs I don't know how many at a time and *hooted* for them all to hear. Then I opened the door to my lovely little chamber and sat down to talk with you.

Remember this day, June 9, 1979. The day of my *first kiss*.

July 17, 1979

Cape Cod

I'm writing this on the last, empty pages of *Stranger in a Strange Land* because it's dark and I can't find the notebook. I hate defacing a book, but if I don't let this out, I'll scream. I'll transfer this entry to the notebook tomorrow.

Morgan and I are living in pup tents next to his mom's big tent here in this campground in North Truro, Cape Cod. Every day we'd hitch to Provincetown and look for girls, but of course never succeeding. We'd practiced trick Frisbee moves all June and half of July in the field next to the church in front of my house. We've been in the campsite ten days already, and even though I'll jump up and catch the Frisbee between my legs right when some sexy girls walk by, they still don't ask my name.

Tonight was no different. We were throwing the Frisbee under the big light by the telephones and toilets. I threw right to Morgan, but the spaz knocked it right into this older, cute, but very white-trashy-looking girl crying in the phone booth. She got off the phone and handed him the Frisbee, then, I swear to God, asked him, "Where's the party?" He just started stuttering and blubbering.

"I'd like some company on the beach. Wanna come?" She headed down the path to the beach, and Morgan tripped over himself trotting behind her like a dog. He misthrew me the Frisbee, and I had to climb a sap-sticky pine tree to get it back.

It's like my absolute favorite movie, *Summer of '42*, where that nerdy guy gets laid by Jennifer O'Neill because her husband is killed in WWII and she's real upset. People say it's not believable and maybe this girl is no Jennifer O'Neill, yet it would still be great *Penthouse* "Forum" material if Morgan loses it tonight. He carries a rubber in his wallet just like me, but I don't know if he changes it every three months like I do. I've heard too many stories about guys opening up the thing after months and finding it like vaporized. I actually write down on my school calendar "Change Mr. C. today," though by the time I ever need one I'll have spent like $867.

You know, I don't think I've ever wanted to be white before tonight. I fall in love almost only with black girls, but there are so few of them around where I hang out that the numbers are against me. If Morgan gets laid tonight, I'll kill him.

I can't wait to see Jenny. We're hitching down to Woods Hole, then taking the ferry to Martha's Vineyard on Wednesday. Wait. I hear a noise outside, I think he's coming back.

Good news. Actually bad news. They went to the beach, her name is Karen. She's *nineteen years old!!* See, Morgan's only fifteen but already shaves once in a while. Well, she starts kissing him on the beach and talking about how rotten her old boyfriend is and all, and she actually takes off her shirt, so he touches bare tit and everything, then, he swears, and the story ends so bad I believe him, she starts to take off his pants when she asks him how old he is. Morgan tells her the truth. "I'm raping a baby!" she says, and freaks out and tells him to leave her there to think. What a rip. Nice guys finish last, and if you tell the truth you don't get laid. I feel sorry for him.

July 19, 1979

Jenny

I'm on the ferry with Morgan and want to paddle over the side or scoot the boat faster so I can be in her arms the sooner. I think kissing Joie really helped. Now when Jenny asks I can tell her I'm the John Travolta of kissing, a regular Lyle Waggoner. The problem is going to be getting rid of Morgan. Maybe Jenny knows someone, but he's already had bare tit on Cape Cod, so now it's my turn. (He's looking over at my notebook right now, so I'm hiding it— you—from him.) "It's just a letter to my grandma," I just told him, and he bought it.

11:15 P. M.

Let me start from the beginning. Dad picked us up at Oak Bluffs and drove us to our cottage in Vineyard Haven. Dad and Morgan were talking and maybe I was saying something, too, but I was like pulling us forward faster with my eyes. This house is better than the one we rented last summer because it's "winterized." Last year's cottage was like a bunch of half-walled office cubicles in a barn. This one at least has dropped ceilings over the walls of the rooms so a guy can have some privacy when he's busy.

Morgan and I had just gotten unpacked and Leslie had just broken out the UNO cards when there was a knock at the door. I studied my Pumas.

Hello, Professor McMillan. Did Austin get in yet?

"Austin? Your little friend is here." He said this on purpose.

I got up from the table in the kitchen and walked to the open screen door as if I were feeling normal.

"There you are. Finally summer can start." Jenny was all smiles, and I would have kissed her right there, I swear I would have, if my entire prying family weren't there smiling like I'd just had a kid.

"Hey, Jenny. How they hanging?" I shook her hand like a dork and walked outside with her. Her kid sister, Gail, was behind her beautiful butt, and Morgan followed me outside.

"You do have a hot bod now, Austin. I thought you were just BS'ing about lifting weights."

I blushed and just about exploded out of my jeans. I couldn't have paid her to say something nicer in front of Morgan. Then . . .

• •

"Jenny. Look, I'm sorry for not writing you back, but I lost your address and—"

"A likely story."

"No. I mean it. Here's the letter I wrote and there's the date right there."

"You could have written it yesterday and faked the date."

"Give me a break! I mean, what kind of a jerk—"

"Cool your jets, big boy. I was only kidding."

She ripped the letter out of my hand and opened it with her long purple nails. She didn't even bother to smell the Old Spice I'd soaked it in.

"You don't have to read it right now. This is my friend Morgan. . . ."

She wasn't listening. She just skimmed the letter right there in front of the whole world. She was frowning. Then she coughed, like she was spitting up something nasty. Then she flipped the letter to her brat sister, who read maybe the first words.

"Oh, brother," and Gail rolled her eyeballs around in her head like they were in a washing machine.

"I—I guess I'll maybe talk to you later," said I, looking around for a picket fence to throw myself on. "Mom's cooking London broil and it should be done . . ." I mumbled the rest and pulled Morgan away. His smile was about to eat up his whole face.

"She's just crazy about you. Can't live without you!"

Back to the house, and I made myself concentrate on UNO instead of suicide, but Morgan must have had all the "draw four/wild" cards because he was killing Leslie and me, making us draw four each turn, so we had half the deck in our hands and he had just two cards, so was just two rounds away from probably winning. See, UNO is like crazy eights but souped up. It's a kid's game, but a blast—when my stomach's not twisted in my guts like a wash rag. Morgan then had one card and I shouted, "UNO!"

"What's that about?"

"You have to pick up the whole discard pile, that's what it's about, Morgan, the guy with a girl's name."

"No way."

"Tell him, Leslie. That's why it's called '*UNO*,' you have to yell '*UNO*' when you put down your last card before somebody else does or you eat the whole deck."

"Austin, why didn't you tell him before? He's your friend."

"I thought he knew the rules. He thinks he knows everything."

"Fuck you."

"Go ahead, pick up the whole pile. . . . Boy, what a sucker."

"Too bad Jenny will never suck you."

I haven't fought, like wrestled fought, with anybody except my sister since sixth grade. My dad had to pull me off him. Though he's younger, like I said, he's always been bigger. Maybe the weights really are working. I can't really tell yet, no matter what lies Jenny tells me.

I've got to go to sleep so she won't see zombie-looking bags under my eyes tomorrow.

3:2 6 A. M.

This must be one of those nights old people have. Now three twenty-seven in the morning and I'm more dead than alive. Morgan's lying there with his mouth like an open toilet bowl. Sounds of backup gurgling up. His eyes are slit open so just the bottom white shows, like he's blind and possessed by Satan. I want to clobber him with my pillow or mattress him to the wall, but then I'd have to explain.

She can't be evil. I love her. Maybe I laid it on too thick in the letter, didn't play hard to get—but fuck games. Most people in the world have probably lost the love of their life by pretending not to care. Why did I think Miss Public School Popular would want a preppie nerd? I don't know how I think sometimes. My heart hurts like something's wrong with it, hurts like I need an operation or a medicine soon or I will die. But die slowly, that's the problem. If I were just shot in the head by a .22-caliber bang stick like the ones meat packers jab cows in the head with, it would all be over in a snap, then I'd have no time to regret dying a virgin.

Like this, however, it's like your life is leaking out of you a drip at a time and you can't stop it.

Showboat, the old musical, was on cable the other night. Paul Robeson has always been my hero. My uncle Fletcher gave me a poster of him in *The Emperor Jones* when I was a kid that still hangs in my room back home. Anyway, in *Showboat*, Paul Robeson sang "Old Man River," and it's actually a great song: "I'm tired of living, and feared of dying, but Old Man River he just keeps rolling along." That's just how I feel.

You read about heartache in books and listen about it in every single song ever written, but before this I said, how bad could it be? It's not like someone *physically* smashed you in the chest with a chair leg. It's got to be less painful than the highs feel good or who'd bother?

I want to claw through my chest and cuddle my heart, stroke it and keep it company even if it would kill me. It's so lonely.

I've got to get out of here. . . .

5:03 A. M.

The night is just beginning to thin. An hour ago I snuck out of the room—Morgan of course didn't even stir. I didn't know where I was going, and the uncertainty gave me a boner. Maybe I'd sneak to her house and pee through the screen on her window. But no. I squeezed myself out of the front door. We're in the center of the island and you almost never smell the sea, but in these dead hours the air is thick with sea smell. The streetlights mumbled hums at me, but I couldn't hear even one car rolling around. I wanted to do something great, something to prove to myself that I'm special and not the asshole dweeb she thinks I am. I pulled the lace on my sweat pants, and they deflated to my ankles. I raised up and off my shirt. I slid my BVDs down my legs and stood on the porch of our prefab naked. I really did. Of course I wanted to get back in my clothes and go back to bed, but I wouldn't let myself, this wasn't weird enough yet. I walked, I swear to God, I didn't even run, to the fenced-in pool across the street and climbed over. The chain link killed my feet and the sharp top almost snagged my balls (yuck!). I "slipped into the water noiselessly," as they always say in Alistair MacLean spy novels, and just floated. Night water is warm. The water was unlit and black, and I worried about sharks and psychos hiding beneath the black, that's how wimpy and paranoid I am. I swear I almost wanted to be caught by some screaming old lady so I'd be committed and finally get some help. Then I jerked off to visions of Jenny, and I hope tomorrow morning she's the first to dive in and gets her hair tangled with my jiz.

The blackness overhead was just admitting whispers of deep blue, so I left. Getting back inside was the hard part. I didn't bring a towel, so I dried off on my sweats and knew my chattering teeth would wake my folks. I'm lying in bed now on my beach towel. The pain in my heart isn't over, but maybe it's not quite as bad.

July 29, 1979

Jenny

I've been trying to see her this past week, but every time I get near she finds some lame excuse and books. Finally I just went over there and asked her what's what. She's leaving tomorrow on the 6:00 A.M. ferry, and I had to know.

I knocked on the door, and luckily she answered herself (if it were Gail, I'd have killed the little brat).

"Can we talk, Jenny?" I'd been practicing that line for a week, and it came off okay.

"We're talking." She didn't seem to want to come outside, and I wanted to get it over with ASAP.

"Would you like to go out with me?"

"What do you mean?"

"You know, boyfriend and girlfriend."

"I already have a boyfriend."

"But what about those letters?"

"I wrote a lot of letters . . . I should pack. . . ."

She pushed herself to smile like she was selling something, then slowly closed the door. If I were cool, I'd have hurled myself at the chintzy presswood door, smashed it down, then carried her off.

I went to our house and played four-square in the street with Leslie, Morgan, and a little girl vacationer.

July 30, 1979

Jenny

I kind of got up at five in the morning and kind of wandered in the direction of her house. I was wearing sweats and sneakers and jogged when I was within sight of her dad, who was packing the trunk.

"Bye, Dr. Sheffington, I was just out for my morning run. . . ." Jenny struggled her ten-speed out the screen door, and the sight of me made her mouth hang ugly and her eyeballs circle her sockets. She pulled me around the side of the house.

"I can't believe you did that. I'm so embarrassed."

"I can't talk long, I'm in training." I was running in place as we talked. "Good-bye, Jenny. You can write again if you want to. This time I won't take it the wrong way." And I ran off before she could answer. I turned left toward East Chop because that's not the way to the ferry and after being halfway cool with her I didn't want to be caught later puking and wheezing by the side of the road. Instead I ran about a mile to the water and trespassed on a little private dock as the sun rose. I watched her ferry pull out across the harbor. I think I even saw their car, her bike and her sister's upside down on the roof like game.

September 9, 1979

Calista

I've been back at Andover a week, helping run the Search & Rescue section of the freshman and transfer orientation. I had taken the course last year, and now as a senior I'm a student leader. They tell me it's good college suck.

It's wonderful to be back at school with no classwork to do. Every day I take another group out to the quarry and lead them up very simple faces. Every night there's a movie or ice cream or something to do. Going through it last year, I was too nervous to enjoy myself. But that's not why I'm writing. I'm writing here in the room (alone! Kurt doesn't arrive until Thursday) after tonight's flick, *Cabaret*, because I'm in love with a white girl.

Today I was putting the ropes and helmets for my section away in the supply cage when I saw her bent low laying her section's ropes on their pegs. Her leader sprained her ankle, so Calista, an upper from New York State somewhere, volunteered to stow the gear. Did I tell you she was wearing blue velvet clogs? The vulnerable underside of her pretty foot yawned at me invitingly as she crouched. I almost kissed it. We just grunted hellos and pleasantries at each other. I asked a friend her story and he said, "She's a bitch, everybody's tried talking to her." I have a feeling she too will get the chance to get her hits in on my feeble heart before this, my glorious senior year, comes to a close.

September 15, 1979

Calista

The finale of Search & Rescue orientation is the bell tower rappel. It was great to see all those kids terrified and in complete awe of me when I calmly scooted over the ledge and rappeled the

113 feet down to the ground. Maybe for once people weren't looking at me and thinking, Virgin.

Our section used one side of the tower, Calista's the other. I was belaying some poor freshman, which you don't even do on a real rappel. So not only was he just sliding down the rope, which is easy, he had another rope attached to his harness that came up to me. Even if he let go and just jumped, I'd catch him. That didn't matter to him. Logic didn't matter. The white bones were about to pop out of his knuckle skin, he was so scared. I asked him to smile, and he scrunched up his cheeks.

"Just take it one step at a time." I felt like the experienced pilot in the control tower talking down the hysterical stewardess in the first *Airport*.

This upper who's real cute but just a friend, Ellen, she looked down the other side, saw Calista, who was already halfway down the brick face of the bell tower like she did it every day.

"Austin, lend me your sweats. I don't want to look like her."

I was paying out the belay rope as the wimpy freshman inched down my side. I could've killed to see what everyone else was looking at, but if the kid freaked out and died, who knows what college would take me. But I heard from the rest of my section that it was great. Calista was just wearing these cutoff shorts, and the harness comes up between your legs. When you're rappeling your waist holds your body weight, and her harness had sucked up her shorts so she looked bottomless. Everybody whispered that it looked real freaky. Ellen was mean, though.

"Ohhhhh," she said, impersonating Calista. "Let me ride again, *please*."

I should have defended her, but I didn't. It was right on the tip of my tongue to say, "That's my future wife you're making fun of."

October 10, 1979

Joie/Toni

Okay, I'm not proud of what I did, but today's my seventeenth birthday and if I hadn't, I might have tried rappeling off the bell tower without *any* ropes whatsoever.

As usual I hovered behind Joie as she waved her Lycra butt over the dicks of every other guy in school. Of course last year's kiss didn't matter and she went right back to torturing me. I hope all her colleges reject her and she goes nuts and ends up in a women's prison.

Anyway, the slow dance came up and I zoomed in, but she wanted to sit it out. Cool, I said to myself, even though it's my birthday, until Akbar asked her. He insisted until she gave in and then practically impregnated her right there on the dance floor.

It was almost eleven and I wanted to get back to Taylor West in time for "Saturday Night Live." I thought I'd tell the gang there that today was my birthday to make them feel bad.

Just then this girl actually asked me to dance. Another first in my sad love life. She seemed cute, though I didn't know her. Slow dancing, she smelled hot and wonderful, fertile. My boner was killing me, but she kept whacking her thigh into it like she didn't care. I was so depressed just a moment before and now I'm about to write to *Penthouse* "Forum"!

Her name's Toni and she's an ABC student. Most of the other blacks at Andover are ABC ("a better chance"), too, but she lives in a house in town and goes to Andover High School.

I walked her home, and we really didn't talk about anything. Then at her house in town she tells me they don't have to be in till twelve-thirty. I have to be in by midnight, so I start to say good-bye when she says, "I'll walk *you* home." I really thought my friends had put her up to it. I'd find out after we made out that she's a man or something. Still, I wasn't crazy about her and was still mad at Joie when, at the foot of my dorm steps, she puckers up. l lean down to kiss her (she's real short), and her tongue whips out of her mouth like a snake and she's like brushing my teeth with it. *First-time Frenching*, and on my birthday. We came up for air once, then I dove in myself to make it really official, then I whipped up the stairs to tell my friends.

Right now, up in my room, I'm not so happy about it. I don't know anything about her, and she didn't seem too smart at all. It was fun to tongue down on my birthday (better late than never), but I really want to be in love with the girl whose tongue is in my mouth. As for the kiss itself, I don't understand the big deal. A good regular kiss, like Joie's last year, practically electrocuted me. This one felt porno.

October 11, 1979

Toni

Right after brunch I had just lowered my butt to the chair and was about to force myself to start my History 35 term paper on the My Lai massacre when Sid, a lower who's got to be gay, knocked on the door.

"A girl is downstairs asking for *you*."

I couldn't believe what I saw.

Last night the Af-Lat-Am lights were red, I could barely make her out. Then on the street and in front of the dorm the streetlights make everybody look awful. But here in the white sun of an eastern Massachusetts Sunday, Toni has got to be the ugliest girl I've ever seen. She was as ugly as somebody can be without having been burned. But I did it anyway. I'm not totally a conceited, superficial creep.

She is yellow-skinned, squat, her sharp nose and her lips smushed into one plug between the twin swells of her oily cheeks. She's like some albino/mulatto experiment that didn't work. I leaned over and kissed her anyway, but in the daylight it was like putting my lips to a pig's snout. I'm not saying I'm Señor Good-looking. The burst zits on my head that I insist on squeezing and poking until they scar horribly look like so many gunshot wounds. But at least people wouldn't describe me as "that ugly guy" (I think). Toni you couldn't describe any other way. But I don't think I let her see all these thoughts on my face. If anyone should know rejection and heartache, it's me.

"I've got to get firewood out by the pond, want to come?" I asked her this, I'm ashamed to say, mainly to get her away from my friends in the dorm, who think I'm a Casanova for Frenching last night. Kurt and I haven't used our fireplace yet, though it's been cold a few days already.

Walking in the woods now behind the dorm, I was two steps ahead of her and trying ferociously to force my heart to like her. I'd actually probably have sex this year, and with a girlfriend squared away I could bear down on the books and on my applications. But every time I'd turn to see if she was all right, she'd stay ugly. Maybe some therapist could train me to like her. They could show me a picture of her and give me some shock to pop a boner like I heard they do to deprogram gay guys. Then I could tell Joie to dance with herself.

Maybe if we Frenched again, I'd change my mind about her. (Why do they call it "French kiss," anyway? I thought they pecked each other on the cheeks. I can't imagine some kid saying "*Au revoir, Mama,*" then snaking his tongue around the inside of her cheeks.) I sat on a tree fallen across the path. She sat her butt right next to mine, then grabbed my head and started picking the food bits out of my teeth with her tongue. I was about to pull back when she laid her hand in my lap.

Wooooooo! Suddenly all the blood and energy sped from my brain and mouth down to my crotch, and the words *hand job* filled every parking spot for a thought in my mind. Then I opened my eyes. If my dick were a balloon, you could hear it hiss its deflate. I'm not saying you have to love the woman who manually stimulates you, but you should at least like her.

Mrs. Lloyd, the cluster dean's wife, came down the path, pushing her three-speed through the leaves and over the dead branches. I don't think it's against the rules to make out in the woods, but

I never bothered reading those sections of the blue book. I knew I'd never need them.

"I'd better get back to my paper."

She walked me back to the dorm. I felt like a jerk. Who'd ever believe that I could break somebody's heart? No more Af-Lat-Am dances for me for a month or so. Bad news.

October 30, 1979

Jenny

I can't believe it! She's coming to Andover for a six-week program in the spring!! Her letter was short but nice: "When I get there you can take me around and introduce me to people so I won't be totally lonely. You talked so much about the school, and it's great college suck." My friends will freak out when they see her.

Today, the Af-Lat-Am led a sit-in at the headmaster's house to get the school to divest from South Africa. He told us he'll work on the trustees.

Halloween 1979

Toni

I finally ran into her. Headmaster Sizer has a haunted house in his basement every year, and I was crawling through some refrigerator boxes painted black and orange when I came into this room with a friend of mine, Marcus Fitch, a cool guy on campus, pretending to be hung from the ceiling. Toni was already in the room and practically throws up when she saw me.

"Where you been?"

"I don't know." I slipped into the next room, where it was dark and they'd hung sheets everywhere so you had to fight through them and there were people pushing at you from behind them. The "Monster Mash" was playing. I hadn't heard it since fourth grade in Michigan.

November 18, 1979

Robin

She's a lower and I talked with her on the bus to Boston a few weeks ago. You never know.

December 26, 1979

My Dick

We're in Dayton with Mother's parents. Christmas was great, I got cool presents (the rock-climbing equipment I asked for and a kayaking helmet). But the day after, I always get depressed. This time it came because I couldn't. I was whacking off in the downstairs shower over the hundreds of Grandpa's *Jet* centerfolds wallpapering the basement. Most are from the fifties, so it's kind of weird knowing that they're all old and fat by now. Actually, even back then a lot of them were fat. I guess they didn't have enough to eat back in the fifties and thought fat ladies were classy. So there I am, my dick in my hand, staring at some by now old or dead lady in my grandpa's sort-of-finished basement. I look up just as I'm about to come and see myself in the medicine cabinet mirror. It was like my life drained out of me right there. I looked so pathetic, my little wiener schnitzel even littler than I'd feared. A grown lady won't even feel it if I ever stick it in. "You'll never get that tiny thing even near ladies sexy enough to be photographed naked, not even when they are old and even fatter." So I stopped without finishing (a first) and went back upstairs to a delicious leftover turkey sandwich on Wonder bread (which I only eat when I'm back in Ohio). Sometimes I think I should just imprison myself somewhere until I grow out of my craziness.

February 4, 1980

C a l i s t a

I think I had a nervous breakdown last week.

I'm teaching cross-country skiing since I was the slowest skier on the ski team last year but my form's pretty good (I think I was the only black guy ever on the Andover ski team, and once again I let down the race). Anyway, Calista's taking skiing, too. We see a lot of each other and are great friends. I wouldn't think of jumping her (maybe if she were black, who knows). It's weird. I brag to my friends about what good friends we are, but when they tease me and say it's more than that, I get pissed. Of course I whack off about her every single night, but the fantasy is always that we're just friends stuck in a tent on a mountainside and one thing leads to another.

I wrote this on a piece of paper last week. I was in AP Physics, but the lesson was a snap:

Austin deluded himself. Natalie ("Nat"), Calista, Sue, Ellen, Jenny, Stephanie ("Stef"), are all beautiful girls he considered his friends, and only one was black and he had tried to make her more than a friend and had just recently given up. Did he choose his girlfriends just because they were beautiful? Did he punish himself by surrounding himself with the very most beautiful women on campus? Austin even fantasized about making love to his women "friends." If he had ever allowed himself to think about his strange relationships, made stranger still by the absence of a steady girl-friend, he would have been puzzled.

I don't know why I wrote that in the third person. I haven't written about Nat, Sue, or Stef, because it's the same old story.

They are gorgeous and popular girls who sometimes let me eat with them. I'm like Pumpkin, my cat at home. I know just how nice it feels to have an animal constantly trotting behind you, ecstatic over the briefest scratch on the head.

March 20, 1980

Ms. Rod

I can't believe it's been so long since I've written. I guess I could have entered "Failure" after every Af-Lat-Am dance, but why waste the ink. Oh, about Stanford . . . I got in! I guess all that grade grubbing and ass kissing was worth it. "California Dreaming!" If I can't get laid out there, I'll donate my dick to someone who can use it (like a Vietnam vet wounded by a VC land mine).

I've called Ms. Rod in Brookline a couple of times. She's teaching freshman English at MIT. She's always inviting me and Dr. Reed, this year's lit teacher, to dinner at her house. We'd finally settled on this Wednesday, and luckily Dr. Reed had forgotten he had to go to see his publisher in New York City that night.

Have I written about my "key theory" to having sex yet? I think any woman in the world will go to bed with any man if the man has the key. I mean, in my case, I talk better than I look, so there is some combination of words that will make Ms. Rod, for example, snatch off my clothes and ride me like a cowgirl. Maybe it's "Ms. Rod, I have ten days to live. Only you can give my life meaning," or "Pipley swing funky Isle of disastrous" (because with my theory, you never know the right key, and maybe what's gibberish to me will jump-start her love engine). In any case, if I could make love with her, I'd be cured. I'd be normal, have a million girlfriends, and my dick would grow.

If I had a fake ID, I'd get her a bottle of wine. Flowers will seem too much. Maybe chocolates. I went right down to CVS and bought a big box of rubbers. I don't see why anyone'd be embarrassed. I took my time and chatted with the salesgirl. I *wanted* someone from school to see me.

So I don't know what the key words will be for her, but here is the fantasy I've been living with since the dinner invite:

I arrive at her door to show her a short story I've written. She is in *the pose*, fuzzy pink sandal and all.

"To understand your writing, I must understand *you*," she purrs. She massages me and stuff, and we dance to old music, then she lets her fuzzy pink robe fall to the floor.

I know it's impossible, but it's my one shot at everlasting peace. Maybe if I explain that to her, she'd do it. It wouldn't kill her, and she'd give a student spiritual enlightenment.

March 28, 1980

Ms. Rod

I've just caught the last Trombly bus back to Andover and will try to tell the story as it happened, but I still can't believe it.

I went to bed last night still unsure of the "key" to winning her over. If she were married, I could've pulled a *Summer of '42* and killed her husband (in the film he's killed in the war), and she'd be so grief-stricken she wouldn't know what she was doing. But I woke up and the splattering of the rain buzzed my brain like a good drumbeat. It was already eight o'clock, but the world had stayed dark. "Terrific!" I said. I knew exactly what to do.

Nerdy guys in movies are always caught in the rain with the beauty who's just their friend. They rush to her swank apartment, where she insists he get out of those wet things. Then her rotten stud boyfriend surprises her, finds our hero in her pink bathrobe that's too short for him, and storms off. She realizes what a jerk Mr. Lyle-Waggoner-hairspray-macho is, and that triggers her love for the nerd (me).

I don't remember going to any of my classes. Wednesday is a

short day anyway, but all I could do was think about her and those pink fuzzy sandals. Then the rain stopped. Bye bye bathrobe.

I was pissed, and I was so close to getting laid. Then, just as the Trombly bus listed to the side of the road and stopped for us Boston-bound kids, the front wheel sprayed gutter water in a high arc shaped like a feather on two girl lowers at the end of the line. They were covered in little flecks of street stuff and gray water. They shrieked like twin Carries, kicked their clogs up and caught them, sprinted barefoot back to their dorms. I, however, was inspired.

It took me forever to find her neighborhood in Brookline. I got off at the wrong T stop, then walked and walked. I was close to being late and hadn't yet found a puddle. Not since pinching Heather Nallabuona's butt had I been so excited. It hadn't rained as much in Boston, so the puddles were mainly potholes filled with fudgelike sludge. Then I found a perfect, relatively sanitary street puddle, only it was right in front of her house. My plan was to throw myself down into the gray street soup and say a bus did it. But of course if she sees me do it, she obviously wouldn't let me inside. I know I wouldn't.

Her lights were on, but I couldn't see her. I also got the idea of maybe catching a glimpse of her naked as she put Oil of Olay on herself after her shower. But I was already running out of time. It was six on the nose and she would be peeping out of her curtains any minute. I stood in front of the water, stared at it, and I only then realized how stupid I was being, absolutely certifiable. What would happen after she asked me to take my pants off? Would she notice my erection and be forced to jump on it? An old lady in her forties roller-skated by. I could tell she thought I was a pervert creep for loitering on her street. Then no one was around, and I fell myself over the puddle anyway and did a quick push-up into it, soaking my thighs. Then suddenly, "*Waaa!*" a speeding ice-cream truck nearly took off my head. I rolled out of the way and jumped up like I was never down.

When I die it's going to be some way stupid like that, being decapitated by an ice-cream truck because I was rolling around in the gutter trying to get laid. Still, my balls were practically glowing in the dark.

I pulled the box of Godiva chocolates out of my knapsack and pushed her doorbell. If I hadn't heard her footsteps so close to the door, I'd have cruised.

"Austin! You made it." She kissed my cheek. Her huge eyes shined more than I'd remembered. She was hypnotizing me.

"Let me take your coat." I handed it to her, and she dangled it from a hook under a picture of T. S. Eliot (I only knew that because it said so).

The house smelled like wonderful food. Creams cooking and roasting chicken. But my legs were freezing and I was afraid of dripping the water from my pants—water like ashtray juice—onto her pretty rugs. I stood helpless in her hallway, my arms out to my sides.

"Oh, my God! What happened?"

"An ice-cream truck splashed me."

"They drive like imbeciles around here, I know. Would you like to get out of those wet things? I'll lend you a robe."

I look at her eyes, her sexy body, her beautiful house with the great smell, and I think, Do I live in the same world as everybody else? How could I think the way I do? I could have been naked in front of her, she wouldn't have had sex with me. She'd have just asked me to put my clothes back on.

"No. That's okay. It's not so bad."

I don't know what we talked about the rest of the dinner. I made her laugh a few times, which was nice. The crazy part was that I couldn't wait to write about it. I'm sort of proud of myself for being so different from the average person. I really did something special, for better or for worse. Maybe I won't end up in a tract house back in Hamden after all.

April 3, 1980

Calista

At school we had talked about John Anderson and how—though he would never beat Dole, Bush, or Reagan for the nomination—he might mess up the Republicans just enough to let Carter win again. Now it's spring break and I'm back in Hamden. She's from Rye, New York, and there's a big rally for Anderson in New York City tomorrow. I called to ask her if she'd like to go, but she said she was going hiking with her parents. Then we started talking about the outdoors, and I let slip my plans to hang glide and get certified to scuba dive this summer. I was thinking of going hiking this spring break myself, I said.

"Why don't we go together?"

I'm sure she could practically *hear* my smile through the telephone wires. "Sure!" I said, my voice fucking cracking for the first time in months. But it didn't matter, joy, bliss, exploding in my insides. The day started so normally. I was almost looking forward to going back to school since I'd lost track of most of my Hamden friends. But her simple sentence triggered a chain of images to flicker before my eyes from a kiss to marriage to kids. I didn't want to even talk to her anymore. I wanted to just sit in my room and feel this wonderful feeling.

"There's a free Judy Collins concert in Central Park Friday night. We could meet there with maps and plans. But the Appalachian Trail is always nice."

I don't remember what else she said. My brain was filling up with ecstasy, short-circuiting all worldly thoughts.

Calista

We met in front of this statue, "The Tempest," by the side of the big lawn in the middle of the park. I was proud of myself for finding it easily. A good sign, I thought.

Judy Collins was warbling and clanking her guitar through her only hit, "Both Sides Now." I can't believe I used to like music like this, Gordon Lightfoot and Cat Stevens, back in the eighth grade. It sounds like Muzak to me now. But Calista is a Judy Collins type of woman, so I didn't mention my cool musical evolution to the jazz/fusion of Chick Corea and the Return to Forever band.

Calista's black hair glistened like lacquered wood, her black eyes seemed a sticky, romantic trap, a La Brea tar pit of broken hearts. I tried to look at her as little as possible during the concert. Lying on a quilted piano blanket, she had brought Stella D'Oro cookies and apple cider. I forgot to bring anything. Every time I looked into her eyes I felt them draw me to her, hoisted up into those eyes by my stomach. We talked for hours, and she laughed constantly.

Nearly every black man there was with a white woman. My folks actually said they expected me to marry a white girl, since after Michigan they brought us up around the poor white ignoramuses of southern New England. Yet I was always determined to prove them wrong. I never even went out with a white girl (all right, all right, I've never gone out with any girl, but I've only *tried* to go out with black girls).

Calista

It's twelve-twelve! Go to sleep! You have to get up at five for the trip—do you want her to see you and say, "Are those bags under your eyes for carrying miniature first-aid kits?" Many trips get canceled at the last minute, so don't get your hopes up until you're actually inside her sleeping bag. Yes, you've packed the rubbers in the real first-aid kit (if she finds them, I'll tell her they're to "isolate a finger wound, keep moisture away from it," or something like that). Besides, with Search & Rescue you shared a tent with a girl and nothing happened then. Of course she was a hateful druggie witch, ugly in mind, body, and spirit. Go back to sleep, creep.

L a t e r . . .

"Austin, I can't believe I'm calling this late, but this is Calista. . . . I . . . I don't know how to say this. . . ." It was one o'clock, an hour ago, when she called. "My parents changed their minds. I can't go."

"Oh. Why?"

"I don't know. They're just being unreasonable. You . . . you know, it wouldn't be so bad if they hadn't waited till the last minute. This thing stinks, I know, but their mind is made up. We've been fighting all evening, but I had to call you before you left for the city tomorrow morning."

"But—"

"I know, but what can I say? Listen, it's supposed to be a freakish day tomorrow, nearly seventy degrees. Why don't we go to Montauk for the day? They'll let me do that. . . ."

We talked until just a minute ago about everything from how to make your life extraordinary, to the worthlessness of money, to sex. Eye bags be damned.

A p r i l 7, 1 9 8 0

C a l i s t a

I took the seven o'clock train into the city, and we met by the Chemical Bank cash machine in Penn Station and caught the 9:02

Long Island Railroad bound for the beach. She kissed me on the cheek hello, and the warmth from her lips heated my whole face. But I wasn't the only one smiling. The freak heat wave had the whole city happy, like somebody had laced the smog with nitrous oxide. On the train, our conversation was light and witty and delightful as always.

She got us off the LIRR at Amagansett, a ritzy fake New England village, and hiked us miles and miles to the town beach. The beach grass was sprinkled with tiny blue flowers, the wind was already kind and warm. How soft the sand, how clean the beach, how clear the sea. We passed three other interracial couples on the beach, older people, and they seemed to wink at us—"Keep on keeping on." Maybe they all have a secret high sign like the Masons that we're supposed to know.

We walked far enough away that the other premature beachgoers were small enough to give us some privacy. Then I showed her my beach trick: I scooped out a deep chaise lounge for her out of sand and laid her towel upon it.

"Thank you, sir."

Then I created a hole for myself. We both kept our clothes on. Then I took off my shirt even though it was still too cool. When clouds curtained the sun, goose bumps sprouted on my arms, my nipples pulled at my pecs. I've been lifting a lot this year—180 pounds is my max, twenty pounds over my weight (lifting your weight is already above average). I tried not to look like I was flexing like a jerk, but obviously I wanted her to get hot and jump my bones.

"You lift weights? You don't seem the type."

"Vat do you mean, I do not seem the type?" I said, impersonating Arnold Schwarzenegger, Mr. Olympia, from the movie *Pumping Iron*. "You tink ve are all ze stupid?"

She laughed until spittle leaked from her mouth. My heart soared like a bird.

"Anyway, you've got a great body." Yooo! I wanted to leap up and do a sand dance, chase and scatter seagulls along the beach, somersault my way across the Sound to Connecticut.

"You ain't so bad yourself." She blushed, I swear to God she did.

Then I did it. I pushed myself out of my sand chair, double-checked to make sure I'd put on swim trunks instead of underwear, dropped my jeans to my ankles, and ran to the water, *screaming*. I hate cold water, and even in the summer the water in the Northeast makes my balls recede up to my chest. But I wasn't thinking about them. Instead I was absolutely focused on this one thought: If I do not see her in a bikini, then I will die. So there I was, splashing through the shallow, splattering myself with needles of melted ice cap just to convince her the water was fine. But I couldn't stop. I felt her eyes on my Speedo. I threw myself forward and in, and all the air from my lungs spat out, and I sank.

Down the beach, a dozen old white people frolicked in the surf as if it were possible. Old white people are incredible; if it were big enough, they could swim in a Slurpee. Then I heard it, a splashing behind me.

I turned and realized I was wrong. My brave dick ignored the cold, my balls hummed and tingled like a tuning fork. She was bouncing toward me in a string bikini I would never have expected from a liberal and a backpacker. I thought then of begging, of giving her my bicycle, sixty percent of what I earned in my *lifetime*, just to make love to me once.

I thought she must have read my perverse mind by the look of horror she flashed, then the wave she had been worrying about slammed the back of my head, rubbed my face into the coarse sand I had just been standing on, flung my feet skyward, and skidded me onto the shore. My terrorized Speedo allowed the interested a view to the top half of the crack of my ass before I pulled it back up. The suit would have sped past my ankles and back out to sea if my boner hadn't held it in place like the nob on a coat rack. I turned to where I had rolled past Calista, but she was gone. Then she surfaced, her bikini top askew to the limit of an areola. But another wave pounded her just as she stood again and tumbled her toward me. She stood up, her long hair masking all her face except her nose like Cousin It. Her bikini bottom low slung, but not very, and her bikini top (yes, her bikini top, go on) was *completely off!* I would have fainted if I could have closed my eyes.

Her nipples were so hard and tiny, the areolas so small and concentric. *My first live naked breast!* She struggled them back into her top, dragged the wet curtain of hair from before her eyes. By that time I had turned away and turned back only after she was decent, as if I had not seen the single sexiest live image of my seventeen years. We got out quickly, all of me except what matters, numb.

"She's just a friend, she's just a friend, she's just a friend," my brain said to me. But I also heard, even more clearly, my dick talking. "Get me inside of her or I'll pee down your new three-piece suit at graduation," it said. "I'll burn, I'll itch. I'll pop a boner in the boys' shower, wilt on your wedding night."

The train back was an old, old wooden-benched car. Gray and black it was, steel and mildewed upholstery.

"I love this old train." Calista loves a lot of things, but this time I knew just what she meant.

"It's pathetic but homey. And at least it's not like the new ones feebly trying to impersonate jets."

She agreed, and from that our conversation progressed to the joys of train travel. (I actually am not crazy about them, but I wanted to agree with her. I had taken the Greyhound across country last summer to visit Stanford. At least buses turn, and they drive right through the middle of cities. Trains are always segregated to the industrial wastelands, the backsides of towns.) We talked about how overpriced and bad prefabricated train food is, finally ending on the subject of how hungry we were. With that, Calista pulled a cucumber from her bag (I'm not making any of this up, I swear!), fresh from her Rye, New York, organic *Whole Earth Catalog* garden (we had eaten the squash, carrots, and tomatoes on the beach). I don't hate cucumbers; who could hate what doesn't taste? I expected her to snap it in two, but she just bit off the end and pointed it at me. I took it, bit off some, and pointed it back to her. The cucumber quickly shrank as it passed between us, and the rules of the game became obvious—give your opponent a final piece, too small to divide. So Calista giggled and passed me a sliver as small as her large black pupils, deliciously shiny from her saliva. I tried my best to bite it in half in her hand but only managed to coat it and her palm in even more spittle.

"Oooow, gross!" she said, and I gave in and lapped up the last of it.

"You win."

At Penn Station she had to hurry off. Her parents wanted her home by eight-thirty. She kissed me on the cheek again but this time added a squeeze to my shoulders. I don't know when I've been so happy. I won't try anything with her because I love her and couldn't stand it if she freaked out and didn't ever talk to me again. I'm determined not to make the same mistake I made with Jenny.

Dad's a sociology prof, and he says, "Adolescents cannot have friends of the opposite sex. These people you may mistake as friends are actually frustrated lovers." But I think that's horseshit. Sure, I don't doubt that tonight I'll whack off to Calista in an "unfriendly" way. But I know, I guess, that she'll never do anything major with me. We're pals now, though I love her.

May 4, 1980

Jenny

I just talked to her on the phone. She'll be living in Pearson House, pretty far from my dorm. She and the rest of the exchange students start next week and stay for just three weeks. "Can't wait to see you, kiddo!" she said. But remember: *She's just a friend now, she's just a friend!!* Don't go crazy again and make her hate you.

....

May 10, 1980

Jenny

She called my dorm's pay phone to tell me she's in. We're about to meet at commons, upper left, with all the cool people. I'm dressed up a bit and have to say I look pretty good: white pleated pants, brand-new Top-Siders, and my cool, tight-knit T-shirt with the cool ring half zipper halfway down the front. I'm about to go brush my teeth for the third time in an hour.

Later...

I'm in trouble. She looked wonderful. Oh, my heart sings like a musical saw inside of me. Friendship this is definitely not. I must have licked my lips 5×10 to the eighth times before going upstairs into the dining hall. I was determined to bring my lips straight on and if she showed cheek, so be it. But she didn't turn, and *wham!* lip to lip for a hot second (well, maybe not lip to lip, but mouth corners to mouth corners). Anyway, that's all it took and I'm back where I started, desperately in love.

Sauerbraten for dinner, one of my favorites, and she couldn't finish hers, so I helped her out. I could feel all of the cool, artsy-fartsy people staring at us, wondering what I was doing with this babe. I made sure I ate slowly and sat up straight. Kurt and the guys had heard all about her, and when she wasn't looking they'd make eyes at me. I was sure she was going to catch them.

"Austin, where's the ladies' room?" Kurt and the guys immediately pointed out in the hall like dogs. "Thanks, guys. I'll be right back."

"Way to goooo!" Kurt held his hand out to slap, but I didn't. "What a babe."

"You guys, if you say anything stupid, I swear I'll break off your arms."

"Oh, Mr. Macho weight lifter now. I thought you said she was just a friend?"

"Yeah? So?"

"So then you won't mind her wrapping her legs around my back, naked."

"You wish, Ben. The only thing you get, you get from your Irish setter back home."

"Look, I'm not prejudiced. Maybe I'll ask her to the movies tomorrow night."

Did I write yet that Kurt and most of the other guys I hang out with are white? Or did you guess?

"I bet she's a great kisser."

"Shut it, willya? Here she comes."

They all turned and mooned smiles at her as she walked up. I tried to play it cool until I saw Marcus Fitch walking back with her. He's one of the supercool guys on campus, going out with Chantal, a famous sexpot. And French. He's also sort of a friend of mine from lit class.

"Austin, where have you been hiding Jenny? She's great."

Jenny tilts her head back on her shoulders and laughs and laughs and laughs.

"So I'll see you two at the movies tomorrow." Marcus went back to his table.

"His girlfriend's a friend of mine, too."

"You've got some great friends."

Kurt, Ben, and the others smile at each other like imbeciles.

I was walking her back to her dorm when she said, "I think I'm going to like it here." I watched her sway up the stairs through the steel grid in the safety glass of her dorm door window. My heart was swelling, and I knew only too well what that meant.

It was drizzling and I should have hurried home, but I felt eccentric and romantic taking the back way back home, opening my mouth to catch the mist, feeling it soak my hair, wet the thighs of my pants so they grip me. Tuberculosis or pneumonia, that's the next logical step. A delicate cough in the morning that matures into hacking up blood and lung, a teary farewell in the infirmary, Jenny squeezing my hand, wiping her tears over her face with my palm.

I got home, opened the door, opened this book, and started writing. I closed the door with my foot.

May 11, 1980

Jenny

The movie tonight was *The Summer of '42.* I couldn't believe it. Jenny thought it was stupid, didn't believe Jennifer O'Neill would actually fall for the nerd.

Marcus and the rest of the cool kids are great. I never hung out with them before. It's funny how the girl you're with here in high school tells everybody all about you. I guess that's because they don't allow cars.

We all snuck out to Pomp's Pound, down the same path where I took Toni to French. The cool kids have so much more fun than us nerds. By the pond they passed around a joint, but it was no big deal. I knew stoners back in regular high school. And Jenny didn't smoke, either, which sort of surprised me. I would have thought they would all jump into the water naked and have a moonlight orgy, but they just smoked and drank Southern Comfort and peppermint schnapps (Jenny drank a little, too) and made out with their girlfriends and snuck back to campus.

May 18, 1980

Jenny

I see her all the time. It's great. People have asked me what's the deal with us two, and I just smile and shrug. The lacrosse jocks at the gym seem to think I'm a stud now. It's pretty cool. Ben and I are going to double-date at the Andover Inn. It'll cost the rest of this month's allowance, but who cares.

Tonight I was a little worried when Jenny didn't show up at the dance until real late. Marcus was with her. I walked her home, and she said they had gotten drunk in the back of a day student friend of his's car.

"Chantal's got the field hockey interschols tomorrow, she shouldn't be getting drunk."

"Oh, you're right. She stayed home tonight to rest."

These have got to be the happiest days at Andover, maybe in my life. I'm going to California next year for college, I'm in love, it's spring. Life is all right.

May 23, 1980

Sunbathing

These two lowers discovered them first. They had passed the girls of North House in the quad when one said, "You psyched for some sunbathing action?" And the other one said, "I didn't bring my bathing suit back from the Bahamas." And the first one said, "Who needs a suit?"

North is actually a house, not a dorm, a real exclusive place to live, only real cool, beautiful girls live there, like Valerie Beridox and Virginia della Chiesa. Valerie I know pretty well because we run the Saturday cleanup program in our cluster together (she's going to Princeton, me to Stanford, so such a shitty job must have been worth it). She's one of the top fifteen prettiest girls in school. Her lips are famous. In the boys' gym someone scratched into the enamel on the hot-air hand dryer, "Valerie Beridox sucks donkey dicks!!" I know it's mean, but her lips always pout like maybe she has. (At my sister's horseback riding camp they had a donkey with a schlong down to his donkey ankles, and you can't tell me none of those little rich girls never experimented on him or included him in some sort of psycho secret horseback riding society.)

For the last week these lowers and a few uppers have actually snuck up in our dorm's attic, climbed out a dormer window onto the hundred-year-old slate roof three stories above the flagstone courtyard below, and surveilled North House with binoculars. Until today they had only seen them in bathing suits or topless but on their backs. Then they enlisted Kurt and me.

We crawled out there, too, and even though I'm a rock climber, I have to say I thought I was going to die. My Top-Siders are real loose, and the squiggly tread under the balls of the feet are totally bald.

So I stepped out of the dormer window and pulled myself around to the peak of the roof. There were about twelve of us up there, our elbows and armpits hooked over the peak, the rest of us hidden down the backside.

Valerie, Cynthia, Virginia, they were all up there. Power chords from their portable radio would waft to us on periodic gusts of spring wind until I could recognize the song as Boston's "More Than a Feeling." But the girls insisted on tanning their backs, and most of us had afternoon classes.

"This sucks."

"We've got to make them turn over."

I had an idea. I deepened my voice with an opera singer's warm-up hum.

"Hey, ladies!!"

All the other guys glared at me like I was a nut, but Hank and Pete started to bolt down the real fast way until they caught themselves. The fast way was way too fast.

"Austin, are you crazy? Whatthefuckdoyouthinkyou'redoing?" Ben hissed at me like a snake.

All the girls suddenly stopped gossiping. You could see them look to each other, then look around.

"Would you rather waste all day up here staring at their backs?" I asked them.

Virginia stood up, topless, to investigate, but the railing to the widow's walk they lay on was at the exact height of her nipples.

"Awwwww," all us guys said at the same moment.

"It's the creeps in Taylor West, look!"

By this time eight of us were already inside the attic. Ben and I were the last down. Just our fingertips and foreheads were visible to the girls. There was no way they could recognize us. Valerie stood up and didn't bother to cover herself at all. Thankfully she's taller than Virginia and her nipples cleared the railing, giving us a wonderful, if very long-distance, view (Hank took the binoculars with him).

"Dream about these, little boys. Dream about these!" Valerie actually squeezed them for us. Ben and I slipped into the attic, where Mr. Geddes was already lecturing the little kids.

"Mrs. Chase at North House just called. You could have been killed. I've never heard of something so stupid. You boys need girlfriends, is what you need. . . . And Ben, Austin. You are seniors, how could you be so dumb?"

When I yelled I don't know what I was thinking. I certainly wasn't thinking that in my next class, AP Physics, I'd be sitting right behind Valerie. (I always chose that seat because she wears Impulse body spray.)

On the way to class I practiced and practiced. I knew that a smile would mean my death. At the classroom door I pushed my cheeks down to a frown. She saw me as soon as I entered, and I forced myself not to look away. All I could think about, however, were her breasts, which, though smaller and pointier than I had imagined, seemed nevertheless pretty terrific (at least from fifty yards away).

"Valerie, I heard what happened. The guys in my dorm are idiots, a bunch of hard-up nerds. Don't worry, I'll talk to them." I sounded pretty nonchalant, if I do say so myself.

"They are so queer. I don't know how you can stand them."

"Well, the year's almost over now, anyway. . . ."

"Stanford. I hate you. That was my first choice."

Luckily Dr. Crabins checked his watch, closed the door, and

started class. I was so happy she didn't suspect. James Bond couldn't have pulled off a better subterfuge. Her body spray was strong today, I guess to cover the sweat from sunbathing. I didn't understand a word Dr. Crabins said. The AP exam was last week, so who cares about the mass of a neutrino at the center of a pulsar. I still have no idea what I want to do after college, but I know you won't see me in a lab coat holding a clipboard. When's the last time you saw a *Playboy* Playmate cuddling up with an astrophysicist?

J u n e   I ,   1 9 8 0

J e n n y

The dinner at the Andover Inn was delicious. I can't afford any more pizza runs, and that's bad with exams coming up, but it was still worth it. I put on my brand-new brown corduroy suit but wore a tie because they're required. The four of us have swordfish and even appetizers, stuffed mushroom caps and shrimp cocktails. We would have ordered wine if we could have gotten away with it. Ben's date was Alicia, a real boring bowser. Her braces are off, finally, but she still has the back two rings around her molars for a night brace.

After dinner I walked Jenny home. Tonight's the night, I'd decided. She leaves in two days because some guy from her real high school asked her to their senior prom. She says she's going with him just because she's a junior and wants to scope out the place for her real prom next year.

Anyway, I was walking her home, trying to nonchalantly bump into her shoulder with each step:

"So . . . how about it?"

"How about what?"

She stops. We were at the bottom of the Vista, the cherry-and-oak-tree-lined corridor ending right at the steps of Sam Phil Hall, the capitol of campus. It was about ten, the pathway lamps lit up all the cherry-tree blooms, and the rest of the world made no sound at all.

"How about going out with me? I know we've been friends for a long time, but I thought, What the hell."

"I . . . I don't think so. Let's not ruin it."

"I . . . I understand."

And I did. I swear. I walked her home and she kissed my cheek, bucked me up with a hearty squeeze and squaring off of my shoulders. I don't feel the heartache of the other time, not at all. I knew this one was a long shot, but I did it. I asked. And there's honor in that.

J u n e   2 ,   1 9 8 0

J e n n y

I can't believe it. I was just back from a kayaking trip down the Allagash (as a student leader I got Calista into river running, too, even though her draw number was awful so she was on the waiting list. She looks fantastic in her wetsuit top. And when it's really hot she'll unzip it like something right out of "Charlie's Angels"). So I was coming up the stairs all covered in mud and feeling like a soldier of fortune when I notice Jenny's name on the parietals board. Parietals are when a girl comes up to your room. You have to get permission from the house counselor and sign her in. So Jenny was signed in, and guess for who? *Ben!!* I ran upstairs and kicked in his door (they have to be ajar when a girl's up). They were sitting on his bed right next to each other, thigh to thigh.

"Hey, Jenny, I'm back. Were you looking for me?" I forced myself to smile. James Bond would never freak out just because one of his women was on another man's bed. She got up and straightened her sundress, pulled it back down by her calves.

"I stopped by to see what you were up to and Ben said I could wait up in his room."

I was trying not to be paranoid and neurotic. I brought her

across the hall to Kurt's and my room (though technically I should have gone downstairs and re-signed her in). We talked about bullshit; all I could think of was her and Ben making out on his bed. I knew it. My life was going too well. Then I'd have to see her in two months on the Vineyard. We said good-bye, and she said how much she liked having me as a friend, and she hugged me and kissed my cheek and she left. I ran back across the hall to Ben's.

"You're right. She *is* a good kisser."

"You fucking asshole. I'm going to beat your head in."

"You said you were just friends now. And she said so, too."

"I can't believe you made out with her."

"We didn't really make out. We just kissed a little."

I would chop off my toes and wear braces again just to kiss her, really kiss her, just once.

"You're not my friend anymore. I hate your fucking guts. I'm glad you didn't even get into BU. Rollins is a fucking loser school that nobody's ever heard of . . . asshole."

And I was getting better, too. Not so crazy of late.

June 13, 1980

Graduation

God knows what'll become of me at Stanford. I guess I'll major in history or English, then maybe law school. People keep telling me I argue so much I'd be a good lawyer. Actually, I wouldn't mind being a professor of something. Fletcher reads, writes, and teaches for a living. That would be pretty fun. I'd always stay smart.

Ben's left. Jenny's left. Calista's left. (I caught her just before she was leaving. We just hugged a bit and cheek kissed. We're going to see each other throughout the summer in New York City. I've got a summer job working in a hospital there. My mom got it for me. She's a gynecologist for unwed mothers. At least I'll be out of Hamden, and I get to stay with my uncle and he's got a Hammond organ.) It's just us seniors, and it's been a terrific day. I wish the girls could have seen me in this new three-piece suit before today. It's brown, wide-rail corduroy. Actually, it looked better after graduation, when my folks let me take off my tie and pull out the points of my shirt. The tag at Marshall's said "irregular," but Dad and I couldn't find anything wrong with it. Maybe I'll dress real GQ at Stanford. What the hell.

We all stood in a circle and headmaster Sizer called our names and passed around the diplomas in a circle until it reached the right person. Real live bagpipers were playing. But the best part came later. Joie, of all people, stopped by my room and, just like last year, gave me a big kiss good-bye. Chantal, Marcus's girlfriend, kissed me on the lips, too. Valerie probably would have, but I chickened out and turned a bit so just the ends of our mouths touched. I don't think I've ever kissed so many girls at one time. Maybe that's a good sign.

June 24, 1980

Ms. Rod

New York is kind of lonely. Every kid in Connecticut dreams of making it here to the big leagues, but to tell you the truth, it's sort of boring. Last week I walked from my uncle's house on 103rd all the way down to South Ferry, where the Statue of Liberty ferry boat is, and back. It was about eighteen miles. After work in the hospital (I'm an "administrative intern," but I couldn't tell you what that means) I go home. My uncle usually goes out "clubbing" with his buddies from the post office, so I might go three or four days without saying to anyone more than "One, please," or "I'm done, thank you. Just the check, please." Morgan came up from Hamden last weekend and we had fun. Calista comes in, but it gets sort of frustrating. She's got a crush on this retardo lifeguard at the pool she goes to up in Rye. "I know it's sick, Austin, but I just keep thinking about him." And she calls herself a feminist.

So about Ms. Rod . . . I wrote a story called "Lawrence Oberti" about a reclusive teacher who's seduced by his student for a better grade. The minute after I mailed it I remembered that I'd named the sexy student Caroline, Ms. Rod's first name. I tried reaching in and getting it back out of the mailbox, but they have, of course, ingeniously designed the stupid mailboxes to prevent just that. Then I thought about waiting for the mailman to arrive and then to beg him to give it back, but I was going to be late for work. That was three weeks ago. No news is good . . .

June 30, 1980

Calista

First, while I was scouring the neighborhood looking for white fuel for my camping stove, I passed a bum sitting his butt in a metal wire trash can on a street corner. His knees and calves and feet, half of his back, and his arms and head dangled free, but the center of him was lodged there. This city is so weird.

We'd planned a camping trip to the Pine Barrens, chaperoned by her two big brothers, who still live in Rye. I met her on the street near FAO Schwarz and immediately confessed to be happy she was wearing a dress. She smiled, then introduced me to her two friends, Maya, who's Indian, and Rich, who's black. They are friends of hers from her old public high school in Rye. It's disgusting, but I was immediately jealous of him. I instinctively wanted to protect my territory from this other black guy.

He was obviously as in love with her as I. He rocked back and forth on his feet and kept staring at her. Where a mustache might someday grow, snot glistened from his leaky nose. He pitched forward, his lips right on course for hers. Thankfully, Calista wagged her head left, then right, converting his clumsy, snotty pass into two very continental pecks.

Looking at him was looking at a mirror.

I pulled her away, to the garage where my uncle's car was being fixed.

Of course the car wasn't ready by five like the mechanic had promised. Calista and I waited on the old front seat of a big American car leaning against a wall. The wall across from us was papered with *Playboy* centerfolds and bikinied and naked spokes-ladies for air filters and fuel-treatment systems. I made sure I didn't look too much. I was wearing my old *Godspell* T-shirt, and I swear I think I caught her staring at my pecs.

At six-thirty the Gremlin was fixed and I drove onto the West Side Highway. I tried not to let her realize how scared I was. I'd never driven in the city before and was positive I was going to kill or at least paralyze us both. On the highway itself the traffic was awful. And then the Gremlin just stopped. Immediately every asshole in New York City was honking at me. Calista didn't scream, though. She was great. Finally, a nice foreign guy (Polish?) pushed us, and I jump-started the car. We went about another half mile when it just stopped again. This time a carful of Puerto Rican guys about my age inched their Electra to the Gremlin's bumper and pushed us over a hill, and with the help of the downhill it jump-started again. This time I got off the highway at the next exit, 178th Street.

Calista's cool the whole time; in fact, she reached up the sleeve of my shirt and stroked my bicep—the first time we'd ever really touched. A wave of goose bumps erupted across my chest, and I flinched away from her. Immediately I wanted to squeeze and kiss her, even in just a friendly way, but I didn't want to make her think I was a studly hound dog, but I also didn't want to make her think I was cold. But I should have done something back, instead of nothing, which is what I did do.

I turned the wrong way down a one-way street.

"Austin, uh . . . I think . . ."

This garbage truck cruising the right way down the street almost took us out.

"Shit! I'm sorry. But if we stop again we'll conk out, and I don't want to stop here."

The car stopped anyway. We walked to a gas station. The night was starting to rise. I felt awful being afraid of my own people, but I didn't even know Manhattan had a 178th Street. I untucked my T-shirt and tried to think tough. We walked past some actually okay buildings to a Citgo. There she called her brothers to tell them we'd be late. I walked a bottle of gas back to the car, expecting to find it already stripped and aflame. It wasn't, but the gas didn't help. I flagged down a gypsy cab (I'm learning all the NYC lingo), and he jump-started the car for free.

I noticed that the guy who ran the gas station, he was white or white Spanish, carried a sawed-off baseball bat wrapped in silver duct tape. He said whatever was wrong with the car he couldn't fix tonight. Calista called her brothers to come pick her up. I called my uncle. Her brothers came first. They snatched Calista home, and I felt like Romeo and Juliet, our relationship torn asunder. Of course I didn't go in for the "Rich"-like, leaky-nose kiss.

July 1, 1980

Angelique

I already told you Mom got me this crappy job working in this hospital in Spanish Harlem. She and Dad put their heads together and came up with this "experience" to send me off to California. I have to wear a tie and jacket, and the office walls are two-tone dingy: battleship gray halfway up, then yellowed white to the ceiling. All the file cabinets are dark green steel. The men wear short-sleeved, button-down shirts. They all thought Stanford University was a community college in Stamford, Connecticut. I want to scream that I turned down Yale. This place is like something out of the Soviet Union or "Barney Miller."

Except for Angelique. She's a secretary and also a model! Janey Peck in river running at Andover was the first real live model I ever met. She was on the cover of *Seventeen* twice, but in person she's a beanpole. But Angelique is black and older, at least twenty-five. We are the only two blacks in the office, so she's nice to me.

(I'm supposed to be figuring out the average number of nonmeat meals requested in the cafeteria for a study my boss is doing on adding more vegetarian junk to the junky menu. It will take forever sorting through all the lunch receipts last month, especially at my lousy $4.18/hour.)

She's just come back from lunch, and she's wearing a slit skirt. She came into work in pants. My little desk is right across from hers, and when I lean back I can see where the slit lets the skirt fall away from her crossed legs under her desk. I know what I'll be thinking about tonight in bed with Ms. Sock. Oops! She keeps looking my way, so it's hard to steal an eyeful. But I'm trying to remember this image for tonight. Under the desk, next to her legs, brown as chocolate, is this big, zippered book, a portfolio like an artist would carry. I bet it's pictures of her. Let's find out. . . .

Later...

You wouldn't believe it!! Here's what just happened:

"Hey, Angelique, do you always change your clothes twice a day? You look great."

"Thanks. I had a go-see (?) at *Essence*. They pissed me off. I did their damn cover last year, and now they act like they don't even know me."

"Oh. Do you have a copy? I'd love to see it."

"You would?"

"Yeah . . . you know . . ."

She uncrossed her legs to reach under her desk and hand me the big leather notebook.

"My book's not great yet. And everything's not in there, but tell me what you think."

She clipped on her special headphones (they yoke under her chin like those on an airplane) attached to a tape recorder that she ran with her foot to transcribe a letter Mr. Cucciarola dictated to her this morning.

....

I unzipped her portfolio and took a breath so deep it closed my
eyes and then opened them and started to look. The first picture
is the torn-off *Essence* cover. Angelique's on a lounge chair in a
bikini. I suffocated my smile and nodded my head very seriously
like I was studying art. I pulled the plastic sleeve around the picture
around the steel spiral, and the next pages showed me (on the left)
Angelique on the back of a speedboat, her fingers in her hair,
which dances high above her in the wind; (and on the right)
Angelique sucking in and eating the insides of each cheek. In the
next one she's sipping champagne with some goon; then she's
skipping through the surf, barefoot, in an evening gown. And
then . . . she's lying on her back, rolling a white stocking off her
calf, the other leg still encased in stocking, her tiny stomach ringed
in a white garter, her loin sheathed in a white silk V, and her
breasts (yes!) caressed by a bra as absolutely gossamer and as see-
thru as a screen door. I kept just nodding my head to a silent,
serious rhythm, but I suddenly realized that I must dedicate my
life to stealing this picture. She looks pretty great in person, but
in the picture she is a dream girl. It would be like making love
with one of my hero Hefner's Playmates, only black and not so
humongous in the chest. I'd be cured for sure.

Another first: *First breasts (though veiled) ever seen in a picture
of someone I knew.*

Only after I'd almost come did I notice Angelique looking first
at me, then at what I was looking at. I closed the book quickly,
zipped it shut, petted off imaginary dirt with my hand, and delivered it back to her desk.

"Well, what do you think?"

"It's very nice. You're going to be a superstar."

"Do you think so?" She reached, held my forearm, and my
lungs froze. Her nails on my skin scared me. Mr. Cucciarola
stepped out of his office ahead of us, and I jerked my hand away
so he could pass. Angelique raised the page she had just typed
above her head, and Mr. C. took it, started reading it on his way
to the lav.

....

"What sign are you, Austin?"

"Libra."

"When's your birthday?"

I told her.

She looked at the wall without seeing it to think for a moment. "You mean you're only seventeen?"

My cock, up to this point in our story, threatened to rip a hole in my new cords. Suddenly it deflated back to insignificance. "You're just a baby."

"But I—I'm going to college in the fall."

Not soon enough. She rolled her chair around, closed herself to me, her back now guarding those breasts.

I should get back to work.

Later...

It's Friday, so everybody is leaving early. Angelique and I are the last ones, and she's just gone to the ladies' room. Her portfolio still leans against the cave for her legs under her desk. Stealing the breast picture would be stupid. But the Xerox machine is in the back. I can't breathe completely, my heart's too swollen. *Don't be a wimp!! Do it now!!*

Later...

I can't believe it. I'm writing this in the office after hours, alone, and you'll never believe it. I pushed back on my chair so hard that I rolled completely across the room. I leaned just my head out of our offices and didn't see her. I ran back and snatched her "book" up inside my jacket, hobbled to the copy machine. Janet, the other secretary, must have turned it off for the night. I couldn't find the fucking switch, then finally did (it's way in the back). The machine said, "Please wait," on its little calculator screen, then, "Warm up," and I was banging on it to make it hurry as every sound in the hall tweaked my guts, made a tiny spurt of pee want to come out and see what was going on. I gave up and started for her desk when the copier beeped a friendly beep like it was saying "Ready when you are, you pathetic freak." I ripped back the rubber flap on the glass and laid down the picture. I pushed "1" copy and "lighten" since it's a smoky picture already and waited. A bright pass of its fluorescent wand and out slid a copy of her image, like something out of a Xerox ad, almost as sexy as the color original. A quick rezip and I was hopping back to her desk.

"You're still here, Austin?"

Angelique smiled from the door. I don't remember how long it took me to close my mouth. I couldn't think. All of my brain was firing signals at the same time, and all I wanted to do was leap through the chicken-wired safety-glass window to the street below. I lowered her portfolio to her desk without it making a sound on landing as if she were blind but had heightened hearing. I wanted to sit down, needed to, but how to explain my guilty hands, my far-flung chair?

I wanted to cry. She looked confused. She slowly, very slowly, picked up her portfolio and held it. Then she looked to my hands and my copy of her image, face up, breasts up. And then she did something that almost made me believe in God again. It was so nice that its kindness tingled my face. She smiled and rolled her eyes.

"If you wanted a copy, you just had to ask, that's all."

She smiled to herself, went, "Ungh, ungh, ungh." She opened her book to that picture, held it out at the end of her arms, examined it. She struggled the picture out of its plastic sleeve and handed it to me.

"I've got plenty of extra prints back at the house." She freed the heavy picture she had held up at the high height of her head (5 feet 10 inches), it surfed the office air right to the center of my desk.

"Thanks."

"Oh! I forgot. Give it back, will you?"

I did.

She trotted into Mr. C's office on her sexy high heels, pulled his Cross pen from its scabbard. She smiled to herself as she wrote something. "Here." This time she delivered the picture by hand. In the right bottom corner, over her toes that were just about to be freed from the white stocking she was rolling down her leg, she had written this:

To Austin,
With much affection,
Angelique Simpson

"You know, that's my very first autograph."
"I am sure it won't be your last."
"You really think so?"
"You bet."
"I hope so."
Something made her twist her wrist and look at her watch. "Oh, no! Ricky's going to flip!" She rezipped her portfolio, slapped it under her arm, hooked the strap to her handbag, and tottered out. "See you tomorrow!"
I can't wait to tell my friends that she's my girlfriend.

July 3, 1980

Calista

We've gone to the movies a couple of times this summer, but nothing's happened to write home about until today.
She's leaving for a bicycle tour of the Basque region of Spain in three days, and today was our good-bye. She had asked me to come along, but Marquita and Fletcher said they couldn't afford it *and* Stanford.
I went to this cutesy gift shop near my uncle's house, "P.S., I Love You," because I had gotten my sister's Christmas present there. It took me forever to decide on a gift. It was hard to choose

something romantic/friendly and definitely unsappy. Then the guy puts it in a pink box and closes it with a big red heart sticker that says the name of the store, "P.S., I Love You," on it. I tried to peel it off, but it was ripping up and fuzzing the box itself. Not even out the door I was already thinking up jokes to acknowledge the sap factor of the box.

I was excited and springy all day. She wanted to go to the Museum of Broadcasting. She said she loved museums, and "most of my other friends aren't the types to go to museums." I wasn't crazy about being called a "museum type," especially since I think of myself more as an "outdoorsy, rugged, macho, mercenary/ mountain man type." But at least she said I was her friend.

In front of the place no kiss hello, but the first thing she said was that I looked "dapper." I could have levitated. I was wearing my brand-new white pleated pants, a long-sleeved, collarless shirt, but I'd rolled up the sleeves, and loafers. She looked fantastic, too. New cowboy boots, stylish lavender pants, and a matching velour top.

After the exhibit on the history of TV news, we wandered around downtown, and I was proud and for once not stoop-shouldered. We came upon a businessmen's minipark with a waterfall with a tunnel you can walk right through, and it was her idea to stop.

My heart sapped the rest of me, and I had a hard time not making any noise while I breathed. The tiny gift box also seemed to swell. I wedged my hand into the pants pocket folded as closed as a purse by my sitting. I had to arch out of the chair to enter the pocket, and a corner of the paper box was smushed.

"Austin, what did you do!"

I thought I had food on my cheek or farted.

"Oh! It's nothing special. Just a going-away present. The sticker is just, uh—"

"I'll be back in a month."

I delivered the little box to the space above her lap, sticker side down. Her hand contacted mine, a lot, while she removed the boxlet from my palm.

"I don't want to rip the sticker, it's so cute."

I don't remember what I said. Probably nothing at all or some unintelligible grunt.

The pink-and-purple ceramic unicorn with the safety pin in its back lay on its side in the cotton batting inside the tiny box as if in a coffin, dead.

"Thank you. It's . . . uh . . . Thanks."

"It's five-fifteen. You're going to miss your train."

At Grand Central I said good-bye as if I were saying "See you later." She stepped into the car, and I said it, the dumb thing only an idiot says to someone going to Spain. I said, *"Adios."*

July 7, 1980

Peep Show

It was another lonely weekend. I spent all day Saturday reading Ellison's *Invisible Man* in Central Park and practicing my Frisbee throws to myself. Everybody, it seemed, was in love; people were practically going at it behind every bush. Summer school kids in identical T-shirts booted a soccer ball around rubber Day-Glo orange dunce cap cones. In the Sheep Meadow, the prettiest spot in the city, the only green grass in the city, fenced off and at the foot of all those old stone skyscrapers, New York women and men actually sunbathe. There's no sand or wave or water in sight, but they just lie there in their bathing suits. I read there sometimes, but I just take off my shirt. I graze the meadow as if I'm looking for a friend, then park it close enough to a babe to get an eyeful but far enough away not to make her move.

Today I saw this gorgeous Indian woman in a yellow string bikini, and I lay down behind her. It was noon, and she was already shiny with sweat. I read on my elbows, indenting the city's precious Kentucky bluegrass with my boner. The Indian woman lay on her back, paddling her skyward calves and beautiful tiny brown feet to the pop radio she listened to. Then she turned my way, and I quickly turned to look behind me. There I saw this short white guy with a huge handlebar mustache and a tiny black bikini bathing suit, ogling me. I must have made a face because he took off.

I turned back around and the Indian woman was now standing, dragging her Jordache jeans over her brown legs. She didn't put on a top, though, and walked away dangling her high, high heels from her hand like a six-pack. Then I left, too.

I watched the roller skaters trace an oval around a wall of boom boxes all tuned to the same soul station. "It's Gonna Take a Lot of Love" exploded from all ten speakers. Some women wore Lycra, others jeans and bikini tops like the Indian woman or hot pants and bikini tops. It was pretty great, and I was getting more and more depressed. I could only think of my calcifying virginity.

I got lost in the bottom of the park and just kept walking south. I pretended to myself that I was just wandering.

"Oh, imagine that, Times Square."

The red neon over the mirrored door was shaped like a giant eye, and a strobe flashed its pupil. If it were my establishment, I'd sketch a pyramid around the eye. Every trip to the city with my parents had us driving past this sign, and since my first erection I knew I'd one day sneak inside. I didn't know if they had an age restriction, but rules in New York are cheerfully broken by all. (In Hamden we couldn't go to R-rated movies until we were almost actually seventeen, here they didn't care. And last year Morgan and I came to the city to see the USS *Eagle* and the rest of the tall ships, and I asked for *Playboy* in Grand Central Station and the guy didn't even blink.)

I walked past the mirrored door and didn't even slow down, then did a sudden military turn—spinning smartly around one leg—that shot me inside.

I thought it would be darker. Everything was fluorescently lit, biological clocks stopped, and instead of late Sunday afternoon it seemed suddenly and perpetually four-thirty in the morning in an artificially lit casino or bus depot. An old lady slouched over the cash register in the corner behind a counter of dildos, black and white (the black ones were almost twice as big, making me feel, as usual, a traitor to my race).

Magazines in plastic with truly disgusting names filled the front room. Undercover cops should hang out there to find out what Boy Scout leaders and kindergarten teachers are buying: *Milk-Squirting Mama* and *Little Girl Review*. Hanging from the ceiling like small, Thanksgiving Day parade zeppelins were these inflatable love dolls with plastic decal eyes and round plastic mouths stuffed with more plastic crumpled around a slit. Their vaginas had identical plastic receptacles. Almost every guy in there was wearing a business suit.

In the back were the peep show booths, like bathroom stalls. Gas station bathroom-style condom dispensers dotted the red walls. I can't imagine whacking off in a little room next to dozens of other pre-suicides, like cows at a dairy.

Anyway, I shopped the stalls; each one had a picture from the minimovie inside and a paragraph description. I thought, politically, I should pay for *Big Black Boom!* but the black girl and the white humping the black stud were skeezy. I don't want to see a giant cock, anyway. Finally I found *Sleepaway Camp* with a picture of two old women (blond and brunette) in their thirties flicking each other's tongues. They wore bows in their heads, kilts, and knee socks.

SLEEPAWAY CAMP. Candice and Leona were two very good teenage vixens, so their parents didn't worry about them at summer camp. No boys across the lake for these two nubile nymphets! But up on the bunk bed one night talking about s-e-x, Candice and Leona tongue down to some raunchy, lip-smacking, juice-oozing, lesbo love action!

I laughed when I read this, and everybody stopped ogling their perverted magazines, the guys in the booths probably stopped beating their meat. It was as if I'd asked for a glass of milk at a Hell's Angels' bar. You don't laugh at a peep show.

I bought a dollar's worth of tokens (four) and escaped inside the *Sleepaway Camp* booth. It was surprisingly quiet and cozy inside. I started to sit on the bar stool provided but thought better of it.

I inserted the four tokens without touching the money opening and waited. A video of two women kissing appeared on the screen before me, and I have to admit, it was pretty great. I love lesbian scenes. No dicks squirting. (I have no idea why the guys finish by jerking off outside the women and come on their stomachs, mouths, or butts. Why don't the women get pissed? And as a customer, it's particularly depressing because the guy with a hand on his dick suddenly takes you away from the fantasy and rudely reminds you what you're doing at that very moment, but you're doing it only because you're not on the other side of the screen with the babe.)

On the screen before me were just women's faces chewing their lips and moaning—all the good stuff. And the women, though obviously not girls, as I said before, were still really sexy. So okay, I didn't actually whip it out in there—who knows what you could catch—but I did rub it through my pants. I'd kill to be in a threesome with two sexy women. If I had a big dick, I'd skip college and audition at wherever it is they make these things.

My money ran out just as the brunette screamed, "No!" and clutched the head of blond hair to her crotch. If they had asked for fifty bucks to continue, I'd have paid it, but I'm sure they have it planned that way. I waited until my wiener schnitzel subsided before turning open the bathroom stall–style bolt and exiting, all serious and mature-looking. Right ahead of me was a stairway studded with flashing lights. Women's moaning filled the down-stairs before an emcee added his voice:

Ladies, loving ladies, upstairs in the rotoroom, gentlemen.
You won't believe your eyes. Only one silver dollar.

A few guys shuffled upstairs as slowly as if they were lining up to be gassed. No one smiled, no one looked at anyone else. No "Howdy, Fred. Fancy meeting you here." None of that.

So I went upstairs. I've seen the George C. Scott movie *Hard-core*, where his good little daughter runs away and falls into the porno world. They show all these skanky women behind Plexiglas talking you through your jerking off via a telephone intercom. But I went upstairs anyway. And upstairs was different. There was a sexual buzz up here. It was dark. The stakes were higher. I bought a silver dollar from a dead-faced African guy on a stool at the head of the stairs and entered a cubicle like the ones below, only each formed the side of this giant polygon in the center of the room. I slipped Eisenhower into the oversize slot, and the shade over the window in front of me motored up. Before me I saw a foam mattress on a plywood platform that rotated. No one was there. Behind the platform I imagined my colleagues standing behind (thankfully) two-way mirrors. A door on the side opened and in walked an old man, blacker than my mother's father, wearing coveralls and dragging a ratty mop and a pail of gray water. He slopped the mop in the pail, slopped the mop around the floor, flipped over the foam mattress to show us a side with even more divets and craters crumbled out of it. Just then my window shade motored back down. Show over.

Outside I said to the African, "Hey, the show's already over."

"Don't you know wait till the light green?"

I shook my head.

He looked past one shoulder, then the other. He dipped into his money pouch apron and picked out a silver dollar, handing it to me. "This time you wait the green, brother."

I smiled. *"Merci,"* I said.

"Merci. You speak French? That's good." He was all white teeth then, smiling sweetly. He looked past me, over my head. "See, green light. Green light."

Pretty green lights were now lit above every slender doorway. This time inside, this time after the shade had arisen, the foam mattress was covered with a black fitted sheet and on it two skinny white women junkies sixty-nined.

Another first: *Sex seen live.*

But I couldn't get excited about these women. You've never ever in your life seen people so sad and unenthusiastic about their jobs. Subway booth guys are more lively. Their tongue waggings and dartings looked snakelike, and the one on top had a dragon tattoo down one thigh and a horrible splotch of a bruise on the other. They were obviously thinking of other things, like their next fix or how to make bail for their boyfriends. Then on cue they switched positions with as much passion as a cook flips over a gristly steak. The nausea I felt when I had snuck into *Deep Throat* with Morgan and the rest of the guys at the Yale Law School summer film series returned. The sadness of their lives, the sadness of *my* life, standing there watching them surrounded by other boys and men similarly unloved. I needed to get out, but the nice African guy would be hurt. I looked away from the blackened crusty bottoms of their ugly feet until the screen motored back down. I opened up and stepped out and almost ran into a woman.

She wore purple high heels and red lingerie and smiled gently at me as she passed. A few other women now milled the upstairs, too. Then they sauntered to the far corner, where I guessed the one-on-one fantasy booths lurked. The woman who smiled at me was a pretty sexy older woman, and if I were at a bar in the Midwest for some reason late at night, I might try to hit on her. It was weird to see the women live and unprotected by Plexiglas. It was scary, and the grown-up men seemed scared, too. They stood straight and quiet. Luckily I had no more money. Besides, there's no way in hell I could jerk off in front of somebody, Plexiglas or no.

I stepped quickly out the front door and military-turned again, joined the regular people in the regular world, pretended to look back at the peep show neon as if wondering what types of pathetic fucks frequented a place like that. *Playboy*, Hef's mansion, that stuff, is much more my style. The women are genuinely beautiful, and there's something sweet and 1950s about the way they don't show off their labia and pubic hair.

It was a wonderful summer sunset, so I didn't mind having to walk the fifty blocks back to my uncle's.

T e l e v i s i o n

I watch too much TV here. While my uncle's asleep I sneak into the TV room and watch "Midnight Blue" cable porn until two in the morning. Or if some "R"-rated B movie is coming on HBO at three in the morning and the cable guide (very thoughtfully) warns "mature theme" and "strong sexual content," I'll set my alarm for 2:55 A.M., tuck it under my pillow so the noise won't wake him up, and sneak out to watch. Usually it's foreign softcore, and the dubbing is terrible, obviously one male and one female actor only slightly changing their voices to play the entire cast of Austrian ski lodge or Greek Isle vacationers. And the German or Swedish ideal of beauty in 1965 is not quite what turns me on today. They are out of shape and pasty, stringy blondes. Everybody's wearing turtlenecks, zip-up boots, and vinyl vests. I know it's a waste of time, but I don't go back to bed until the foreign credits show up.

I slump back to bed at 4:15, exhausted and frustrated. My eyes are already droopy, but with bags hanging under them like wet drapery I look particularly awful. Every time I look in a mirror the next day I remind myself of the wasted night before. My uncle's talking about getting a videocassette recorder when the prices come down. I hope he springs for one before the summer's over so I can finally get some sleep.

I'm also sickly this summer. I go to the gym, but I'm always coughing from the pollution in the city, and the bloody noses are coming back. The new white sheets have rusty splotches on them in the morning.

···

July 15, 1980

LaShawna

Life just got easier!

I'm one of seventeen hospital interns. The rest of them are in college already. Once a week we all get together at Lincoln Hospital in the South Bronx for no real good reason. Except LaShawna. She's at NYU Hospital, a nice clean one, and she's gorgeous. She's from the Bronx, but a nice part, she says.

I'm proud of myself for talking to her and walking her to the subway after our meeting. Some big guy tried to pick her up ("Say, you're beautiful. What's your name?"), and then he asked me if I minded. I felt great! I'm going to see her at Lincoln Hospital tomorrow, and I'm going to get her last name. I know she lives at the last stop of the Number 2 line. She's a sophomore at some city college. I told her, "Me too."

July 16, 1980

LaShawna

Can't believe it!! I got her last name at work, then just called her up a minute ago. I asked her if she wanted to see the harbor festival tomorrow. She's got my number from the intern participant list, and she'll call me at work tomorrow. We could walk around the Battery or just see the fireworks at nine-fifteen and the movie *Airplane!*. You should have seen me when I called her. No hemming and hawing. I just picked up the phone and dialed before fear had a chance to strangle bravery.

J u l y 1 8, 1 9 8 0

L a S h a w n a

Called her. She wasn't in. Will call again. No more intern meetings till next week.

A u g u s t 1, 1 9 8 0

T h e T a n g o P a l a c e

Morgan came into town for the weekend. I should have seen it coming.

We cruised Times Square looking for a place to go. We were both curious, but Morgan was more hyped up than me. He especially wanted to go to this grungy, seedy joint at the back of an alley. I wanted to go to the Mardi Gras because it seemed the most respectable so would probably have the prettiest women. We passed a place called the Zoo. The sign said "Free Details Inside." Many men stopped and read the sign, almost went in. Morgan walked right toward the creepy bouncer and said, "We're here for the 'free details,'" as if "detail" meant "sample." The guy said it'd cost sixty bucks to join this sex club, where we can have as much sex as we want till four in the morning. We left. We didn't have fifty bucks between us (which is probably as much as we'd ever had in our lives). I again suggested the Mardi Gras, but Morgan liked the Tango Palace because it was seedier. On the walls going up the stairs were strips of masking tape saying things like "Oooooh! I want you" and "You'll have a ball."

As we got to the top of the long, almost scary stairway, the signs got hotter ("Fuck me now, big one!"). At the top was a ticket booth. Only two dollars to get in. Three women in garter belts or bikinis lounged behind tables on the dance floor. They looked like a trade-school/women's prison production of a *Guys & Dolls* nightclub. They were all alone, and a green wooden, ornate railing separated us and the rest of the guys in booths from them. The walls were hidden by metallic wrapping paper, a nearby column was spray-painted blue with large pink dots, there were various mirror balls around the room and many lights (but none either bright or white). A flashy jukebox mumbled Barry Manilow's "Copacabana."

A fat bartender, who was also the ticket taker, asked us if we wanted some beers.

"I thought these were just strippers. Let's eat the two bucks and cruise."

Morgan didn't hear me. A pretty black woman in a red garter and matching top was staring right at him, hypnotizing him. She beckoned him with her finger (I swear) and drew him from his seat to the rail like a magician.

Immediately she snaked her hands around his neck and held him close. She whispered in his ear, then nibbled it. He twisted away, blushed like a baby, and held his ear as he returned.

"Your turn."

I went up and we made small talk as she put her arms around me. Her sugary perfume welled in the back of my nose and throat and camped there like the sugar smell that filled the air the day my elementary school class in Michigan toured the Kellogg's factory in Battle Creek.

"Don't you want to dance with us, sugar? Aren't we fine?"

I wanted to tell her we just wanted to watch, we didn't think people really *did* it in here, right in the middle of the city, but I just mumbled something and escaped back to my seat. I could feel my green nylon sport wallet miraculously rising out of my jeans and floating overhead on a barely visible wire to her soft cleavage.

Now one of his own, a white lady, called Morgan. Her breasts were huge, unlike the black's, whose were small but whose nipples were erect. This new one grabbed his hand and put it on her waist. When I met her, up close I saw she was as old as my mom, but sexiness radiated out from her, and I almost blurted out we were minors to make them kick us out, make them break the spell. But I didn't, and the woman wiped my chest with her breasts. Then she reached low through the railing between us and squeezed my dick.

Another first! *First penis-hand contact.*

But I was too scared to enjoy it.

The black one called back Morgan and squeezed his dick and called him chicken. "I want to fuck you," he said she said to him.

"Jesus, what did you say back?"

"What do you mean, what did I say? I said, uh, I don't know what I said. What can you say?"

"Let's get out of here. I don't want to lose it this way."

"Twenty dollars an hour."

I looked at him. Actually, that's not an unreasonable fee. My heart and my dick leeched my brain of much needed blood. I was terrified of doing what I'd dreamed of doing so often. I'm tired of practicing. Sometimes I can't sleep and just bang my mattress with my fists because another night's about to pass and I'm still a virgin. At least this way I'd get it over with and maybe then I'd be normal.

"If you tell anybody, I'll tell them it was your fucking idea, Austin." Morgan didn't look like he was having any fun at all. I'd never seen him so serious.

"Look," I told him, "I know what my life will be like if I chicken out, the exact same as it's been, which isn't so good. But I don't know what it will be like if I go through with it. So if you're in, I'm in."

Morgan nodded very seriously, his arms tightly knitted over his chest. The black lady rubbed her pelvis on the wood railing at him. I didn't think of it till now, but it's ironic he went with a black lady and I was going after a white one. But just as I was going to go after the old white lady with the huge, smearing breasts, a short old guy bumped past me, and he and she went to a restaurant-style booth in the back.

"Let's skip it, Morgan. I don't want to wait an hour and I don't want to put it where that guy has."

"What about her?" He pointed at this bubbling, fatty one; she must have been for weirdos who had rail-skinny wives. "They'll be like that in Italy. You'll have to get used to it." He can be so

stupid. See, Stanford has this overseas studies program in Florence,
Italy, and I'm planning on going there my sophomore year.

"See you later on the other side." Morgan smiled and let himself
be conveyed to the railing by his woman's power.

I hardly had time to feel sorry for myself when this lady I saw
in the beginning in a wide-striped bikini came back from the way
back. I met her at the rail, and soon we retired to a booth behind
Morgan and his date. The ticket taker/bartender immediately took
my twenty bucks, then asked me what we'd have to drink, and I
said nothing for the both of us. I'm broke, I told him.

"Let's dance." She took my hand and pulled me to the back
side, the prostitute side, of the railing. Morgan's was pulling him
out there, too. I thought we were just waiting for a room to open
up, but these curtained stalls in the back with mattresses and old
travel agency posters all looked empty.

Maria was good-looking, Hispanic (Spanish, she said, not Puerto
Rican), small but nicely shaped breasts and *bronze* skin rubbed
with so much perfume that she shined and her skin practically
squeaked when you touched it. Her perfume was the same last
Christmas's candy-cane sugar scent as the old white woman's with
the large breasts. There's probably a dispenser in the back next to
the Lava soap and Janitor in a Drum. I expertly fingered down
her back, then boldly squeezed her butt.

"This is my first time."

"First what?"

"Uh, fuck?"

"You don't fuck me for twenty bucks."

Curses, foiled again. But almost immediately I was sort of glad
(I swear). I had fun anyway, squeezing her butt and feeling her
breasts *(a first)*. I didn't kiss her, though. Who knew what she had
growing in there? We returned to the table, where she continued
to try to cajole $100 from me to have sex with her, then we returned
again to the dance floor.

"I'm so horny!" With her accent it came out "hoeny," almost
Chinese. I had ten dollars left in my wallet, and I was hell-bent
on keeping it there.

At the table I asked her about herself. She said she was a legal secretary, originally from northern Spain, not Castilian. They speak a dialect in her town, she said. I asked her if she knew the Basque country, and she said no. Then she said she lived in Manhattan. Later she said Queens. Did I write yet that she was wearing a rusty red wig?

Back dancing, I reached down and pressed her vulva, and a moan gurgled out of her throat that practically made me come. If I had a hundred bucks right then, I'd be that much poorer now. I played with her breasts inside her shirt some more. She tongued my ear and I squirmed.

At our table she lifted her tiny breasts out of the bikini top and presented them to me. *Another first.*

Touching them was nice, but actually seeing them was unbelievable. Some drool must have escaped because she smiled as if she'd won our war over my wallet. She scratched a hand down her belly and must have been fingering herself right there under the table.

"See how my nipples harden, honey?" And indeed they did. "I just came."

She removed her hand and licked her glistening thumb and thumbnail (painted the same purple as that striping her bikini). The tremendous thumbnail extended her thumb past her middle finger. "You know I'm wet down there. See the drops?" She stood and leaned over our table, lifted her breasts with her hands as shelves and delivered them to my mouth. "I want you to suck my tits." *Another first.* I did and it was wonderful, the texture, the smell, I could feel her body all rev because of me.

"Oh, you just tease me," she said. She dragged me back just to dance. She rubbed my dick hard through my pants, and I was so close to coming but tried not to moan because I knew she couldn't let me finish for free.

"Look, I just lost my job and have just a hundred dollars to my name. I'm just not sure yet."

It worked. I could see the shine come to her eyes. I slipped my hand up her leg, touched base, then she backed off and fingered herself. I stroked her again, and she really was wet. I'm still impressed by her biological acting. I stared into her eyes (beautiful, beautiful brown things, big and deep). She asked what was the matter, and I told her how wonderful her eyes were and that she must hear that daily. She cupped my head in her hand. "What can I do to make you fuck me?" It was the sweetest, most tender thing a woman or girl has ever said to me. I peeped through the window of love for one flash. She batted her eyes again and kissed me softly, no tongue.

By now her bag of tricks must have been near empty. At the table again she took a big, noisy breath. "Dinner's served." And she sat on the table, flopped her pretty legs over each of my shoulders, shoved her bikini bottom over to actually show me her vagina. I looked, but I felt a bit like my mother must feel at her OB-Gyn office.

"Listen, honey. I want to fuck you, but I got to make a living. Aren't you going to tip me ten or twenty bucks?"

"I'm jobless." Which was sort of true. Summer internships don't count.

She stood up, huffing and muttering, "Shit."

I saw Morgan back in front of the railing, all ruffled and sweaty. We waved good-bye to our women, who were back in the exact positions they'd held before. They waved back.

Morgan tried to buy two cocktails but couldn't afford them, so he and his date had to share a beer.

We walked all the way to Greenwich Village since we were broke. In Washington Square we crossed this herd of girls, teens. This pretty black girl suddenly screamed in Morgan's ear, "Booo!" Very meanly. We both jumped and shrieked. The girls giggled, then looked stern. We listened to a pack of throwbacks singing "Miss American Pie." The crowd seemed to compete to see who knew the most words. Who's the least phony. On Bleecker Street a bum pissed. All night long I couldn't smell the summer New York night, just the candy sweetness of her perfume. Breathing it made your nose twinge. Old flowers, alcohol, and maple-flavored syrup.

August 18, 1980

Calista

She got back from Spain three days ago and I'd already called her mom three times. I'm leaving for Stanford in four days—orientation wipes out any hope of seeing Jenny on the Vineyard—and Calista will have to go back to Andover for her last year in a week. Every ring of my uncle's phone triggered my practiced, unstressed conversation with her. Finally she called today. The words "I love you" and "I can't live without you" barely stayed down with the entire box of Pop-Tarts I had just eaten. She's house-sitting for her old t'ai chi instructor on Eighty-eighth Street and invited me over for "a drink."

It wasn't the first time I'd bought booze, but I was still pretty nervous. The Indian guy didn't care and even asked me if I wanted the Freixenet gift-wrapped. I did. She said to come over at eight, but I was late trying to find a newsstand with decent breath mints. I couldn't wait for them to dissolve, so I crunched six, and for some time my molars were so clogged that my mouth couldn't close.

Her door opened and her hug nearly broke me, the heat from her cheek I still feel in mine.

"I wasn't back an hour before my mom said, 'Calista, I have to talk to you.' I thought she was going to talk about sex, but it's a little too late for that."

The world then fell away from me. I couldn't hear whatever it was she continued to say. I was all heartbeat. I forced my face into what I hoped was an unshocked expression, but she caught on and backpedaled, embarrassed. I teased her about it, congratulated her, and tried to impersonate a laugh by huffing out quick exhales. I think I said things like "Way to go" and maybe even "Welcome to the club," but I honestly can't remember. As she talked, all I saw in front of me was Calista under a Spanish oak, under a Spanish man.

Sabino. The bastard Basque shepherd/terrorist was herding his sheep on horseback just outside Pamplona when the American cyclists tried to pass. They did it in a youth hostel.

"Don't they have rules against just that? Don't they separate guys and girls?"

"Austin, it's a youth hostel, not a prison."

I waited as short a time as I could, then checked my watch. "Oh, my uncle's taking me out to dinner. Then I have to pack my stuff to take back to Hamden, then repack for school."

"I'll miss you, *laguna*. That's Euskera for friend. Euskera is what the Basque speak." She opened the front door, stepped close enough to bump my knee.

She kissed my cheek (actually, closer to my ear). Still, my heart fluttered and I must have been smiling foolishly by the sad smile she gave back. Her lips were rose petals near my ear.

August 22, 1980

Stanford

I hugged Mom and Dad good-bye at JFK, but it was easier this time than at Andover. Back then, as they drove away, my little sixteen-year-old self drained from my body, scampered after the station wagon like a yelping dog. This time I'm ready. I'm really going to change my life this time.

I'm writing on the fold-down TV tray in front of my seat on the plane. The stewardess is a man. I fantasized sitting next to this gorgeous vixen, striking up a scintillating conversation, then discovering she too was beginning Stanford. Next to me is a large white businessman whose skin has the smell of all fat people—oversweet, like a hospital or bus bathroom disinfectant.

> Priorities at Stanford
> 1. Fall in love
> 2. Get laid

3. Become cooler
   a. dress better
   b. dance better
   c. be more charming, less assholish
4. Graduate Phi Beta Kappa

I'm not going to be shy anymore. I mean it this time. I'll find a girl I like and swoop in mercilessly. Slay her with jokes, wit, romance, and if it doesn't work out, fine. Off I'll fly to another.

I'll be living in the black dorm Ujamaa. It's really only fifty percent black, but that's about sixty people. It will be good for me. I could have had a black roommate at Andover, but I thought it was stupid, reverse racism. Now I'm sick of being on the outside of everything, the black world and the white. That's probably why it's been so hard to get laid. I'm going to be normal, finally, and then we'll see if my life shapes up.

October 6, 1980

Sheryl

She's beautiful, intelligent, feisty. I've been spending a lot of time with her but haven't yet gotten the guts to ask her out. She, this senior, Howard, her friend Jewelle, and I had this big long college-type argument. As usual, all were against me. I like being the underdog, but I could tell by the end I'd taken it too far and she started thinking I was a creep. She reminds me of Joie. Sometimes I think this is going to be the big one, the one true L—e. Craig, my roommate, says she's an abrasive bitch. I'm also pissed because I got a C on a Chaucer quiz that I thought I aced. I'm the only freshman in the class.

Whanne that Aprille, with his shoures sote . . .

....

S h e r y l

Same problem as at Andover. My big mouth, my opinionat-edness. Got into another argument, all against me. The first was about the FBI's versus Exxon's influence on the world. I was a real asshole. Vietta the RA said I always talked about what I didn't know anything about. Our resident fellow, a doctor, was talking about ATP, adenosine triphosphate (or something like that), it's basically gasoline for the body. Sheryl said, "What's ATP?" and I said, "Didn't you take biology in the tenth grade?" She looked right at me and said, "You're an asshole." She tried to smile a bit afterward, but it didn't help. I feel like shit.

O c t o b e r   1 1 ,   1 9 8 0

S h e r y l

I've been following her around for a week like a lapdog. I'll wait in the lounge and pretend to be studying, when really I'm just waiting for her to pass by to eat lunch or dinner. I wait just enough not to be too obvious, then follow her into the dining hall. Today I followed her to her table, where she and her cool friends laugh too loud. There was a chair next to her but hardly any room.

"Is someone sitting there?"

"Yeah, the Invisible Man." I don't know if I'd call it a smile, but the ends of her lips were upturned. Her cool friends snorted laughs, then grumbled as they scooted over.

....

October 23, 1980

Sheryl

Believe it or not, she's acting friendlier. But today I went over to her dorm. She was right there, ten yards down the hall. I yelled, "Sheryl!" She turned, then I (swear to God) tripped right on my face. She and her friend Jewelle just turned back around. My life is a Jerry Lewis movie. And I hate Jerry Lewis.

Halloween 1980

Sheryl

She's been friendly lately, so I asked her if she wanted to go to the museum.
"I'll think about it." I'll think about it. Think about it. It. What a lovely chain of words.

After lunch...

I just asked her again. . . .
"I don't think so."
I went to the museum anyway. It was nice. All of Rodin's "Burghers of Calais." I remembered them from the Museum of Fine Arts in Philadelphia, where my father's mom lives. Their tortured, hollow cheeks, empty, dying eyes, their shackled grief, all reflected how I felt for a minute, then I laughed. Fuck her.

After dinner...

A lot of people in the dorm are going to San Francisco to see the Gay Pride Parade. The upperclassmen say it's wild and fun just for normal people to watch. I asked Sheryl if she was going. She said yes but said there was no room in her car. I hoped to see her there, but she didn't tell me where she'd be.

1:15 A. M.

Jewelle

Marching out of the shower room, I clenched my pecs as I always did, hoping some girl would have strayed up to our floor. But the hall was silent, and a wind from somewhere hurried me back to my room. I was just drying my testicles (a little too thoroughly; if you want to know the truth, I was weighing them and the idea of masturbating over a fantasy of Sheryl changing her mind).

Knock! Knock! Knock!

The violence on the door flashed the image of an uninvited fraternity-initiation Nazi lightning raid of goons capturing me nude and forcing me to pick up hard-boiled eggs with my ass cheeks.

I opened and leaned around the door.

"Hi. What are you doing?" This supercute girl named Jewelle Blake, one of Sheryl's clique, was just smiling at my head giraffed around the door.

"I dunno. Just taking a shower."

"Are you going to the parade?"

"Uh, yeah. I guess."

"Who are you driving with?"

"Uh. I dunno."

(You've got to remember, I don't think I'd ever really talked to her before. Her smile raced my mind forward to images of a honeymoon, of driving our kids to soccer games.)

"Look. You get dressed. I'll find us some wheels."

Jewelle's from the island of Grenada and has a pretty Caribbean accent like my mom's aunts in St. Thomas. Darker than I am, with skin so richly brown it seems deep. She doesn't straighten her hair, either. Bigger curls than my Afro, and not brittle and uneven like mine, either; her hair glistens and must be soft to touch, but it's definitely natural. She's very political.

I pinged against the walls and bunk bed of my monk's cell. My struggling heart wouldn't let me think, wouldn't let me breathe. What would I wear? I didn't want to be too dressed up but didn't want to be El Slobbo, either. I put on my polo shirt because it was clean, then whipped it off. At lunch Sheryl had asked me if I had *The Preppie Handbook* and all her friends (including Jewelle, I guess) had snickered. Right after lunch I threw my Top-Siders in the trash, then had to get them back out and wipe off the trash juice. They're the only shoes I have besides my sneakers.

I put on my lucky old *Godspell* T-shirt and pulled my jeans from the dirty clothes and tried to stretch out the wrinkles. I spurted too much toothpaste in my mouth. It made me queasy the rest of the night.

I walked down the stairs like a beauty queen or something, trying to play nonchalant. Jewelle was waiting with Gus and his girlfriend. Gus hates my guts. He's a sophomore and thinks all the new blacks are conservative rich kids and he's some Malcolm X militant. He's my next-door neighbor and thinks that I, the prep from Andover, am the worst of the lot. He and his girlfriend screw all the time. She's loud. I've never heard a woman moan live before. It's incredible. When Craig, my roommate, isn't there, I lean against my door, close my eyes, and pleasure myself.

We were driving to SF, just the four of us. Like a double date. Fortunately his Datsun B-210 is so tiny that Jewelle and I were right next to each other. I tried the old "thigh pressing" routine, and I *think* she responded, at least on the way back. Matter of fact, I'm *sure* she did.

The parade itself was disgusting! Cowboys and Indians in jock-straps. Men in gorilla masks, and that's practically it. Transvestites galore. Our group shuffled down the street as one, terrified. A pack of teenage boys stumbled down the street in just towels, drunk. An older man tweaked one of their tits. But Jewelle was more shocked than any of us.

The four of us crossed the street right into Sheryl and her gang.

This junior named Antoine, short and ugly, drove them. I was embarrassed being with Jewelle, but I could tell Sheryl was embarrassed also. I think I did a good job acting friendly to her.

A man dressed like Queen Elizabeth II walked right up to Jewelle and puckered his lips. She stepped back, then slipped her arm in mine for safety. Now I was the frightened one and cranked down on her arm bone like I was cracking a nut. She said, "Ow!" and jerked her arm out of mine. I don't know what the fuck I was thinking. I wanted, started to explain, say I was sorry, say I'm not always a lunatic, say her advance caught me unawares. But I said nothing, and that was probably better. As I wrote before, on the way home I'm pretty sure I got some leg action.

I was going to walk her back to her dorm, Roble, just down the road but reasoned she'd think me too forward.

November 1, 1980

Sheryl and Jewelle

Saw Sheryl this morning and felt supersad. It's amazing how my heart would leap before when I saw her, now it sank. I went by Jewelle's room late tonight, Saturday night. She and her *dizzy* friends were there. They act so childishly, talking about *Playgirl* (giggle) and moaning over all the dumb disco songs. They are all boy crazy, but not for me. Two other guys came over. They said they were freshmen, too, but looked like grad students. They had mustaches and were very GQ. I was in a pair of corduroys so old it'd lost all of its treads. I was also on the ground and thought, God, these guys are humongous, but when I stood up and nonchalantly (I hope) sized them up, I saw I was at least as tall. The girls were evidently taken with the looks of one, comparing him to Teddy Pendergrass. He was all suave and cool and flirtatious while I was shy and reticent and my jokes were not very well received. This awful thought surprised me: God, Sheryl, I made a mistake! This Jewelle is a completely different person in public.

I left them all laughing too loudly at nothing and happened to swing myself past Sheryl's room. She wasn't in.

The dining hall squats in the middle of our Lagunita residential cluster. Sheryl lives on the west side, Ujamaa is on the east.

I don't know why, during the week, I ache for the weekends. At least in the week I'm couched in study so can't think about life, about girls. Saturday nights alone at Andover felt just like this. Nothing's changed. I remember tonight's pretty sky and its shiny, shiny moon.

Cutting through the dining hall to Ujamaa, I liked its darkness. Its screen door rapping closed behind me hurt my ears. I walked to the hall's center, dimly warmed by that moon, and I sang. Even to me it sounded bad, but it felt good. An impromptu medley of corny James Taylor songs. (Everybody in Ujamaa swears they only listen to P-Funk and the Sugar Hill Gang, but they all have Carly Simon or Pure Prairie League eight-tracks in their rooms. I've seen them.) I loved the confidence in my voice, there alone, acting so crazy so near dozens of people so quick to ridicule. Catching me singing off-key soft rock in the dining hall alone on Saturday night would be their windfall. But I thought of Sheryl catching me and understanding somehow through the awful but sweet timbre of my voice that I wasn't really an asshole. At least not an irredeemable one. I imagined that as I neared the end of "Fire and Rain" or "Sweet Baby James" I would sense something behind me just before I would feel a soft hand smooth around my waist to my chest, hug me from behind, and lean all her weight and her tears on my shoulder. I know the medicine I need.

November 2, 1980

Jewelle

I ate brunch at her table, but we didn't talk much. I think I should have, I think I might have made her sad. I think she likes me. Uh-oh. I feel the pull of the love tide. *Here we go again!!*

December 10, 1980

Mistletoe

The incident involves Vietta, the RA who said I talked about what I didn't know anything about, and Liz Eversohn. They are both gorgeous, black and white. Vietta dangles mistletoe from her door, and I'd been hanging out in the TV lounge waiting for her to go back to her room after "All My Children." She and her friend Liz were arguing about some stupid character named Tad right in her doorway when I joined them and bluffed my way through the argument. About every ten or fifteen seconds I'd not so casually flash my eyes above their heads to the green weed with the red bow. At the same time they looked at each other and frowned.

"Come here." Vietta held up her index finger, then flexed it back at herself.

What a kisser. Wow. Then Liz gave me my first white girl kiss since the nursery school "Kissing cootie." Nice. Then they both kissed me again. They must have liked the retarded, drunken smile they were bringing to my face. If only Hef could've seen me.

December 20, 1980

Jewelle

Dear Jewelle,

Merry Christmas! I think someone told me you were going back to your relatives in Grenada for the holidays, but I obviously don't have your address there, so I'm sending this to your Phoenix address. (Duh. You already know all this because you're reading the letter right now.)

Anyway, this is all to apologize for this Christmas card not getting to you until after Christmas.

Hamden, CT, my home, is okay. No snow (and no sun like you must have experienced down there, of course). All

*three of my parents' parents are flying in, so I'll be thrown
out of my room to the lumpy couch downstairs. The only
positive side is seeing Grandpa and Grandma sleeping in my
old bunk bed like little kids at summer camp.*

*Well, I'm sure I've bored you long enough. It will be nice
to see you in '81. I hope we can hang out some more. The
first half of frosh year was a little disorienting, but I'm now
ready to loosen up and enjoy myself. I hope you are, too.*

> *Happy Holidays once more,*
> *Austin*

The card itself was a cartoon of regular deer falling to earth like
rain. (Get it?)

I don't know why I love her so much, but I keep envisioning
our kids—cute and brown and brilliant, with lilting Caribbean
accents. Jewelle and I will be downstairs, cuddled before the fire,
when we'll hear loud thumps from directly overhead. "Honey,
you look in on them this time. I don't want to have to kill my
own children." I'll kiss her and sneak up the stairs. Jewelle will
calm when she hears the ruckus cease, but after just a few moments
it will start up again, even louder. She will blast open the door
and instantly freeze little Austin, Joanna, Derrick, Cindy, and me,
their supposedly grown-up daddy, in the midst of an explosive
pillow fight. The kids and I will all cower from Jewelle's scowl.
Then she will bite her lower lip (as she often does), and very
slowly, and very reluctantly, she will start to smile. "Yeah!" shout
the kids. "Yeah!" shout I as Jewelle herself grabs a pillow and starts
whacking away.

Eventually we will all settle down on the floor and the kids will
beg us to tell them, for the zillionth time, the tale of our courtship.

"When I first met your father I thought to myself, Oh, no, he's
so quiet, definitely not for me. Then one Christmas he sent me
this letter, and I don't know how to explain it, the letter was so
awkward and sweet that something inside of me flew out to that
cute little dork and I knew that I had to take care of him."

"Yeah!! Tell us again! Tell us again!" squeal the kids.

··

January 18, 1981

Jewelle

She hasn't yet mentioned the letter. I triple-checked her address, so I'm pretty sure she got it. She's often busy. But that's okay. Unless she transfers, I know where to find her.

Valentine's Day 1981

Liz Eversohn

She's Vietta the RA's best friend, and now she's one of my best friends, too. She lives in Naranja, next door to Ujamaa, but she's over here all the time. You can spot her angry red hair across the dining hall. She looks like that old actress Rita Hayworth, a lot. Just as curvy, only Canadian, from Vancouver.

I guess all that kissing under the mistletoe did it. We tell each other everything, and she's a junior. She was bitching about not having a boyfriend for Valentine's Day, so I did something sort of weird. I wrote her this letter on red construction paper:

Dear Liz,
Even though we just met I think we'll be great friends. I'm sorry you don't have a boyfriend on such a romantic day such as today, but hey, I don't have a girlfriend, either. But you are so beautiful, you don't have an excuse. We both know that all you have to do is wink once and half the guys on campus will come groveling. I know I would. I slipped this under your door because I am too chicken to hand it to you. But you're a great person, so don't be depressed today. Promise?

Love,
A. McMillan

P.S. If you're really awfully lonely and can't like go to sleep or anything, I could come down and stay with you, maybe, on the floor or wherever.

Around twelve-thirty in the morning she knocked and woke up Craig. Outside my room she handed me a dopey kid's valentine and said my valentine was sweet. Under her coat she wore just a nightgown. Her breasts kept the flannel from touching the rest of her body. She wore running shoes with no socks. And hugged me hard.

March 22, 1981

Spring Break

It's spring vacation and I'm in Marin County at the cottage of a friend of a friend. There are four of us, all from Ujamaa, but I'm the only black again. (Why is that?) We hike Mount Tamalpais, pick our way through sprawling cliffs of flowering ice plants, come within yards of herds of mule deer as quiet hawks slide in circles overhead. At night we talk college talk: geopolitics and sex. The girls with us I am not interested in. I'm so horny I could scream. An electric feeling is ever-present in my groin. Last night I found out there's a thriving prostitution ring on campus. Tonight I find out they're beautiful and live in the graduate student trailers. I'm broke but real tempted.

Some older guys I know from the *Chaparral*, the humor magazine I write for, told me about the Lilly, down El Camino Real. It's a topless show where they might blow you up on stage if you say you're about to get married. I'm sorely tempted to ride my bike over there.

The thing about me is I don't look like I've done so little. The only other freshman virgins are pepperoni-faced jet propulsion laboratories summer interns who'll never screw what they don't pay for. My virginity is getting a bit ridiculous. Each day drives

···

me deeper and deeper to the exteme of the bell curve. If I don't get laid by spring quarter, I will die.

June 8, 1981

Annual Report

Didn't lose it. Didn't even come close. Didn't change my life. Jewelle and I are fairly good friends, but I'm not going to write her this summer unless she writes me first. She has still never mentioned my Christmas card.

How long can I keep losing? By now, to give me just an *average* amount of girl luck, tomorrow I deserve some Playmate nympho stewardess to screw my brains out in the aft lavatory on the plane home. Instead, I'm sure I'll end up beating off in the twisted and narrow, smelly lavatory over a Virginia Slims ad in *Money* magazine.

Perhaps all this heartache is good for me. Your heart is a muscle, and torture can only make it stronger. Maybe when I get older I'll have a big advantage. Maybe I'll live longer than the loved people with their lazy and fatty hearts.

July 5, 1981

Calista

This summer I'm moving people for a company called "For This I Went to College?" It's run by Dianetics devotees, so the other movers tell me to double-check my paychecks. I'm getting stronger lifting pianos and refrigerators up New Haven's countless five-flight walk-ups. Maybe I will inflate, and maybe that will help me in my expedition to Mount Calista this summer.

Yesterday, my first attempt. I took the train into the city to see her. We went to a fucking Gordon Lightfoot concert in Central

Park. She couldn't see over the crowds, so I hoisted her up on my shoulders. Her thighs were so deliciously warm around my neck and ears that I longed to turn around, listen to her squeal with delight. The good-bye kiss on the lips was longer than the hello.

September 24, 1981

Mustang Ranch

Jack Lewis, another black guy from Stanford, and I have been driving across country back to school for four days now. *On the Road* it ain't. We speed past billboards for the "Museum of Twine" in Sandusky, Ohio, or the "World's Largest Exhibition of Barnyard Oddities" in Grand Island, Nebraska, and he doesn't even slow.

"Hey, it's my car, man."

I should never have mentioned the Mustang Ranch, though that is probably the main reason I agreed to help him drive. We are actually in a hotel room in Reno, ten minutes from the ranch, and I've seriously changed my mind. He's in the shower getting ready, but I don't want to lose it this way. It's pathetic.

But Jack, who as recently as Colorado said I was a freak, suddenly changed his mind.

"Look, we just ask a taxi driver where it is. They probably tell guys a thousand times a night. It was your idea. Don't be a pussy. If you don't want to go, I'll leave your ass in the motel and let you sniff the condom."

He's a real pig, and if he weren't a varsity shot-putter, I'd kick the shit out of him.

Our motel, the Pioneer, has a giant cowboy smoking a cigarette and winking in neon on its roof. I made Jack stop there. He usually pulls into every motel on the strip and comparison shops for hours. The lobby was cluttered with slot machines, and I played a dollar's worth, lost, played another dollar's worth, and won five dollars in quarters.

....

L a t e r . . .

He came out of the shower and kept smiling at himself in each of the room's mirrors.

"Jack, I don't see why you can't just ask the motel owner."

"Why don't you ask the motel owner? It was your idea."

"Then are you going to pay for the cab ride?"

"Hell no, I ain't going to pay for the cab ride. What's the matter with you? It's not like it's our first time."

"Uh, what are you going to wear?"

"What I got on. What do you think, I'm going to get dressed up to go see some whore?" Jack's parents are both from the Bronx, but he grew up in Bridgeport, a half hour from Hamden.

I didn't know what to wear. I didn't want to look "virginal" or poor, but I'm both (if she charges more than $60, I won't be able to spend more than $8/day on food for the rest of the trip). I borrowed an iron from the motel and sort of pressed my white pleated pants on the rubbery bed.

Jack flagged down a taxi cruising up the strip to the real hotels, and we got in. I had my hand on the door handle in case the cabbie pulled a piece on us or called the cops or something. Legal, shmegal, if you ask me, paying for sex is still seedy and compromising. The admission of inadequacy, the . . . Aw, don't get me started.

"You boys headed to Circus for the smorgasbord?"

"We were actually looking for the Mustang."

I was studying the neon, just now turning on in the late summer dusk. I willed my soul out of the cab.

"Phhhew! That's one long and bumpy cab ride, but not half as long and bumpy as the rides they offer inside!" He laughed and looked in his rearview to see if we were laughing, too. I looked away.

"Well, we've got a car, but we thought you just might know."

"Shoot. You all find yourselfs a Nevada cabbie who don't know how to get to the cathouses and get a good hold, because folks'll pay money to see that fool!"

So he told us and dropped us back at the Pioneer and didn't even charge. "Just kick her once for me, fellas!"

My mother's a feminist. I circulated petitions for the ERA.

The brothel has its own highway exit, "Mustang," on official Department of Transportation green-and-white-painted steel. We circled down from the lit superhighway into an abrupt darkness of dirt. Jack's rusty Impala bottomed out and exploded dust in our headlights.

"Maybe it's closed for repairs. This can't be the regular road."

But Jack wasn't listening. He was driving with his dick. Since Connecticut, he only let me drive when his eyes started to cross. He sweated over every tiny highway crack I rolled his bald tires across. Now here he was churning rooster tails of cowboy dirt high into the Nevada night. We drove and drove through what must have been an organized-crime burial ground until Jack stopped, desperate, before a thin, swayed, and rickety wooden bridge. He cut the engine and we rolled down our windows to listen.

The Nevada desert quiet tonight was perhaps the most absolute silence I have ever heard.

"It's gotta be right over this fucking bridge, goddammit."

"That bridge couldn't hold us walking, let alone this boat. Besides, it's a bridge over dirt in the middle of the desert. Who goes to whores more than truckers, and you think an eighteen-wheeler can make that?"

Jack's eyes shined in the dark. He turned his car back on and creeped it over the Japanese garden–like wooden bridge without incident. Fifty more yards, at the crest of the hill, lights from ahead reached our windshield. A prefabricated compound, like a secret LSD factory, sat below us, ringed in chain link and barbed wire. In front of the gate waited dozens of pickup trucks, big rigs, and a crowd of taxis. A beautifully asphalted road stretched out behind them back toward the white-and-red jewels tracing the highway.

"Where did we take the wrong turn, I wonder?"

A television eye watched the only opening in the gate. I smoothed my windbreaker over my chest and opened my mouth to breathe with less noise. I remember trying to remember the floodlit parking pit because I wanted to see if I saw things differently after coming out, deflowered. Jack pushed a button by the intercom. Before he could lean his mouth to the slices in the plastic that covered the tiny microphone, the lock buzzed and a ghost suddenly edged the closed gate ajar. We pushed inside and courteously closed the gate behind us. I could be wrong, but it seemed like the roof was studded with gun turrets. I imagined the National Organization of Women's Rapid Deployment Forces parachuting in and torching the place.

Before we could open the front door it opened by itself, and inside at least a dozen beautiful women were busily scampering to attention all in a line just for us. A man in a real cowboy hat and flannel shirt stood by the door.

"Welcome, fellers. What's your pleasure?"

Jack immediately picked a trashy-looking blonde. I picked a black woman, though she wasn't the youngest or prettiest. But I did it. I lifted my hand and pointed. Immediately all the others fell away and our women stepped to us, took our hands, and escorted us down the velvety wallpapered hall.

Joie (let's call her) opened a thin door, stepped inside, and immediately unclasped her earrings and tossed them on the Formica nightstand.

"Calm down," she said. But I was calmer than I had thought I'd be. "A blow job will be twenty, and forty dollars to sleep with me, and both—which is what I recommend—will be sixty."

I have never dreamed a world less real than the one I was experiencing. I wanted to leave, until my own damn stupid philosophy bubbled up in my short-term memory: "If you have a choice between the safe and the new, always, always, choose the safe—I mean, the new." If I left with nothing, I'd be once again disgusted with myself for cowardice. If I did something, I'd be differently disgusted with myself. I couldn't speak, but I did rip sixty smackers out of my wallet.

"Make yourself at home. I'll be right back." She seemed like a nice lady. Older, maybe twenty-eight, twenty-nine. I snooped around, sure cameras monitored my every move. A queen-size bed. Palm trees and sea, spray-painted on the stucco in front of the bed. Three rolls of Bounty paper towels ("the Quicker Picker-Upper"). Boxes of Kleenex everywhere. And Jergens lotion. In the bathroom a bidet (I knew about them only from Italian class last spring). Above the toilet, another spray-painted mural, this time depicting a topless Hawaiian woman rising from the surf.

She came back in and scared me.

"What's your name?"

"Fred."

"Fred, could you drop your pants and stand over here in the light? I have to check you for bugs." She clasped my dead dick, pinched it, and rolled it in her hand. When Dr. Damato, my pediatrician, poked around down there I was petrified I'd accidentally pop a boner. This time was about as sexy. She waddled me over to the bidet and washed my pubic hair with Ivory soap.

She pulled a purple beach towel from a cabinet and let it parachute smoothly to the bed. Then she pulled off my windbreaker, tugged off my polo shirt, stepped me all the way out of my pants, and pulled my underwear off my ass. She guided my hips to the towel, laid me there face up, and touched her lips only to my dick. This, I must admit, was wonderful. The warmth all over me was tremendous. I looked down between my legs where for years lay only disappointment or perhaps, occasionally, my own right hand, a cored tomato or sock, but now the top of a woman's head rose up and down over me just like in the movies. I wasn't rock hard, but I was up, and after a long time of this I asked her something. I got up the courage to talk.

"Ma'am. Could you lick my balls, please?"

My toes curled and uncurled, I was crawling up the bed, and she was wrestling me still.

"Would you like to be on top?"

She was about to stick it inside her. Would that be the official end of my virginity, or doesn't it count until I come?

"Oh, how about a little of both?" I envisioned us screwing like porno professionals, up, down, all around. She straddled me and hobbled up my body on her knees until her target hovered above mine. She lowered herself, and I heard the end more than I felt it. She rose and fell above me, I fell out a few times, but she quickly hid me inside her again. There was no crescendo, no unbelievable pleasure. It was just weird. I wanted the strength to tell her to stop, to tell her that it wasn't right. I'm still a virgin because this cannot possibly count.

She stopped only later. I saw sperm on her and my dick was now again dead. I came, I guess.

She was about to rise off me, but I stopped her with my hand.

"Do we have to go right now?"

She flicked her eyes to the electric alarm clock on the nightstand, collapsed on top of me. I held her naked to me and her warmth eased my heart a bit, but I still had to measure each breath like medicine in my open mouth. So unloved. But when I just held her to me, felt her breasts on my skin, I did what you are supposed to do with a call girl. I imagined she was my girlfriend. I imagined being in love with a naked woman whose breasts puddled against my chest, whose breath braised my neck. I felt for just a subdivision of an instant the insuperable joy that must await me somefuck-ingday of lying in bed with the woman I love. Maybe you'll be all right after all, was the thought that came to me just then, and I smiled.

She peeped again at the alarm clock but kindly tried not to let me notice. I released her. She wiped herself off with a wad of Bounty towels, washed me again at the bidet, and we left.

"Thank you," I said. Jack was at the bar, frowning. He only had a blow job. He said he couldn't go through with more.

Another first: *No, the only first that really matters. But I won't even count it. Paying for it doesn't count. I know because I feel the same.*

I don't know why I didn't think of this before I went there. At least on television, prostitutes often put up their children for adoption. I wonder if my mother ever worked here?

....

October 14, 1981

Liz Eversohn

She's a great friend and always giving me pointers on how to pick up girls. That doesn't stop me from noticing and commenting upon her unbelievably curvy, now senior bod. She's the most frequent focus of my nocturnal role plays. Jewelle (who hugged me the first day of school) will be my wife someday, so Roto-Rootering over her could bring bad luck. I've only got three months till I go overseas, and I don't want to have a nervous breakdown before my transformation.

November 24, 1981

Linda Babb

(As I sit down to write, my two roommates are already asleep in the other room.) I directed two scenes of Goldsmith's *She Stoops to Conquer* instead of writing a final paper. She played Kate Hardcastle. One day during rehearsal I noticed her wonderful breasts. Moderate-size and nicely shaped. Then and there I decided to ask her over to my room so we could write a prologue so the two scenes would make sense. She's white, a junior, and in some sorority. Everything I don't want in a woman.

Anyway, she came over tonight, and I fantasized about the wild sorority sex we would have. Sitting next to her on our floor, I kept massaging my own neck and groaning. Then I added a wince to each moan. Finally I just up and said it.

"Oh, my aching neck. I must have pulled it at the gym."

"Would you like a massage?"

I lay down on my stomach and she helped me wheedle off my T-shirt. Her fingers were strong and soft. My hard-on nearly levered my butt off the floor. I was *this* close to turning over and kissing her.

"That was wonderful. Now you've got to let me reciprocate."
"Some other time. The neophytes are baking cookies."

November 27, 1981

Jenny

I just got a letter from her. She's in her first year at Vassar and didn't think she'd miss boys so much. She talked a lot about how the Vineyard last summer wasn't the same without me. But the great news is that she's invited herself to stay with me one weekend during Christmas break before I split for Italy. "I owe you at least a kiss for your birthday," she wrote. Wish me luck.

Jewelle

Jenny's letter gave me the courage to call Jewelle. I asked her to the Sunday flicks, and she said sure. When I showed up at her dorm, three people, two jerks and her friend Gloria, joined us.

The four of us marched down the aisle, dodging the computer-paper airplanes launched weekly by the nerds in the balcony. Jewelle waved to her many fans as we passed. I stopped, started, danced, and shoved to maneuver myself next to her before we filed down the aisle of her choice. I succeeded, but when she slouched on her seat she leaned her head on the side of her chair closest to one of the jerks. I didn't care a whole lot. I wanted to see *Tender Mercies* and not be distracted by counting heartbeats before trying to hold her long and perfect hand.

. . . .

November 28, 1981

Linda Babb

Tonight was the night of the play, and I think it went pretty well. People seemed to laugh at the right places—especially at the jealous duel I staged like a Three Stooges routine.

At the end of the evening Linda said this to me:

"Austin, you're a genius! Ours was by way far the best."

"Well, Goldoni's *La Locandiera* in drag was pretty funny."

"I guess. . . . Hey, listen. Could you walk me home tonight? I don't trust the bushes around here." She lived only about a hundred yards from the little theater.

I guess I should tell you that a rapist was on the loose on campus, so it wasn't as obviously forward as it might read.

She leaned into me as we walked, though the pathway was plenty wide.

November 29, 1981

Linda Babb

I've just come back from the Costume Department! I had to return all the swords and leggings and tights I'd borrowed. I was unloading the articles from a paper bag to a kindly old lady who guarded the warehouse of clothes when I pulled out a pair of powder blue panties.

"Sonny, I don't think you got those things from here." Everybody's a comedian.

Linda was the only actress in my cast! She didn't leave a pair of socks, or a dickey, but her panties. You don't forget them by accident! It's probably right out of the horny sorority girl party book. I'm about to call her and ask her what's what.

L a t e r . . .

"Hey, Linda. . . . Yeah, the show was great and the monologue really made the difference. You know, you should seriously consider acting professionally. . . . No, I'm not just saying that. . . . But the reason I called, other than to congratulate you again, was that you left something in the costume bag. . . . No, I'm pretty sure they're yours unless the other guys are not what they appear. . . . Now calm down, I wasn't embarrassed at all. I just thought you might want them back. . . . I hadn't really inspected them, but now that you mention it, they appear extremely clean, brand new, almost."

She's coming over at six.

5:57 P. M.

I asked my two roommates to leave, and they were cool about it. I moved the box of condoms from my sock drawer to right under the bed. I opened it up to make her think the box wasn't new and so there wouldn't be too much downtime between when she says yes and when we start. Carly Simon's singing now, and Chuck Mangione is on deck. Sorority girls like music like this. I just brushed my teeth and made the bed.

My game plan will be to whip open the door and give her a big macho kiss before she has time to think. Then I'll insist on massaging her this time and then just go for it. All systems seem go this time. It's six o'clock already. I'm sure she hasn't forgotten. Right now I'm double-checking the hydraulics.

Knock! Knock! Knock!

"Coming!" I just said this and just wrote it, too. She's actually just on the other side of the door! My ticket to free sex.

I'll write again when I'm able. Maybe after she falls asleep.

6:02 P. M.

I forget who it was who wrote "The best laid schemes o' mice an' men / Gang aft a-gley." The last part is Gaelic and means go to shit.

I opened the door and had my lips puckered. My heart was beating at a dangerously high rate.

"Hi, Austin! This is my soror, Binky!"

Binky actually curtsied hello.

"Linda says you're a brilliant director. I do a little acting myself."

Like a robot on "Lost in Space," I mechanically rolled myself to the bedroom, where her panties lay folded in a plastic bag. I extended them to Linda.

"Do you really have to go?"

She rolled her eyes. "Homework," she said. "*Quel* drag."

And she was gone.

You know, I couldn't concentrate all day long. I would get rushes of hard-ons and erotic daydreams. There was a ninety percent possibility of something happening if not screw, I had thought. Still, I've been down this road enough times before to keep an ounce of myself in reserve to pick the rest of me up afterward. That's the part that's writing this right now.

December 10, 1981

M i s t l e t o e

Just a week of exams, then I'm back east, then on January 5 I leave for Florence, Italy! After six months of overseas study I'm sure I'll return an Afro-Latin lover. But in the meantime, I'm pulling out all the stops to get laid stateside for real. I figure the more change I go through here, the farther along I'll be in Europe.

Lea Clarke is a cute, white yearbook editor. Her hips are a bit wide, but so what. She's always working late and flirting with us

Chaparral humor magazine guys. She seems the only woman in school who doesn't know we're a convention of sexually repressed geeks.

Because of what happened last year, I've been looking forward to Christmas at Stanford for eleven months. Mistletoe is actually a parasite that happens to grow high in many of the Spanish oaks on campus. Last week my roommates and I went out back and chucked Frisbees into the trees to dislodge clumps. I've kept mine in my pocket to be ever ready for the dozens of girls on campus who keep making the mistake that we are "just friends."

A half hour ago I passed through the *Chappie* office like I always do, and a few guys were playing pinball on the machine we just bought.

Lea was hanging out in the inner room drinking our beer.

"Hey, Aussie!"

"Lea. Let's go to the back room, I've got a surprise for you."

Her eyes widened and she looked like an elf, all mischievous cuteness and surprise. Annie, a *Chappie* staff writer from New York and another "just friend," must have sensed something in my voice.

"Lea, watch out for his mistletoe."

I swear I was pushed. I didn't trip. But Lea was already in the back room, so I had to follow her in. I silently closed the door behind us and held it shut.

"What's up, big guy?"

I scraped the now crumbled and powdered mistletoe along with the mulch of lint from the lining of my nylon bomber jacket pocket, and I presented the lint/mistletoe potpourri to her in the palm of my hand.

"What's that!?"

"Uh, mistletoe." I held the crumbled magic above her head.

She shrugged and tilted her head up to me, then opened her mouth wide. I felt I was her mother robin and was supposed to drool predigested worm goo down this chick's gullet. But I just smiled to myself and watched her waiting, then lowered my lips to hers. The seal set, her tongue violated me and scrubbed my uvula. Yet as unromantic as it all sounds, she gave me a boner that nearly made me swoon. We must have kissed for about fifteen seconds. It was super.

"I've a good-bye card I want to give you tonight." She said that just before running out the back to see her "hum bio" (human biology) TA.

I came back into the main room, and Bruce, a senior, raised his eyebrow like Spock. I swear being teased by guys (and Annie) about what a stud you are is almost as good as doing it. I proudly told them all what transpired and of course Bruce told me that he's messed around with her, too.

"Well, I'll do more than you tonight."

"Austin, you can't do more. You can only do it better."

Later...

She came over and handed me a going-away card with a photo of two puppies tripping over their ears. We made out until she said, "That's it," in midkiss, as if, somewhere, an egg timer had just dinged.

December 16, 1981

Jewelle

She had to come to the Coffee House sometime. I'd been camped there this whole week, only leaving to take my history of Africa exam. (The course was incredible. What King Leopold of Belgium did to the Congo made Hitler look like a mama's boy.) Today she was cutting through alone, and I gave her the old "I'm leaving on a jet plane, don't know when I'll be back again" routine.

"My little brother collects stamps, so why don't you write me sometime?"

··

Jenny

She came for the weekend and just left.

The doorbell rang and Austin Pavlov scurried through his usual routine. I scooted upstairs to my parents' bedroom to reexamine my hair, running on tiptoes to muffle the noise.

Jenny looked the same, and we hugged. She took a cab from the train station but didn't have enough money, so I had to pay the guy. I must admit that in a stupid, old-fashioned sexist way it made me feel like a man.

Immediately we talked and talked and talked. I even turned off the TV. Mom came back and let us use the car. I drove Jenny to the New Haven green, and we walked around the college bars in the cold. Now that I am in college myself, this town seems so dinky. I can't believe I used to worship college students. The drinking age is still eighteen in Connecticut, so we went to the Anchor Bar. In California it's twenty-one, so you can only drink at school parties. We were carded at the door, but luckily Jenny turned eighteen this summer.

She was still full of incredible stories. For her birthday last month she went to Philadelphia and was supposed to meet some friends at a discotheque there but couldn't find them. She was broke and didn't have their number, so she just asked a guy leaving the place if she could crash on his couch. She swears she didn't sleep with him. They just messed around and when she said she had to get to sleep, he was "totally cool about it."

Then this other guy from Haverford College came to Vassar for some party, and by the end of the night he had punched her in the eye. "But, Austin, it was no big deal. He was shitfaced."

Dinner with the family (except Leslie, who was away on a ski trip with her goony jillionaire friends), and Jenny was telling cleaner but nevertheless incredible stories about professors accusing her of cheating right in the middle of class and one about a senior woman sending two hulking field hockey goalies over to her room to tell her to lay off the senior's West Pointer. Mom and Dad hardly touched their food.

"Austin, change the sheets in Leslie's room for your little friend." I hate it when Dad says that. Then the 'rents went to bed.

She helped me stretch and tuck the sheets. I turned on my sister's color TV. I closed us inside my sister's pink room.

"So the TV won't bother my folks." I don't know why I was trying to outsmart her, the queen of seduction. "Would you care for a massage?"

She stretched over my sister's bed as if she had won it. Leslie's *Willard*-era Michael Jackson poster grinned over Jenny's back and my hands. I massaged inside her blouse and purposefully ran into her bra strap again and again, hoping she'd give in and spring her back free. With each pass of my hands, knead of my fingers, she moaned like she was coming. I hoped she didn't notice that I stiffened and angled an ear to the door and inched Leslie's pillow closer to Jenny's open, twisting mouth. She moaned louder, dragged her purple nails up the sides of my jeans.

"Your turn, tiger." I rolled off my T-shirt, and she actually sighed! My boner swelled and swelled in electric waves until I felt this twinge down there. Overstimulated, but who cares. How can you be "over"-stimulated, anyway? (I'd find out later.) After rubbing deep into my muscles, she began whispering just the pads of her long fingers down my back. Vast fields of goose bumps miraculously plumped to life behind her electric sweep. My hands swallowed the bedspread. I reached back and caressed her calves as she had mine. Her body stopped. I pushed myself up and was proud of the point my crotch now made.

"Jenny, do you want your birthday present?" I stared at her through my lowered eyebrows, wiggled my head a bit in a sexy way.

I moved in and kissed her without hesitation. Pretty long and with tongues.

"You're a better kisser than I thought."

"Teach me to be better." I kissed her again.

"Not here, this is your own sister's bed."

"Exactly."

"You're sick."

"I know."

"I've got to go brush my teeth. Then let's go downstairs."

We inched out of the room. Sounds from the "Tonight" show and the gray TV light leaked out of the crack at the bottom of my parents' door. Jenny left me for the bathroom in the hallway, and I eased down the creaky stairs.

The TV room's burnt-orange, steel-cone fireplace, Mom's mystery books insulating the walls, the wicker coffee table, and the expired *TV Guide*, they were so much a part of my normal life that to see them there unchanged by my change seemed bizarre.

Somehow I didn't hear her until she was crossing the kitchen.

We lay next to each other on the rug and kissed and kissed and kissed. I caressed her sides, swept down to her butt, then up to her breasts through her shirt. She kissed my neck and chin, and which way was up just then I did not know. She stopped.

"I wonder what's wrong with me?"

"What do you mean? You're fantastic." You never know when Jenny's going to go off the deep end.

"Thanks, I needed to hear that."

My fingers lay between hers, and I noticed we were the identical brown. The peace I felt with her then I had only imagined in Reno.

Then I noticed the nightgown in her hand. She rose to change in the little bathroom off the kitchen. As soon as she was gone I noticed that I wasn't up and that I had to pee. I waited twelve minutes for her to change. Maybe she was new to putting in a diaphragm.

I didn't want to chance creaking back upstairs to the bathroom. I opened the side door to go in the garden, but it was fifteen degrees outside. Pumpkin's kitty litter box sat at the landing to the basement stairs. I peed and peed, until the box looked like a Barbie doll swimming pool. You don't realize how much bigger a human's bladder is than a cat's until something like this comes up. I emptied an entire fresh bag of Kitty Litter on top.

Jenny stepped out of the bathroom.

"Sorry it took so long. We'd better get to sleep. I'll go up first." She kissed me good night and crept away and up. Still, I went to bed more happy than confused.

Yesterday we spent the whole day walking around New Haven. I took her to the British Art Collection and we made fun of the ugly old paintings of pasty women with rosy cheeks fondling bowls of fruit.

(Jenny just called from the Hartford bus terminal. She took a Trailways back up to Springfield, Mass. She said, "Thanks, Austin. I just had to call you. I had a great time. You've got sexy lips."!!!!!)

So anyway, yesterday we did all this stuff, but she was actually a bit cool. I tried to hold her hand, but she wasn't into it. I forgot to mention that after breakfast I tried to sneak a kiss when no one was looking, but no dice.

That night I took her out to eat at Edge of the Green, one of the fanciest places in New Haven. I ordered wine, and we were not even carded. I put my arm around her a few times, but she didn't seem to care. At home I was shitting bricks. Mom was asleep and Dad was at a conference in New York. Jenny and I were lying on the rug downstairs again, but she just kept reading my dad's GQ as if I were dead. I put my arm around her and kissed her ear. I tried to rest my head in her lap, but she pushed me away. I drew the magazine out of her fingers and rolled her onto her back. I dangled myself over her and kissed her lips and her neck. I pressed my tongue between her lips. Andover flashed back to me, CPR class when I shot my tongue down the rubber throat of "Resuscitation Annie," the waxy, dead dummy you practice on.

"Isn't this like making out with a log?" Jenny said. "I just don't feel like it." Her voice was weird, entertained. She smiled as she talked. "Look, Austin, yesterday I didn't get the reaction I wanted."

What?? My answer was to try to kiss her some more, but she pinched my face. I extended my lips between her pinch so they looked like a sea creature inside its shell.

"Listen. What do you expect out of this?"

I expect marriage, children, a lifetime of bliss with you, the first and last woman I will ever love.

"Nothing," I said. "Just a nighttime of fun between friends."

I kissed her, and this time she kissed back slightly.

"And what was the matter with last night?"

Her crazy look seemed to say, "You mean, you really don't even *know!*" But this is what she did say:

"Analyze, think, then act or react."

She likes being cryptic and in control. I told her as much, and she agreed.

"Analyze," I said, and screwed closed my brow, focusing my brain on the problem at hand. "Think," I then said with a silent movie–ish pensive scratch of my cheek. "Act or react." I then sprang and smothered her, kissing her whole face. She let me kiss her and responded a tad more, then she got up to get a Pepsi and drank it slowly.

"Hurry up already," I said.

She just flipped only her eyes away from that aluminum can. She finished with a contented "Ahhhh." She rose, snatched up her toothbrush and paste, swung through the TV room door.

She returned, and we were making out for a bit when she said, "Move on top of me." We dry-humped for days and days, she moaned like a porn star, I felt her breasts through her dress, felt her nipples awaken.

"Oh, my pants are ruined." I hadn't really come in my pants, at least not officially, but I guessed that was the "reaction" she had wanted to eke out of me last night. And I guess it worked because she smiled big and locked her legs around mine and play-fucked me hard. I tried sneaking hands down the V of her cleavage, up the slits on the sides of her dress, but it was too tight all around.

"You don't know what to do with my dress, do you?"

I faked a pass for her boobs up her narrow sleeve, and she laughed. I am actually being aggressive and charming, like James Bond or something, I remember thinking. Then she unbuttoned my shirt and tingled my body with her hands.

Just then the front door closed.

"Your dad!" She jumped to the bathroom. I clumsily buttoned one button of my shirt and waited, mummy rigid on the edge of the sofa, to be caught and destroyed. I could hear him standing on the other side of the TV room door, wondering why I was up so late. Then he must have turned and stepped up the stairs to bed.

Jenny peeped out of the bathroom and wouldn't do any more kissing. It literally took more than an hour (from two-fourteen to three-twenty) to get her back to where we were. But now she was wearing her nightgown, so access was eased greatly. The granny nightgown buttoned from toes to clavicle, so I started at the top, each button affording a better and better view of her beautiful brown swells. When I finally saw her small, full breasts and saw her nipples hard as nipples can be just because of me, I wanted to stop my life right then. That's enough, I was thinking. Quit while you're ahead.

I kissed her chest and tasted her nipples, sucked on one as I'd seen in *Deep Throat*. Gently I pinched the other while my other hand squeezed her butt and traced its crack. It was an out-of-body experience, and I saw myself working on her expertly—yes, expertly, I had found a groove, found my calling, and transcended the everyday shittiness of my usual reality. I tried a hand for her panty's elastic.

"Austin, I don't want to get all slimy."

Instead, I retreated to suctioning her breasts, and she clutched my head to her chest.

"Oh, God. Oh, God . . . Sorry, honey, but I have to go to the bathroom." When she returned she said, "Now it's your turn."

I hoped to God she would touch it.

"Actually, Austin, I'm pretty beat."

My eyes flew wide and she smiled. "Psych your mind!"

I smiled until she moved her head down my chest and her hands up my leg.

"You're horny," she said.

"Are you ever horny?"

"I'm horny now."

The touch was almost painful, it was so exquisite. She squeezed everywhere near it, then dragged her head lower and lower until she was nuzzling the waistband of my underwear! Somewhere, alarms went off. Emergency teams scrambled. The impossible suddenly seemed possible. I moved to unbutton my belt, and she suddenly raised her lips from my belly button.

"Don't push it," she said.

Relatching my belt reignited her, and her chin actually brushed my pubic hair. I twitched down there, but it didn't feel as though I'd come. She rose from my stomach.

"Sorry for torturing you like that, sweetheart." But her smile held no apology at all.

For hours we vaguely watched TV, lightly napped in each other's arms, rested easily together. Marriage must be like this, I thought. Once in a while my hand scouted the world near her crotch but was always attacked by her closing legs.

"I haven't had this much fun in a long time, Austin."

I couldn't have paid her to say sweeter words.

"Jenny, I can't believe this is happening." She was lying inside my opened legs. If we were naked, I would have been inside her. I can't remember how many times we told each other we should get some sleep. I looked inside my heart and found there for perhaps the first time in my life nothing but shimmering joy. I kissed through her nightgown just past her belly button, and she jack-knifed around my head but urged it away.

"Someday we will make love," she said.

At six twenty-three I tucked her in with a thousand kisses.

Four hours later, after brunch with the 'rents, I drove her to the train station and we kissed on the platform, then kissed through the open window. I prayed some New York-bound friend would have seen me. Our last kiss was the best.

She, an internationally known expert, was supremely turned on. I think I will be a good lover, maybe even great. Unless she was faking it. . . . Naaaah. But I am concerned about not coming. Why am I really excited but semiflaccid? The time with the whore I was also semiflaccid and didn't know when I came.

It's still so unreal. I remember back on the Vineyard, a lifetime ago, biting my pillow and screaming, "I'm in love, I'm in love!" Delectable pain flushed me. I was so shy back then. Could the dark days be through?

January 4, 1982

Sachsenhausen

All of us Stanford-in-Florence students first flew to Frankfurt, West Germany. We had eighty seats in the back of the plane, and it was an in-flight *Animal House*. I'm the only black, and I didn't know a single one of these people from school. I feel like a Mafia informant who was witness relocated. I can be whoever I want to: jock, gigolo, nerd, or creep. It's up to me.

They found us a hotel in the Sachsenhausen, the historic part of the city, the only part left standing after the war. "Dr. Mueller's Sex Shops" brighten nearly every corner with their neon and strobes. One porn place has stairs that light up when you step on them. The men scamper upstairs as quickly as possible, their advance broadcast by colored lights for blocks. But trust me, I didn't go in. My new friend Jay and I went to a jazz club. At the door we had to convince them that we weren't military. The U.S. bases around Frankfurt are huge, and the only Yanks they see are GIs. I guess they get wasted and wreck things because nearly every club said it was off limits to U.S. military personnel.

We were drinking our first German beer, and the trio was pretty good. Jay said they were doing a lot of Charles Mingus.

Jay's a junior, but we get along great since he's girl-crazy himself. More than me he bitches about how lonely he is.

"Austin, I'll tell you something, but swear you won't tell anybody. I'm not weird, you know me, right? But last year, I was going nuts. And there was this guy at school, one of my best friends. I knew he was bi, and I guess I knew he had like a crush on me. I didn't do anything. I swear, but I thought about it. Those guys are so fucking lucky. They just go to a public bathroom, write

....

their name on the wall, and sit by the phone. I wish it were that easy for regular guys.

"I hear gay guys have this code with bandannas, like whether you want to give it or get it, whip or be whipped, things like that. It would be pretty awesome if girls were like that. If you could just walk into T.G.I. Friday's with a bandanna in your back pocket and get a free blow job from a girl."

I don't usually like beer, but I have to say, the German stuff is better. Then around midnight, this blond German lady, at least forty, sat down right next to Jay before she even said, "Hello, boys." I imagined her as Marlene Dietrich, the ex–Gestapo chief's mistress, now looking to hook up with the conquering regime.

" 'Ohhh, say can you see! By the dawn's early light! What so proudly we hail! At the twilight's last gleaming!' . . . *Sehr gut, ja?*" She wobbled like a cartoon drunk. Leaning on both our arms, she told us of her American husband, a journalist with *Stars & Stripes*, who was killed at the battle of Hue, in Vietnam.

"My son looks so like you." She petted Jay's cheek, then kissed it, then kissed the corner of his lips, then his lips. Some man appeared and peeled her off Jay and guided her outside.

January 9, 1982

The Villa

I haven't masturbated since I've been here (four days), and I hereby vow not to touch it until I'm back over North American airspace. I've got to change everything if I want to change my life.

The villa was built in 1548 and sits on the top of a hill overlooking Florence. You can see it from miles away. The driveway is about a kilometer (⅓ mi.) long and snakes steeply up the side of the hill past straight and skinny cypresses and squat and round maritime pines. My bed lies before my ten-foot-high keyhole-shaped window, which overlooks the entire valley of tiny Tuscan red-tiled roofs. In the center of the spill squats the outsize one, Il

Duomo, the cathedral. If you want a better description of this same view, read the beginning of Milton's *Paradise Lost*.

We had a wild toga party. I wouldn't think of attending one stateside, but when in the Roman Empire . . . It was actually fun to pretend to be a carefree and brain-dead frat boy, and the girls looked great in sheets. I didn't really talk to any of them, foreign or domestic. Jay, on the other hand, met this pretty Italian, who by the end of the night was calling him "my little cowboy." He's from New Mexico and thinks he's in love.

February 11, 1982

Jay and Valeria

"Austin, it was our second date. We were having hot chocolate at Gailli's. I told her I loved her."

"What are you, nuts? You never *ever* do that so soon even if you feel it. That's lesson number one. Even I know that much. You probably scared her away."

"Well . . . she said she loved me, too."

March 14, 1982

Francesca

She looks exactly like my rich, high-yellow cousin (I'm always tempted to tell her I was adopted so it's all right if our genes commingle). Long black hair, light brown eyes, a movie star mole studs her perpetual pout. Jay and I had first met her sister when we had snuck into Pitti Lingerie, a lingerie fashion show, masquerading as two reporters from *Seventeen* magazine (with my *Stanford Daily* press pass). The sister is cute and blond and older, mid-twenties. Then at a costume *carnevale* party, their family's, the blonde recognized me and was sort of pissed I'd hoodwinked her. Then she laughed.

"Devi conoscere mia sorella, anche a lei piace degli scherzi."

She said I had to meet her sister because she was a practical joker herself. Francesca heard herself being talked about and turned. My black-and-white cow mask slung low, cradled my chin. Francesca wore a black-and-white minidress and a matching floppy hat. I talked only with this sexy Harlequin the rest of the night. My so-so Italian improving by *passi grandi* because my heart was so intent. Usually, after an Italian party, my brain hurts and I retreat to English with someone who's studied stateside. Tonight I ended the party with two warm kisses on my cheeks.

I called her today without too much planning, but it turns out I should have. I suddenly forgot all the Italian I knew and sounded like a retard. I could tell I was paining her to listen to me.

"Ma, Aus-tinn, tu parli francese?"

I only speak one word of French—*chagrin*.

For some reason I still asked her if she wanted to go to dinner tomorrow night. She said she wasn't sure, but that I should call tomorrow at two.

Right.

March 15, 1982

Francesca

From one forty-three to two-eleven I waited with my hand on the receiver (I didn't want to appear too anxious). At two-twelve it was busy. I waited three minutes because I think I remember from "Hollywood Squares" that the average phone call is that long. I called every three minutes until two-thirty when her mama answers and says she's already gone back to school. I leave a message saying I'm off to London for spring break and I'll see her when I get back. But, truthfully, I don't think I can take any more of this love bullshit.

Jewelle

I was still pissed about Francesca and the state of my life when I triple-checked my cubbyhole in the mailroom and found a letter from Jewelle! It only took three of mine to make her respond. She signed the letter "Love."

My friend Liz Eversohn, on the other hand, has written I don't know how many times. She just got accepted to Berkeley's biz school. It seems like law school isn't that different and both are definitely not for me.

April 20, 1982

Francesca

Ricardo, some other Italians, and I drove through Chianti country today and just got out where we wanted to and rambled through some stranger's vineyards. I love this country. Nothing's straight and flat, all the views are sweeping hills striped with grapevines and their wire grid, or tiny and twisted olive trees as perfectly planted as the corn rows I'd get braided into my hair as a kid during Dayton summers. Ricardo and I talked mainly of Francesca, in Italian, until I gave up and let my head rest and his English flex.

As soon as we walked back into Ricardo's house he picked up the phone and dialed.

"*Ho telefonato a casa sua.*" And he handed me the phone.

"What! Why'd you call her house? Hang up!"

"*Pronto? Pronto? Chi è?*" I heard from the phone.

"*Sono io, Austin.*"

"*Ah! Austin! Come stai? Ti porta la Francesca.*" Her mamma is great, and at least it seemed like the family had discussed my prospects. I hope it's not just because I'm the only *nero Americano* in the city.

Francesca was an angel on the phone and understood most of

what I tried to say, and I'm pretty sure she invited me to dinner tomorrow night.

April 24, 1982

Francesca

Life is wonderful. I see her nearly every day. We haven't kissed yet, but who cares. Ricardo tells me that she has never worn makeup in all her life, but now she does. I was late once for dinner at her house and Ricardo was there, and when I called and said I was on my way, she ran upstairs and changed her clothes.

Tonight I had Francesca and Ricardo and Lanie, his latest American girlfriend from the villa, over for dinner. I made hamburgers and french fries (frozen). Ricardo and Lanie left early, and Francesca and I simultaneously got cravings for hazelnut gelato (both of our favorites).

My bike is an old mailman's bike from the fifties. Its brakes aren't even cables, they're metal rods. It's beautiful, right out of De Sica's *Ladri di Biciclette (The Bicycle Thief)*. I mounted it and patted the top bar for Francesca to sidesaddle onto.

"No, Austin, guido io."

So I let her pedal behind me while I balanced on the bar. She zigzagged a few meters before crashing into a Vespa. We laughed. I couldn't breathe, I was so happy. Then it was my turn to pedal her. They call it *in canna*, and you see lovers all over Italy riding this way in the spring. I hug her so she won't fall (of course) and purposefully ride wobbly to make her shriek and claw my arms with her pretty nails. I feel like Paul Newman riding Katharine Ross in *Butch Cassidy and the Sundance Kid*.

At the gelatería, staring into her eyes across the table, I felt vertigo grip my stomach and my heart, and I snatched at the table's edge to hold myself up. She is as shy as I, but sweet. She left without even kisses on the cheeks, but I don't care. I feel so pure.

....

April 28, 1982

Francesca

She pulled a small flower from the villa's swimming pool–size flower bed.

"Guarda, Austin, che profumo!"

From my nose she pressed the flower into my hand. It was no big deal.

On second thought . . .

Another first: *A romantic gift from a girl!*

May 1, 1982

Elba Shell

I missed her each step on the rocks amid the tame waves nudging the coastline on the island of Elba. Jay and Valeria held hands. I delicately hopscotched the biggest rocks ahead of them alone, like a couple's only child or Irish setter. "Ceca" (Francesca) leaves in eight days for a summer job with an uncle in Milan. An oral exam kept her in Florence this weekend.

First I saw only its crown and thought I'd again be disappointed. Parts of shells on the beach always look perfect, then, drawn from the sand, reveal their chipped edges and mysterious holes. Yet this swirled and dappled shell looked *nearly* store-bought. Later, at a trattoria overlooking the slender yachts and complicated fishing boats in the harbor, I had an idea.

I just wrote a message to her on a tiny sliver of paper from this notepad, stuck a needle in one side, and sewed a thread to the end of the fortune cookie–size note. I insinuated the note in the shell so that just the tip of the black thread dangled free.

"She'll never find it. That's crazy," Jay just told me. He also just told me that he is engaged.

I envision Ceca cleaning out her girlish things on the eve of her wedding to some Milanese industrialist. She'll start to throw out the too perfect shell, then musty memories of me will waft from a forgotten puddle in the back of her brain. A smile will bloom between her cheeks, and the ghost of my face will make her slowly collapse to her bed. Then the tiny cord will reflect some light. Suspicious, she will gently tug, yet holding the shell an arm away. I too shall be married by then, and her phone call will disregard the time zones and wake Jewelle. Francesca and I will share a long-distance smile in the dark. . . .

Maybe I should go into advertising. My romantic dribbling would make a great ad for AT&T.

I told Jay my vision, and he thinks I'm high. He is staying in Italy for the summer to be with Valeria. The rest of the school is off for a field trip to Greece before they summer topless on the islands in the Aegean. As for dear Austin, a Howard classmate of the folks forced on me an internship with Pittsburgh Paints' public relations department. If this weren't happening to someone I know, it would be hilarious.

M a y   9 ,   1 9 8 2

F r a n c e s c a

I waited for Ceca to finish her oral exam. Sitting there in Piazza San Marco this gorgeous spring, I noticed lovers amid the pigeons everywhere, and none, I thought, were any happier than me. We walked our bicycles through San Lorenzo market, between the stands and their striped awnings, we walked between the immense Duomo and its dwarf baptistery, and I couldn't help but feel I was being filmed. Somebody somewhere was making a training film on being in love, and I was its star. We stopped and sat on the side of the Loggio di Lazzi, the atrium of bronze and marble Renaissance statues in Piazza della Signoria. I scooted my butt only a little bit closer. Later, crossing the Ponte Vecchio, I slipped my arm inside hers, softly. We sat on the bridge and watched the rowers slice the river. She rose to light a cigarette, then returned to find my arm still there, inviting her to nestle in. Ricardo tells me I am her first boyfriend so don't expect too much. But being with her already gives me more than I'd dreamed of.

The sun colored the Arno the same red as the tiles on the roofs of the four-hundred-year-old houses lining the river. I cannot believe that I changed my life and found this place. I cannot believe that now it's near time to go. I had wanted to wait until we said good night to hand over the shell, but Florence, the Ponte Vecchio, sunset in spring, is the only time to hand over such a gift.

"Per me? È bellissimo! Che colore!" She bounced her eyes from the shell now in her palm to my eyes and down again. She immediately noticed the string. She backed away and looked to me for help. I gave her none. She yanked out the note and uncrinkled it.

"Ma sai, Austin, c'è un biglietto qui dentro."

As a matter of fact, I did know there was a note inside.

" 'I lick you sooo mooch. It's sooo vary hard tuu lif'?" I wrote it in English because she doesn't speak any English at all. Her brow was a wrinkled mess.

"Cos'è 'lick'?"

" 'Like' is *mi piace*."

"Allora 'sooo'?"

" 'So' is *tanto*."

" 'Mooch'?"

" 'Much' is *molto*."

" 'Hrd'? No, 'hard'?"

"Difficile."

" 'Lif'?"

'Leave' is *"partire."*

"Mi piace tanto. Partire è tanto difficile."

"Sì, esatto," I replied.

"Grazie. Altrettanto." ("Same to you.")

She drew from her own pocket her own gift. A tiny Renaissance lithograph of the Duomo. I could only stare.

I held her handlebars as she got on.

"*Arrivederci, ti voglio bene,*" I said softly. ("*Ti voglio bene*" is just a shade from crazy, heart-bursting *ti amo.*)

"*Ti voglio bene, anch'io.*"

I leaned dead on for her lips. She turned four degrees east, then west, semiprofiled left, then right, one lip's edge, the other, then left.

Pedaling home past the soccer stadium, the spring carnival was closing its rides early. In Italy they call it Luna Park. And *luna* means moon.

May 20, 1982

Calista

She's somewhere in France. She's again cycling across Europe, but this year as a leader. She has called three times, but I was always out courting Ceca. I would love to hook up with her over here, but I don't think it's going to work. Her plans are not to reach Florence until August. Maybe Ceca and Ricardo could show her around.

June 12, 1982

Airbus

I'm on the airbus from Athens back home.

"You did your little European thing with all those white people, now it's time to get yourself a J.O.B."

Thanks, Dad.

I just did something weird. I went to the bathroom in the airbus, and it's huge for an airplane. I took off all my clothes just because I thought it would be an experience to be naked in a plane. It was. Jewelle was the first one to float to the top of my brain. So Jewelle it was for the first time. Bad luck be damned.

Atlanta

When they'd told me Pittsburgh Paint I had assumed Pittsburgh, PA. But they have this small office here in "Hot-lanta, the Paris of the South." It ain't Florence, but it ain't Pittsburgh, either.

I live in the basement of this nice old lady. My mom's mom met her at a Links national convention. She cooks dinner for me almost every night, and she's nicer than my own mom's mom. She seems to want to get me married off to some southern black belle.

It's wonderful to see so many black people around me. I have to get used to not being stared at as I was in Italy *("Gurada, mamma, un nero!")*. Mrs. Landestoi is evidently one of the black aristocracy here because this neighborhood is swank. New silver-and-burgundy Cadillacs, Electras, and Lincolns stud almost every driveway. I feel like the gardener. And I like it.

Mrs. Landestoi, on the other hand, seems to think I am some sort of big-shot wunderkind in the Pittsburgh Paint operation. I didn't tell her that I share a desk with a temporary secretary in the product labeling division. "The poets of paint," the division head likes to call us. Our department thinks up names for the new shades of oils and enamels. On Monday I'll find the tint of Jewelle's skin on the latest paint chip chart and suggest "Cocoa Perfection."

July 18, 1982

Lynn

Mrs. Landestoi introduced us at a party, but it turns out her parents and Marquita and Fletcher all went to Howard together. I've done a few things with them, like watch the Peachtree Road Race over a brunch of champagne and cheese grits.

She's very cute, but more important she's real smart. If she were

a guy, we'd be friends anyway. Last week, she invited me to see
E.T. because it came out when I was in Italy. We had fun until
she started moaning about her boyfriend at Hampton Institute.
Still, she flirts a bit. I think a little "summer lovin' " might just
be in the cards.

July 22, 1982

Lynn

She suggested it, I didn't. I wasn't about to say no to a woman
who asks you to take her to *The Story of O.* It was pretty fucking
sexy, no gross cum shots like American porn.

Anyway, it played at the only foreign-film movie theater in all
of Atlanta. I brushed her arm every few minutes to try to wheedle
a rise out of her, but I had to be careful to time them not to
coincide with the really hard scenes.

After the film she drove me right home. I wanted to go out to
a bar or something, but she said she was tired. In front of the
house I saw that Mrs. L.'s Electra wasn't in the garage.

"Would you like to come in for a sec and see the house?"

I think I'd already started to say, "Well then, maybe some other
time," when she opened her side of the car and got out. I turned
away from her and silently screamed, then got cool again and
ushered her up the snake of flagstones to the house.

"Would you like a nightcap?" (Lesson number one from the
"Love, American Style" school of bacheloring.)

"Scotch on the rocks." She's pretty cool.

I opened every cabinet in the living room, dining room, and
kitchen but couldn't find any booze at all.

"I've got orange juice, prune juice (that's Mrs. Landestoi's, but
I'm sure you're welcome to it), or chocolate milk."

I delivered the two chocolate milks on a tray with some nacho
cheese Doritos.

" 'She was an innocent farm girl whose so-called cousin "D'Ar-banville" seduced and impregnated her.' "

I didn't know what the hell she was doing until I saw she was reading from a book of Mrs. L's, *Shrinklits*, a tiny bathroom book "wittily" encapsulating famous works of literature.

"Well, Austin, you're an English major, too. Who is it?"

"Tess of the d'Urbervilles. I hated that book."

" 'His last name was the same as his first and his rival for the young maiden's attention was Claire Quilty.' "

"Humbert Humbert from *Lolita*. That's one of my favorites, we read it in high school. 'Lolita, light of my life, fire of my loins, my sin, my soul. Lo-li-ta . . .' "

"Just answer the questions and stop showing off."

My hands shot to ring her neck, play-strangle her. Then they softened to a caress. I left my arm over her shoulder, and she let me.

"Oh, first you batter women, then you try and make nice."

I gave her my hound-dog eyes of love and leaned in for the kiss. She let me.

"Why did you do that?"

Fuck.

"I don't . . . I—I—I don't know. It seemed like a good idea at the time."

"But I'm not pretty like your Italian girlfriend, Francesca?" I had told her everything.

"Are you crazy? You're beautiful. And smart, too. And . . ."

I just kissed her again, and this time her mouth opened and we were really going at it. I reached for her truly large boobs, and no problem at all; I reached inside her T-shirt and rolled her nipples in my fingers, and she just moaned. I slid my hand down her jeans and swooped into her crotch. She was already wet and widened her legs.

Luckily Mrs. L. can't ever get into her garage without scratching the side of the car or clanging a trash can, and the noise gave us an early warning. Lynn stretched her bra back over her nipples and left. I'm sure Mrs. L. was happy to see me with Lynn because her folks are so loaded. Andrew Young's always over at their house to watch football. We could sixty-nine on her Persian rug and she would just smile and bring us lemonade.

July 23, 1982

Jenny

I'd been waiting for a telephone call from Lynn for two hours. I was getting madder and madder when the phone rang. My hand caught the receiver in the middle of its first ring, but I suavely didn't pick up until the third.

"Hi, Austin."

"Hi. . . ."

"You don't know who this is, do you?"

"Jenny?"

"Sweetie, you're such a brainiac."

"I've got this incredible secret and I haven't told anyone yet."

"Okay. I'm ready."

"Maybe I shouldn't tell you. . . . Okay, okay, okay, I'll tell you, but just not right now, okay?"

"Whatever you say."

"You think I'm so queer, don't you?"

"I'm used to it by now."

"Everything okay down there?"

"Yeah. I've got a girlfriend. It's nothing serious."

"Way to go, killer. . . . Well, I'd better cruise. I'm calling from the 'rents'."

"Thanks for calling, Jenny."

"Check you out like a trout."

August 2, 1982

Lynn

"Look, I'm leaving in just twenty-five days and I don't want to be tied to anyone."

"Neither do I. That doesn't mean we can't still be friends . . . and maybe, you know, mess around once in a while when the moon is full."

"I'll call you."

August 6, 1982

Mom and Dad

Dad talked first.

"So, are you all right? Do you need any money?"

"No, Dad. I'm fine."

"How's your little friend?"

"You mean Lynn?" I had told them about her weeks ago. "She's fine."

Mom asked me about her, too.

"I remember when she was a baby. The Potters were living in Detroit and we drove up from Ypsilanti to see their newborn."

I didn't have the guts to tell them the truth. I know they're going crazy because I've never had a girlfriend. They probably think I'm queer, but they're such liberals, they probably brag about it to their friends. "Oh, I can't wait for our dear Austin to come out. I've already asked for membership information from Mothers of Special Men."

....

A u g u s t   8 ,   1 9 8 2

L y n n

I just got off the phone with the bitch. I don't feel anything. Zip.

"Oh, maybe I haven't told you yet. Perhaps me and my ex-boyfriend are getting back together."

I feel angry and sad at the same time, which is certainly better than just sad. I've got to find somebody new before I leave. I don't know. I don't know shit.

Oh, and I got a letter today from Jay and Valeria. The wedding's in Friuli in August. If I could afford to jet back over, I'd be the *testimone*—best man.

It was already ten at night when I decided to run. If I had a car, I wouldn't be in such fucking pain right now. In Florence I bought a pair of Supergas, Italian tennis shoes, so some pretty American would ask me where I got them. Their canvas is as rough as burlap.

I wore a bright yellow T-shirt so I wouldn't become a road kill and set off jogging for the first time since high school cross-country ski practice. I wanted to stop after a block but did not. I never take things to the end, with women or the world. This run was to have changed my life. The sides of my feet soon felt as if they were over flames. But blisters always feel worse than they are. They swell in my mind as an excuse to stop.

"But I won't stop till blood seeps through the shoe."

The kudzu vines lining the unlit road were slowly strangling the trees hidden behind them. Last year, Atlanta child murderer Wayne Williams dumped two bodies somewhere along this road. One of the "children" was nineteen. I'd forgotten the groove you get into running, after your "no" side gives in to the "yes." You didn't know that girl, really. You got to second base after only a few dates. You should be proud. It's all practice for Stanford, where you'll be completely refashioned.

I felt good until I looked down to my feet. I wasn't sure until I was right under a streetlight. Then I was sure. The sides of my white shoes were pink.

I walked home in just my reddened tube socks. My sneakers are soaking in cold water and baking soda (Hints from Heloise). After I finish writing this I'll find the Band-Aids so my sheets will stay clean.

August 15, 1982

Pittsburgh Paint

I'm still hobbling to work, then taking my shoes off under my desk. I'm sort of proud of the ripped blisters. If Hef ever hosts a talk show for his fellow romantically/sexually obsessed, this will make a great anecdote.

They've rejected all of my latest ideas—an almost Day-Glo red I wanted to call "Abject Fear," a sickly pale yellow I wanted to call "Mineshaft Canary," a pale olive, "Boredom," and for a slate gray, the color of no color at all, I suggested "Despair."

September 9, 1982

Rubydee

YAHOO!!!!!!!

I just came in from a Georgia football game. My boss got us field passes, and we met Herschel Walker. I walked into the house hot and sweaty and found Mrs. L. and fifty or so rich black ladies sipping tea.

"Oh, here is my boarder. Austin, come meet the Peachtree chapter of the Links. Austin is a junior executive for the Pittsburgh Paint people."

"Ohhh!/That's beautiful, baby/Fine, that's fine/And a handsome young man, too/Yes, he is. . . ."

I shook their hands while trying to clamp my armpits to my side to hold in the b.o.

"And Austin, I'd like you to meet Mrs. Loretha Henderson, she used to help me out when my husband and the girls were living here. And this is her daughter, Rubydee Henderson." I didn't laugh. I fell in love with her at first sight.

She's twenty-five!! And has a two-year-old boy!! (Named, I swear, Ossie Davis Henderson.) She's gorgeous, tall, regal, even browner than me. She studied at the University of Georgia but had to drop out when she got pregnant. She's going to study computers somewhere this October.

As soon as I saw her I hoarded thoughts of her, I scraped my stool next to hers in the kitchen, but she was in the middle of a Stephen King novel. I gave up and went down to my underground.

What a bitch, I was thinking as I dropped my pants, splooched Jergens in my palm, and advanced on the pillows on my bed.

Knock! Knock! Knock!

The door has no lock and my heart ricocheted around my rib cage. I smeared the blop of lotion on my thigh and jerked up my pants, buttoning only the top button of my jeans fly as I hobbled to the door.

"I broke my nail, and Mrs. Landestoi thought you might have a Band-Aid."

Why ever make up a bed when you're the only one who will ever see it? She must have noticed the two pillows laid end to end down the center vertical line of the bed, my summer surrogate. I turned her around and urged her down on the chair at my desk.

"I think I have some in the bathroom, I'll be right back."

Band-Aids in hand, I whipped shut the medicine cabinet, and its mirror shook. My eye bags draped halfway to my chin, nubs of something white but hopefully dead polka-dotted my Afro. I leaned out of the bathroom, smiled to her, and shut the door. I picked my hair slowly so it was noiseless, smeared raw toothpaste on my teeth and tongue.

"These might be a little big, but I'm sorry, they're all I have."

I squatted at her feet, propped my knee against hers, held this stranger's hand as I circled the Band-Aid around her finger.

"They're working you too hard up there."

"Oh, my nails break on me whenever I'm nervous."

"Are you nervous now?"

This is when she looked at me. She hoisted her eyes from her finger touched by mine, and I saw something in the bottom of the brown melt and glow.

"I have to finish the dishes."

I let her leave my room first, then jumped back and threw the pillows to the top of the bed, ripped the tangled rope of sheets off and passed them to the closet, soared the bedspread over the now naked bed like a cape.

Upstairs I rinsed the dishes she washed, sidling closer with every saucer or tureen. I felt sure, for perhaps the first time in my life, that someone liked me as much as I liked them. I felt calm and right in an invisible groove. I had to go back downstairs with her and was frantically trying to conjure an excuse.

"Shoot, your Band-Aid came all undone with the water and all."

Down, down, down we returned to the must, dust, crippled Ping-Pong table, water heater, boiler, and wet lime smell of the basement. Inside my room, the dropped ceiling of white fiberglass ceiling panels and the recessed opaque Plexiglas fluorescent lighting fixture never seemed so homey. I put on a Lucio Dalla tape to impress her. I lovingly dried her finger and changed her bandage. I then sat on the bed. She chose a chair.

"That music, it's not Spanish. I took some in high school."

"It's Italian. I was studying there this year."

"I always wanted to learn it."

She pressed herself standing, leaned over my desk, and fished through my piles of books. She picked up *Marcovaldo* by Italo Calvino.

" '*Un-a noti di . . . di . . . d'estate . . .*' "

" '*Una notte d'estate,*' 'on a night in summer . . .' "

" 'Ch-chera un ce-cert-o typ-o . . .' "

"Tipo. 'C'era un certo tipo.' 'There was a certain type, I mean, this certain guy . . .' "

She laughed and squeezed my arm. She sat on the chair, and again I squatted at her feet.

"Would you like to learn how to count to ten?"

"Unos, duos . . ."

"Pretty good. *U-no, du-e, tre, quat-tro, cin-que, sei . . .*"

"*U-no, do-e, tray, quat-tro, chin-kway, say . . .*"

"You're excellent . . . *sette, otto, nove, dieci.*"

"*Set-tay, ot-to, no-vay, de-ay-chi . . . uno, duo, tre, quattro, cinque, sei, sette, otto, nove, dieci!*"

"Perfect!" And I did it. I kissed this beautiful stranger's lips.

"You're fast." (Imagine, me!!) "Are you going to kiss me every time I get it right?"

"And even when you're wrong."

I am so cool!

She read more of *Marcovaldo*, and I was amazed how her southern accent dropped away and Italian better than most of the villa's frat boys filled her mouth. But the paragraph was too long, I couldn't wait, so lifted the book from her eyes and kissed her hard. We made out like hungry people, lots of snorts and bites. Then she sweetly pushed me back.

"I think we'd better read some more Italian."

"Here's how I teach. . . . *Questo è un bacio,*" and I kissed her softly. "*Il naso,*" and I kissed her nose. "*Le guancie,*" and I kissed her cheeks. "*Il mento*"—the chin—"*le spalle*"—the shoulders— "*i capelli*"—her hair . . . "*il collo*"—her neck—"*e finalmente di nuovo le labbre,*" and finally her lips again, and I kissed these, too. We held each other too tightly, floating together in the desperate shipwreck of my room.

Again upstairs we went before someone came down. Most of the women were gone, but silver bowls of cashews still pocked the living room. We collected them all, turning bowl after bowl into the first we collected. I ate most of the ones we retrieved.

"I love cashews," I said.

"I wish I were a cashew."

I couldn't walk, I couldn't breathe. I couldn't speak, I couldn't think. How could words affect me so physically, capture my legs and my lungs?

"Rubydee, I like you so much."

Mrs. L. drove her home, and I went along. We held hands in the backseat, and I walked her to her door, shielded our kiss from Mrs. L. with my back.

"So I'll see you tomorrow." We'd decided to see *An Officer and a Gentleman* at the mall.

I returned to the car and couldn't look Mrs. L. in the face. I felt trapped in a bad episode of "Father Knows Best."

"Nice girl, son."

"Yes, she is."

"She would have already risen out of her station if she hadn't had the baby."

Back home Mrs. L.'s guest from New Jersey, Mr. deCollette, was home from his dinner party, his white-looking, knuckled feet on the coffee table, a water glass full of Scotch next to the bottle in front of him. I'd never before met a real-live black Republican. He talked to me only of Andover and couldn't believe I turned down Harvard for Stanford. I tried to sneak downstairs without speaking more than "Good night." If he knew I was going to marry a "peasant," he'd burst a valve. I can't wait to find a way to tell him. But not tonight; I want to carry my great feelings into my sleep. Who knows what kind of golden, magical dreams will sprout from such a perfect day?

"Austin!" He had to shout over the classical music he blasted. Mrs. L. looked to me with pity and excused herself good night. "Austin, where are you?"

I circled into his field of view. "Austin, I'm trapped in black skin. I fence, I shoot, I sail, I ski, I dress white, and I think white. Negroes are an ignorant and foolish tribe, and look at me. I am not one of them." From our similar talk last night, I know that

....

he calls society blacks "Negroes" and poorer blacks "niggers." He wants to cut all welfare benefits and thinks rock & roll is garbage.

"Mr. deCollette, you should get some sleep."

"Don't tell me what to do, goddammit."

"Well, I have to go to sleep, sir. I am in love."

I don't think he heard me. Or did not believe his ears.

September 10, 1982

Rubydee

I've been waiting at home for her call for forty-five minutes. I've called her house twice. I feel nothing, as always.

I just called again, and her mom answered. She's on her way, but the buses are slow. She wants to meet right in front of the theater in the mall.

I scrounged five drugstores in the mall on my rubber hunt before I found some displayed where I could snag them without asking. I pretended I couldn't speak and just paid and left. I don't know why I was so shy about them now that I finally need one.

She arrived late, and though I'd already seen *An Officer and a Gentleman*, I hate missing the beginning of a movie.

"We could just walk back to my place?"

"No."

It was a great date movie. We held hands. I really wasn't watching any of it at all, I was concentrating on Rubydee. My hand slid from her knee to between her thighs, and she didn't clamp down until very close to the strike zone. I gave up and ringed my arm around her back until it fell asleep.

At her bus stop I kissed her again and again, and again she called me "fast." Then she said exactly these twenty-one words:

"Austin, since Saturday when we first met I've been wondering what it would be like to make love to you."

• • •

After her bus left, I sat down on a mall trash can painted like fake wood and shaped like a wooden barrel on a ship. I was so scared. After the dinner we'd planned tomorrow night at Steak & Ale I suggested a nearby motel. If it weren't for TV, I wouldn't know what to do or where to take a date. Here now in my cellar I still taste her lips, still her perfume wanders my nose.

I guess I don't really love her. We're pretty different people. But it's more than just lust between us. And I'm leaving in a week for school. She's said she'll write me every week. I told her I couldn't write so often. I think I'm going to tell her I've made love only once before (but I can't tell her with whom). I hope, if I tell her, that she'll help me out. I've no doubt that I will prematurely ejaculate or whatever it is I'm doing wrong. I'm petrified.

September 14, 1982

Rubydee

Both our bus lines let us off in front of the Steak & Ale.
"Would you like to eat or go right to the motel?"
"Motel."

I'd made reservations at the Dixie Motor Inn from work today, hoping my boss would hear and tease me about it. He loves me after the department head okayed two of my names: "Blizzard" and "Tequila."

The motel room is blue—the walls, the drapes, the two queen-size beds, the fishing seascape, the mirror scribbled over in thin blue lines to look, somehow, like blue marble.

Rubydee didn't seem gorgeous anymore, just sweet and nice. There was sadness and loneliness in the room with us, but there was also some romance. There was that.

"You might not believe this, but this is the first time I've ever been with a woman except once with a . . . a prostitute." She just nodded. I kissed her again and again, but I wasn't hard, it was all so strange. I wasn't even afraid. Then she stopped my hands on her sides.

"Maybe this doesn't make much sense. You're leaving so soon."

"Memories are everything. If we make love for a day, or a week, or a year, in the end they'll all collapse to memory. A memory is an instant, a moment. . . . You don't know what this means to me. For the rest of my life this room, your lips, your smell, will stay with me and make me smile. No matter where I go I'll have this moment of you with me."

Shut up. I believed what I was saying, and I still do.

She let us kiss and she let me unbutton her dress, then she freed the rest herself. I unbuttoned my own shirt, dropped my pants from around me.

"I, I don't know still. . . ."

"I don't want you to do what you don't want to. I'd feel worse if you regretted staying with me than if you left right now."

"You sound like an old saint."

"I've just been hurt so many times myself that I know how it feels. Like someone broke your arm or smashed your leg. I couldn't make myself do that to someone else."

She kissed me now and gradually widened her mouth. Shuffling to the bed, I fell on her gently, kissed down her body to her bra, and undid it faster than I'd feared. Her nipples were already hardening before I sucked them into my mouth. Kissing down her belly, I felt it undulate as I passed. She wriggled herself to help the panties down.

I smelled her before I tasted her. I was an animal lured by a scent, and I wallowed in it, licking her everywhere porn movies had told me to lick. It worked. Her body churned and boiled, she pinched and twisted her nipples, ground her butt into the bed. I started to think she'd forgotten to tell me about her epilepsy. Then the noises, deep noises, revved deeper than her high voice could possibly have produced. She reminded me of Linda Blair in *The Exorcist*. She came.

Another first.

I still fiddled with her breasts with one hand, tried to open the condom with the other. Finally I ripped the package with both hands and lowered the disk to my dick.

Half-hard at best, white shit dribbled from the opening as if alive.

"Uh, we've got a situation here."

She opened her eyes and leaned up to look. I'd been lifting all summer by sneaking into the Holiday Inn near work, so here I was, a well-muscled eunuch. I decided there and then to see a doctor my first day back at school.

I tried to convince her to lick it. Instead, she tinkled her fingers past my chest and stomach. Almost instantly I was pretty hard and guessed the right side of the condom and easily unrolled it down the shaft. She reached under and guided me in. The rhythm was tricky—I suck at dancing—and it kept falling out. But she was so wet. Gradually I learned her moves and mirrored them, and she actually locked her legs hard around mine and grabbed my waist tight and pushed and pulled me inside of her like a demon. She practically ate my ear off and cried loud when she came again and convulsed sharp. I came, too, and it was much better than in Nevada, but it didn't make my eyes cross and my whole body shiver like when I'm fantasizing well. Bizarre.

I went down on her again, and though she didn't come this time she did go crazy again.

"Let's make love again," said I.

She was on top of me then, wiping me with her thighs and vagina. I tried to get to my pants for another rubber, but she locked me to the bed with her body.

"Don't get up."

"I have to get another condom."

"It doesn't matter."

I wanted to lecture her. I wanted to remind her that's exactly how Rubydee got stuck with little Ossie Davis. I forced myself past her, slung on another condom, and slid back onto her. This time I was determined not to fall out, to measure my strides and try to drive her crazier still. I did much better, but she didn't come. I knew I didn't love her, and though I felt relieved and satisfied, I wasn't overcome by joy. It wasn't like kissing Joie or Jenny or even a sweet kiss on the cheek from Francesca.

"You know, Austin, with a little more practice you could become a great lover." And my sadness vanished. Unbelievable, those words.

Now I'm not a virgin.

I walked her to the last bus and slept alone in our motel room bed.

September 16, 1982

Calista

Mom forwarded this postcard. It was a close-up of the *David's* groin circled in red lipstick and the word *Oooauuu!* which is the Italian translation of "Wow!"

The bike tour is going wonderfully. I see why you love Italy so. Your friends in Florence are angels, especially Ricardo. I think he will become this year's Sabino. This continent is lucky for me.

Love, Calista

Oh God, Sabino was that Basque bastard. If Ricardo makes love with her I will die! I can't wait to get back to Stanford.

October 1, 1982

Liz Eversohn

Jewelle is in D.C. for the semester. That's good. It gives me more time to improve myself. Liz and I've been friends forever (see October–January 1980–81). My freshman year she was the white Canadian senior I kissed under the mistletoe with Vietta the RA. I once slid a Valentine's Day card under her door, asking if she'd like me to sleep over. Now she's at Berkeley's B school. Jay says we'll start going out. He and Valeria are living in the married students' housing. It's actually a pretty nice apartment. The twins are due around Christmas.

Liz and I go out all the time. We're always flirting heavy-duty, and she takes my arm or squeezes me for no reason. Her boyfriend is a little creep in the business school here. And her body is better than a Playmate's. I try not to stare, but when the strain on her blouse from her breasts popped open a button, I nearly fell face first on the table. But what's great about her is that she's a girl but I can tell her everything. At the Coffee House, I told her the story of Rubydee.

"And then I kinda went down on her. Are you sure you want to hear all this?"

"Go ahead. Maybe I'll learn something." Liz's always giving me shit. Like a big sister.

"Well, of course I'd never done it before. I'd never done anything before."

"Except at the whorehouse."

My eyes and head shot around the Coffee House in opposite directions to make sure no one had overheard.

"I knew I shouldn't have told you."

"Awww, poor baby." She reached over and scrubbed my arm with her hand, then stroked my cheek. "Go on. I'm all ears."

"I had seen it done in a porno movie and just sort of winged it. She went crazy, locked her legs around the back of my head like a professional wrestler. She made so much noise I thought the vice squad would burst in. Do all women like it that much?"

"I've never gone down on one."

"Don't break my balls. You know what I mean."

"For me it's okay, but I like giving more than receiving."

I looked at her hard to make sure I was understanding her right. I was. Oh, boy.

"What time is it, Liz? I promised I'd help finish pasting up the *Chaparral*." I really just wanted to rush home and beat off over Liz going down on me while the image was still fresh.

October 10, 1982

GQ (Gentlemen's Quarterly)

Marquita and Fletcher got me a subscription to GQ magazine for this, my twentieth birthday. So maybe I did wear an Afro well into 1981, but they aren't much better. Dad still wears khaki safari jackets, and Mom hasn't thrown away her culottes.

October 17, 1982

Rubydee

I've written her twice, but no response. I guess it's for the best.
Last night, three o'clock in the morning, the guys were still waxing type for the fall *Chaparral* and pressing it onto page boards. I sat on the couch in the other room, the typewriter on my knees. Perhaps not one of the words in the paper I handed in this morning was spelled correctly. Instead of typing, I frequently pinched cold erasers of cheese from the roof of tonight's Domino's Pizza box, stretched the cheese into lines that soon snapped, and ate them. Springsteen was groaning something loudly on KZSU. Lenny Barth, the editor, threw his running shoe at my typewriter.

"No real work in the office! You know how I hate that."

"It's due tomorrow morning."

"It's bad luck. I wrote a paper in here once. Milton. I got a No Credit for the course."

"Thanks."

"Did I tell you I slept with the Angel last night?"

"Did you sleep with her or sleep with her?"

"Everything, man, it was great."

The Angel is his Jewelle. Len's a senior and has been her best friend for four years.

"I'm telling you, man, it works. Just be their friend for a couple of years, and one day you'll be sleeping on their floor like you've done a hundred times, and she'll pull back the sheets and let you in."

Couple of years!

I can live with that. I'll still be youngish when Jewelle comes round.

"And, Austin, here's something else I've figured out, and if you think I'm wrong, just say so. All guys if they're around any girl not their mother, grandmother, or sister for a long enough time will eventually want to have sex with her, even if she's ugly, just to clear the air. Am I right?"

I would have objected if at that instant into my mind had not been projected the stained and jagged smile of Mrs. Turnov, my disfigured seventh-grade English teacher and once the object of my affection.

October 20, 1982

Liz

The rumor is that Jewelle, away this quarter at Howard in Washington, is engaged to an heir to the Johnson (Afro-Sheen) fortune. She hasn't written me back yet, but I don't believe it.

Instead of going to sleep in class today I studied this Indian (from India) girl. Her brown legs were crossed and fidgeting inside her white jean skirt. I composed this poem:

Oh, are her eyes so beautiful from within as without?
Doth she know her power?

....

That every pump of that expos'd cross'd thigh doth pump my
    member full?
Those lips so plump, God made for kissing long,
Oft turn to smile and warm my heart most full.

Of course this is Renaissance poetry class. Too bad she only
dates Nazi-looking blond swimmers.

Later, Liz called.
"Can you talk?"
"Always."
"I just wanted to say I'm still pissed with you about our con-
versation last night."
We talk every night. I raced to catch up with her, to remember
what stupid thing I'd said this time.
"Austin, you're such a sexist pig. All you think about is sex,
and you have this Neanderthal attitude. You were so sweet as a
freshman. What happened?"
"Uh. I don't know. The little boy grew up, I guess."
"Fuck you. That's just what I mean. I can't talk anymore. Good-
bye."
It was so weird. Then I remembered that Liz once said she
wanted to learn Italian, and the first thing I said was *"Che poppe,"*
about a passing student—"Nice tits." I just want to die. She's
right. I'm a pig. I only care about how pretty or stacked a girl is.
I've been told that before. I must think about sex every minute
and a half. And I thought I was getting better. It's more than
disgusting. It's sick. She practically called me an irredeemable
shit. And she may be right.
I've got to change. No more jerking off. That's it. *Finito.* No
more "sore shoulder, won't you please massage it" routines. No
more conniving for a kiss. I've got to stop thinking of women as
prizes. That's why you've never been really in love. That's why
you will die alone in a home.

....

October 27, 1982

Jewelle

She just sent me a letter! She loves D.C. but says the Howard men are uptight and boring!

Francesca's also written a few times. She's fine as always.

November 1, 1982

Chaparral

Typical Saturday night of hell. Andover rehash. I don't know how many girls I hovered around to slow dance with at the Ujamaa dance. Anyway, none of them said yes. I wandered the campus with my windbreaker unbuttoned in the cold of the night to hasten death. A huge frat house, SAE, I think, squatting like a wedding cake, swelled with music and squeals. I stepped inside and sidled between the drunken, hooting frat boys and unsteady sorority girls before their midnight trains. Every single person in the room, it seemed, bumped into, then spilled an overfull and flimsy, tall plastic cup of keg beer on my hands, pants, and T-shirt. Every one of the white boys did a double take when they saw me and said, "Hey, sorry, man," and twice, "Hey, sorry, bro'." I struggled through to the back door, and the absolute and sudden silence outside was as shocking as the noise just before.

Nobody I knew in the Coffee House.

The *Chaparral* office again. I'd slept there three nights ago with the rest of the crew, trying to get the fall issue out before the Big Game. Tonight stale beer vapor was its atmosphere. Popcorn and Doritos bits speckled the rug. I turned up the radio. Quincy, a friend of mine at KZSU, was playing a Return to Forever marathon retrospective. I called him up and talked to him for a while. Then I played pinball until one, when people would start filling the streets again and march home.

....

January 11, 1983

Jewelle

She's back. She came by the Casa Italiana for lunch. She came up to the room to talk. Grover Washington, Jr.'s saxophone had no effect. Still, it was wonderful. But I'm afraid the usual will happen. I'll make one date with her, and if she turns her cheek, fine, I'm outta here.

February 2, 1983

Jewelle

We see each other at least twice a week. We haven't kissed yet, but it's only a matter of time. We saw Twyla Tharp's dance company when she came to Mem. Aud., *Sophie's Choice* at the Sunday flicks, *The River Niger* for the Black History Month film series. We talk for hours in her dorm room or mine, usually about the state of Afro-Americans.

Yesterday, after *The River Niger* I wanted to kiss her or at least walk hand in hand. I'm tired of this gray area, and if I don't try something soon, she'll just think of me as a friend and start telling me about some jock she has a crush on.

It was raining and I tried to scoop her with my arm under my umbrella.

"It's not raining that hard." And she spun out of my reach and walked in the cold rain.

Back in her room, I sat on her couch in the exact position that would give her plenty of room to sit next to me without feeling too crowded. The only chair in her living room was covered with her poli sci books. She pressed herself backward onto the dining room table.

Before I left I borrowed a baseball hat from her since it was raining harder and louder. Of course I really just wanted an excuse to stop by her room today.

His name is Bart. Big, black Bart. They were studying together, though I bet he can barely read.

I left her dorm congratulating myself aloud for how cool I was. Two stupid girls stared. Jewelle and I are just friends, fine, fine, fine. And maybe she and the stupid guy are just friends. And even though we never kiss, we act like girlfriend and boyfriend, and that will be very useful practice. Perhaps she can fix me up with one of her friends. I'll be all right.

February 3, 1983

L i z

Tonight we saw *Emmanuelle* at the *Chaparral*'s film series. Her goony boyfriend is in midterms, so he's never around.

After the film we went back to the *Chaparral* headquarters. There's always beer in the fridge, but this time only Old English 800 malt liquor and Thunderbird. I had bought them for our Wednesday meeting as a joke, and nobody had touched them.

"Let's see what all the fuss is about." And with that Liz unscrewed the top and swigged the Thunderbird. I snatched it from her and chugged myself. We stared at each other, waiting to see if stubble would suddenly sprout on our chins, if fingerless rag gloves would materialize on our hands.

"Kind of good. Sweet, like schnapps."

She had been touching me a lot that evening. She flopped her hand right on my thigh throughout the movie, and I just grew and grew; she had to have noticed. While we were walking over here she rested her head on my shoulder.

"Austin, you used to wrestle in high school, didn't you? I bet you were awful."

"I could kick your butt with one hand."

• •

"You think so?" Sparks twinkled violently from her violet eyes. I set wide my feet, outstretched my hands to attack.

"No. Let's do it right. Don't they get in some position on the ground or something?"

My hands on her shoulders guided her knees to the carpet. I bent her palms to the carpet till she was all right angles. At her side, one knee up, one down, I circled her waist with my right hand, gripped her wrist with the other. I felt electric. Energy pure.

"Ready, gentlemen . . ." I mimicked the deep, official-sounding voice of Doc Kirchoffer, my seventh-grade wrestling coach. "Wrestle!"

She collapsed to the carpet, and I blanketed her from above. My hands vised her wrists wide; my penis, feeling huge now for perhaps the first time, pinned her butt. How could she not notice? We grunted and strained, and the noises themselves nearly got me off. Then, in a tactical error, she suddenly flipped herself over but not out of my body's fall. Each of my body parts smothered hers, but she continued to fight back and fight back hard. She's a jock and a feminist and probably the strongest woman I know. She arched her body to buck me off. I then sat up on her, my knees on her shoulders.

"Pinned! You're pinned! Give up before you kill me."

"Grrrrrr-awwwww!!!"

I've never heard a woman growl before, and something inside me snapped. This thought came to me then: If Liz and I do not make love tonight, my heart will implode and thus I will die.

"Grrrrrr-owwwwwwww!" And she bit my thigh.

"Owww!"

"If you don't get off me, I'm going to bite someplace else."

I sat back off her shoulders and lay down alongside her.

"Let's get out of here. Haven't you guys ever washed this rug?"

Her Subaru hunched in a corner of the parking lot behind the student union. She ran. I ran after her. She'd locked the doors, so I beat on the glass.

"See ya."

"I don't think you should drive. Let me in and let's wait a while."

I spoke loudly and opened my mouth wide so she could read my lips.

"I'm not one of your little undergraduate 'friends' who fall for lines like that." The engine whined awake and started the car forward. I hopped on the hood, and it buckled in under me with a loud, crumpling noise.

"You asshole!" She was already out of the car. "You dented Mildred."

I sat off the car, and its hood exhaled and my dent was gone.

"See? I just really don't want you driving yet."

"Okay, Austin, get in. I've got another competition."

She turned from her bucket seat to mine, her chin in the cradle of her palm. She just stared at me angrily. I was afraid, and I blinked.

"Ha. I won."

"Wait, wait. I didn't know the game until I lost. Let's do it again."

Again we stared at each other, and I knew I would lose. I know what happens when I stare at a woman long enough. But I controlled the vertigo and brought my nose to hers and felt the connection. Still her eyes refused to blink. I extended my lips to hers, and she let me. We weren't exactly kissing, but I wouldn't do any of this stuff with a guy friend. Then I blinked and blinked, blinked again, and kissed her smile.

Then she attacked me. She sucked my lips and my tongue, then my fingers! I tried to touch those breasts I had so dreamed off, tried to stroke her crotch. Each time she grabbed my hands and held them away. She pulled off my (now lucky) *Godspell* T-shirt, sucked my nipples, licked down my stomach. She twisted around the emergency brake, still licking. *Not even I, who have been the unluckiest of the unlucky, deserve this much luck.*

But she nuzzled under my belt like a foraging animal, slid free my web belt, popped open my jeans. *When she stops, as Jenny had stopped that sweet night in my parents' TV room, do not be disappointed. Already this much is too much joy.*

When I arched off the seat she worked my pants off my butt,

put me in her mouth. The unfair world I had lived in all my life I was allowed to leave for a moment. I stayed hard forever. I watched it disappear and appear, saw her cheeks hollow and fill. Then she pulled off and hushed this to me, through long red hair that draped one blue eye:

"Come in my mouth, aye."

But I didn't come. I'd never before noticed the "Ay" of her Canadian accent. I don't know. I guess it was too weird, this dream coming true. It was too wonderful to enjoy, as if that makes any sense. A sharp clank from the dark near the bowling alley sprang her lips from my dick. It was nothing, but it was over.

She kissed me and we smiled.

"Why are you smiling, big guy?"

"You're smiling, too."

"Just answer the question."

"I'm pretty unbelievably joy-filled right now." Then I giggled like a fool and I laughed. She held me and we were laughing together when she started the car again and drove.

I bought a long tube of Baci Perugina candies for Jewelle for St. Valentine's Day. I opened one yesterday to see what romantic messages they held. *"La differenza fra l'amicizia e l'amore è un bacio."* ("The difference between friendship and love is a kiss.")

February 14, 1983

Liz and Jewelle

I gave them both valentines. Liz and I are even better friends than before. It's as if we share a secret, a special memory. Like buddies from the war.

Jewelle gave me a nice Valentine's Day card. No present, though.

Okay. I'll admit it. I think about making love with Liz constantly. I haven't jerked off in days. I'm saving myself. I want to be rock hard and in top form when (if) we do it. When I gave her her Valentine's Day card we kissed a bit until she stopped.

February 28, 1983

Jewelle

She just called me for no reason. We talked and laughed for an hour and twelve minutes. What am I going to do?

March 9, 1983

Jewelle

I just read *The Sorrows of Young Werther* for the third time, and it wasn't even assigned. I like the idea of a romantic youth so heartbroken he dies of TB. I wish I could do that, except the dying part. Maybe I could fake my death, see if then she'd cry.

I live for her crumbs. Last weekend it rained hard and she let me slip my hand around her waist under the umbrella.

Then yesterday Liz drove me to Jewelle's in the rain. Her light was on and Liz said, "Good luck, tiger." I knocked and knocked on the door, but no one seemed to be home. I ran back to Liz, but she was already driving away and couldn't see me in the night and in the rain. I circled Jewelle's trailer, expecting to see her being humped by Bart by the glow of her clock radio, but no such bad luck. I walked home slowly, resigned to the rain, wanting to hold a movie camera at arm's length and film myself, as I was being soaked. Pneumonia is pretty romantic, too.

Liz

She cooked a delicious carbonara and we drank lots of Chianti. Her boyfriend hates me and so didn't show up. She was too tired and buzzed to drive me home, so we slept it off in her bed. Soon we were making out and dry humping.

She stopped in the back of the Italian House, and I might have said something about Jewelle and my hopes for spring break.

"Get out of my car."

I couldn't even talk to her. Now, 1:15 A.M., I decided to write her a letter:

> *Dear Liz,*
> *You may be mad at me, but I'm also mad at you in return. You are too important in my life to have the nerve to say, "Get out of my car." You are my best friend and especially now when I feel more alone than ever, I cannot take your abandoning me. I swear if we're not friends when I get back from break I'll go crazy. . . .*

Wait, the phone just rang, there it goes again. It must be her.

I, Mr. Asshole, just read her the letter. First there was complete silence, deadness from her world, then uncontrollable sobbing. I feel like shit, and without a car I can't whip on over to hold her.

"I'm going to call Rick. He'll hold me and tell me all is okay."

Jewelle

We'd just come back from the play *Woza Albert* about South Africa when Bart knocked on her trailer door. They mumbled in the doorway for a bit, then she came back holding a smiling teddy bear clutching a heart. For the rest of the evening I had to stare at that fucking grin.

"Jewelle. Can I ask you something serious?" Then I made myself laugh to leaven the moment. "Ever think of me as a boyfriend?"

"No."

I understood the words before I heard them.

"You're like a brother. Like Bart."

We joked about something, until I felt I could leave. I felt and feel almost good. At least that jerk's in the same boat, and he wasted money on a teddy bear. In the words of the old Negro spiritual: "Free at last, free at last, thank God Almighty I am free at last."

PART TWO

"Love Junkie"

Jenny

Austy baby,

I can't believe you didn't keep hounding me to tell you that secret last summer. You didn't even care?

Thanks for the Christmas card, kiddo. If I had sent any out at all this year, you know you would have been first on the list. Anyway, here's the secret:

I was psycho for this French guy, ponytail, Gitanes cigarettes, the works. He really wanted to stay in the country because he was making beaucoup bucks at his business. See, he deals a little bit and in France all people do is hash and who wants to sell that smelly shit. Anyway, I married him so he could get his green card. Nobody else knows but you. We're not even going out anymore (the guy scene here at school is très ennui*). We have to meet with this creepy lady from the Immigration and Naturalization Bureau every six months, and I have to pretend I can still stand the guy. It's crazy, but in the end it was worth it. He paid me $5,000 to get hitched and $500 each time we go in for the checkup. Between that, and some extra student loans, I'm rolling in moola (especially since I've transferred to the University of*

Colorado at Boulder. You must have already figured that out by the return address).

Which brings me to you, sweetie. I keep thinking about you. Boulder is great, I needed to get out of that East Coast scene. But this entire frat here hates my guts and keeps writing in bathrooms that I'm a dyke. I think I'm going to take next semester off and I was wondering if I could visit you around May 5th.

I started dialing Boulder information before her letter had fallen back to my desk.

"Hi, handsome! I was just about to call you since I was such an airhead and spaced on leaving you my home number."

She's coming here!! May 5th will be the best day of the year. She'll be staying in my room, and I have only one bed!!!

I've heard of people marrying greasy foreigners for money before. No big deal.

April 19, 1982

The Queen of England

She just came to visit Stanford, and the entire school was in a tizzy begging President Kennedy to be invited to her reception. The staff of the *Daily* was invited, but the staff of the *Chaparral?* Not a chance. To protest the event and to sell issues, we bought an inflatable love doll, a tiara and a dress, and propped the float in the middle of White Plaza. What kind of disgusting old man sicko child molester would actually inflate one of these things and fuck them? We made all kinds of jokes about her in the office. Her mouth was a hugely round "O" filled with some sort of plastic membrane. Identical membranes had been installed in her vagina and anus, but of course the dress concealed them. "Meet the Queen," said the sign around her neck. We got in a little trouble.

The dean of admissions spotted us in the middle of a tour of prospective patsies.

Then came tonight, Saturday night, and Liz wasn't around, Jewelle was on a date with her "brother" Bart. At night we left the queen inflated in the coffin in the office. I've always prided myself on being open-minded. That's all I'm going to say. If this ever falls into the wrong hands, I don't want to be forced to take my own life or flee the country.

May 5–8, 1983

Jenny

Jay and Valeria lent me their used yellow VW squareback to pick her up from the airport. I sort of wanted a nicer car, but can you believe I can't rent one till I turn twenty-one?

I was sure she'd come out of the gate talking to some goofy old rich guy she met on the plane.

"Austin, this is Gordon, he owns the San Francisco Forty-niners. He invited me to stay at his Napa ranch for a few days. You said you had only a single bed anyway."

In real life she walked out of the beige, accordioned tube from her plane with her arm around this thirty-year-old white guy.

"Here's my friend I was telling you about, 'bye." And he disengaged and disappeared.

"Austin! What gives?"

"What? What do you mean?"

"You look great."

"Gee . . . I'm sorry I shocked you."

"I mean, I guess I forgot how hot you looked."

We walked past people running the other way to planes about to fly.

"The weather's great out here. The sun helps clear up my skin."

"That must be it."

I'd just left the VW twenty-six minutes, but parking still cost me $5.75.

I had planned everything. The first night we saw Toni Morrison read at the law school auditorium. As this beautiful, salt-and-pepper-haired woman spoke in this brilliant and sexy voice, I just kept squeezing Jenny's shoulder. I'm sure anyone who cared was shocked to see me with a cute girl (she's not gorgeous to me anymore, but she still has chains over me that never seem to weaken).

Then the night came. We'd brushed our teeth, I'd snuck some cologne onto my earlobes (I guess that's where you put it), I'd crossed my fingers a thousand times, knocked every plank of wood in the Italian House. I got an extra pillow from the RA and propped my sleeping bag beside the bed.

"Are you going to sleep in your bed?"

"Yes."

"Should I?"

"Yes!" I shouted, just like that, just like a dork. She settled back into the bed and smiled. I actually had two more hours of history reading, so I hoisted my daypack onto a shoulder and started out the door. (Did I tell you I'm a double major now, English and Afro-Am history? The English is for fun, the history is for grad school. I guess I'll follow in Fletcher's footsteps and become a prof. I hear young college professors are right behind rock stars and test pilots for ease of "date-ability.")

I don't know if I've ever felt so delicious. I wanted somebody to tease me, to congratulate me. I wanted somebody to question my constant, born-again grin. I stared at the same page (a transcript of the Supreme Court's *Dred Scott* decision) for twenty-three minutes, luxuriating in the swell of my healthy boner before I inched back into the room.

Pulling my clothes off myself slowly, I hoped she'd sense me in her sleep and see through my brand-new white BVDs. The present wasn't rolling forward fast enough. Just standing there, I willed the future and saw and felt myself inside her and knew that it would save me forever.

Gently I lowered my underwear, raised the sheet and sat half off the bed, and kissed her baby cheeks. I don't know exactly when she woke, but soon we were making out through the flannel of her floor-length granny.

"Austin, how about one of your famous massages."

My letter to *Penthouse* "Forum" was already half-written in my head.

She helped me raise off her nightgown, and she wasn't wearing any panties. I sat on her back and massaged her, my dick hotdogging the crack of her butt. I whispered my fingers down her side as she had taught me and watched the field of goose bumps rise and spread along the chocolate of her back.

I guided her to roll, kissed from breast to breast to belly button and below. She went nuts and soon came hard around my head.

"I want you to be the first to make love to me." I saw her face over the mound and between the mounds of her breasts. My grin was wet.

Springing my bureau's top drawer in the dark, I miraculously didn't stub anything. The condom slipped out of its foil without incident, but of course, when I leaned to roll it over my dick, I found it flabby and uncooperative. I tried to stuff it in anyway, hoping, as Marquita and Fletcher had hoped when they used to buy me shoes three sizes too big, that I'd someday soon grow into it. But it would be twenty-six minutes at least before the batteries recharged (my previous personal studies had concluded). Jenny leaned up and watched it.

"It's all right . . . well, it's not all right, but I understand."

She turned to the wall and again slept instantly. Surprisingly, I fell asleep right away myself.

An hour and a half later, at one forty-eight, I awoke to perhaps the hardest hard-on I or anyone has ever known. It almost hurt, the skin was so tight. I kissed her neck and she swatted me away. I slipped it between her thighs and gently, then urgently jiggled her shoulders.

"What *time* is it? I'm exhausted."
Again she slept.
If I were Japanese, I'd have been dead hours ago.

T h e   n e x t   d a y . . .

We drove to San Francisco and promenaded Fisherman's Wharf.
A white-faced mime saw Jenny pass, clutched his heart, and threw
it out to her. I saw him, he saw me see him and pretended to be
petrified. I liked it. We held hands sometimes, sometimes she
decided not to. We slept naked together, but she wouldn't even
let me go down on her.

Another first: *I've actually spent the night with a girl. But if it's
always like this, my wife and I will have separate bedrooms.*

Last night I was ready and had decided to get it in while it's
good and can the foreplay. We got naked, I kissed her, then she
stopped kissing and spoke:

"I think I'm in love with this Italian guy back in Colorado. I
love you, too, but in a different way. I'm afraid of you, but you
two are the only two guys I could make love with right now. . . ."

"Why didn't you sleep with your husband?"

"Yucck! He wasn't my type. I don't know why I ever went out
with him."

The next morning, today's morning, our last, I stepped out of
the shower room thinking that at least people *think* we're sleeping
together, which is something, isn't it? Then I saw dots on my white
towel a color the Pittsburgh Paint folks could only call "Blood
Red." As I trotted to my room, red dripped from my nose to the
carpet, to my chest, more to the towel. My first bloody nose in
four years. Jenny came in from the girls' shower, saw me on the
bed naked with my head tilted back, squeezing my nostrils shut,
and didn't say much of anything. Throughout the day we were

not even holding hands. I put her on the plane and left the airport before it had even retreated from its stall.

We're so different. She said I was the first black guy she had kissed since the tenth grade. "I'm into Jewish and Italian guys," she said. She hangs out in white frats, listens to cheesy new wave technopop.

But she is gorgeous to me now. All week long she wore this miniskirt. Her breasts are small and brown and shaped as if designed. And since the night on the rug in my parents' TV room, I have never forgotten her smell.

Oh, in the car on the way to the airport she said that she doesn't think she loves the Italian guy in Colorado anymore. I don't know what the fuck that means.

And maybe I learned something about cock maintenance. I'm just supernervous with girls at first and prematurely ejaculate. No big deal. The second and third nights with her next to me I was hard when I went to bed and when I awoke I was hard still, and now sore.

May 14, 1983

Jenny

Austin Darling,

Stanford was rad. It's so much warmer and nicer than Boulder. I sort of wish I had transferred there instead. I love you, kiddo, but you scare me.

You were such a gentleman, and I'm sure we will make love one day and I bet you're really good at it. (I didn't think you'd be so well hung. Dicks usually gross me out, but yours is sort of handsome.)

Anyway. Thanks again, kiddo. You're great.

She's so fucking weird. But what if she's telling the truth about the little wiener schnitzel? When it's angry, sometimes I do think it's close enough to average, but "well h—"? Only the instant before I come. And only in my imagination. . . .

Get a grip! I hate her for knowing exactly how to lie to make me love her again.

May 27, 1983

Liz

She's got an exam right now across the bay in Berkeley, but last night she needed books from the Stanford biz school so studied there until it closed (midnight). She called me when she was ready.

"I've got to get a good night's sleep. I'm tying a knot in the bottom of my nightgown."

"You don't trust me?"

"I know you."

"What's that supposed to mean?"

"You're probably still saving that erection that your little friend Jenny didn't let you use."

"Fuck you."

"You dream about that, don't you?"

"Yes."

"Austin!"

"I can't believe you're still seeing that creep."

"I'm coming over right now, and I've got to get some sleep. Constitutional law is a bitch."

"I'll leave the door open, I have plans this evening."

"At midnight?"

"Toodaloo."

The *Chaparral* had to go to press, so I helped lay out pages until two. She was sleeping in my sleeping bag but on top of the bed. I wheedled into the sheets beside her.

She woke me up at six.

"I can't sleep. I'm too nervous."

"You need your rest, Liz. Come inside the covers where it's warm."

And she did. We hugged and I kissed her whole face, except her lips. That she would not allow. Her body, however, cooperated. Through my white cotton and her flannel geese we pantomimed with vigor.

May 29, 1983

Jewelle

So I called her and so two guys answered the phone, laughing. They put her on, but she couldn't catch her breath between giggles and squeals. I don't remember why I called, but I kept it short.

June 15, 1983

Handyman Videos

My boss from Pittsburgh Paints now runs Handyman Videos. They're working on these home repair videos they think will sell in hardware stores. Their office is in Stamford, Connecticut, only an hour's train ride from New Haven. I'm the "office coordinator." I call up the actors and make sure they arrive on time at the studio or at some fancy house under construction.

The actresses are from New York and sometimes beautiful before they make them look like typical housewives. One of the actresses said she was on a poster for Snap-On power tools. She has a boyfriend, but I swiped her head shot, keep it under the mattress with the *Playboys*.

J e w e l l e

I'd promised myself that I'd never write anything more about her since I'm not trying to be anything more than J.a.F. with her anymore. But I always feel better after I write it down. It's as if after I see it before me, my problem becomes fiction.

She came to New Haven for a three-week-long public policy program at Yale. She stayed in a beautiful, fake-Gothic dorm room with a carved and working fireplace. After movies at the law school (where Morgan, the rest of the nerds, and I, years ago, would loiter the hallways until the law student ticket takers had left, *Deep Throat* or *Behind the Green Door* had started, then we'd twist around the heavy, red-leathered door and slip into back row seats before the band of bright light we had just let in from the outside was again strangled by the door's close), after these countless, friendly dates, Jewelle and I would sit on her room's floor and I would goad her into talking politics just to watch her lips move.

When I realized I'd known her for three years but had never seen her in a bathing suit (and more important, she had never seen mine, and my body seems to be the only thing that ever fools girls into going out with me), I took her to the beach under the East Haven lighthouse. I also tried to impress her with one of my best war stories:

"Lighthouse Beach is much nicer now that I can drive. As a kid I had to sneak and run and creep all the way here from the bus stop, a mile away. Once, a half dozen moron Italian high schoolers, real Guidos, who had seemed huge to me when I was in the seventh grade but now can't be more than five seven, shouted, "Go back to the fucking Congo, ya fucking mouli!" and ran at me, hounding me through every backyard, every rusted swing set, and around every fucking aboveground swimming pool in their lousy neighborhood.

"I could hear them gaining on me and wondered why the hell was I coming out here alone instead of waiting for my friend

Morgan and some of the other guys to get out of summer band practice.

"I admit it, I started screaming. I could just see myself on a spit over a huge hibachi, being turned into a couple of feet of spicy Italian sausage. But I finally made it to the beach, and the lifeguard back then was this huge black guy with this really pretty Italian girlfriend. He jumped from his tower to the sand like a flying rock. The Stallonies just stopped dead and shuffled away, grumbling. Before, I'd only nodded very suavely to the lifeguard, as I'd imagined black guys did all the time except I didn't know since my sister and I were the only black kids in my neighborhood. . . ."

"Me too, in our ritzy compound on Grenada." She was laughing and gasping with every turn of my story. I almost stopped in the middle to memorize the sound of her laugh.

"Anyway, after I catch my breath and say thanks, I ask him, 'What's a mouli?'

"He laughed. 'Mouli is short for *moulignan.*'

"Then his girlfriend said, '*Moulignan* means eggplant. But they don't mean nothing by it.'

"I'd like to go to the car wash where they all probably work now and attach their gold neck chains to my bumper and drag them around the city."

She touched my arm to steady herself while she laughed, then said: "Gosh, I have never even been called a . . . a . . . nigger."

"I can't remember how many times I've been called that. The last time was at Andover, by a six- or seven-year-old shouting out of his school bus window. That was the worst since he was so young. When *Roots* came out I was in the fifth grade, and this bully in the ninth grade saw me raking up trash from our front yard that people parking at the pharmacy next door would throw. He said, 'Nice work, Toby.' "

"And what did you do?"

"I said, 'It's "Kunta Kinté," muthafucka.' He kicked the shit out of me, but it was worth it."

"Really?"

"Scout's honor."

....

"Damn."

I can't believe she believed me. In real life, after he had said, "Toby," and glared down at me, I just sort of grumbled something and hurried inside the house.

She came to dinner at least once a week and I was sure my folks were going to say something like "So, Austin tells me you two are head over heels in love." But Marquita and Fletcher were pretty cool and haven't been bugging me about her as much as I'd like.

August 28, 1983

Calista

This past weekend was the twentieth anniversary of the march on Washington, and Calista said I could stay in her dorm room at Georgetown. I'd like to think I would have gone anyway.

High school and college students masquerading as 1960s-era hippies, nuns, the Red Communist Youth Brigade, and various black Baptist deacons and deaconesses filled every seat on the Amtrak and every spot in the aisles. I stood between the cars with the noise.

The heat and the wet and heavy air along the Potomac weighted my lungs. Calista led me quickly from the station to Synergy, her dorm/deadhead commune (once some frat house before they were kicked off campus for peeing on a pledge). The white, be-tie-dyed communards all stood up with finishing school grace and reverentially shook my hand with both of theirs.

"How *are* you?"

Their wide eyes looked so sad. They must have all just watched *Sounder*.

They all painted "Reagan! Stop the Lies!" and "Imagine" placards and staple-gunned them to halved broomsticks. Calista and I made one quoting Elvis Costello: "What's so funny about Peace, Love, and Understanding?" I tried to feel like Paul Robeson in the Spanish Civil War, but the whiny John Lennon music kept spoiling my mood.

I bought a pair of blue, bikini-style underpants at Woolworth's in New Haven just before boarding the train. Her futon on the floor was small. When she leaned over to open her window wider to let enter the only fractionally less muggy outside air, I noticed down the V of her nightgown her gently hanging breasts. The vision of Amagansett, Long Island, and the angry waves' scorn for her bikini top instantly replayed in my mind.

"We'd better get a good night's sleep. Tomorrow might get a little rough."

You know that wasn't me talking.

The shower room is coed and communal. She'd told me about it on the phone weeks ago, and it'd given me reason to live. This morning, however, Calista had woken before me and snuck out and showered while I slept. When I finally went in, there were only woolly, bearded men and this stringy, junkie-looking pale girl with breasts sharp and thin like an animal's.

The march was inspiring and wonderful and all that. Hundreds and thousands of people—a lot of black folks, but I'd wished there'd been more. Busloads of union people, old civil rights and Hollywood celebrities, Buddhists, Spanish Civil War veterans, and Rastas lined the long reflecting pool before the Lincoln Memorial. A stunning, topless white hippie waded through the water on the shoulders of her tall and naked boyfriend.

Jesse Jackson spoke at the end, and everybody, all the hundreds of thousands, held hands and sang "We Shall Overcome." Calista held my hand high as a TV camera panned the crowds. She was crying. I only let myself feel the tiniest wave of a chill.

At the commune it was Calista's shift to wash dishes. The (surprisingly delicious) tofu spaghetti sauce was burnt and fused to the pot and the stove top. We didn't finish cleaning until it was time for bed.

"I don't know if my shoulder is sore from the march or the pots and pans." I windmilled my arm and winced every once in a while.

· ·

"Oh."

I waited while she brushed her hair in the mirror under her "IRIE!" Rasta poster.

"You must be sore, too. Would you like a massage?"

"I'm going to fall asleep as soon as I hit the pillow, but thanks, sweetie."

Later, no matter how much I kept shifting and scooting around on the futon, she wouldn't wake up. Luckily, the night air was hot and dead and declared a stage-five pollen alert by the TV news. You could almost see the millions of ragweed bits surfing the air like tiny dry snowflakes. She woke up coughing. I handed her a Kleenex before she even asked. She squeezed two hits of nasal spray up each nostril. She squinted at the clock radio and huffed: 3:10 A.M.

"Would you still like to give me a massage, or is it too late?"

She must have noticed the physical manifestation of my exuberance, but she just kept on sighing and groaning in sexy comfort as I pressed away the knots in her muscles through the cotton of her nightgown. I slid my middle fingers over the sides of her breasts, the parts that swelled and spilled out from under her body. And she let me.

Then she massaged me, and while she worked on my shoulders her breasts massaged my back.

"Oh, right there. Ohhh!" I tried to make sexy sex sounds so deep they'd reverberate my chest cavity and hence vibrate her straddling thighs.

"You have the body of a god."

I forced myself over, and she rose up as I rolled. She rolled the muscles in my arms between her thumbs and the rest of her fingers. I kissed her hands.

"Let's get some sleep."

"I'm not sleepy."

"You're so sweet. But those antihistamines are really knocking me out."

She leaned off me and slumped to the pillow at my side.

Late for my train, the next morning I woke suddenly to a weighty wetness in my underwear, smelled the bleach and mowed summer lawn of more spilled and wasted life.

The shower together was cruel. At the station, in front of the long and stainless-steel-sided American Zephyr, she patted my butt good-bye.

The body of a god? Maybe Shlemiel, the seldom-worshiped god of failure, premature ejaculation, and drizzle.

September 1, 1983

Jewelle

I just got back to Palo Alto, twelve days before the start of school, to help put out the freshman issue of the *Chaparral*. I'm finishing up early, in December, and want as much of a senior year as possible. She's back early, too.

"Do you want to go to the movies tonight, Austin?"

Wow. And later she said:

"I want to have dinner with you."

I picked her up at her off-campus apartment. I wore a tank top even though the "overnight lows" (my lifetime companions) hovered around sixty.

"Austin, you're shaking."

She lent me a Mickey Mouse sweatshirt that fit. I was wondering who it belonged to when she said, "You look cute."

It was the nicest thing she had ever ever said to me. Walking into town, I felt, for perhaps the first time, that we were on a "date."

Between dinner and the movie we killed time in Walgreen's since it's open till nine. We wandered the toy aisles and pointed play guns at each other and laughed. We held up the disgusting nylon floral shirts and plastic sneakers and pleather high-heeled shoes and plastic flower wall hangings and giggled.

The cheesy theme song from *Love Story* started in my brain, and I almost tried to stop it.

....

September 13, 1983

L i z

She invited me over to eat. We had too much Chianti and like last year decided to sleep it off before she drove me home.

"We're going to rest, *rest. Capisce*, Austin?"

Then she crawled into my arms and slept on my bicep. Then she started hugging and kissing me. She stretched off my T-shirt and my pants and then my underwear. She wouldn't let me take off any of her clothes, then kissed most all of the bits of my body again and went down on me again. I felt great, but not as great as if I were imaging it all. Maybe it was because she was wearing corduroys and a thick sweater. She looked sort of like a guy. And I felt weird being naked when she wasn't. Maybe it was because I was buzzed.

September 18, 1983

J e w e l l e

She's on the campus steering committee for the Jesse Jackson campaign. They're starting early. Fletcher says he came over for dinner once when I was a baby and we were living in Michigan. I told Jewelle I remembered it. Yesterday, all day long, we registered voters, door to door, in sunny San Jose. In December, after I graduate, and before I start working wherever it is I'll be working, I think I'll do some more volunteer work for him back east.

"Keep Hope Alive!" Words to live by.

· ·

October 6, 1983

Jewelle

We were in the Coffee House. When she got up to say hello to some guy, she smacked my cappuccino onto my hand. Immediately she forgot about the creep and held my hand, and wiped it, and kissed it. I almost splashed the rest of the scalding coffee on my face.

October 9, 1983

Jewelle

For my birthday we went to SF to see Alvin Ailey. But before that we went shopping in I. Magnin. She tried on miniskirt after miniskirt, and I was getting dizzy. I wished I had brought a camera. It was all so romantic, so married. Then she grabbed my wrist, and for a moment I thought she was going to tell me she loved me.

"I want you to smell my favorite perfume."

She pulled me down the escalator to the fragrance world and sprayed her wrist with Wind Song by Prince Matchabelli. I knew it from the ultraromantic commercials they run every Christmas. A goony male model guy is leaving on a train. He presses his hand against the cold train window, and his beautiful wife, circa 1977, standing outside, matches her hand to his through the glass.

"Do you like it?"

I burned to scoop her in my arms and swing her around and around until she laughed and cried, "Oh, Austin!"

She opened her change purse but didn't have the fifteen dollars for the eau de toilette.

"Damn." And we walked away. Then suddenly, "I'll meet you right here, I've got to go to the bathroom again."

"I'm glad I'm not a girl."

She shoved her LeSportsac at me and escaped. She was menstruating and had to run to the john often. See how much she tells me?

When she came back I handed her her bag, and we hadn't even left the fragrance stands when she weighed it, squeezed the floppy nylon from outside, and hurriedly unzipped it. She pulled out the eau de toilette and relaxed and sighed.

"Thank you! This is so great! Wow!"

And on she walked. No hug, no kiss, no affectionate squeeze of the awaiting bicep.

On the bus back to school she stayed away and silent.

October 15, 1983

Young & Rubicam

God knows what I'm really going to do with my life come December. Marquita and Fletcher keep "suggesting" grad school right away, but I think I'd like a few years away from books. I've been thinking about advertising because it's sort of like writing, which I like. I know I don't want to be in the home video biz my whole life, and sometimes ad people get famous and win awards and stuff. In "Bewitched" it looked sort of interesting. They worked in a neat office building and drank martinis.

Young & Rubicam is a fancy New York ad agency, and they were holding interviews on campus today. Their director of personnel was a babe.

Rising from the desk in the career planning and placement center, I think she heard me sigh when I saw her calves. Instantly I forgot all nervousness. Sure I said stuff about being a go-getter and a people person, and I handed her some funny (I think) pieces I'd done for the *Chaparral*, but what I concentrated on was pushing back in my rolling chair to sneak gazes at her crossed legs through the papers on the glass top of the glass desk. When she unfolded a folder and the spread manila wings blocked my view, I shifted with a cough till I could once again see the sweetly wrinkled arch of her foot peeking behind the side of her suede spiked heel. It would have been so amazing to have picked up this thirty-year-old Italian-looking lady. After drinks in the city we'd have wild older woman sex in the Airporter Lodge.

October 19, 1983

Jewelle

She says she's got too much work to keep campaigning for Jesse, so I barely see her anymore. We haven't talked since my birthday. Yesterday I decided to confront her. I went by to pick her up, but she had also invited her friend Gloria. We three went to the Coffee House, where somehow the subject turned to beating your kids. They were both for it and I'm against.

"Well, then you two will never marry."

I thought Gloria was on my side. But Jewelle changed the subject before checking her watch.

"Oops, AKA meeting. You two stay here. See ya."

I don't really know Gloria, but I asked her anyway.

"Why doesn't she like me?"

"Why don't you like me?"

My life is so fucked up. I don't know how serious Gloria was. She doesn't even know me. But she didn't say "What do you mean, 'doesn't like you'? Jewelle loves you and has been waiting for three years for you to kiss her, you big dope." Oh, boy.

And what's Jewelle doing in the AKA sorority, anyway? She's the darkest woman on campus, political, and has nappy hair!

I just got Gloria's number from the student directory:

"So, she hates my guts?"

"She doesn't hate your guts."

"Then does she love me?"

"You'll have to ask her that."

"I wanted to settle things before I go back east."

"Then don't go. If you love her, stay and fight."

"I shouldn't have to fight for someone. If I love them and they love me, then why should we play games?"

"Maybe if they play games, they don't love you."

This music major talked like this, like fucking Yoda, for eighty minutes. And she's right. How can I leave school when I'm so close? I'm staying and fighting.

October 20, 1983

Jewelle

I decided to confront her. I wore my cool, tight Mexican shirt with the stripes down each chest and got my hair cut in black East Palo Alto. This afternoon, when she opened the door to her room, looked up, and saw me, a smile ignited.

"Nice haircut, honey."

I sat on her desk and she touched me a lot, much more than usual. I don't understand. Maybe she's so nice because she's happy to know I'm leaving in six weeks. She had another AKA meeting but invited me to eat at her dorm tonight.

About six hours from now I'll know whether I swim or am sunk.

Later...

The guest dinner spots in her dorm are booked for tonight.

"There's always tomorrow," she said, and hung up.

I stared at the phone and said to myself, "Now is the time." I even pulled you out, and a pen, to take notes while the news comes hot off the press. Wish me luck.

. . .

"Hey, it's me again."

"Hey, you again."

"I . . . wanted to say . . . that I've never liked somebody as much as you in my life, and uh . . ."

"That's so nice."

"I just wanted to tell you."

"You're sweet."

"So when will I see you again?"

"I don't know . . . how about tomorrow, after gospel choir. Around eleven."

"At the *Chaparral*?"

"Sure."

I don't know what the hell just went down, but at least it will all be over twenty-four hours from now. When I let my brain roam, I foolishly, idiotically, childishly, think she's going to say, "I love you, too." When I hear those words from that mouth in this brain, I smile like it really happened. I know it's wrong, or at least the chances of that answer are just 30 or 40 percent, but I figure I might as well dream the nicest dream I could possibly dream now, have a day of sweet though unrealistic thoughts, if twenty-four hours from now I'm going to be emotionally disemboweled.

Part of me is watching from far away, watching on television. It's like "I Love Lucy." I can't stand it now. I scream at the set, "Lucy, you fool! Ricky told you not to go to the club tonight!" But I know she will and I know she'll get in trouble and cry. I always immediately have to pee. But there's nothing you can do to stop Lucy but turn to football. For me, turning the channel on Jewelle now would be forgetting her altogether. But I'm betting everything that this one time Ricky will invite Lucy on stage to sing.

October 21, 1983

Jewelle

Greg, my RA: "The drum is talking, my friend. It says *you're* pushing Jewelle Blake."

"Who told you that?"

"Two or three different Ujamaa bigmouths. Who would think a brother who shows up first day looking like a black Thurston Howell the Third would end up jocking Jewelle Blake! We're all very impressed."

"I'd love to keep talking to you, Greg, but I've got to be somewhere."

"And I think I know where."

My smile made me run faster to the office.

In the magazine's playroom, where Liz changed my life, I turned on KBLX, the Quiet Storm, and crammed the old pizza boxes and near empty beers in the trash in the other room. I opened all the windows and made myself play pinball, made myself not stare at the door. I imagined her stealing up behind me, snaking her hands around me, hugging me from behind, and, on tiptoe, kissing my neck. At eleven-three I saw the image of her open the front door behind me on the painted bikinied girls on the lighted glass face of the "Joker Poker" pinball display.

"Hey."

"Hey." I made myself not turn away from my ball, I made myself play pretty well. I made myself exclude her presence, but she came right up to me on the left side of the machine. And on the right side came Gloria. The three of us didn't talk about anything that I can remember.

....

October 25, 1983

Lesa Biltmont

The last thing I needed. She's this supercute frosh with huge boobs. We've been flirting all fall, but that's it. Then yesterday she told me she was baking cookies for a dorm fireside chat and asked me my favorites. I told her Rice Krispies marshmallow treats if they count as cookies, but I wouldn't be around at the chat because I had to work at the magazine.

"I'll save you some and bring cookies and milk to tuck you in tonight." I'm a senior and she's just a freshman, for God's sake.

Jewelle hasn't been returning my calls. I slumped back to Ujamaa around midnight and saw on my notepad next to my door this message:

Austin, I have your treat. [smile face]

I went to Lesa's room cautiously and knocked. The light was off, but her roommate woke up, said Lesa was out but handed me a large marshmallow treat on a plastic plate. I went to bed.

I thought it was a fire or a fire drill when I heard the angry knocking on my door some crazy late hour later. I threw my robe over my shoulders like Fellini and opened the door.

"How could you just eat your treats and not try and find me?"

"Hello? Uh, you weren't in."

"I was in the lounge studying."

"I'm sorry."

"If you had found me, I would have given you these, too."

She held forward a plastic plate with homemade chocolate-chip cookies.

That was last night. I just got back to the dorm and found this on the notepad in gold marker:

Came by again to say hello and maybe bring another treat. I won't be back.

....

I don't have time for this crap! The girl fell in love, then in hate with me overnight? But tomorrow's a full moon. I shouldn't have, but I called her up and offered to make her a "Stanford Woman." They say that if a senior kisses a freshman in the middle of the quad during a full moon, she becomes this "Stanford Woman." She said yes. At least this will make me track down Jewelle and find out once and for all what's what. If Jewelle is really going to be my wife, I've got just twenty-three more hours of the bachelor life.

October 26, 1983

Lesa

She says she's got a psych paper due tomorrow and can't make it to the quad.

Jewelle's in the city for the day with her sorority girlfriends. My new plan is to ignore her for a week and see if she misses me.

December 4, 1983

Jewelle

I ran into her at a Christmas party, and then we studied together. Somehow I got around to calling her "cold."

"No, I'm not, Austin. I was thinking about that Friday when you helped me make yams for Kwanzaa. I'm different with you than with others. I'm much more touchy-feely with other people. I would have hugged anyone else who helped me so much, but I felt I shouldn't have hugged you. *You're* not very warm."

....

December 11, 1983

Jewelle

We'd set the tenth aside for a "date" for a week. But when I called her up to go to the Coffee House to hang out, she said she had too much work to do. I went anyway, and there she was, with this midget white guy with bad skin. He conned his way into the gospel choir and now look at him. When she saw me she waved from across the place, then turned back to his grated skin.

Today she called and explained that he was feeling sad because his rich father was late paying some bill so the registrar yelled at him and he's so stupid he was failing some course and might be on academic probation, blah-blah-blah. (She might not have put it that way, but that's the truth I gleaned.) I asked her to go out tonight to the Sunday flick, but she said she was busy. I went and there she was, again with the runt shit with the boiled face.

I spent forty bucks on a little green mechanical leprechaun because we had passed it once in the Stanford Shopping Center and she thought it was adorable. I'm going to set it by her door, douse it with one of those fucking blue margaritas she likes to drink, and light it on fire. Then get this, after I graduate two weeks from now, she's coming back to New Haven to interview at Yale for their public policy Ph.D. program. I'd already promised she could stay right in my house for four days.

She just called. That's three days in a row, a world's record.

"Why did you say you couldn't go out, then went out with other people?"

"Austin, you're not insistent enough. You should know I'm a pushover."

I'd like to push her over a cliff.

···

December 13, 1983

Lea Clarke

Remember she was the cute white girl who worked on the yearbook but hung out in the *Chaparral?* I mistletoe French-kissed her my sophomore year.

I happened to be sitting next to her and her frat-boy friends at the big game against Berkeley last month. She asked for my number, but I didn't give it. She called me last week anyway, and she made a date for tonight.

She picked me up in her swank black Rabbit convertible and took me to the Dutch Goose for beers. She's actually *Republican*, and her nose is so upturned you could hang a coat on it. (Maybe she's not really all that bad, but I wanted out of this night.)

I don't know what happened. I sort of asked her if she wanted to go for a drive. Winding over the Santa Cruz mountains, we soon looked out from the moon-swept palisades into the black of the night and the sounds of the invisible Pacific. I sort of put my arm around her as we left the car and wandered the night fog. The angry wind twisted our clothes around our bodies. The sea you couldn't see until it splashed white. We Frenched like desperate people until the cold pushed us back to the car, where we made out some more. I gently tugged up the hem of her sweater, and her lips disengaged as smoothly as an automatic record player arm at the end of an LP.

"Well, Austin, time to go home."

December 15, 1983

Jewelle

Listen . . .

Gloria, Jewelle, their friend Larry Coleman, myself, and three silly AKAs drove to a Bennigan's in some mall near San Jose.

Even I ordered one of those disgusting blue toy drinks. Larry likes to ask personal questions:

"Okay, everybody, who were you in love with and who did you date these four years?"

"Let's not even talk about it."

"What are you afraid of, Gloria?"

"Jewelle, I'm not the one who's afraid."

"Look, it was my idea, so I'll go first."

And Larry named a bunch of girls whom I had only vaguely heard of.

"Austin?"

"Uh, nobody. I just worked on the magazine, really."

Not a creature was stirring, not even a mouse. But under the table I'm pretty sure the AKAs pinched each other.

"Well, who did you *want* to go out with?"

"Sheryl [Jewelle's friend], Gladys Washington—"

"Ughhhhh! She looks like a Barbie doll."

"Jewelle, and you . . . ?"

I swear I tried to will myself transported far from that tacky, godforsaken, tasteless, and cold Spicy Zing Wing–serving singles bar. I cheated by disappearing the bulk of my body in a slouch under the tabletop laminated with ugly Victorian newspaper ads.

"Why do you ask questions like that? I don't know . . . Cleavon Derricks my freshman year, Brooks Atkins, and of course Fritz all last year and part of this year. . . ."

I don't know what she said after that, I don't know what anyone said. I didn't even know they knew each other. He's a fat, white frat guy who was Jay's roommate when we were all in Florence. He showed me how to tie my sheet into a toga for our first party. He is living in the Italian House this year, and we went to see *Ghostbusters* together. I'm sure I've mentioned my love for her. It informs all that ever leaves my mouth. If I'm the last off the bus from SF, I have the driver in tears over my love life. They joke about it at the *Chappie*.

At the table over the eerie blue crushed ice in our "Texas-sized" goblets, it was as if I were back in Florence at my first Italian parties. I heard but didn't understand any of their spoken words. My mind explored ideas far off from the loud middle managers surrounding me as they slid their already loosened ties high on their heads to rakishly cinch their temples. I would periodically and arbitrarily smile, frown, and localize my eyes so no one would know that I wasn't there. She must have known what she was saying to me, that she was . . . fuck it. I've got to lie down on the bed, though I can't even dream of sleep.

Later...

Each time I lie down, something else to write blooms in my brain. Just out of sheer masochism I asked her, after the Bennigan's, who was the last person she kissed. Of course it was the midget shithead white gospel singer. "If he weren't so short, we'd be more than friends." This has got to be good for me. All this. All this pain, this closing of my throat, swelling of my heart, choking dry heave of backward tears.

December 18, 1983

Me

I'm back home and am doing better than I'd thought. I'm still not sleeping more than two hours at a stretch, but I'm definitely mending. Of course when she arrives tomorrow she'll promptly rip right off my three-day growth of scab.

December 19–21, 1983

Jewelle

We moved too fast.
This is the most important entry of my life.

. . .

Back in Hamden. My goddess was dead, and I just wanted to start my life again and make up for the wasted years. I know they're not real, just the out-loud fantasies of nerdy guys like myself, but in the movies, after so many years of attention and of begging, the guy *always* eventually gets the girl.

I was cold to her. When the doorbell chimed I held back my body from flying to the mirror and checking, once again, the state of my 'fro. She hugged me in the doorway, and I gave her nothing. I took her to a yellowing diner that smelled in the shopping plaza around the corner because I knew she'd hate it. I was going to confront her at dinner, but I didn't know how either of us would react, how loud we'd get. I didn't breathe involuntarily, not once, all day.

At home, she lay in my sister's bed. Leslie doesn't get back from school until tomorrow. I stood before the mirror in the bathroom at the top of the stairs, rehearsing my words. I couldn't let her leave my house without attacking. Satan had to be exposed even at the expense of my life. I knocked, then stepped into her room.

"Jewelle, didn't you realize that if you had told me about Fritz, you would have saved me a whole lot of pain?"

"What do you mean?"

She stepped back into one of the pink poles of my sister's ten-year-old pink canopy bed. "I honestly wasn't trying to lead you on."

"What about the hugs and the smiles and the flirts?"

"I thought we were just friends."

"And friends don't tell friends about their love life?" Good one, I thought. "I've kept a diary of my trouble with women since the tenth grade. I've never been so fucked over in all my life."

"You write down everything?"

"You should read about yourself."

"I'd like to."

I jogged out the door to my room.

"Everything all right, son?"

"Fine, Mother."

"You are sleeping in your room, aren't you?"

My left shoulder led my crash into the left edge of my doorway.

"This isn't a bordello, you know. If you two would like to spend the night together, you, your father, and I would have to discuss it first. I won't have any sneaking around in my house."

"Yes, *Mother*."

She must have already pinched her contacts out of her eyes because she was wearing these thick black Poindexter glasses I'd never before seen.

"Don't laugh, Austin."

"I'm not."

Then she pulled you from my hands.

"The Mustang Ranch? I never thought you were the type."

"Don't read that part, read about you. . . ."

I reached for you, but she turned and held you away.

"Sixty dollars! . . . Did I meet your little friend Jenny? And you think *I'm* a bitch. . . . Liz is your friend who lived in Naranja when we were freshmen, right? . . . Hmmm, I don't remember doing that. How weird."

Then she cried. Then she held my hand. She held my hand.

"I wanted to kiss you when you bought me that perfume, but I didn't want to lead you on. God, I'm so, so sorry."

"Jewelle, are you a virgin?"

"No."

"Did you sleep with Fritz?"

"I can't answer that."

"Are you going to sleep with the midget?"

"I don't know . . . probably."

I thought I had loved her before, but the fullness I felt with her then, holding my hand, leaning against my shoulder, I could never have conceived.

"Don't cry. You didn't lead me on. It was my fault."

"I'm not ten thousand percent sure."

"I never liked you more than tonight. We'll be great friends forever."

"I love you a lot, Austin." She smiled so hugely, her whole body smiled, and the hug she gave me, it was as if our hearts hugged.

I don't know who asked who, but we slept together, in pajamas, hugging through the night. I wanted to kiss her, of course, but didn't want to spoil such greatness. I was hard and blue-balled and in heaven.

I strode to my room at six-twelve in the morning. My footsteps smacked flat and loud, but not so loud as my smile. I would have been proud to have been caught. The eight-oh-five Conrail carried us to New York City, the capital of Christmas.

We held hands, we hugged *each other* down Fifth Avenue and past Rockefeller Center. I used to hate the skating couples.

Back home at dinner with the folks, we held hands under the table. Mom and Dad smiled.

After they'd gone to bed, we watched *The Philadelphia Story* on channel eleven till two in the morning. She slept through most of it, her head in my lap.

"Austin, I'm going to bed."

Upstairs I tucked her in and slept in my own.

The next morning, after the folks left, I snuck in to watch her sleep. She awoke to my face and smiled without thinking.

"Where were you last night? I missed you."

I didn't scream. I didn't spring through her window headfirst into the dirt two floors down in the backyard.

"Well, now it's eight-thirty. You'd better get up or I'm coming in with you." Jewelle patted the mattress at her side, sidled over. I hinged out of my shoes, lay long beside her.

She had interviews at Yale all afternoon. At night I borrowed some money from Fletcher and took her to Edge of the Green, the same swanky restaurant I once took Jenny to. Back home I helped her pack for her train to Princeton the next dawn.

"Jewelle, should I sleep with you tonight?"

"Yes."

We cuddled in bed.

"Jewelle, should we kiss?"

"It wouldn't stop there. I thought we'd make love tonight, but I don't want to hate you in the morning."

"I knew I had a lousy reputation."

"No!" She laughed. "During my period I get way horny. I'd want to sleep with anybody in this situation."

"Nicely put."

"Oh, you know what I mean."

"A couple of women have said I have, um, sort of a nice body."

"I guess, but you could use a butt transplant."

I didn't want to make love with her anyway. I was sure I'd be too nervous to hold off. The humiliation of lying over her just-warmed-up body with my wet wiener schnitzel rapidly shrinking out of her would kill me dead. I'd hear her suck her teeth and study the underside of my sister's pink canopy until I got off her so she could wash me away. I just wanted to hold her, kiss her, maybe even go down on her.

We talked forever about how no matter what happened in my sister's bed, we'd still be friends.

We kissed before I could get nervous about it. It was okay. I sucked her breasts, and her nipples seemed about to shoot off, they were so hard and black. She kissed down my chest, then actually sucked my dick. Oddly, I felt her Afro tickling my thighs more than I felt her mouth. It's not like I think only sluts do it, it's just . . . oh, I don't know. I didn't expect her to be so good at it.

"Austin, I feel awful. As bad as if we'd actually done it, only without the fun. I don't like you so much now. . . . I'm going to try and pull away from you, but don't let me." I noticed then that her once rich, syrupy Grenadian accent had almost completely given way to generic Palo Altonian.

"I won't let you. You're never going to lose me."

I massaged her topless back. I tugged off her pajama bottoms and massaged her feet, her calves, then lingered on her beautiful thighs and butt. Many inches from her crotch, I touched the wetness that had spread. My dick nosed the back of her legs, the back of her knee. I was stupid to continue! We talked more and somehow decided to make love. I smuggled the rubbers in from my room. She went to the bathroom and extracted her tampon. She slid under me, and my hardness evaporated. We both thought it strange.

I don't think I was sad or embarrassed. I knew that if I made love with her, we wouldn't ever be friends again. My past obsession would seem casual, I'd race back to school, and with no more classes to attend I'd trot behind and watch her date midget and amputee white guys.

We slept apart on the bed, nude, for an hour. At five she had to get up to catch her train to Princeton. She knows a guy there.

"Don't fuck him."

"Funny, I was just thinking whether I would or not."

She also said that when she's married, she can't imagine being faithful. I was hard as a tree.

"I guess we shouldn't make love. But I'd love to see you orgasm. I've been told I'm very good at cunnilingus."

"You mean 'going down on someone,' doctor?"

"I like it. I like the control."

"I think that's why I like going down on guys."

"I like zeroing in on the clit and making them squirm."

"I've only had it done to me once."

"Did you like it?"

"Of course! But I'm on my period. I don't want to gross you out."

"I don't mind."

"You're hired."

I laid a towel on the bed, and she weighted it with her butt. She came easily but not forcefully. It was fun for me, but not so spiritually rewarding. My dick throbbed. It begged and pleaded to enter her, but I don't know what would have happened to me after she left. It could have been anyone's clit. There was no blood at all.

She had told the truth earlier. Suddenly she got up and showered, alone, she insisted. She never again looked in my eyes. I drove her to the train station, but she wouldn't let me wait at the platform.

"Listen, you're doing just what you said, you're pulling away from me like you said, so why don't you just stop it?"

She said nothing, and I got so very scared.

"Jewelle, why don't you call me in two weeks?"

"I'll call you when I feel like it."

"What if you never feel like it?"

"I'll miss my train."

She delivered her body for me to hug, but she was already gone.

Back home, I don't remember a stoplight, or how I got through the terrible intersection of Whitney and Chapel, or parking the car. I slept in my sister's bed and hugged the smell of Jewelle in the pillows and gagged on my tears so my parents would not hear. I want to page her in Penn Station but won't.

December 22, 1983

Jewelle

Christmastime this ain't. I don't leave home much waiting for her call.

"What's the matter, son?"

"Oh, nothing."

"Everyone feels a little blue right after they graduate. All your life you've been a student, and now, suddenly, the real world comes knocking."

No one in the world can help me. Maybe my birth mother. If she's alive. If she's straight. I still would've been smart if she'd kept me. Still gone to college, maybe. Probably not Stanford. Who wouldn't rather be a junkie bastard made good than a twisted buppie-to-be?

I stay away from my parents because I don't want to start crying in front of them. Marquita is especially nosy. They tried for three years before giving up, going out, and picking me up at the store.

Two years later, my sister growing in her belly, must have been such a lovely surprise.

When I feel tears surging behind my eyes I pull on my sweats and go for a run. The icy wind would have made its own tears anyway. I think I like their warmth streaking toward my ears in the cold.

Dakota Staton, this aging jazz singer, performed at Woolsey Hall last night. I'd never heard of her, but Mom says she could have been as famous as Billie Holiday. Before the show, the folks took me out to dinner and tried again asking what I was going to do with the rest of my life.

The old grandmother minced on stage in her tight and bulging sequined, floor-length golden dress. Her high, Supremes-ish wig was cocked at a rakish angle as if the fake hair were a hat. Her band leader was older than she was and looked like a fat smile balanced on top of a thin black wire.

How did he look, and did he ask about me?

This phrase shut my eyes and kept them closed throughout the rest of the concert. I didn't care who gawked. Ms. Staton's voice and the perfection of her band understood. When shitty pop love songs rise from the radio, I twist it off. "Oooh! You hurt me, yes, you did. Now I just wanna flip my lid. . . . "If you were really hurt, you wouldn't share your pain with backup singers and a drum machine.

January 13, 1984

Jewelle

She just called and she loves me again! Or at least we're still friends. I can breathe, the foot is off my heart! Yet she continues to deny.

"You were so dead when you left. I was petrified."

"Everyone's dead at six in the morning."

I didn't even answer her lie.

"Okay . . . at Princeton, I couldn't even talk to the interviewer. I just kept thinking of you."

After Marquita and Fletcher left for work I opened up my old toy chest and threw thirty pounds of *Playboy* and five years of *Sports Illustrated* swimsuit issues in the drugstore's dumpster up the street. I've never read Hef's autobiography, but he must have had a similar breakthrough/turning point just before he founded his publishing empire. So the next time I orgasm I swear it will not be at my own hands. I'm going clean.

January 18, 1984

Julia McNaly

Rewarding myself for stuffing over two thousand envelopes for Jesse at his New Haven campaign office, I took off this weekend with Morgan. We went to Northampton to cross-country ski with a friend of his who's now a friend of mine. Larry is finishing up Hampshire College but has been *living* with his girlfriend in her dorm at Mount Holyoke all year long. I hate him. His girlfriend's place is a swank condo that she shares with three other women (I made the mistake of calling Holyoke a "girls' school." About fifteen of them simultaneously screamed, "Women's college!").

That night after skiing Morgan and I slept in sleeping bags in their living room. Julia MacNaly is one of her roommates. Her grandfather was the first black mayor since Reconstruction and an air force pilot (one of the famed Tuskegee airmen) in WWII. She's pretty cute, but not skinny and certainly no Jewelle. Morgan wanted me to go for it. He was always urging me to go after any black girl, no matter what she looked like. I said forget it. Besides, she was out on a date.

I was asleep when she came back and turned on the downstairs light. Morgan was snoring.

"Oh, I'm sorry, fellas!"

"Don't worry about it. How was your date?"

"Good. I dumped the jerk."

"You must have been truly in love."

"It was just physical."

I felt we could make out if I made any effort at all, but it was late, and also, if I failed, after the shit with Jewelle, I might have set their condo on fire.

"Good night." She hiked up the stairs very slowly.

"She wants you. I can feel it."

"I thought you were asleep."

"What are friends for?"

"I don't know. I don't love her."

"You don't know her."

"Exactly."

"Her bed's better than this floor. And at worst it's practice."

Practice?

We heard, then saw her at the top of the stairs.

"The Three Faces of Eve is on TV."

"Great! We'll be right up."

"Morgan!" I whispered. She disappeared.

We pushed out of our sleeping bags.

"I'm telling you, Morgan. I'm not going to do anything."

"Well, if you change your mind, just say 'atavistic' and I'll scram."

His mom once called him that when we were kids. Neither of us know-it-alls knew what it meant and were impressed. It's been our running joke since the sixth grade.

She sat in the center of her bed, Morgan and I sandwiched her. If she wanted us both at the same time, she was barking up the wrong tree.

I snuck looks at her, at her body. As always, one minute I'd decided to proceed, the next to retreat. But she seemed experienced. Maybe she could give me some pointers so the next time

I'd be able to deliver Jewelle two dozen rapid-fire, bone-shaking multiple orgasms before she passed out from pleasure. When she came to she'd be in love.

"I like black-and-white films, but I find them so . . . so . . . atavistic."

Morgan stage-yawned. "I'm out of here." Like a robot he rose and left.

The emptiness that was left waited obviously to be filled by a kiss, but of course my resolve again fled. I didn't love this one.

And I didn't want to cheat on the other.

"Hey, bitch. Isn't that *The Three Faces of Eve?* I adore this flick." Cindi, one of the other housemates, just got in from her date. "Oh, shit. I didn't see you had company."

"Enter, wench."

Cindi stayed for two hours. I was going to go to bed, but by the time three o'clock pulled up I steeled myself to score. Besides, Morgan would be impressed.

"Do you want me to close this?" Cindi held the doorknob in her hand. I didn't see what Julia did with her face, but Cindi dragged the doorknob behind her. Before it had even clicked shut I kissed her, then slid my hand right for her crotch. Bingo. No coy begging off, nothing. I felt wicked, like running from first base straight across to third, no angling up, wasting time on second.

I was terrified of not being hard, but it was wood, it was wood wrapped in leather. Inside her, safe and hard, I wanted to control my strokes and last awhile, but I came sooner than I'd planned. Still, I smiled. I went down on her and drove her nuts. We hugged, and I don't remember falling asleep, but my new hard-on woke me at dawn and we made love again. This time I lasted forever and she came hard and all of her skin simultaneously exploded into sweat.

I didn't get it before. I didn't see the point of risking my health and getting naked in front of a stranger. Never too quick, never too small, fantasies were always better than life.

But this time, coming, my orgasm made my dick a rumbling

rocket gathering strength to finally explode with my soul. For a moment I stopped seeing, and an electric shiver swept up my body to my face and tingled the roots of my hair.

When I landed, however, and when I looked at her and kissed her face, my only thought was this rotten whisper: If this had been Jewelle, there would be no one on this planet happier than me, and no one that had ever been.

The next day she gave no sign, no wink, of our night.

March 16, 1984

The Future

I've been reading a lot of great books, gone skiing twice, and generally just wasting my life.

Senior year is supposed to be your best, but by graduating early, I missed two-thirds of it. I think I'm going to go back to Palo Alto for the spring and just have fun before graduation. Of course Jewelle is still there and . . . and don't even think about it.

But, seriously, a new chapter in my evolution begins today (I mean it this time, I swear). The old plan of picking one person and nagging them until they fall in love with you didn't work. Of course that doesn't mean that it would *never* pan out. I could try it again, but I don't know anybody else to lash my heart to. . . .

My God, what are you saying! You are truly an idiot. You are twenty-one years old. If you camp out another four years at the doorstep of some girl's heart and even if she does eventually say yes, you'll be *twenty-five years old!* Now you need to enroll in the slash-and-burn school of romance management. First date: She says she hates kids and *boom!* You're on to the next. First date: She can't read the menu and her feet aren't even all that fine and *boom!* bring on the next dancing girl.

I only wish that we lived in a world of arranged marriages. A young Beijing professional's bride was selected for him in utero.

He probably never has nightmare flash-forwards of life at forty in his one-bedroom efficiency:

The oven timer chings that dinner is served. The prostitute, older than you, rises from between your legs. You offer her half of your Hungry-Man turkey pot pie, but she says she has promises to keep and miles to go before she sleeps. However, at your dented steel door she does turn and wish you a Happy Thanksgiving.

There's gotta be somebody else out there I missed in that great big school.

April 6, 1984

Calista

I'm on a 727 bound for Santa Fe. Seat 12D. She's doing independent study at a women's center for Hopi Indians in Gallup, New Mexico. We're going to travel Mexico together. I haven't seen her since last summer's march. I'm hoping we'll at least make out.

I needed to get out of Hamden. I was so bored with the winter so snowless, dry, cold, and cracked. The black streets were grayed by dead salt. I thought the spring would have healed me. Instead, I sit up until two or three in the next day, quietly beating off under the ugly orange caftan Marquita's mother crocheted to whatever R-rated garbage is on HBO. I almost want to get caught by Mom and Dad so I'll stop.

Gay guys just go to bars, wink or nod knowingly, or wave their bandanna semaphore, and they've found someone for the night. Their hangouts are sex factories, so their bodies, at least, never have to be lonely. I never understood their promiscuousness until I realized they're just acting like any other bunch of guys. Imagine the Zeta Chi frat house if somebody subliminally piped in old Cole Porter musicals for a week and they all turned gay. They'd be boffing each other twenty times a day. ("Yo, Brantly! Last one

• •

to chug his brewski blows the neophytes!") Before AIDS their lives *seemed* so ordered and neat.

A stewardess would be terrific. It's a shame that today almost all are either ugly, old, or male. When I was a kid I remember a stewardess was a stewardess, none over twenty-five. When they tried to put them out to pasture they must have sued and won. So the same ones I ogled in the sixth grade are the same moms now shoving a microwaved towel in my face.

I hope I don't fuck up this friendship, too.

April 7, 1 9 8 4

Calista

Last night, lying there next to her, on my back, the sheet making an obvious tent pole between my legs, I tried to will her to kiss me. I tried to psychokinetically draw her lips to mine. It didn't work. Maybe if we talked about it?

"Water beds make me horny."

"Austin, they're actually awful for making love on. You can't ever find a good rhythm. It's like this. . . .

And she, also on her back, jerked her hips into and out of the waves, activating the bed with ricocheting surges from foot to headboard and craziness in between. It didn't calm for minutes.

"Calista, do you think our making love would be a good idea?"

"Wow!"

"My thoughts exactly."

"Oh, I don't think so. We're friends, and I've tried that with other friends and life just gets too complicated."

"It doesn't have to be if two people are clear with each other in the beginning."

"Maybe you're right, but not tonight, anyway. I'm telling you, water beds suck. It just came with the apartment."

April 8, 1984

Calista

Mexico is fantastic! So close and yet so far. It feels more foreign than Italy. And before coming I'd been watching the Spanish stations on TV, and with my Italian I can pretty well let them know that I'm hungry or sleepy. Of course Calista is so fluent they think she's one of them.

We took a Greyhound to El Paso, Texas, then a cab across the border to a Mexican train that wheeled through the desert and La Barranca del Cobre—Copper Canyon. It's deeper than the Grand Canyon, carved by the Rio Grande. We spent the night in Chihuahua, home of Zapata. I think she asked for two beds, but I'm not sure. Anyway, we got two beds in a cute little *posada*.

"Would you like to make love tonight?"

"Oh, I'd feel strange because—oh, I told you. One of my clients at the women's center went back to her husband and he put her in the hospital again."

April 9, 1984

Calista

We slept on the train across the country to Mazatlán. I tried to hug her every once in a while, but she wasn't too into it. This trip might have been a horrible mistake.

April 10, 1984

Calista

Mazatlán. What a wonderful place. We're in the old, colonial part of town, away from *la zona dorada*, where all the drunken

Stanford students pound margaritas and ceviche. Our place has a kitchen, four beds in two bedrooms, a terrace overlooking l'Avenida del Sol and the Pacific, prettier here than up north. We're on the beach all day long, and I could swear she's wearing the same bathing suit she fell out of that magical day years ago in Amagansett. She fell out of it here also, today. I took it as a sign from God.

"I'm so happy to be out of Hamden. I was drowning there of loneliness."

"Why don't you go back to Florence?"

"I'm thinking about it. I've got the rest of my life to sit behind a desk, or make sure actors arrive on time for instructional videos. I don't feel like I've had enough fun yet in my life. . . . Speaking of fun, how about tonight?"

"Do you always have to talk about it? Fine. But just wait till I'm ready."

It's twelve thirty-three. She's in her own bed, very asleep. I leave the door open and flush the toilet a couple of times. I aim my reading lamp's light on her eyelids. I'm about to open the French doors in the front, hoping some late-night drunken *taxista* will honk.

April I I, 1984

Calista

Never have I felt a sun so hot. It presses you to the sand. You feel the sweat pool, then run down your sides past your armpits. After a day of heat, wonderful people, and lime-cooked raw fish, making love with a good friend would be the perfect, perfect night for these sunny days. On the beach I lie next to her, thinking of how she will look orgasming under and above me, just in case she can read my mind. I mean, if you like someone, don't you want to make them happy? If she only knew that I *will die* if we don't do it, I'm sure she'd give in.

....

Wait, I have to stop. She's coming back from the straw-hut bar with our Tecates.

"You know, after sex with my old boyfriend, we used to masturbate each other."

She just said this, out of the blue. We were just talking about ceviche and how magical it is that lime juice can cook fish. She also said:

"You're a god. Look at your body compared to these men around here."

Back in the hotel, she dug the sand out of her bikini bottom.

"Oh, if I'd done that any more, I think I'd come."

I didn't close the door before I stepped into the shower, and before stepping out, I played with myself a bit just to get it less stubby, but not yet hard. She passed the open door just as I was drying my balls. I peeped in the mirror that she didn't.

April 12, 1984

Calista

It's our last night. She's flying back to New Mexico, I'm taking the overnight train to Mexicali, on the Mexico-California border (right across the invisible line from California's Calexico).

We ate at a wonderful restaurant right on the beach, candlelit and straw-roofed.

"I've had more lovers these four months in New Mexico than ever in my life. Some of the Indian men are amazing."

"Almost all black Americans are part Cherokee."

"Really?" She smiled. "On peyote especially, they last forever, and you come before they do, which of course is the best way. . . . I can't believe I'm telling you all this."

"You know, in Washington I wanted so desperately to make love with you, but I didn't want to scare you. And also, I haven't done it much and I was afraid I wouldn't be, you know, superhard, or I'd come too quickly, or, I don't know . . ."

Walking back to our hotel barefoot on the cold night sand, I held her waist and leaned my lips down to hers. She turned and I struck cheek. I left my lips there, sadly stranded on the side of her face like a boat whose keel is stuck in the mud at low tide. I tried again, but this time got the other cheek. She started walking again.

"Oops."

"Austin, I don't want to, all right? It's weird. When I was house-sitting in New York and had just come back from Spain, I wanted you *a lot*. I dreamed about your muscles for months. But now it's just not right."

This gorgeous friend was warm for my form *five years ago!!* I could have been laid when I was *sixteen years old!!* I wanted to scratch and claw, chew my way back to the past. If we had made love back then, I'd be a suave stud even Lyle Waggoner would envy. I'd be a flesh-and-blood, smoking-jacketed, gourmet-cooking *bachelor* that Hef would call for advice.

"Austin, are you all right?"

"I'm just going to take a walk on the beach."

Mexican beaches in the moonlight, alone, fill your mind with dark wisdom.

I thought about how fucked up I have behaved. I've ruined our vacation. I was *exactly* like her sniveling black friend years ago in New York City, begging for a kiss on a street corner while snot drooped from his nose to his upper lip. The only way you can sleep next to a body you like for nearly a week and never want to play with it is if you are absolutely repulsed by the personality of the attached brain.

I wanted to sleep on the beach, curled into the cold sand by the side of the road. Instead, I snuck back inside our lovely room.

Calista called out, "You can turn on the light. . . . I got roasted today. I can't believe you didn't burn."

"If I were still in Africa, I'd be under this sun every day. For you this is unusual, a tan, but for me, New England winters are the unusual, the 'antitan,' or 'pale.' "

"Wow. Anyway, could you put suntan lotion on my back?"

She rolled over on her belly, hoisted the T-shirt of mine that she was wearing high up her neck. Her breasts puddled beneath her. I was already in just my white BVDs when I climbed on her back. I rubbed it in daintily, struggled to avoid the sides of her breasts.

"All done." I climbed off her, pushed off the overhead light, and found my own twin bed in the dark.

"I'm mad at you."

At first I couldn't locate her voice in the black.

"I'm mad at you for making me feel guilty. If we do make love, it won't be out of pity. I've got to think, by myself."

Of course I don't want it out of pity—unless that's the only way.

She left our room overlooking the water, for our wasted bedroom in back (all for just $5 a day). I was waiting for her answer when I fell asleep. When I awoke it was one-thirty. I snuck into her room and peeped. She was asleep. I guess that was her choice.

In the morning I woke up and sat on her springy bed.

"Calista, if you want to hit the beach before your flight, you'd better get up."

"I'd rather stay in bed." She yawned and smiled sweetly, stretched her arms, her body, long as if diving into a pond. Under the sheets, she was naked. "I'm really fried." She held the sheet to her breasts, presented me the bottle of Sea & Ski, and turned on her breasts. I drew down the sheet just to the low valley of her back. Then I massaged her, okay, a little sexily this time.

"I'm sorry for mucking up this vacation. I could make it up to you by going down on you." That way, she wouldn't have come out of "pity."

"No, thank you. But I was just going to ask you to make love."

"Really?"

She nodded, rose from the bed, nude, snatched up her purse on her way to the bathroom. She had brought her diaphragm. That made me happy (unless she thought she might have met some tourist or local).

My dick wasn't doing so well. It wasn't soft, but it wasn't su-perhard. I helped it as much as I could manually.

She came out, pushed me to the bed, and smeared herself over me as we kissed. She cried when I sucked on her breasts. I rolled her over, entered her, and she moaned for a minute before I came.

Same as it ever was.

I always thought the guy was supposed to ask, "Did you come?" It was all pretty horrible, but I deserved nothing less. I was mad at her for not letting me go down on her first, to guarantee her at least one good orgasm.

She was already up and off me, had already grabbed her towel for her shower.

"I wish we had more time. The second time I'm not so, you know, whatever."

"I'll miss my plane."

"Isn't there another one in the evening?"

"Can I borrow your shampoo? Mine's already packed."

Big black muscle man of her dreams prematurely ejaculates. I know the second time around she'd go crazy or at least come before I did.

If I hadn't read *One Flew Over the Cuckoo's Nest,* I'd have committed myself years ago.

April 22, 1984

Jewelle

I'm working off campus at a print shop. I'm what they call a stripper. I take special photographs of the stuff to be printed and develop them and mount them so the offset printers can run off thousands of copies. It's pretty much like what I did when I was pulling all-nighters on the *Chaparral* for free. Mike, Steve, and the rest of the printers are pretty cool, working guys. In our bathroom in back they've pasted dozens of cutouts of centerfolds, Snap-On power tool girls, and bikini-clad motorcyclists. It's sort of pathetically comforting to know you don't stop being a pervert after you leave your twenties and get old.

I'm a boarder at the Alpha Chi frat house. It was the only room in town I could afford. They're all white and always drunk. When I think that these guys can someday be the president of the United States or of United States Steel and I can't, I want to torch the place.

I've been back on campus two weeks, and Jewelle only last night made time to see me. She said she's been busy because the midget's mother was in town.

May 27, 1984

Liz

We see each other all the time, but she's still going out with the businessman creep. I think the Canuck might marry him just for the green card. She invited me over to Berkeley for risotto and Chianti. Then we went to her room and started making out, then we made love like wild weasels!! I purposely didn't drink too much, just enough to put me at ease. Besides, I've fooled around more with Liz than with anyone else in the world. I don't even remember how many times we did it that night. I looked down on her, maybe the third time, and saw a body sexier than most Playmates. She pulled me in on invisible strings, summoned me like a witch. She reached between my legs and caressed my balls and dick as if they were holy. I entered her magically, in one stroke as I descended. Our rhythm worked us to the top of the bed, but I used my strength to raise her up, one-handed, and guide her rotation like a magnet guides a compass needle, and we worked our way down. Finally, we slid off the bed to the rug, yet I stayed inside her. We came together, just like a *Penthouse* lie. A surprising explosion.

I wonder if I could get her to write Calista.

J u n e 1 5 , 1 9 8 4

G r a d u a t i o n

Why'd I come back? I knew that none of the women here would be my everlasting love. But as soon as the diploma hits your hand, your life meter starts running. I have to move somewhere, maybe the city. There are so many people there that the odds, even mine, should skyrocket. I've only known about twelve women in my life, and out of those twelve, I fell for Jewelle. If I have a date a week in someplace new, that's fifty-two women, or more than four times the chances of meeting another Jewelle. Before, all I could think of was losing my virginity, then for a bit it was getting at least not laughably, pathetically awful at sex. After the last bout with Liz, I know that under the proper conditions I can garner a passing grade.

So now I have to move on to the most important quest of anyone's life—the "wife hunt" (as my thirtyish friends Mike and Steve from the print shop call it). From this day forward I'm looking for a companion for my golden years. After the grandchildren are too old to baby-sit. I want a spunky old bird to say, "Time to go to bed now, Father. You know how you get when you stay up past eleven."

"Yes, Mother." And she'll help me out of the La-Z-Boy and we'll help each other up the stairs.

A u g u s t 5 , 1 9 8 4

C i n d i B r o w n

Only temporarily am I living at home. Unfortunately, the instructional video business is booming. *How to Saw* sold over fifty thousand copies. Once my raise goes through I'm moving to New York and reverse commuting to work. They offered me more money than Young & Rubicam. Maybe I'll stay a year. The folks want me to take the GREs and the LSATs now before I forget whatever it is I was supposed to have learned. The tests are good for a few years. Who knows.

When the regular woman can't make it, Cindi Brown works makeup. She's a friend of Michelle's (the only other black person on the show and practically the only one who knows a quickset trowel from drywall—including me). Cindy's twenty and a sweet brown. She'd be a top model if she were a few inches taller. As it is she's signed with Elite Petite. Right now she's got a print ad for Shakey's Pizza running in the Southwest. It was nice how we met:

"They didn't tell me they were using black actors. . . . I guess you'll have to use my makeup, we're about the same shade."

"Oh, I'm not talent. I'm the assistant field producer. I talked to you on the phone. Austin McMillan."

"Oh, how embarrassing."

"No. I'm flattered."

"You should act. You've got a good look."

"Thank you. You do, too."

"Do they ever need black actors?"

"Sometimes. Maybe you're too pretty to be one of the first-time homeowner housewives, but you'd be perfect as the beautiful daughter of a family remodeling. I'll put you on the list."

She squeezed my arm in thanks. My whole body hummed. I've heard the real producer, who's married, feed similar lines to actresses when his brother-in-law/partner was out of earshot. Maybe I felt a little bit like a rat, but at least like a normal and time-honored American rat instead of a crazed, perverted Willard who should never have been let out of the laboratory.

"Here's my head shot. That's my service's number on the back. Here, let me write my home number. Do you have a pen?"

Cindi Brown

She lives with her mother in Queens. This afternoon, I met her at a boho cafe in the East Village. I'd never been there before, but I'd read about it and I'm thinking about moving to that neighborhood. I can afford it, and I'd feel a bit more like a rebel, a little less like I'm wasting my years of book learning.

Sure, everybody wore black, but the cafe's mudcake was delicious. Cindi didn't sit, really squatted over the half-painted folding steel chair. Her nails, as red, curved, and hard as the hood of a sports car, seemed alerted to attack and pith the brain of any rat foolish enough to scamper over her shiny high heels. But her lips were as red and as wet as her nails.

"Do you come here often?"

"Sure. It's kind of a hangout for young people in the entertainment industry. You know how artsy people crave that air of dirt and danger."

"Uh. I think I know what you mean. I myself am very risqué. I just love to take risks."

And here comes the truly weird part, the part that shows me that I will always, always, be at least a little odd. No, I didn't laugh. I didn't leave. Instead, my dick inflated under the table like the emergency life raft/slide on a jet, sapped my eyes and lungs of blood, pinned me to my chair.

I am sure this is a phase I will soon mature out of. After about thirty years of wild Playmate/model sex and all my friends finally respecting me a little, I'll settle down with someone who can read and write.

"I've got a go-see in a half hour. It's a national ad for Soft Sheen, the hair relaxer. I hope to God I get it—it would be so great. But I'm free later on."

"Is a go-see the same as an audition?"

"It's for models, for print ads, catalog, runway, stuff like that. It's so stupid. You walk right in, hand them your book, and leave.

I don't see why you can't just send it to them except I guess they want to see what you look like in person."

"I could go with you if you want me to. Since it's not going to take long."

"You're sweet."

The building was so ugly, the elevator and the lobby, too. I never would have expected what I saw. The particleboard cubicles in the black ad agency's offices were blotched yellow from (perhaps) spilled coffee or had holes and chunks missing from late-night deadline punches and pencil pokes. Two cubicles had been emptied of desks and blotters and filled with mismatched chairs. In each of the chairs dangled the crossed legs of black women so beautiful that I held my mouth. I sat Cindi down, and all the women smiled up at me at the exact same instant. Instantly I'd forgotten Cindi. The woman in the red mini would soon be my wife. Then I noticed that five of them were wearing red minis, the other twelve black. It must be somebody's job to look at them all day long, to be paid for saying which one is the best. There's no way I'm going to spend the rest of my life making sure vans arrive on time to carry middle-aged actors most known for their work with antacids to construction sites.

Yes, I looked around the room and said, There they are. They are all that I've ever wanted in this world. Their beauty still beats my heart, still fills my lungs. My future must lie in this city.

Was it Jane Austen who wrote that you can fall in love with a rich man as easily as a poor man? Well, I think you can fall in love with impossibly beautiful and sexy international *models* as easily as you can with short, waistless women with lonely faces and difficult skin.

September 28, 1984

Jewelle

She's going to Princeton instead of Yale, but she stopped by on her way to grad school. We took the train to New York and had a great time together. I did keep thinking of our last trip to the city, the happiest days of my life, but I wasn't at all sad. There was a familiar, gentle, bluesy bittersweetness in the air. We sat on the edge of a fountain in Central Park as the dying sun reddened like the first of the dying leaves. It made me throw seventy-five cents in the water, and within myself I let Dinah Washington sing:

> *Peace on earth, to all mankind,*
> *Understanding and peace of mind,*
> *But if it's not asking too much,*
> *Please send me someone to love.*

PART THREE

"Two-by-Four Stud"

Jenny

I feel like my record's been stuck in the same groove since puberty. I was happy before stubble started to sprout on the underside of my balls, before my armpits and feet began to stink. I was a star athlete in elementary school, played Gale Sayers (who else?) in our videotaped version of *Brian's Song*. I was popular. Then one day my newly sized nine and a half feet tripped up the stairs. So it's been downhill ever since the sixth grade.

Maybe that is why I had stopped writing for a few months. I wasn't learning anything except how little I learn. Today I begin again only because I can't afford much needed therapy on my salary, and here in this dirt-colored studio apartment on First Avenue of the East Village of New York City I have few close friends.

I moved here two months ago. I could hear my mom whooping and cartwheeling inside our house as I closed the front door. I lived with my uncle in Manhattan for a week before the stink of the insecticide bombs in my new place had subsided enough to move in. It's very dirty and drug-ridden, but often, coming back from Connecticut on the train after work, it matches my mood.

I immediately called everyone I knew to proclaim my change. Jenny's mom gave me her new number in Baltimore, where she lives with a Greek banker named Taki. Less than fifty seconds into our catching up, she told me about her upstairs neighbor.

"Lance is nice. He's half black, half Persian and has a hot bod. Most mornings, after Taki goes to work, we practice oral sex on each other."

"I think we could have some great casual sex, though I can't really see us going out."

"I don't know, Austin. I could see us dating. And my whole family's convinced we're going to get hitched. I told them you wouldn't even consider it. I've been such a bitch to you all these years, I can't believe you still even talk to me."

"Till death do us part."

"Can I come up this weekend?"

I cleaned the apartment, begged Jerrold, a commercial director and a cool playboy friend of mine, for the address of the newest club. She was supposed to have arrived at Penn Station at two in the afternoon. By five-thirty I had called five times. Her neighbor Lance kept answering the phone. "I don't know what to tell you, man, but I, I gotta go." Three days later . . .

"Do you hate me?"

"Yes." And I hung up. I did, I swear it. That was probably the first time I smiled in those three days.

She called back.

"I was there listening in when you called all those times. I'm just afraid of you. You're too smart for me. But all you want is sex."

"And all you want from me is a victim. You're a fucking sadist."

I had never heard her cry before.

I shouldn't blame her. How much can you blame someone for kicking you after you've taped a "Kick Me" sign to your own ass?

Sabrina / LaShawn / Angelique / Gwen / Shirley

I now hire talent for the shoots. I've got stacks of actresses' head shots and modeling agency catalogs and waste hours every day memorizing their names and stats. Of course the really famous ones won't do an instructional video, but I don't let a week pass without my heart stopping at the sight of some angel summoned to my office.

My friend Michelle from work says I'm hopeless. She's right. (I thought she was a lesbian because of her flannel shirts, but she says she's seeing some guy. I'm happy for her. She's a sweetheart.)

Anyway, after each black beauty dumps me and takes up with some New York Met, or former Shalimar bassist, I vow to find a nice, intelligent, non-"PPG"—professional pretty girl. It never happens. But Gwen was the longest.

She can't shake her Haitian accent so didn't get the part, but I asked her out and we dated sixteen times, my *personal best*.

"Bite my breasts . . . no, bite them! Harder!"

I thought I was biting as hard as I chew meat.

"Harder!!"

I knew I was going to draw blood. (Do nipples have blood inside of them? They seem too solid.)

And later she whined romantically, "You mean you came already?"

Like the rest of my infatuations, she calls whole basketball teams by their first names. I asked her out one night and she said she was too tired, she'd been out till four at ——'s New Jersey estate. He gives her a floor ticket to all their home games. She says his wife doesn't mind.

So I went alone to Jerrold's screening of his commercial reel last week. I'm trying to get him to direct some of our shoots.

At the screening I thought I saw Sade. I whispered to Jerrold: "That there, will be my wife."

After the screening we all went to dinner. Jerrold's current model is at the same agency as Shirley. I stood and posed and double-checked that my shirt's top button was still buttoned (as seen in the April *GQ*, pp. 178–184) until he introduced us. At the end of the night, *she* gave *me* her number.

"Now you're going to call me, you promise?"

I thought it was a trick question.

December 14, 1984

Shirley

Yesterday I called Shirley, and that night I took her to see Miss Betty Carter at a buppie dinner club. Shirley did not look like Sade that evening, just another pretty face. Then, unfortunately, back in her apartment, she handed me her head shot.

If I had seen this picture in a magazine, I'd have dedicated my life to tracking her down. I fell in love with her airbrushed likeness.

I didn't want to keep it. I didn't want it in my room.

Masking-taped to her mirror was this handwritten sign:

YOU ARE SPECIAL!!!!
DO WHAT YOU SHOULD!!
EAT WHAT YOU SHOULD!!
DON'T STOP UNTIL YOU'VE REACHED THE TOP!!!!!
YOU DESERVE EVERY GOOD THING THAT COMES
*   YOUR WAY!!!*

"Nice exclamation points."

"You're so funny."

"Thanks."

"My acting teacher makes us say that every day when we wake up. This business can be so hard on a person's ego. Well, I don't need to tell you. You're a producer!"

. . .

In my brain somewhere I pulled out a tape. I'm not sure, but it probably commiserated with her on the shamefully few number of jobs for talented black actresses, said of course she was more than a mere model, she was a dramatic artist, she had a "craft." It probably told her that her acting teacher was right. She *is* special.

What I was thinking was this: Oh, God, please let me sleep with her. If I did, then every time I saw her holding up a can of Roachpruf, or waving from a Mercury Cougar, or beaming beautifully under a Wendy's visor, I'd think I'm not such an asshole after all.

"They can't take that away from me. . . ."

"I know what you mean, Austin." (I think my brain had automatically mentioned something about the importance of first impressions.) "Sometimes I meet a guy and immediately picture myself with my legs wrapped around his back."

December 27, 1984

Shirley

"Hi! Let me call you right back. My mother's on the other line."

That was three hours and forty-three minutes ago. It's still busy. The third call this week that she owes me. Could she have possibly taken the phone off the hook just on my account? It's flattering, in a way.

The dignified, sane part of me understands when he's being blown off. Unfortunately, that faction in the parliament of my brain has yet to come to power. I'm going to write her a letter:

Dear Shirley,
*   Don't think of me as some sort of pestering psychopath or even a typical "black macho male" tending his ego wound.*

I'm writing you because, stood up or not, I care about you and would like to maintain some sort of relationship. . . . I don't understand what happened last Sunday or why you were so very afraid to talk today. I sensed some "cooling" at the end of our day together (the sixteenth), but was not quite sure.

Of course there are two motives behind this letter. The first has to do with respect. Respect me enough to explain to me by phone: home (212) 460-7878/work (203) 430-2500 Ext. 4325, or by mail: 155 East 9th Street, New York, NY 10019, or even in person what went wrong.

The second reason is the more slippery one. I want us both to change our minds. I want us both to give each other another chance. I know this isn't done in New York. "New York relationships" are cool and surgical. No one admits emotion. For me that is death. It's not every day that I meet a lovely stranger who pleasantly surprises me with her wit and her charm and her laugh and her smile. I'll stick my head on the chopping block one more time to chance rekindling something within you.

> With my fingers crossed (and blushing),
> Austin

My bathroom scale tells me that I've just purged the house of thirty-six pounds of pornography. The *Playboy* and *Sports Illustrated* swimsuit issues broke open the first trash bag, so I then used three. The triple-bagging also made them less visible through the plastic. I (reluctantly) taped over my two-years-in-the-making, two-hour-and-twenty-four-minute compilation videotape of all the sexy scenes from all the sexy cable movies with some self-motivational infomercial. I'm going clean.

December 28, 1984

Francesca

My sweet, unkissed love from Florence and my best friend there, Ricardo (who also schtupped Calista, undoubtedly much better than I did), are now engaged. I told them they should name the baby Austin. I think they sort of liked the idea.

January 3, 1985

Shirley

Came home from work to a message on my machine. *Yahoo!* I'll call her now.

"Write more like that! Wow!"
"I just . . . I don't know. I guess I'm romantic."
"Are you free for dinner?"
"Sure."
"Would you mind picking some things up and I'll cook."

She cooked wonderfully, and the night was all smiles, though she did say, as all the PPGs had said to me, "I wouldn't wish it on anyone to begin a relationship with me." And, "I lived my whole life for other people. Now I need to live for me. I've got to be a special person for *me* for once." Still, a nice full kiss good night.

January 18, 1985

Shirley

We've gone out a couple of times, but no sex and nothing more than tongueless kissing. Morgan and I are going to Mexico for six weeks. (We just finished the first series of videos, so there's not much work until spring. But in May the boss says there might be some big changes.) Our good-bye dinner was so romantic. She used to work in this restaurant, and the owners gave us a free bottle of champagne. We made out in her hallway, but she has an early audition tomorrow morning so couldn't let me upstairs. She asked me to bring her back a big bottle of Kahlúa. She's going on vacation herself. She made $12,000 last year, but she's skiing for two weeks in Cortina d'Ampezzo with a *friend*.

February 20, 1985

Isla Mujeres

Morgan and I have been hitchhiking Mexico for three weeks, and Cancún is the only disgusting place we've found. The main disco doesn't allow Mexicans and almost everybody is white trash from Southern Methodist University.

The first ferry in the morning chugged and gurgled as it creeped us from Cancún to Isla Mujeres, an island just off the coast and the size of a zoo. The tourists here are mainly non-American and call themselves "travelers." Except Berneice and Catherine, nineteen and twenty, from Saginaw, Michigan. Berneice sat Indian style on her Budweiser towel in the sand. Another beach towel covered her lap, napkinlike. Since she was topless, I asked her the time. Reaching into her blond hair, she pinched her headphone pads off her ears like clip-on earrings.

"What?"

"Oh, you're American. Do you have the time?"

Topless women have too much control. I talked with her forehead, because the symmetry of her eyes reminded me too much of what I really wanted to see.

Morgan had met Berneice's sister, Catherine, at the bar shack at the edge of the beach, and together they pressed through the sand, balancing four margaritas. Berneice stood up, and the towel in her lap slid to her knees, then tumbled and fluttered to the Bud towel. There's a jellyfish that looks like her thighs, but I can't remember its name. Catherine, on the other hand, and despite her beautiful name, was unattractive from stem to stern.

"Oh, hi, Ca-ca. You finally made it back. What number does this make?"

"Fifty-three, I think."

"It's your day to keep track, remember? Our goal is ten margies a day. This is our fifth day. . . . Miguel! Get your ass over here."

Their friend Mike is an old gay guy and cook for movie stars when they fish in Montana. He asked Morgan and me at least five times throughout the day, "Neither of you is gay, right? No, I didn't suppose so." And, "You are very attractive young men."

Berneice, the pretty one except for her thighs, seemed to like Morgan more than me. She was a talker:

"These two creeps, you might meet them on the island, they tried to drug us and like rape us on their boat. Oh, my God, it was so scary."

Catherine looked away.

After the sun had cooled they showed us the youth hostel. Miguel went to the post office to check on his mail. One of the hard-core European hippie travelers had heard of a party on some wild American's boat. Catherine said she was beat. Berneice pulled her behind a thatched cabana. We could hear their angry mumbling, but still Berneice came back alone.

"She must be on her period, I swear."

I didn't care. She was ugly and mean, and I want to stay faithful to a future with Shirley. And if Morgan got lucky with Catherine, good for him. A group of now twenty, including Morgan, Berneice, and me in the rear, marched outside of town along the coast. Miguel is offering us all mescal to celebrate the happy results of his AIDS test. He's actually a pretty cool old guy. I'm happy for him.

It took me a while to realize that the host of the party, the owner of the boat, Matt, was the same guy who had tried to drug the girls. His crew, Len, leaned to kiss Berneice hello, but she frowned and turned completely away. Miguel drew three new bottles from his daypack and delivered them to the deck of the boat with noise. Matt rolled seven joints and blasted Jimmy Buffett from a speaker swinging from the mast. Sometime later Morgan and I noticed that we'd missed the last ferry, and the youth hostel was full. Matt invited us to spend the night on the deck. We knew siding with Matt would squash Morgan's chances with Berneice, but she didn't even invite us to sneak into her hostel and sleep on her floor.

Once all the others had filed off the narrow gangplank and Miguel's singing in the dark could no longer be heard, Len, the crew, told us the story.

"Dude, I couldn't fucking believe it when you brought that bitch with you. Last I heard she was bringing the *federales* down to bust our asses."

"But her sister, she was quiet but cooler about it." Matt extracted a Ziploc bag of pills from his duffel bag, offered, but I, at least, declined. "Mexico's a great fucking country, man. I been sailing from Carmel to Key West and back, but Mexico's got the easiest *farmacias*. 'La Giallita,' that's Mexican for Quaalude, and they sell you fistfuls, man, for a dollar."

"That's why the bitch sisters are pissed with us. They been here a fucking week, man, and flirting with all the guys, I saw how you dudes was checking her out. So we invite them over and offer them some 'ludes and they take them, no problem, then we offer them margaritas (which they're like fucking addicted to), but we mashed like a shitload more 'ludes and other downers in the drinks, too. They drink, and in like ten minutes Berneice's going like, 'Oh, it's so hot in here,' and takes off her top. You saw how cherry her tits were, right? So now they're both taking off their clothes. So Matt and Catherine do it down in the hole, and I go after Berneice, but she like freaks out and goes schizo on me."

"Then in the morning Len tells them we put more 'ludes in their margaritas and they go off, 'You raped me, you mutherfucker, I'm going to call the police, I'm going to kill you,' blahblahblah. And that was Monday, I think, and here it is, Thursday?—is it fucking Thursday, man?—and one of them's back drinking with us on the deck!"

"And what about that lady chick you picked up in Cancún?"

"Oh, yeah, that was fucking wild. I just saw her at the bar of the Miramar Hotel, nice place, and we get to talking about the tequila buzz versus mescal, so I tell her about the *farmacias* down here and about my stash on the boat. I motor her over in the little Zodiac raft, and we gobble like half my stash and she's rubbing herself like a cat. The bitch of it was, I was too fucked up to do anything!"

"So I come home, drunk, but not *that* drunk, and there she is, naked and rubbing herself on the deck, and Matt's like glass-eyed in the corner—"

"So I said, Shit, if I'm not getting some, *somebody* ought to. And I let Len have her and just watched the show from the cockpit."

Eventually they went down below to sleep. Then the silence came. And the stars. Black was the night and white the stars. Town, this late, glowed just a few quiet and shapeless yellow specks. The water, a mulatto born of the Caribbean and the Gulf of Mexico, smacked the side of each of the catamaran's pontoons. I almost wished I could think as these men think. Hearts like theirs can never be broken.

February 28, 1985

Puerto Angel

Two nights ago Morgan left at Salinas Cruz, just south of here on the southern Pacific coast. He took a first-class bus because our butts were damaged from the Guatemalan wood-bench school buses that Greyhounded you through that country, the prettiest I have ever seen. The same day I took a regular bus here to Puerto Angel, where I thought I had slung my hammock above the path of the passing backs of the pigs that roamed my posada until a large one charged under me, speared my side with his snout (surprisingly dry), and sent my hammock rocking for the rest of the night.

The next day (yesterday), I checked out of my posada and into "Harry's Camping" because Harry didn't have any pigs and because his campground is right on this tiny cove called Xipolito and written up in my hippie guidebook as the prettiest beach on the planet. "Harry" was born Julio, but some drunken American called him Harry like twenty years ago and he liked it. I swim all day alone, stuff myself with ceviche, and think back to what a jerk I was to Calista the last time I was in this country.

The second morning (today), while I was untying my hammock, a cutish European-looking girl extended her head through the zipper of the mosquito netting of her tent and started flirting. She sounded half German, half Valley girl.

"Hello, fellow traveler. You mean you do not have a tent?"

"I didn't have this hammock until I bought it in Mérida."

"Wow. And where are you heading off to from here?"

"Puerto Vallarta. Just to catch a plane to Los Angeles."

"I am an au pair girl in Los Angeles myself. Und ve come from Puerto Vallarta now. You should be nice to my friend here so he maybe take you for free."

"Are you German?"

"Naw! I am Austrian."

Katya, nineteen, reminded me painfully of Leza, an Icelandic au pair I knew in Florence and another she-wolf of the SS. Instantly, I understood that this Katya is immensely skilled at hurting guys. Later I met her patron, Bart, thirty, a San Diego surfer, and her girlfriend, Ute. Bart met the girls in Mazatlán and invited them to stay in his dad's place in Puerto Vallarta. He's paid for their whole trip. I envy their tent, but if it rains, I'm pretty sure they'll let me squeeze in with them. Katya is evil, but cute. Ute, not so cute.

The girls hiked down the beach to topless sunbathe. Bart and I drove up the coast to study the waves.

"Fella, you could really help me out. Katya's always saying she doesn't want to mess around because Ute will get all bummed. I'm not saying you have to date her or anything, but if you like talk to her, I can make the moves on my chick."

•••

From one love junkie to another, I couldn't say no.

In the afternoon the four of us drove to a beach outside of town in Bart's decapitated Bronco.

Bart circled after her through the sand. Once he wrestled her to the ground and kissed her. She never struggled, but she just died in his arms and scowled. He said she'd been like that for a week.

At a restaurant in the market at night, brightened too bright by lights fed by a chortling generator, Katya ogled the waiter.

"The boys here are so very fine and nice. Two boys dove for coral for us today in the morning. See?"

Bart didn't even look.

"Where will the ladies' room be?" Katya pushed away from the table and up, wandered the tables to the kitchen. Fifteen minutes later doom was settling upon our table.

"Ute, where the hell did she go?"

"I do not know what to tell you."

Fifteen minutes after that, Katya returned through the front with two Mexican boys maybe even younger than she. Katya pulled off her plate, which was between Ute and me, and lifted it to a fresh table with her new friends. I looked to Bart, but he was already leaving. I tried to politely half wave to Ute and follow him out.

"Bart, wait up. . . . When people say they know exactly how you feel they usually don't, but believe me, I really do."

"I'm going to kill that little bitch. I'm going to rip out her fucking heart."

Back at the campground he emptied the Bronco of all their belongings. Their bathing suits, towels, toiletries, everything he shoved to the sand under the tall palms of the campground. But not Katya's brand-new Nikon. That, he held in his hand like Yorick's skull—he, a surfer Hamlet. Harry/Julio approached, flashlight first.

"¿Qué paso, amigos?"

"Nada. . . . Mira, esto es para ti."

He couldn't believe it. He tried to push back the camera.

· ·

"No. *Para ti.* A gift. *Feliz Navidad."*

Harry/Julio's smile was a joyful and wondrous one. He squinted behind the viewfinder and pushed our flashless picture in the dark.

Bart and I drove next door to another campground and rented a thatched hut for the evening.

"If you still want a ride to Puerto, I'm leaving in the morning."

"You know, Bart, you're my hero."

We hitched our hammocks from the beams in the hut and traded women stories for hours.

"You should write yours down, Bart. Like me."

"Maybe I will, man. I could write a fucking book."

The banging alarmed me out of my sleep. I shifted and wormed, but the cocoon of the hammock wrapped me tight.

"Bart! Bart! Open this thing. I have to speak to you." Bart is completely free of muscles, his chest is concave like something's wrong with him. He'd been sleeping in his bathing suit and un-latched the hut door to Katya, the moonlight, and two big foreign-looking guys.

"Where is it!"

"Where is what?"

"You goddamn, you know what. My Nikon, what did you do with it?"

"Uh, this lady here says you took her camera, mister. All she wants for is it back." The big foreign guys were standing well behind her in the shadows of the moon.

"Look, fellas, if you want to dance, fine, but first you ought to know about this bitch you're protecting. You got some fucking nerve coming back here after all I've done for you. I don't know where your fucking camera is. I piled all your shit in the sand for you and your new boyfriends to pick up."

Katya looked back to the big foreign guys. They stepped back into deeper shadows.

"Listen, mister, we did not know it was this personal thing. She told us you were just a thief. We are very sorry for this."

And they left.

"Let me search your car, you goddamn!"

"Fine."

．　．　．

Neither of us could sleep, so we celebrated in a bar in town playing old tapes of football games. The big foreign guys passed by. We both hailed them, but only eventually did they come. One was Swedish, the other German. They had actually been in Isla Mujeres a week before Morgan and me and remembered Catherine and Berneice. We all four talked women as the bar closed around us.

March 2, 1985

Puerto Vallarta

Bart's father's place overlooks all of town. The condo itself is still under construction, so I'm sleeping on a mattress on the floor of the master bedroom next to ripped half boxes of hand-painted Mexican tiles. Bart is upstairs in the guest bedroom because it's more finished.

Puerto Vallarta is not Mexico anymore, it makes Cancún look rustic. Everyone is Canadian or Minnesotan (you can't tell, they all say "Aye" after everything like my friend Liz). Last night, after dinner at this great restaurant of a friend of his, back at his father's place, there was a buzzing of the buzzer. We looked to each other. Bart pressed the intercom.

"¿Sí?"

"It is Katya and Ute."

And he let them in.

"Man, you were so strong before. Don't cave in now."

"I'm just going to talk to the bitches."

I waited downstairs, stared at the lights of the cruise ships through the jagged hole where one day will be a window. I heard someone coming down the stairs, turned, and saw Katya.

"Bart says you told him to be mean to me."

Oh, shit.

"I told you to become his friend to come stay here, and now you tell him not to let us stay here?"

"I told him you didn't like him as anything more than a friend."
"So, if he is my friend, he should let me stay here the night."
Her Nikon necklaced her neck. She saw me see it.
"See, all is done."

Today at the beach, Bart attacked her again and kissed her, and she again died limp in his arms. As I am writing this, the three of them are sleeping in the queen-size bed upstairs. Bart is in his underwear, the two fräuleins in clothes.

March 5, 1985

Shirley

She squealed when I called her. On the other end I smiled. I asked her out to the party tonight to celebrate the premiere of "Our House," our new PBS syndicated TV show. We rented out this awful discotheque. All night long she held my hand, caressed my neck; it was wild. Then they stopped the party and showed parts of the first show on the monitor.

We got the rights to this sappy Crosby, Stills, Nash & Young song for the credits. We dissolve from still to still to still of Seth, out host, picking at the skin under his Rusty Jones red beard, scratching his head, then smiling up at the sunny sky, rolling up his plaid shirt, and slinging on his work belt. The actor I'd hired to play the young homeowner was so coked out of his head that drool shined his lips after every rapid-fire and unintelligible sentence. PBS needed the pilot in a week, so my boss had me do it.

It wasn't acting, really, and I didn't even have to pick up a tool (because I wouldn't know what to do with one anyway). I was adding a new bedroom to my dinky split-level in a middle-class neighborhood in Darien. The GC (general contractor) told me about the stud separation, the thickness of the preset for the tile floor, the cost of the paneling per board foot, etc. I just nodded, then asked him, How much will all this cost me? After he said the figure, I whistled.

....

That was Seth's cue. He stepped into frame and told me, as he will tell every homeowner every week, "You know, Fred, many of these home repairs you can do yourself and save a pretty penny."

The GC looked a bit sad when he said, "I hate to admit it, but your friend's absolutely right."

Some lady whistled when she saw me, I think. My friend Michelle yelled, "Take it off!" Afterward, a lot of people recognized me, and this fat lady asked me if I was ever on "Miami Vice."

"Austin, maybe you should sign up with a good acting coach. I know a lot of them that take amateurs."

Still, Shirley's kiss good night fired my insides like whiskey.

March 10, 1985

Shirley

She's busy all weekend. *Fuck her!* She says she'll call when she's free.

The awful part is that I don't love her and know that I never could. More than anything I feel we're in a battle for her body. I ache to sleep with her, but she always parries, dances away. Maybe rapists feel the same way. I don't want to hurt her. I don't want to force her. But I do want to fuck her and make her come till her toes curl. I want to have to drag my leg to the door because she's clinging to it like an ankle weight.

Michelle promises that if I ever call her again, she'll stab me.

March 12, 1985

Models

I am sicker than I had feared. I found out that this Ford model was playing a realtor in our next show and that she went to Andover. I didn't need to be on the set, but of course today I made up some excuse to check her out. I don't know how many tall, plain, expressionless women (whose bodies seem made of the same wire hangers that replace them once the dresses are inside the stores) I will have to see before I can ignore them.

Shirley and the other "models" I know aren't really full-time models, they are "P.P.G." commercial actresses who work behind perfume counters or sell clothes (they are always in debt to the store owners despite the discounts). They'd be just as happy married rich or as a movie star or recording artist. They don't know what they want to do, they just know how they want to live. If they are lucky, they might have their picture taken for *Black Elegance* or *Blacktress*. No matter how yellow their skin, they always complain they are too "black" for *Essence*.

Joanna Tobin, today's real model, for one thing, is extremely white. She's six feet tall, straight black hair, and blue eyes. I didn't recognize her at all from boarding school. She named all the people she knew at school, and I named all the (seven) people I knew, and none intersected. She was really nice to me anyway, so I tried to make myself ask her out. The worst, most shallow, and shameful part of my soul liked her better because of her title.

"I'm finishing up at Yale—better late than never—so I'm pretty busy, but still, we should hang out sometime?"

She couldn't find a piece of scrap paper. "Do you mind?" And she lifted my hand and drew her number at the end of my palm's lifeline. Michelle teased me about it all day.

"You're like Tom Jones at Caesars Palace," she said. "Soon they'll be tossing you their room keys and panties."

I couldn't even answer her. Could I ever turn into an actual stud? You think? Naw. But it was nice of Michelle to tease me.

March 15, 1985

Amyl Nitrate

I've got to write this down while I still believe it. A friend kept raving about amyl nitrate and sex. "It enhances the orgasm," he'd say. For me, the orgasm is the only thing in the world that doesn't need to be enhanced. Anyway, he gave me one, a little capsule wrapped in a yellow net, and told me to pop it under my nose and my partner's as we approached orgasm. It's a powerful smelling salt cardiac patients carry around with them. They pop it under their noses, and their heart rate soars.

I didn't feel like waiting a year before Shirley gave in, and I don't feel like calling the white model girl, Joanna, so I tried out the thing with blond Kathi Rae Walker, *Playboy*'s Miss March ("Turn-Ons: Honesty and Hank Williams, Jr."). Believe me when I say that I will never do one of those things again. But also believe me when I tell you that just for an instant, Kathi Rae's eighteen-inch-tall centerfold came alive. This tiny, three-D holographic leprechaun hovered inches above the glossy page. Kathi winked at me as I came. But I think I might have hurt myself.

March 18, 1985

Good News

My boss is going to test *me* out as the host of the whole show! Seth, the guy we've got now, turns out to be not only macro-biotic, but also a drunk. The boss says I'd be good, but it depends if PBS will take a chance on a black guy, and pretty young. Seth is a licensed contractor, looks perfect, like a house-building Jim Henson. I can barely saw a plank. But, actually, that doesn't matter. It's all scripted. The guest homeowner always says, "I've never been good with tools." And the host always says, "It's easy. Here's my friend Jim, a licensed plumber. He'll show you a few tricks of the trade that will not only save you a pretty penny, but make you feel good and emotionally invested in your lovely home."

If I could only grow a beard, then maybe I'd have a chance.

I don't know what I want to do for the rest of my life, but if I get the job, my salary triples. I'm not nervous at all in front of the camera. Who watches TV at five-thirty Sunday morning, anyway? The fishing shows have a higher share.

Oh, the bad news is that I've still got a sore from that night with the three-D leprechaun. I hope it goes away on its own because I can't go to a doctor. What if I become famous and then die of the thing?

March 22, 1985

Shirley

She called! She said *she* was near suicidal, that's why she's been avoiding me. I invited her to dinner tomorrow. I'm going out right now and buying two Cornish game hens from the Ukrainian butcher. I'm not going to make up the bed or pud pull tonight for luck. I've been researching this for over a decade and I'm pretty sure it brings bad luck before a date.

March 24, 1985

Evil Shirley

Midnight. I've put the hens in the freezer. They'd been out of the refrigerator for seven hours already and were starting to change colors. If Shirley does show up one day, I'll try to serve them again. Maybe they'll make her too sick to fuck whoever it is she is fucking.

I'm writing this from the Burger King on Second Avenue. I want to kill her, kill myself in the act of killing her. I wish I'd admitted to Michelle that I'd called her again. I wish somebody would yell at me. Marquita and Fletcher were too seventies. They never raised their voices.

I wish I could convince myself to pity myself. Yet by now she must think I get off on her games. She probably just did it for the new letter.

It's like a "golden shower." Sure it's repugnant to you, but if you have to pee anyway, and the pitiful creep is always hanging around the bathroom and whining for it, what's it to you if you shoot a few squirts in his face?

I know I love only beauty and have yet to realize that beauty and evil often very peacefully coexist.

But why haven't any of my supposed friends told me that I have become a shallow, vapid asshole? (Okay, maybe Michelle and Jerrold did try to warn me a few times, but I thought they were just kidding.) But I wonder how long I've been this way. I was a nice enough guy in college, I think. But I must be a creep now. How else could someone, even this Antichrist, treat me so badly?

As each day passes without your ever having had a real girlfriend, your assholish pathologies and eccentricities continue to calcify. I give you less than four months before you become hopelessly maladjusted.

Austin at forty: My constant refrain to all my long coupled friends will be, "You sure you don't know anybody else you can fix me up with?" Thanksgiving and Christmas will find me called "Uncle Austin" by the many children of my happy friends. Some of the wives will watch me playing with their Buckys, Jamils, and Sweet Peas and whisper among themselves in the kitchen, "Gee, he's so good with kids, and you say he's not gay. I can't believe he's still single." The other wives won't let me baby-sit: "I don't care if he is your best friend, I just don't want him around our children!"

Anyway, Austin Jones, asshole no more.

Bring on the ugly girls.

I'm wearing my Walkman headphones so the other bums and crazies will leave me alone. The Walkman itself is busted, so I left it at home. I just tucked the headphone's plug into the hand-warmer tube at the belly of my hooded Stanford sweatshirt. This nice old black guy, who looks just like the photo of my father's grandpa on the piano, has propped a yellow "Wet Floor" sandwich board in front of my section and is mopping.

"Don't get up, son. This way you get the whole section to yourself."

Do I look so much like I need it?
I guess I do.

April 21, 1985

Genevieve

At CBGBs a Black Rock Coalition band was covering Elvis Costello's "I Just Want to Be Loved" when I first saw her. She's not that cute, a proofreader for the *Nation* and a poetess. Just what the doctor ordered, except I'm not in love.

"Well, I don't see why I always have to come stay over at your place. Why can't you ever come to Queens?"

"You live in your great-aunt's basement, for chrissakes. . . . Okay . . . Genevieve, let's flip on it."

"Over the phone?"

"Sure. Heads or tails."

"Uh . . . heads. Wait! How can I trust you?"

"You shouldn't sleep with anyone you don't trust."

"All right, all right . . . flip."

"Tails. Come on over."

"Two out of three. C'mon, Austin?"

"Okay . . . choose!"

"Tails."

"Wrong again."

"You're lying! Let me do it."

"I don't trust you."

"I trusted you."

"No, you didn't."

"Look, Austin, heads or tails."

"Heads."

"Shit. Two out of three."

"Heads."

"Bastard."

. . . .

.   .   .

See? There's no guarantee that a nonmodel will be noncrazy.

April 28, 1985

Michelle

No, it's not like that. But all the guys on the show think we are made for each other. It was the same in junior high. The year before busing there were only three black kids in the school, me, my sister, Leslie, and Stefanie, this nice girl, pretty smart but plain. My friends were always trying to fix us up, though they wouldn't ever consider dating her.

Actually, Michelle reminds me of Liz from school. She's my new, unaccredited psychotherapist. I tell her everything and she tells me how messed up and superficial I am.

Anyway, we finished taping a season of shows with the drunk and they'll be deciding on next year's host in the next few days. Michelle bet me a lobster dinner that I'll get the job. But if I don't, I'm definitely going to grad school. Fletcher talked to Yale's Afro-Am Department and they're saving me a slot, just in case. Maybe I'm ready to go back to school, get smart again. On the other hand, daily I find myself daydreaming witty conversations between David Letterman and "the hottest rising star on pre-dawn cable television. . . . Please welcome Austin Jones, the Fix-It Kid!"

They were concerned that "Austin McMillan" sounded more like a British prime minister than a home repairs adviser, so I suggested Jones. If I do get the job, Marquita and Fletcher will freak out a bit, but I don't think they know that I know my real mom's last name. I'll just tell them that the company picked it out of a hat.

··

M a y 4 , 1 9 8 5

P a r t y

I had a big party to celebrate my new job. PBS didn't renew, they said they were working on their own show (but even the boss thinks it's just because they think I'm too young and too black).

I don't care because now the USA cable network is going to air little old me (Sunday mornings at four-thirty)! They're changing the name from the Vermont hippiness of "Our House" to the Dayton, Ohio–styled "The Home Repair Show." I like the cheesy honesty of the latter. We're the lead-in for fifteen-year-old reruns of "The Galloping Gourmet." Manhattan doesn't get the channel yet, but maybe by summer. I invited every pretty girl I've ever met, and they were all nice to me. But I'm not in love with any of them. Michelle didn't bring her man, a Greek aluminum sider she met on the show.

"Hey, Austin," Michelle whispered to me out of the side of her mouth like a spy. "So you won the lobster, but I'll bet you another dinner I can name all your women here tonight."

"You're on. You don't even know how many of them showed up."

"Here goes. That one in the black mini and the weave must be . . . oh, wait, there are three, no, four of them."

"Hardy har-har."

"Okay. The one tugging down her hem is Gwen."

"You talked to her."

"She just looks like someone who'd want their nipples bitten."

"Shhhh!"

"Let me see, Cindi Brown, Sabrina, and LaShawn I remember from the shoots, so they don't count, but the pitiful one on your ratty old beanbag chair—throw that thing out tonight—that must be Genevieve. Go on and talk to the poor girl."

"I've got to mingle. I'm the host. But you missed the most important one."

"Oh, the red mini, good weave, who's been squeezing the boss's bicep all night can be none other than Evil Shirley."

"You bitch."
"You better be talking about her."

May 10, 1985

Homosexuality

All guys wonder sometimes if they're gay, right? I mean, I don't look at guys and get a boner, but what else could expain how fucked up I am with women? Sometimes my mind tortures me with thoughts of jamming the hand of the guy who makes my papaya smoothies into the blender, of doing it with my sister, of making out with some guy. I don't want to do any of it, I think, but sometimes these thoughts come into my brain. Especially now, when I'm down. It was much easier being depressed when I was behind the cameras. Today the makeup lady said I looked like shit and had to have her assistant go out for more cover-up for the bags under my eyes. It took me five takes just to get through the opening:

"Hi, and welcome again to 'Home Repairs.' Last week we laid the hardwood floor in a parquet pattern. If you remember, that left a jagged border that we said we'd get to later. . . . Well, now it's later, and Jim and Candice are going to show us a few tricks of the trade on how to finish off one of the most beautiful jobs in home remodeling."

"Trick of the trade." At least six times a day I spout that phrase. I'm sure it condemns me to a week more of hell every time I say it, every day I spout shit.

I don't know. My director is gay, but very cool. It was his idea to take a chance on a twenty-three-year-old Negro. Nobody else besides Michelle believed in me. Still, personally, I don't want anything up my butt. Gwen, one of those models, thought she was turning me on by straying her fingers up there. In the middle of everything I had to keep my butt clenched shut and squirm it out of her reach. Afterward I handed her a moist towelette.

I don't want my dick up anyone's butt, either, male or female. The vagina's dimensions, texture, and consistency have been per-

．．

fected through a million years of Darwinian selection. I don't want a blow job from a guy because I don't want a blow job from anybody I wouldn't kiss, and I don't want to suck a dick because I know where they've been.

June 21, 1985

Lesa Biltmont

She was that freshman in Ujamaa with a crush on me my senior year. She was in town for just the night and called out of the blue and asked to sleep on my sofa. She left this morning for Paris to study political science at the Scienze-Po'. So maybe I tried a little something late last night, but she said she didn't want to be even more jet-lagged.

July 27, 1985

Didi

I was sitting in the apartment noticing how saddle-backed and cracked were my window sashes, how I haven't even installed the paper towel holder I swiped from the set three weeks ago. I was sitting sideways in the now dirty white, family hand-me-down chair, shredded by years of Pumpkin's cat scratching. I was sitting sideways so the chair's arms cradled me at both the back of my knee and the middle of my back, like a fraying bum hero struggling my body out of a building's fire. Not a friend was free, and I was feeling particularly unloved. Rising, I rolled the cable TV dial through all the stations, two through thirteen, A–W, and as always could find nothing to watch. USA cable, my new network, was syndicating an old black-and-white sitcom that I'd never even heard of.

The clock on the VCR glowed a green 7:57, five minutes and

thirty seconds from the 8:02:30 promo for "The Home Repair Show." Finally out of the chair, I kicked at the clothes on the floor until the brand-new cable remote slid out from under an undershirt. But where was that complicated instruction manual?

I covered most of the mismatched linoleum on the kitchen floor with the new *Village Voice* as if I were preparing to scrape the thousands of flakes of peeling paint from the ceiling. Instead, I pulled the plastic ex-grocery, now garbage sack from its cave below my sink and sprinkled the trash over the paper. The pages of the manual for the cable remote were waxed translucent by garbage juices. The "Parental Channel Lock" pages pulled free as easily as greasy butter paper from its stick. I turned back to the USA network. I pushed all the buttons the manual told me to, and voilà, the USA network disappeared into a funhouse mirrorlike warp, the sound suddenly an unintelligible and irritating *shush*. Now I can't watch myself unless I figure out how to deactivate the parental lock. Marquita and Fletcher keep hinting that they know it was more than a coincidence that I changed my TV name to Jones, but I won't admit a thing.

I was finally starting to clean the place when the pretty little phone bleated its electronic chirp.

"Hi, this is Didi. Is Lesa there?"

"No. She left this morning."

"Shoot. I knew I should've called earlier. You're her friend from college, right?"

"Yes."

"I met her at Affluence, this store I work at sometimes, and I'd promised I'd show her around the city before she left."

"I'm sorry. She didn't leave me her address in Paris."

"She would've liked the party tonight. It's one of our biggest of the year."

"You throw a lot of parties?"

"Not me. Ford."

"Oh." *Get thee away from me, O Satan!* Be strong! Battle stations! Deflector shields on full! Do not—I repeat, do not—under any circumstances whatsoever meet this evil being fresh from the bowels of hell.

"Didi? You know . . . I know just what it's like when you want to invite a friend somewhere but you just miss them. All my plans tonight fell through. Every single one of my friends had to cancel. It's the worst luck. I really want to go out tonight, but there's just nobody around. There's nothing to do tonight, I'm so bored but I really feel like going out, I'm all dressed up and everything and—"

"You're welcome to come out with us if you want."

"If I wouldn't be intruding?"

"Listen to you. Come on."

"How will I know you?"

"My three girlfriends will be wearing black and I'll be wearing a peach miniskirt. . . . And how will I know you?"

"I'll be wearing a . . . a . . . white shirt and brown pants. I'm about six two . . . black."

"Me too."

Me and my big mouth. My only white shirt didn't smell but was stained and crinkled. I ducked my nose under my underarms, wiped each armpit, and smelled my finger. I wet a hand towel and rubbed each pit till I hurt myself, sprayed cologne on my chest, but the spray valve stuck and kept on spraying all over me and the room. I was buttoning my shirt still hot from the iron as I triple-bolted the front door behind me.

Young shitheads in moussed ponytails ("dork knobs") and many too many beautiful women laughed and hugged each other in the velvety restaurant. Foreign languages were flying. I kept searching for the huge eunuch bouncers who'd catch, humiliate, and expel me.

"Hey, I saw you on TV. You're that house guy on cable. I watch you on the Island when I get in from clubbing in the city."

"Thank you, thank you very much."

"Where's your plaid shirt? How many of those things you got, anyway?"

"You'd have to ask wardrobe."

I leaned around a five-foot-eleven-inch preteenage girl in a micromini and ordered a drink at the bar. Maybe I should just go home, I thought. Spare yourself, for once. So Genevieve wasn't perfect. Find another *smart* girl. There are literally tens of millions of them on the planet. Then I actually looked at all the models in the room. Hardly any of them made my heartbeat quicken. I knew they were mainly ex-gangly, nerdy girls getting back at all the popular guys who passed them over for the prom. Like me, they bloomed late in life, and like me, they were neurotic and petty.

If I leave now, before she even shows up, I will be once and forevermore cured, I remember thinking.

"Austin!" And this tall white girl hugged me.

"Joanna Tobin. I worked on your show once. We went to Andover together? Congratulations, Mr. TV Star. Whenever I'm back at Yale or on Long Island and up that late I watch you: 'You can save a pretty penny with a few tricks of the trade. . . .' You're great. But why'd you change your name?"

"You know . . . showbiz . . ."

"Here's my number again, in case, you know, you lost it."

I don't know what I did with her number because my brain and my soul were already fixed on the restaurant's door.

The thin column in the doorway was Didi, dressed in a peach mini and white stockings and white shoes. Along with her three plainer, shorter, and heavier friends all in black, she looked like the lead singer of a Motown girl group.

"Uh-oh," I said to myself aloud.

Didi smiled so big when I neared her. Her friends air-kissed the various fops they knew.

"You must be Didi. I'm Austin."

"Austin? Oh, my! I didn't even ask your name on the phone. Isn't that an unusual name for a black man?"

"I was born with the name. I don't know where it came from. Uh . . . would you like some gin and tonic?"

"Yes! I've had a horrible day."

I handed her my half-empty glass.

"I—I thought you were going to get me a new one."

"Oh, my God! . . . I mean, I'll be right back."

I shoved through the poseurs and jetted toward the door. Never once have I been so stupid. I was about to double-check my wallet for cab fare when I realized she was following me.

"I didn't want to be all alone over there." She touched my arm to steady herself, and it was as if she'd injected adrenaline right into my aorta. "I'm sorry I'm such awful company today. I'm so darned depressed I just want to get drunk, and I never get drunk."

"Do you want to talk about it?"

"Willi Wear offered me their fall collection in South America. Then guess what! My stupid passport expired just last month, but I didn't know till they were booking my flight."

"That's no big deal. If you pay extra, you can get one in twenty-four hours."

"Well . . . my birth certificate was with a friend back in Florida, and it was all real messy, and they liked this other girl just as much, I guess, but shoot . . ."

"The important thing is that someone liked you. That means it will happen again."

"You think so?"

"You are as beautiful as anyone on the planet. Of course you'll be a success."

"I needed to hear that now. You're a sweetie."

"It's true."

A second drink in her hand, she led me to her friends in the back of the restaurant in a booth. She leaned into me, I think. I rested my arm on the ledge above her with only a few minutes of strategizing.

Her friends wanted to go to Nell's. I had vowed never to return with anything less than a pipe bomb after the time Morgan and I were turned away at the door.

Inside, I bought her another drink and we danced downstairs. Each of her rhythmic steps brought her closer to me until our legs were between each other's. We didn't need to touch to feel the sex. At least five times she tripped onto me. Each time I caught her but held her baby waist longer and longer until that was how we danced, my hands on her hips, her arms yoked around my neck. I tried not to look at her so I could keep on my feet. She is not only beautiful, but sweet, like an ugly girl. And she likes me, of this I am sure.

"You know, you have a very sexy voice on the phone." All night long she said things like that, things that I say to dates but that they never say to me. At three Tuesday morning they drove me to my door and I kissed Didi's sweet cheek.

"It's funny how you meet folks. I had a fantastic time. I really like you, I'm not being so friendly just because I'm drunk."

I'm at home writing this. I can't go to sleep. Pregnancy will make her look more lovely still and should help her keep on some weight. Our children will be beautiful. Or at least tall.

July 30, 1985

Didi

We'd already made a date for this Friday when she called and invited me to her friend's birthday tonight. Her friend having the birthday worked for the NAACP Legal Defense Fund. He was nice to me and I was nice to him after he introduced me to his girlfriend. I tried to save Didi a seat next to me, but she was two hours and four minutes late.

She wore a wild red floral halter-topped dress, and her three sidekicks, as usual, tagged along. The only seats left were far from my end of the near endless chain of shoved-together tables for two. But she winked at me when she entered. I tried to talk to whoever it was I was sitting next to, but all I was doing really was raising my chin to make my jaw look stronger for her. I made the people around me laugh so she would want to join us. It was delicious to be so far away but so close to her. We'd look to each other over the people between us at exactly the same moments. She was

••

sitting next to some high-yellow pretty boy with Italian hair who blabbered on about nothing.

After dinner I boldly walked to her and squatted by her chair, mooned into her face like a dog. But she mooned back. I don't know how long it took somebody to say, "This is ridiculous." Musical chairs played out, and a seat opened up for me like the sun between sliding clouds. The gigolo kept talking about how they make Brie like he had just caught a PBS documentary on the history of cheese. Didi excused herself, turned away from him, and asked me this:

"Did you miss me this week?"

"I thought about our date every day."

Her blush made her turn away, and a marriage proposal only barely stayed down in my throat. After dinner, nobody (including me) wanted to go to Nell's except Didi and her friends. This time I swaggered past the door people, wishing for a better sneer to flash them. Inside, her friends danced downstairs, while we sat at a table above deck where an old jazz combo played "A Cottage for Sale."

"Your hands are beautiful."

I didn't know what to say.

"What's the matter, Austin?"

I looked down and measured each word before releasing it gently from my throat like a series of weather balloons launched skyward from a wide field on a sunny day: "I was just thinking how much I'd like to kiss you."

Now, she looked away. "You're crazy. . . . Wait a minute, let me stop blushing."

I pushed up from the table and leaned forward just enough to let our lips meet. Her lips are red and soft and the bottom one so sweetly plump it's creased in the middle. While my eyes were closed she stole a large piece of my soul. An old black lady singer, not Dakota Staton, but of the same school, joined the band, tugged her too tight sequined spandex gown back past the bell of her hips, and began "Moody's Mood for Love."

"There I go, there I go, there I gooo . . . "

Instantly my new favorite song.

I've never seen *Lady and the Tramp*, but I've seen that Italian restaurant scene where Lady and the Tramp dig into the same plate of spaghetti and end up eating opposite ends of the same piece of pasta until their lips meet in the middle and they lightly kiss and blush. Didi's hair is almost red and wild like dogs' ears, and that Lady dog was awfully cute.

Later that night she was driving me home, her friends in the back, when we passed some busy unmarked awning and her three friends suddenly got the urge to visit their friend who works the door at that club. It was two-thirty.

"I'll pick y'all up at . . . four?" Didi looked at me to see if that was the right answer.

As I sat down on my unraveling couch and asked her her pleasure, whispers of the dozens of dates I'd brought here disoriented me until I remembered that we'd already kissed. After the first kiss you know you can at will, so you can luxuriate in the electricity of anticipation. I felt the blood full blasting through her lips, plumping them even more. After our lips again separated, dizziness crowded my sight with buzzing shapes.

"Wow. I don't like a lot of science fiction, but—"

"You don't? It's my favorite."

"I mean, I love what little I've read, and in Robert Henlein's *Stranger in a Strange Land*—"

"I love that book."

And I love you, I thought. "It's wonderful. Anyway, remember the E.T. guy is this great kisser because he focuses his entire being into his lips."

"So that's your secret."

"I don't mean me. I mean you. Your lips make me dizzy."

And we kissed, just kissed, until it was time to pick up her friends at the awning.

It's five-twelve. She's coming over tomorrow for a rooftop barbecue. I miss her already.

. . . .

July 31, 1985

Didi

On time from her faraway Queens apartment, after our kiss of the day, she balanced and rotated a pie tin covered in Reynolds Wrap from around her back and delivered it to just under my nose. I peeled back the foil with my teeth, but the aluminum buzzed my fillings.

"Oh, I love marinated artichokes." At least I do now.

On my dirty roof, on folding chairs and milk crates passed up through the blackened skylight, I fed her hamburgers and potato chips and beer. Across the street an even bigger rooftop barbecue toasted us. They tried to throw us their extra marshmallows, but the wind curved the bag down into the crevasse of the alley between us.

Later we walked. When she hung on my arm I instantly straightened my back. We promenaded past the faux derelict bars and Indian restaurants. On a bench by the river, the sun only now setting red, we didn't kiss. We held each other.

"Austin, it's all going so fast."

"It's only good when it's fast."

I've never been more nervous making love, but my hydraulics didn't malfunction. We weren't savage with each other, we were slow and strong. She's nearly as tall as I am, though scarily skinny. I stayed hard forever, but not for me, for her, for the privilege of watching spirits possess her face. When I came I wouldn't have minded just then dying. I had experienced greatness for the only time in my life.

She is asleep next to me. I taste the artichokes still, confuse them with the taste of her kiss.

Didi

We hadn't seen each other in three days.

"I can't believe how much I missed you."

"Didi, some wonderful things have happened to me in my life, but you are easily the single most wonderful. Thank you."

We made love for hours, as usual. It's the first time I think that I didn't feel that I was just practicing. I feel that this moment, this night, is what all the misfirings and masturbations had been in training for. She told me she'd been in New York for two years (from Miami), but as soon as she saw me she said she was struck. When she talks she sounds like me. I didn't think anyone, especially not one of the very most beautiful women in the world, would ever feel what she seems to feel for me. In the shower she slid down my body and fellated me. I might have cried, I'm not sure because of the spray of the water in my face.

Didi

"I was stopped at a stoplight and I just started thinking of you inside of me and I got so excited, so wet, it was wild! When I looked up I saw the light just turning red again. It's a good thing nobody came up behind me. Austin, you're dangerous!"

Didi

Last week she spent the night four times. We make love for so long that we rest, me still inside her, and just talk. One time, from the stereo, while we were making love, a beautiful Sonny Rollins solo colored the room:

"You know, Austin, when you're inside me like this, I'm the saxophone and you're the sax player. You make me do whatever you want, make all these crazy noises and faces, it's wild!"

We hold hands in the house, like imbeciles.

"I feel sometimes like you're inside my whole body, coming out of my mouth."

"Wait. You're too big."
Little old me.
I haven't touched it myself in fifteen days. *A personal record.*
After lovemaking, once, while I was peeing, she kissed my neck.
"Hey!"
"Can I hold it?"
"Now?"
"I'd love to be able to pee standing up. Just let me pretend."
"What's mine is yours."

Modeling here is slow. She's got an offer to work in Hong Kong, then she'd like to try London and Paris for a few months. I will wither when she's gone.

September 9, 1985

D i d i

If I ever find the cocksucker who said "Every rose has its thorn," I'll gut him with this ballpoint.

Eddie, her *boyfriend*, is some kind of Cuban gangster back in Miami. He's serving thirty-five months in a minimum-security prison in the Florida Panhandle. She won't tell me her age, except that she's older than me. I guess around twenty-seven. She thought ours would be just a fling, but now that I'm planning our future together, she's scared. Her old agency in Miami just called and offered her catalog work for a month. She needs the money and is leaving me.

September 13, 1985

Didi

As I'm writing this I'm taping the sexy parts to this stupid movie called *Hardbodies*. She's back in Queens, packing. Here's what she said an hour and a half ago:
"I want to pack alone."

It's two-thirty in the morning. She just finished packing and wants to come over. With my luck, even if I do win her away from the gangster, a week later I'll end up slumped over a barber chair with a bullet where a Hindu dot should be. Michelle says she's not going to hang out with me in public until Didi officially dumps me.

We made love until she had to drive to the airport. She'd lost an earring in the sheets. I hid it under my mattress like the princess's pea.

September 28, 1985

Didi

She flew from Miami to the Panhandle to visit him. She was also grouchy with PMS, she said.
"Him and me've worked some things out, for now."
Before I had even hung up the phone I was reaching for you and a pen. They are talking about her opening up a disco in

Miami. He'll bankroll it from the slammer. I see inside myself, see my heart corroding, see holes in it expanding until whole chunks bubble and drip into my body cavity. The weight of my own rib cage will implode upon the emptying hole unless I keep forcing my lungs full of air. Soon I'll be fucked up and sick again.

I couldn't quite bring myself to ask if his prison allowed conjugal visits.

September 30, 1985

Jewelle

She just called. She's breaking up with her current man. Who gives a fuck.

Didi

She called again. (She won't leave me a number where I can reach her.) She's not sure whether she'll dump me or not. She still cares about Eddie the gangster and thinks he'll change.

"I feel I'm in a tug-of-war between you two."

"You're right."

October 3, 1985

Didi

I just talked to her again. I'm not euphoric, but the Ginzu knife is off the wrist. She's coming back for a week just for my birthday before she leaves for Hong Kong. Marquita and Fletcher bought their own cottage on Martha's Vineyard two years ago. If Didi'll go for it, I'd like to take her there for the weekend. I won't tell anyone where we're going in case Eddie's contacted some north-

• •

eastern crime family to come after me in exchange for a Florida hit by his boys. Somewhere I read about these kinds of deals, something like hitmen time shares.

October 10, 1985

Didi

I spent the entire day pacing. Twenty-four is as old as I've ever been, and I couldn't stand to face it alone. Michelle was nice enough to host the party in her loft. (It's the opposite of my place. It's right out of *AD* magazine: glass bricks, double-pane windows, a terra-cotta kitchen floor. Of course she did it all herself.)

Nine o'clock. My show is now on at noon, Sundays, and Manhattan cable now subscribes to the USA network, so my minuscule celebrity has ballooned my tiny roster of friends. We all flattened soft cheeses on stone-ground Wheat Thins. She knew the address and number to the loft. Somebody I barely know and now hate said, "So, when are we going to meet the mystery woman?" It wasn't until forty minutes later that the buzzer buzzed and I opened the door and saw her again. I closed the door behind us, and out in the dirty hall by the freight elevator we hung on each other. Her smile was just there to calm my anger, and it worked. She was late because she'd scoured the town for the same chocolate cake I'd forgotten we'd once had at a restaurant. Then she handed me a large box from Sony.

"Oh, my God. Baby. What did you do?"

"You work in television, so I thought you should have your own video camera."

"You can't afford this."

"Shhh. Just say thank you."

"Wow."

It's the best gift I ever got. It zooms, does its own titles, fades up and to black. I can't wait to try it out.

Then inside the loft she asked me to show her where the bathroom was, then jerked me inside and kissed me for minutes and minutes.

October 17, 1985

D i d i

We've spent the last few days running the city, buying supplies for Hong Kong and a new bathing suit for her week-long stopover in Hawaii (an ex-model girlfriend of hers runs the Hard Rock Cafe on Maui). I love her and will be faithful, but part of me wants to protect myself so hasn't slowed its incessant girl watching. Whenever she catches me checking out someone else's sweater or miniskirt I just say, "Isn't that Gladys Steptoe? I think she went to my high school."

Being apart, even for months, won't be so awful if I can keep remembering that we're going to spend the rest of our lives together.
I'm going to tell her I love her, but I do not know when.
If Eddie the gangster wins, I will die. What can someone so evil appreciate about someone so wonderful? He can only love her beauty. Of course that's what I first saw when I first saw her, but now, when she's tired, her eye bags hanging lower than my own, her skinny, brittle rib cage straining her skin, her hair stinking of the cigarettes she sneaks when she's away from me, when she is all of these ugly things, I love her no less.
She won't talk about it, but the finality I feel to this parting is sinking me.

October 19, 1985

D i d i

Yesterday, after packing huge bags for her trip, we packed one little bag to take here to the Vineyard. Last night, we missed the last ferry to the island. But the steamship authority bent the rules and let us sneak her car on a midnight freighter.

Marquita and Fletcher's tiny cottage smelled so sea musty—the pure essence of melancholy—that I nearly cried when I opened the door. Firelit lovemaking in the soft, old bed. Afterward, she told me this:

"It feels like a honeymoon, but I don't remember the wedding."

Today we roamed Gay Head, the wild side of the island. The leaves were as red as the red cliffs. I snuck away from her and mailed a postcard to her Hong Kong address:

I am scribbling fast because you are about to come out of the RumRunner sweater store. I love you so very much. I wanted you to arrive in Hong Kong to word from over here so you won't be too lonely over there.

4:34 A. M.

"It's my birthday present."

"No."

"Please . . ."

That was around midnight. I begged her, sucked each of her toes until she let me tape us. I propped the camera on the dresser and just let it run. We made love and each of four times came together. There's no TV in the cottage, so we'll watch it when we get back to New York.

Just a half hour ago, I woke up hard again and wound myself against her, then slipped inside her from behind. We'd done it this way before, but this time, as deep inside her as I could, she howled from someplace she'd never howled from before and I worried about her as she continued to tremble and come.

"I love you," I said after she finally opened her eyes.

"I love you, too," she said between breaths, before wiping the sweat off her forehead, nose, and cheeks with her palms.

She's back asleep again while I'm writing this by the nightlight's light in the bathroom. I could spend a lovely life just watching her sleep. And for the first time in my life, if a genie gave me a wish, it would not be to be anywhere else.

October 20, 1985

Didi

This morning, back in the city, we watched our movie. Strange it was to watch, so different than it felt. Clumsy and hilarious, boring, severe, and absurd.

"Oh, my God! Austin, give me that tape right now!"

I rushed it out of my VCR and held it over her head.

"I swear I won't show it to anyone. I know it's stupid. We'll throw it out after you get back."

"If I ever see that thing in some video store, I'll kill you."

It was time to go to the airport.

In front of her gate, I couldn't let her go. Again I said it:

"I love you."

I didn't expect her to reply again. Not really.

2:46 A. M.

She just called from her girlfriend's in Honolulu. I feel much better.

October 24, 1985

Didi

I've been writing her every day. I've also been sending audiotapes. I won't bore you with the details. I just tell her everything

I've told you. So far, however, from neither Hawaii nor Hong Kong, no word at all.

November 1, 1985

Didi

October 20, 1985

Dear Austin,
  Hello . . .
  My wonderful saxophone player. I've been trying to leave your face back at the airport, but I keep seeing you. The flight is so long that we're already on our second movie. Have you seen the old flick That's Entertainment? *Gene Kelly is dancing around Paris, and his movements make me think of you.*
  I'm frightened like I know you are, too. My heart burns (not heartburn, you know what I mean). I can't tell if I'm happy or sad. But I know I could cry at any second. Don't be mad at what I didn't say at the airport. You know how I feel.
  I know (and you know) I avoided all your millions and millions of questions about, "What's going to happen to us?" Who knows, but you need to know that I will never ever forget you. I know you won't let yourself believe that, but it's true.
  I hate hurting you, but I can't live your life and mine, too. I'm getting too old to have this many problems.
  Even if you finally decided I'm no longer worth the bother, you will have helped me more than anybody else ever has helped me. My life is better, baby, just because of you.
                                        Love, Didi

Personal First! My first received love letter. Am I reading too much into it, or am I winning? My heart's in such a dangerous place, on the railroad track playing chicken. I'm about to make her a tape. I'll blast Nat King Cole's "Unforgettable" because that's exactly how I feel:

> *Darling, what is so incredible,*
> *is that someone so unforgettable,*
> *could think that I am unforgettable too.*

November 10, 1985

Didi

Dear Austin,
   Your postcard was waiting for me on my tiny little bed. What a sweetie you are! I'm listening to Sonny Rollins as I'm writing this to you. Oh. I have an idea. STOP! Go to the stereo and put on old Sonny yourself. Maybe then you'll understand my crazy state of mind more.
   I needed Hawaii. I got so brown I'm shiny. You'd love it. Devon was as crazy as ever, millionaires throwing themselves at her feet as usual. We never got to bed before three.
   Hong Kong is so far so good. But I'm in this itty-bitty model's apartment and two of the other girls are just seventeen years old! But Romy, from Germany, is cool. She knows every single person on the scene. All the coolest clubs let models in for free and give us free drinks and food.
   Every day I have another audition. The shows are just starting up. The agency is pretty excited about me. Knock wood, baby.
   You saved my life in New York. I don't know what I'll do without my legs wrapped around your back! (I can't believe I just wrote that, but it's true.)

                                        Love, Didi
                                        XOXOXOXOX

November 19, 1985

Chocolate Singles

I can't remember the last book I read. I can't remember a single class from college. I wonder if one day researchers will discover that acne makes you smarter. I swear to God when I was a neurotic pizza face back in high school I was sometimes brilliant. But if you ask me would I rather be the smartest guy in the world or the handsomest, I'd definitely say smartest. But between the smartest and the sexiest? I wouldn't think twice. I'd trade in sixty IQ points for one large dose of animal magnetism.

What got me to thinking about all this is that *Chocolate Singles*, the black dating newsletter/magazine, said I'm the twenty-second of the fifty most eligible black bachelors in New York. Next year Didi and I probably won't be married yet, we'll just be living together—so I want to be in the magazine's top ten.

Christmas Day 1985

D i d i

She just called and we talked for fifty-three minutes! A friend of hers, some Japanese guy, a model hanger-on named Yukio, traffics in stolen corporate MCI cards. I'd forgotten how small her voice is. I rubbed my chest as I listened. She got my gold bracelet (insured up the wazoo) and says she wears it every day. I still haven't received her gift, but she told me today it's a stuffed good-luck dragon. Still no definite date of return. When we finally hung up I had to sit down on the couch. I missed the train to Connecticut and made everybody wait two hours for turkey and yams.

D i d i

I haven't heard from her in years. She's working in Tokyo now. I keep trying to pin her down about the day (or month) she will return. But I just bought a Japanese phrase book in case I have to go over there and kidnap her.

I had been good. I hadn't looked at it once since she left. But today, after twenty minutes of trial and error, I figured out how to patch my video camera to my VCR, played back our tape. I don't know why I didn't cry when I saw us come.

L y n e l l

For some reason, the cool New York black people invite me to their parties even though "The Home Repair Show" is about as uncool as you can get.

Triumph Television picked it up, and next year "Home Repairs with Austin Jones" will be on broadcast TV Sundays at noon. It was their idea to add my (pseudo) name to the title. The bookshelves in Marquita and Fletcher's TV room are filled with cassettes of all my shows. More and more often, people bother me on the street. ("Hey, you're the fix-it kid, am I right? Do you get a commission on all those 'barroom-styled ceiling fans' you're pushing or what? What the hell is it, anyway? 'Barroom-styled.' What is that?") And this time I'm *seriously* talking to a realtor about finally moving out of this hellhole.

The Studio Museum of Harlem was having a benefit, and they offered to give me a free ticket, but I paid. Lynell was obviously not a model or actress, so I asked her to dance and she said she'd seen me on cable. I was so lonely that just the smell of her as we danced replenished me. Then she took me home and fucked me.

Didi told me to see other people, but as I was inside this woman, a bright and pretty ophthalmologist, I couldn't come. Finally, I had to conjure Didi's lips and cheeks to mind. I hurt myself biting my lip not to whisper her name.

Valentine's Day 1986

D i d i

I was tired of the fizzle. I wanted a bang-up ending. I just now reached her (she's always out) and made myself not say "I love you." I just asked her if she had any idea at all when she'd be coming home. She grunted something about going straight from Tokyo to Milan and staying in Europe for at least a *year*.

Maybe crash isn't the right word. Crash implies surprise. For me it's more like they cut the cable on my elevator months ago, on the 110th floor. I just pretended I believed in miracles because it didn't matter if I prepared for the landing or not. It makes no difference if you jump up just before impact or brace yourself against the sides, the cables and pulleys and motor on top of the elevator car are going to crash down upon you anyway and in less than a wink will squish your body till you burst.

That brings to mind a few more words. I just bought a new roll of airmail stamps so have to unload them somehow. Maybe if I plaster the envelope with ten dollars' worth (instead of forty cents), it'll get there before it's too late:

> *Dear Didi,*
>
> *Your cowardice disappoints and angers me. Why are you running away from me and my incarcerated colleague, Eddie?*
>
> *Or maybe it's just me? You haven't told me exactly when he gets out, and you haven't told him about me, so if (when) you decided to see him again, I'd be just another silent skeleton in your closet.*

All you ever say is "Live for the moment" and "I don't
know about tomorrow." Only children and animals can think
like that. You try so hard to avoid conflicts that you create
even worse ones.

Besides, New York is the fashion capital of the world. Don't
sabotage your promising career just on my account.

I still do and will always love you.

Love,
Austin

February 28, 1986

Stewardess

A friend of mine has this friend who's a stewardess. She told
him that she tapes my show just because she thinks I'm sort of
cute. I said it was okay to give her my number.

March 1, 1986

Didi

This, her longest letter, should be her last. I'll give you just the
highlights:

You don't even deserve a response. You were always so
sure all along that you'd win. Well, you didn't. It doesn't
always work out like it does in the movies. "She'll change
her mind, she will, she will, no matter how many times she
warns me." Your romantic wet dream came crashing down
on you. I'm sorry. I tried my best to open your eyes gently.
You knew from near after the beginning my situation but still
took the chance of going full steam ahead. I wish it had
worked out for you. But don't worry, it didn't work out for

him, either. It worked out for just three people. ME. MY-
SELF. AND I. I wish the best for you. I always will. Please
wish the best for me. Who knows if the future will ever bring
us back together. I hope so. Take care, Love, Didi.

R e b u t t a l

I'm going to call everyone I know and date the world. I'm going
to pitch the boss a special series on remodeling the bathrooms of
several months of Playmates.

Okay. It's not like her letter was a total shock. I thought mine
would either push her on a plane and into my arms or push her
away so I could get on with my life. I feel better than I thought I
would, all things considered. Sex with Lynell got me ready. The
Pretenders sing this song: "Back on the Chain Gang."

I called Jewelle just to talk, but she wasn't in. Jenny's mother
gave me her new number in New Orleans. She squealed when
she heard my voice, told the cotton trader she is now living with
to turn down the TV.

M a y   2 5 ,   1 9 8 6

L o s t

I'm writing this on the back of some take-out menu because I
have to write it somewhere. I don't know what I'll do if I don't
find you. I'd been carrying you around with me everywhere to
help me get through Life After Didi. Even though I haven't written
anything because I'm sick of whining, it was nice to know that a
good, long neurotic rant was just a pen stroke away.

However, I don't know why it doesn't hurt as much as it hurt
with Jewelle. The highs with Didi were so very much higher. I'm
disappointed with myself for not hurting even more.

It was weird having a girlfriend, being one of the happy ones for once. I never really felt comfortable. I never thought I could ever really be one of them.

I'm glad the fucking book is lost. Writing hasn't helped me at all. Fuck it. Try and live without reflecting for a while. *Go clean!*

June 6, 1986

Evil Shirley

(I don't know how this book landed behind the stove. I don't remember ever throwing it.)

Evil Shirley called out of the blue last week, then actually showed up. I defrosted the Cornish game hens for old times' sake. The orange glaze camouflaged the freezer burn. We made out on the couch, she even reached her hand into my pants, before she said she had to go. I so wanted to fuck her, just to get it over with, just to put her back in the past where she belongs.

If you haven't screwed someone you want to, there always remains something untidy in your life. Like a good book you lost before you could finish, it's a perpetual anchor to the past. And when it's someone you have grown to hate, you want to free yourself of them all the more desperately. Sex, like a photograph, steals a nugget of their soul.

Lynell

She called while Shirley was over. I feel sorry for her.

June 8, 1986

Mount Ukulele

I can't remember its real name. We've been filming here in Kauai for four days. We share postproduction facilities with a no-money-down real estate swindler. The beach house we fixed up lorded a small pineapple grove by the sea. I'd assumed all of Hawaii was grandmothers tilting poo-poo platters down their flabby, veiny wattles, while their husbands drunkenly hoolaed too near, then tried to dive upon, the undulating grass skirts of young Polynesian girls.

But our corner of Kauai is peace. I need this place so badly now. Today was our last day of shooting. I'd finished my last voice-over ("And as the sun sets on the lovely island of Kauai, we say aloha to the McGullicks' enchanting bungalow by the sea"), and I asked the recording engineer, a local, to point me to the nearest gym.

"Gold's is real far, man. But, hey, if you want a workout, take my mountain bike for a spin up Mount Ukulele [not its real name]."

Twenty-one gears, and every Day-Glo green tube and strut be-stickered with some brand name or a decal of a shark in sunglasses. It looked like a pot farmer's bicycling tractor.

The graveled fire trail tried to gently worm up the ridges of the mountain, but it never lowered close to an easy horizontal. I stood and stomped each pedal like a soldier in mud. I thought of my summer in Atlanta. How, after some girl (what was her name, anyway? Glenn?) had dumped me, I ran till my baby toes bled. I remembered that I had liked it. Then I thought of the Old Man in the Sea. Then I fantasized I was in a brand-new episode of the "Superstars," competing against cheesy, has-been celebrities, network vs. network, in a televised race up Witch Mountain. When my chest started to hurt so badly that I couldn't hear the Jim McKay sports announcer in my head color comment on my race, I braked and leaned off the bike.

Below me sprawled the sea. Above me two-thirds more green mountain.

Surely it would have been faster to walk. The gravel shot from my wheels, digging me more in than up.

"It looks like the mountain is just too much for Austin Jones. If his feet touch the gravel once more before the summit, he will be disqualified and Gabe Kaplan will take the event. . . ."

....

Asshole Gabe Kaplan, shithead . . .

Mr. Kotter kept me going.

Finally, beyond the high ridge up ahead was nothing but royal blueness. I sprinted to the cheers of Charlie's Angels. But the summit was false. The rest of the way up looked like a giant's staircase, and the end of the uphill of each step always pretended to be the mountain's final pinnacle. Sweat watering my hands slipped me off the straight handlebar, and my chest smashed metal.

"Ouch! Unbelievable! Jones didn't fall! He didn't fall!! He slipped right off the handlebar onto an unpadded bolt. He is indeed worthy of the title 'Superstar.' But it looks like he could use a little 'home repair' himself right about now. Let's see that again in slow motion. . . ."

It was forever that I saw from the summit. Forever in every direction. Huge and green folded slopes of forever, then forever blue.

This can't help but change me, at least a little. . . .

My sudden and ferocious hard-on made me grin. I checked anyway, but of course I was alone. I ripped the cord that loosened my shorts, pushed them down and my underwear. I stepped out of their circles and rose my T-shirt off my chest. I gamboled and cavorted for perhaps the first time in my life, clicked the heels of my sneakers like a big, naked black leprechaun. I was alone and happy. I grabbed my dick, and it felt weighty. My right hand worked it well, while my left punched fists in the sky. No one but the world was in my thoughts, and I was fucking it well until I was seized by the swell of an orgasm. An electric jolt lit my arms and the top of my head, my toes dug the volcanic earth, and then she appeared and was everything. Damn you, Didi.

When I reappeared, I was merely a naked loon atop a long-dormant volcano. From imperial to absurd in a series of uncontrollable contractions.

J u n e   1 5 ,   1 9 8 6

M o n i c a

She's not a model. I swear to God. But . . . maybe . . . she is
a highly successful local actress. She recognized me at the gym
on the Lifecycle.

"Hi. I hate to bother you, but my father is, like, your biggest
fan. He's always saying, 'Monica, that young man is a credit to
our race.' So . . . could I have your autograph?"

"Could I have yours? I love you on 'The Young and the
Restless.' "

"You watch the soaps?"

"It's on in the trailer while we're taping."

"Wow."

We went to dinner and a wonderful South African play at the
Public Theater. She's not political at all, but we still had fun.
Afterward, crossing streets, and whenever someone, anyone, approached, I'd slip next to her and guard her with an arm around
her waist. She didn't tense up. She didn't twist away. I took her
home in a cab to her place in Gramercy Park and in the doorway
she reached up on tiptoes, steadied her hands on my shoulders,
and kissed my cheek like a princess.

And she did it. Her eyes made me begin to forget Didi, they
began to drag my heart from the ashes.

E a r l y   t h e   n e x t   m o r n i n g . . .

D i d i

The ringing at three-fourteen in the dark panicked me instantly.
The crackle and periodic *ping!* told me it was long distance.

"Hello?"

I've never known a prettier voice than Didi's.

"Hello? Didi?"

She hung up or was disconnected, because after another electronic *ping* a loud BAH-BAH-BAH-BAH signaled something very wrong and hurt my ear. I tried her old Tokyo number, though I had heard that she had moved.

" もじもじ . . . "

"Hai, sumimasen, Didi Bond, o-kudosai?"

" もたもた . . . "

"Didi Bond."

" もりもり . . . "

"Domo arigato, gosaymashta . . . sayonara."

At least I got my money's worth from that phrase book.

June 27, 1986

Jewelle

She's in town and right this very moment sleeping on my couch. Monica's over at her apartment and a bit pissed. I can't wait till I can relate to Didi as I do to Jewelle. The pain is now just welcome, sweet nostalgia.

July 4, 1986

Monica

We flew to my parents' place for a family reunion on the Vineyard. Didi's ghost never left, but we had a wonderful time anyway. She wouldn't let me make love with her yet, but in the *amacca matrimonial* ("matrimonial hammock") that I'd brought back from the Yucatán slung by the pool, face to face, a heavy blanket over both of us, I taught her how to drive a stick shift as my family barbecued. This is what cool fifth-graders must have done back in Hamden. Monica held me hard as she gently practiced shifting from reverse to overdrive.

Monica

My new apartment is just three blocks from hers. She helped me find it and decorate. I'm proud to say I didn't once lift even a scraper or level. Rickel's Hardware footed the bill for all the remodeling. Either they or True Value or Snap-On keep bugging me to be their spokesman. Didi's boxes only half fill a spare closet.

I see Monica three or four times a week. It's weird; I'm falling in love with her, but she never comes. Last night, after eight minutes of sex, she squeezed me, rolled onto her pillow, and closed her eyes.

"Uh, Monica? I can't sleep. It must be the chocolate in that mudcake."

"Do you want me to stay up with you, honey?"

"No, no. Go to sleep. Sweet dreams."

It wasn't the mudcake. It was *Emmanuelle Goes to Africa* on Cinemax.

Still, she is an angel. Her beauty keeps surprising me. She emanates the soul of pure beauty. No Cuban gangster ex out there ready to kill me, no hangups. I'm not used to this. She takes my arm or flops her legs over mine when we sit as if I were her personal couch. And I love it. She is so sweetly normal and our dating is so sweetly normal that I'm starting to feel sweetly normal myself.

August 1, 1986

Didi

She called. She's in town. She's on her way here with her car. I can take her on today. I feel strong. I just told my agent to turn down a $100,000 contract with True Value. I know what I do has no glory, but if I sell out even more, my already spotty soul will become absolutely irredeemable. My contract is up in January and I'm thinking about a big, big move.

• •

The bluesy bittersweet that clouded the room around us seems to be (or seemed to be before Monica) the timbre of my life. We hugged hello, but weakly. We worked together efficiently, loading her boxes onto a cart lent us by the doorman. I bought her a present, *Sula* by Toni Morrison.

"I didn't get you anything. I'm sorry."

"You weren't supposed to. I just thought you'd like the book. I bet we'll get back together, maybe years from now."

"You'll be married to this new girl."

"I don't think so."

My new chandelier winked reflected light from the small diamonds in the bracelet I'd given her last Christmas.

She held her wrist out to me. "Do you want it back?"

"Of course not."

I'd told Monica that I'd take her to dinner tonight at eight, but Didi and I were running behind. Parked in front of my building, she thanked me for helping her pack. I kissed her lips. She didn't kiss back. I kissed her lips again and again until I began to feel something inside her shift, I think. In her rearview mirror I saw Monica enter my building's alcove.

"Write me from Milan, tell me where you're staying. You know how I love to travel."

I ran to Monica, licking clean my lips and teeth, kissed her with a breathless, "Sorry I'm late."

In my life I have seldom been naughty. But naughty, sometimes, is fun.

August 15, 1986

Monica

We're joined at the hip. Sometimes we bicker like an old married couple, but even that I like. Then, last night, another *personal first*.

"I love you."

I didn't know what I thought it would sound like when a woman finally told me she loved me (the time Didi said it right after multiply orgasming doesn't count), but it sounded scary.

"I love you, too."

I meant it, I guess, but not the way she does. No single person or flower or mountain is prettier on this earth, and she loves me. In the morning, before I sneak out of bed and go downstairs to the car waiting to take me to work, she rolls to me in her sleep and hugs me. Even her subconscious loves me.

Thanksgiving Day 1986

Monica

Of course my folks call her "daughter." I want us to live together before we get married, but she's already lived with three guys and says when you love someone you love them, no need for a test drive. Maybe she's right. She's not educated the way I am, in Latin and history; instead, she understands people better than anyone I've ever known.

December 8, 1986

Monica

"Austin . . . Austin . . . which skirt makes my legs prettiest?"
"Huh? Uh, didn't I go to high school with that girl?"

Christmas Day 1986

Monica

I got her some small diamond earrings. She didn't get me anything like a video camera (I rarely use it, but it's still the best gift I've ever gotten). She got me clothes. Her friends think even off the set I dress like I was adopted by Vermont all-natural ice-cream entrepreneurs (instead of upper-middle-class academicians). She didn't get me new underwear, however. They probably come next year.

Michelle (she's now my associate producer) asked me if Monica were disfigured in an auto accident or fire, would I love her as much, and I didn't know what to say. She is so sweet, so good to me, so giving and loving, but if her beauty didn't still, to this day, disturb the rhythm of my heart, I know that I wouldn't still be seeing her. And Didi and I never squabbled. Our stopping-and-starting relationship was a perpetual honeymoon. Maybe a regular relationship with a regular woman is the only kind that can possibly last. And Monica will be a wonderful mother.

Valentine's Day 1987

Monica

She still hints about marriage. I hint back. Some days I'm resigned to it, but other days I panic that I'm settling for an imperfect fit. On the other hand, maybe I'll never love again as I loved Didi, and if I lose Monica, I'll just spend years and years chasing my tail until I die a suspicious and lonely old bachelor.

If our love life weren't so suburban, maybe I'd be more content. Thrice a month, max, and then only when she says, "Poor baby, you must be very horny." She never seems to get horny. It can't be over fast enough for her. If I was Didi's saxophone player, I'm Monica's kazoo.

When she goes down on me she is happy to make me happy. I, on the other hand, usually fantasize about her Haitian friend Kathy helping her out. Or replacing her. One of Jerrold's latest, Candice, a Kenyan Princeton undergrad, also often materializes on the inside of my eyes.

If Monica and I broke up, I wouldn't die.

March 14, 1987

Monica

I love her so much. We haven't fought in a while. We're either at my place or hers six nights a week. I get up early to edit the day's script, and maybe around ten she'll waddle into the room, screwing the sand out of her eyes like a tiny girl, walking so softly on her perfect little painted toes, wearing my robe with the sleeves rolled up. Without asking, she shoves me away from my desk and sits on my lap, collapses onto my neck. I protect her. She makes me feel strong, traditionally normal.

I never thought I'd become "well adjusted." Perhaps I'll ask her soon. Our babies will be adorable. But I won't let them model, except for the occasional MENSA calendar. I can't believe I'm not going to end up a lonely loser dialing 970-PEEE just to talk to someone on Christmas Eve.

June 1, 1987

Montego Bay

I just got back. Monica was supposed to come. Triumph Broadcasting, the syndicator of our show, had a two-week convention in Jamaica for every independent station in the country. They'd brought down all their "talent" to schmooze the programmers into renewing contracts or finding us better time slots. They call it a "chew and screw" because Triumph tries to stuff them with better food and get them laid by prettier "hostesses" than Tribune or any of the other big "vendors."

The last time I was in Jamaica I was maybe twelve years old, sharing a room with Marquita, Fletcher, and Lauren, my sister, in some bed and breakfast on a hill. All I remember of that trip is a drunk French guy who had tried to pick up Marquita while

Fletcher was paying the bill and a lovely, flirting Jamaican girl exactly my age (and my silence that I even now regret).

This time, our resort was just out of town, a kingdom unto itself. Chandeliers and fountains, white marble and parrots in white cages, was the lobby. Lines of little white lights, like beads, trimmed the edges of the glass elevators. I was the only black in the lobby without a helmet or gold-braided epaulets, at first.

"I wondered where he was ever going to find work again, the interior decorator of Caesars Palace."

I was laughing before I turned.

I still can't believe Lola Banis is not much older than me. I used to think she was the little girl on "Julia," but she swears that was somebody else. I remember pleasuring myself to one of the last episodes of "The Jeffersons" where Lola was a special guest star they met in Hawaii. A falling coconut clonked her on the head, she got amnesia in her bikini, and when Weezy wasn't looking, George tried to convince her he was her boyfriend.

And of course the sexy outtakes from her movie they ran in *Playboy* last year.

She has been out of the clinic six months and just disentangled herself from her scumbag heavy metal drummer. She's trying to make her comeback with an exercise/talk show that Tribune is trying to air this fall.

"When Monica comes down, the three of us will tear this island up!"

"I can't wait to meet her."

When Monica called and said she'd booked this Bacardi ad and couldn't come, Lola fingered my hand.

"Poor baby."

That night we took her jeep to a restaurant overlooking the bay. Jerk chicken and rum punch eaten, she slipped her hand inside my shirtsleeve and massaged my bicep.

I won't say yes, but I won't say no, I'd decided.

"If I weren't in love, I could easily fall in love with you." She was referring to the white Laker she had met in the clinic. She was on the phone to him nightly.

The next day, outside, on a round terrace overlooking the sea, the programmers filled just assembled bleachers. We sat before them on a couch in a fake, outdoor living room. Shannon, the call-in psychic, guessed the TV programmers' car makes and models, then predicted that they would all soon subscribe to his show and air him prime time. Chef Zack cooked regional specialties from "every major market and from quite a few of your smaller markets." Dr. Block sensed tremendous sexual tension between the programmers and the hostesses.

And me? What did a guy who turned down Yale "early admission" do for these men from the heartland whose paunches bowed their green burlap ties? I buzzed in half a telephone book–high stack of Nielsen breakdowns on a table saw.

"Gents, 'Home Repairs' will cut through to your core audience and deliver the time slot."

And they all applauded as if I'd just said "I love Jesus" on Oprah.

Since Lola's show is new, Triumph taped the actual pilot episode down there in Jamaica. After all her very public problems, none of her Hollywood friends would consent to be guests. So believe it or not, yours truly had the highest Q score of any "celebrity" they could afford in the Miami/Caribbean area.

"I've been a big fan of my next guest for, gosh, I don't know how long. Oly, I mean Oliver Stone, first turned me on to this guy when I was finishing up that last little picture of his. Anyway, please give a *Lola* welcome to 'the Fix-it Kid,' Austin Jones!"

I trotted through the potted plants on the stage and air-kissed her cheeks. "Charming home you have here, Lola. But did you ever think how lovely a set of barroom-styled ceiling fans might look in the foyer?"

[Laughter.]

"Oh, you can never stop, can you?!"

She recrossed her legs, and her skirt fell away from her thighs at the slit.

"You're so young to be such an expert on home repairs!"

"Well, some people are born with a silver spoon in their mouths. I guess I was born with a silver hammer. . . ."

[Laughter.]

"No, seriously. I have always loved tinkering, changing the blade on the lawn mower, fixing the other kids on the block's bicycles, helping some neighbor put up a basketball hoop, things like that. 'Home Repairs,' our show, I guess, is just doing what I used to do as a kid, but for a bigger neighborhood."

[Applause.]

"All right, ladies and gentlemen, when we come back Austin and I will have changed into our workout wear, and now you should, too!"

Okay, so they made me wear Lycra cycling shorts with a ballet codpiece and tank top. Weekday daytime is 89 percent female. The rest are sick school kids and unemployed drunk guys who never buy anything but generic beer anyway. We quickly changed in empty rooms on the floor. Lola entered mine without knocking.

"I can't believe they loved your line about a 'bigger neighborhood.' "

"I stole it from Bert Convy on 'Win, Lose or Draw.' "

"What a great ass." Through the Lycra, she held a cheek in her warm, long fingers. "I bet you have a huge cock."

"Places, folks . . . thirty seconds . . ."

The stage manager sat us on mats facing each other, legs veed wide, the bottoms of my socks flush with the bare pink soles of her pretty brown feet.

"Now here's a wonderful stretching exercise you can do with a friend or hubby. . . ."

And she stretched my arms, which pulled my head toward her fragrant crotch. I could smell the wetness of her movie star vagina. Then when I leaned back, she strained herself, mouth first, toward my codpiece.

Logically, it didn't make any sense. Who cares if she was in *Playboy*? My love for Monica has never been stronger. And a vision came to me during the next commercial break: my Monica, her ankles wrapped around the back of some male model after their Bacardi shoot. I've waited twenty-six years for a normal, gorgeous woman to love me. If I cheat on her now, I know someday she'll dump me and I'll end up back in the pit.

July 7, 1987

Monica

Why didn't I sleep with Lola! She's in this straight-to-cable movie every single time I turn on fucking HBO. She plays a lady cop who goes undercover as a stripper to catch a psycho. Every time Monica and I make love (every twenty days!) it's Detective Lola or Loala stretching in Lycra that I come to.

Last week, as I left Monica's apartment, into my head jumped B. B. King's blues. All of a sudden I found myself singing "The Thrill Is Gone."

The strange part of it is, I'm looking forward to being single. Maybe it's as crass a reason as now that I'm even a very minor celebrity, meeting women is easy. And last week Michelle told me my advancing age is a plus:

"You're the last person I should be telling this to. If the National Organization of Women finds out I squealed, they'll kill me. But here goes. Remember how teenage girls like, what was the name of your fantasy at Andover, Jenny? Just as she terrorized the little teenage boys by withholding sex, mid-to-late-twenties guys like you can terrorize late-twenties women by withholding marriage."

And I thought there was nothing positive about growing old.

I'm not as sad now as that night at Bennigan's, when I discovered the identities of Jewelle's loves. I'm not as sad now as when I realized that Didi was never coming back. Maybe I'm about as sad as the last time Evil Shirley stood up my Cornish hens. No. I'm sadder than that. I'm sad because I am not sad enough.

···

August 8, 1987

Monica

I'm nervous. No one's ever broken up with her before. This is going to kill her.

Later...

Her brother stopped by. I didn't do it.

August 9, 1987

Monica

"Austin, I'm feeling lazy. I don't know if I want to come over tonight."

"I think we should probably talk."

"Oh."

"Hi."

"Hello."

"I just . . . you know . . . we fight all the time, it's awful, we decided we wouldn't be together forever, so it's unfair to you to lock you down now."

"You're right."

"I'm so sorry." My throat threatened to close, tears swelled to the back of my eyes.

"Austin, this is the easiest breakup I've ever had. We'll still be friends. I'm not even crying."

She held me as I cried on her neck, then we watched *Top Gun* on HBO. At midnight I thought she'd leave, but she went to my bedroom and got in my bed.

"Do you think this is a good idea?"

"It's late. I don't want to go home by myself."

I held her and we kissed. I fingered her to orgasm.

"One for the road." I push-upped over her.

"No, Austin, it wouldn't be right. . . . I'll pack your things at my house tomorrow."

"Can I keep the black sweater? It's a men's extra-large, anyway."

"That's from Charivari. Forget it."

"You can keep the leather jacket."

"Still forget it. But you can keep my blue shirt."

"Thanks."

August 14, 1987

Martha's Vineyard

I'm happy here alone. I hadn't read a book in months, but in these four days I've read four. Naked all day, I drag on sweats only to shop in town. But I have forbidden myself to masturbate. I'm ready to begin phase III of my life.

Phase I . . . childhood to college.

Phase II . . . postcollegiate anxiety.

Phase III . . . the rest of my life.

And the rest of my life just might be a good one.

September 7, 1987

Miscellaneous

I went out twice with a friend of a friend, and we've kissed sweetly. If anything more happens, it will only be for the sex. But dating again is sort of fun.

Tonight I'm going out with Katrina Billings, an ad sales rep for CBS. And I just spoke with Jewelle. She's single again. I'm thinking of going to Munich in October and asked a friend of Didi's for her address there (she's moved from Milan). Candice, the Kenyan head of the black students at Princeton and one of my friend Jerrold's ex-girlfriends, is coming Saturday. He always told me she had a crush on me, and he was never very serious about her. In fact, he gave me her number. I've left four messages for Lola in Los Angeles. She must be out of town.

Today I was Michelle's dummy for the day, trying on clothes because she says I'm about the same size as her "friend." No one at the show's ever met him, and she still doesn't call him her boyfriend, though they've been seeing each other for eight months. He's some preppy black lawyer, so we went to Brooks Brothers and I modeled ugly, Republican pants for her.

"My price for modeling is that you fix me up with somebody."

"I'm sorry, sir, but we're fresh out of bitchy, anorexic, human coat hangers."

"Michelle!"

"What? You're my best friend, but I wouldn't wish you on Ivana Trump."

I couldn't believe it.

"You look so cute when you pout."

Later, spinning out of the store's revolving doors, Michelle saw her first.

"Oh, hi! You worked with us once a couple of years ago."

"I remember. I keep running into Austin, though he never calls. Here—" And she grabbed my hand and wrote her number on my palm again. The fire started, she disappeared into the store.

"Austin, is there something you'd like to tell me?"

"What can I say? We went to high school together."

I called her, Joanna, right before writing this down. She's back at Yale, getting her masters in international relations. But she lives in New York this semester because she's doing fieldwork at the UN. If she were black, she'd be made to order: tall, part-time Ford model, full-time intellectual. She speaks Portuguese and French and has just started Italian, she quotes James Baldwin and Zora Neale Hurston.

L a t e r . . .

K a t r i n a

At dinner tonight she couldn't eat. I asked her why. She said she always gets nervous on first dates. I kissed her and held her hand. She said I have beautiful hands. She lives in Rye, New York, and by the time the date ended it was midnight.

"I'm on my period. I don't feel so good."

"You shouldn't travel so late, especially in your condition. I've got an extra bedroom. You're welcome to it."

"Well . . . Are you sure? I don't know."

I felt like the evil witch spreading a trail of bread crumbs. And I liked it.

Back at the crib, I broke out the sherry and we made out. After both sides of Sarah Vaughan I pulled back from her lips and suddenly, the shy woman who couldn't finish her food had steam curling out of her ears. I almost laughed. Her lipstick now rouged all of her lower face, and the rattle of her breathing was deep and measured.

"Things are going too fast, too fast."

"You don't want to sleep in that other bedroom. It's a pigsty."

"Austin . . ."

"I'll be good."

"But what about me?"

I lent her a T-shirt but soon coaxed it off. I was possessed by thoughts of sex and angled my hard-on through my underwear over her panties. I sucked on her nipples and she cried. I walked my fingertips over her breasts and she shivered and squeezed her legs together. I felt deliciously devilish. At 2:20 A.M. she rose to draw her tampon from her body.

We screwed ferociously. She locked her ankles behind my back and jerked herself up and down on my dick. I felt perfectly huge, like one of the rotten, sexually confident assholes I had dedicated my adolescence to hate.

September 8, 1987

Candice

We had only met once before, two years ago, but even back then, despite being one of Jerrold's girls, she was someone I lusted after nightly. The entire date tingled. And the idea of making love with two different women on consecutive nights, a *personal record*, appealed to my stupid machismo.

We kissed when we met, then quickly kissed again. Her eyes skittishly studied my left eye, my right. She snatched my hand and held it to her side as we walked. She is twenty.

"You know, your hands are absolutely gorgeous." Her British, boarding school accent made me hard.

Back at home, though, after holding my hand and rubbing my back through dinner and a blues band, she said this:

"I hope you don't mind. I'm not feeling too sexual this evening."

Nevertheless, I enticed her to receive a massage. When I came back from the kitchen with the warmed olive oil, she was already naked on my king-size bed, her body as black and as tight as black wood, her Kenyan butt an edible mountain in my very own bed.

Now naked myself, I massaged the warm oil into her hands, arms, and shoulders, into her back, her butt and legs. Then I greased her thighs until her butt rose to a rhythm. I lay on her and, without entering her, pressed the head of my dick on her clitoris.

In every position we simulated sex, and in every position she eventually came.

"We need to make love. You realize that."

"Austin, I don't want to make love with you because I think I'm in love with a woman at university."

Sometime before graduation, every leftist woman in college "falls in love" with another leftist coed.

"Close your eyes and pretend I'm her."

"I don't think that will work."

"Look, she's not here now and you seemed to be enjoying yourself."

"That's just it, don't you know. I am so confounded."

"You're probably just bisexual. Next week invite your friend down here with you and we'll find out."

She didn't go for it, and we finally slept.

September 11, 1987

Katrina

I was a bit distant from her tonight. I'm afraid she's falling for me and I'm not at all ready.

"I understand, Austin. You just got out of a relationship."

"Exactly."

I said exactly, but that wasn't it, exactly. I know now that it would never, ever work.

I should have let her go back to Rye, but we made out in the taxi to my house.

"Everyone tells me you're a gigolo. They always see you with different beautiful women."

"I'm not a gigolo. I'd *like* to be one, but I'm not."

"I could see you dating starlets."

"Me?"

Back home she didn't really want to make love again.

"Things are going too fast."

"Too late."

I had a taping in the morning, so afterward we went to bed.

At some dead hour in the middle, middle of the night I thought I felt fingers around my dick. She had pulled another condom out of my drawer and had it on me and had me inside of her before I was even conscious. She ground her hips on me, sucked up my dick, and squeezed an explosion of joy from it that made my head tingle and sweat spontaneously erupt from all of my pores.

This just might work out after all.

September 15, 1987

Joanna

At her apartment we spoke Italian all night long. I took her hand. I can't believe I didn't know her at Andover. But she says she was an ugly duckling, too. A gangly, JV basketball failure. She was one of only two whites on our team. Anyway, fuck the world. I like her a lot and don't care who stares.

September 17, 1987

Monica

If she wanted to get back together, I would. But I called her and she told me she's off to Paris with a new "friend."

Later...

Katrina

We went to the movies, then I sent her home. I wanted to see what we had when we didn't have sex. Not too much. I feel sorry for her. I know exactly what she's going to go through.

Later...

Candice

While I was talking to Katrina to make sure she got home all right, Candice called on the other line. She never says who it is, so I end up saying things like "Hello! How . . . how's it going?" waiting for the girl to mention school, or the TV studio, or the UN, something to reveal her identity. When I told her I couldn't talk right now she slammed down the phone.

September 22, 1987

Joanna

"Ebony and I-vo-ry . . . !"

I am so fucking happy!! I picked her up at her door to go to some party for some photographer she knew. She looked fantastic, like Paulina Porizkova. The party was in a swank loft in Chelsea, and every famous model of the world was there. Joanna was still one of the very most beautiful. It's funny, I never thought so before. I guess because she's sort of a tomboy usually, wears jeans and no makeup. Tonight, her six feet in a miniskirt, dancing and flirting with me, falling on me as Didi did at Nell's, gave me joy. The DJ had Marley sing "Could This Be Love." I kissed her right there on the dance floor, and right there on the dance floor she smiled.

"I had fourteen dates before I met Vance in college, and you're my fourteenth since I broke up with Donnel, my last boyfriend."

We shared a taxi to the East Side, and en route she massaged my hands.

"Has anyone ever told you your hands are gorgeous?"

"Why, no . . ."

My stop was first, and I started for my wallet.

. . . .

"I wonder what the inside of a home repair expert's apartment looks like?"

"My dad is a general contractor back in Lincoln . . . Nebraska. I told him I was going out with you, and he got all excited."
"He's a very liberal guy."
"He's used to it by now, but I'd better be going home."
"Nope."
"How are you going to stop me?"

I lay at her feet as she massaged my neck. Her fingers seemed almost as long as my own. I closed my eyes and purred. I felt her shadow pass over my eyelids. I opened my eyes just as she leaned her long neck down to me like a doe to water and laid a kiss to my lips.

I convinced her to stay over, promised I'd be good, then kissed under her black hair, down her neck, until I saw a shiver shoot down her side.

"I want to know you inside, before I know you inside of me."
"Nicely put."
"It's not a line."
"I know it's not a line, but people are so damned careful, too careful. I feel something here, I feel joy with you, and if you leave now, we'll both feel disappointed because a perfect moment, something that happens to people only rarely, was spoiled. And what's worse, we spoiled it ourselves because Miss Manners wrote somewhere that nice girls don't on the first date."
"Nicely put."

In my bedroom I unzipped her minidress and sailed it to a chair. She's six feet tall and as curvy as a short girl. We fell to the bed kissing, and my heart was not only moving faster than my head, but moving faster than my dick. She unbuckled my pants, and when I was just in my underwear she stopped.

"Your body's too beautiful for BVDs. You need silk boxers."

We kissed more than a thousand times. She went down on me so hungrily that I was scared. I twisted into the sheets and stroked her shoulders.

. . . .

"A-a-a-a-are you getting tired?"

"You have a beautiful cock."

Then I went down on her and she came.

"Would you like to make love, Joanna?"

"Let's sleep."

In the morning, she'd changed her mind. Not since Didi had it been so long and so wonderful. I thought Katrina and Candice were multiply orgasmic, but Joanna is truly. Riding atop me, she'd rock spastically and in thirty seconds she'd come. Then she'd go slow. Thirty seconds later she'd come again. I don't know how many times she did this, but at least a dozen. Then I rolled her over and pinned back her three-foot-long legs with my shoulders. She anchored her hands on my butt, yanked me into and out of herself. I loved my body, what my strength could do. I felt like those very mortal and ordinary Trojan men hiding inside that magnificent wooden horse.

We rested, but I stayed inside her.

"Have you read Charlie Mingus's biography, *Beneath the Underdog?* He seemed like he could make love like you do."

"I've got it, but I haven't read it yet. Maybe I'll go get it right now."

I faked to leave, but she gripped me with her thighs.

"You're not going anywhere till I let you."

From seven to eleven we made love again. I can't remember it ever having been more wonderful or honest.

"Austin, when I saw you again, coming out of Brooks Brothers of all places, I just couldn't help myself. I can't believe I was so bold. Your friend must think I'm a slut. But I just kept looking at your hands and imagining them on my body."

"I've never been talked to like this before."

"Do you like it?"

"I love it."

"But we've got awful timing."

"What do you mean?"

"Donnel, my old boyfriend, is coming into town and he'll be staying over this weekend, on the couch."

"Oh."

"We haven't been together since April. It's no big deal."

"You could stay at my house while he's here."

She shrugged.

At breakfast at the Cuban-Chinese, we just stared at each other. I'm not calling Katrina anymore, and Candice is coming in town tonight for a concert (the morning after), but this will be our last date.

We held hands waiting for her cab home. She growled like a dog and kissed me hard. It was as if we'd kissed for years and always, always enjoyed it.

I don't care if my friends freak out that I'm dating a white girl. (Though Joanna is *very* white. She couldn't even pass for part Italian. But at least she's not blond.)

September 24, 1987

Joanna

I'm dying inside! I've tried not to call her, but I have, twice. She has yet to call back. Donnel's a fourth-string lineman for the Houston Oilers and, with a name like that, undoubtedly Black Like Me. If she goes back to him, I'll die.

She called.

"If I just met a guy and he suddenly said his ex was staying over for the weekend, I'd be pissed."

"And I am. But I, I shouldn't be telling you this. I don't want to scare you. But I keep thinking about you."

"Me too."

....

September 26, 1987

Joanna

Sleep isn't happening. I keep blowing my takes at work. I just met her, this makes no sense. I'm more upset with the thought of losing her after one night than I was about Monica, whom I'd known for over a year! I bought a Frank Sinatra tape just to hear "Witchcraft." And a Nina Simone. I'm sure he's out of her life. She's so strong and smart.

12:06 A. M.

Finally! It's bad, but not awful.
"Well?"
"It's like he never left."
"Oh."
"That's good and bad. We fought. Our relationship was awful back then, and nothing's changed."
I didn't have the courage to ask her now many times she came on his hips.

September 27, 1987

Joanna

I'm on my way to her place. I'm nervous. But these silk boxers feel nice. I'm battling my best, though losing the strength, to keep my heart corraled. It so wants to go out and play.

Analogy #2:
I'm like a moth who knows the ultraviolet bug zapper means a sizzling death. "Don't worry, guys, I'm just going a tiny bit closer to take a better look. You know, research. Ultraviolet's my favorite

color. Hey, c'mon. Don't worry. I went to college. . . . *Ahhh—* " *Zzzzapp!* That minute burst of smoke was me.

We made out a bit, but she wouldn't let me spend the night.
"We went too fast, Austin."
"Too late."
"No, it's not. We need to get to know each other better."
"But—"
"I can't believe you're still so romantic and trusting after all the heartaches you've told me about."
"It's the only good part of my life."

October 1, 1987

Joanna

I am crazy about her!! A model getting a masters. What more can you want? Friday we hung out, but she didn't want to stay over. We fooled around and she went down on me, but she didn't want to make love so went home even though it was past two. She wanted to slow everything down and doesn't want our relationship based purely on sex. Saturday I stayed over at her place, but again she didn't want to make love. Little by little, however, we did more and more, until, sixty-nining, we grazed each other like goats. That's when the phone rang and rang and rang until her machine beeped.

"Hello! *Hello!* Joanna? Are you home? If you're in the shower, *pick up the phone!* This is long distance, Joanna. Oh, well, now you know I called."

I've never heard a voice so deep and so black. Barry White would need surgery to get a voice so deep. I didn't ask. But I did try harder. To make her happy. I rotated back up to face her, and I was never harder, bigger or gentler. I imagined him watching us and weeping. She later said she'd never come from so deep a place. Even with Didi it took a few times to get our bodies truly comfortable with one another, but with Joanna it was comfort at first sight.

Since we've made love again she's back with me. She said she's not usually so driven by urges, but once, after not having seen an old boyfriend for months, she picked him up at the airport and they rutted right there in long-term parking.

"Donnel?"

"Yes. Listen, Austin. Here's this little letter I wrote you. Why don't you read it at home."

Uh-oh, I remember thinking.

October 5, 1987

Joanna

Dear Austin,

Mobuto Sese Seko, the leader of Zaire, is speaking before the entire GA (General Assembly). As you know, he's one of the richest men in the whole world while his country is one of the poorest. I should be listening to him more intently, but he's a creep and his words make my skin crawl and my stomach turn. Only Ron-boy Reagan makes me sicker. I can't think about world affairs anyway because I keep thinking about you.

But don't get carried away. I don't want to encourage you too much, not yet at least.

We need to slow down. We were crazy. No, you're crazy, but that's one of the things I like most about you.

You don't know how hard it was not to stay over with you those first few nights this week. I shouldn't tell you this, but if you had just stood in front of the door, I would have weakened. I hate to be weak.

I've got a lot of male friends here in New York. Some of them like me, and I'm going to tell them that I'm not available "that way," but I'd still like to be their friends. I hope you're not going to be too possessive. But you seem like the jealous type. I know I am.

I think too much. I should just have fun. I love your touch, your loving, and talking with you late into the night between our bouts in the bed.

mil besos,
Joanna

P.S. Rereading this letter, I wanted to throw it out and write a colder one, but this is really how I feel.

People had always assumed that since I'm (sort of) preppy, I'd marry a white girl. I spent my whole life proving them wrong, then *wham!* I'm zapped by a brilliant farm girl/model/diplomat-in-training from Nebraska! Our little mulatto (no, "mixed race"— mulatto means "little mule") children will be smart, tall, and beautiful! I deserve this happiness.

After Didi I didn't think I could feel this way again. However it ends, at least I know I'm alive again. I feel delicious.

October 30, 1987

Joanna

October hasn't been a great month for us. I've been mailing her love letters, we've been sleeping together, but I can smell poison in the air.

"Austin, I'll be right over, but I can't spend the night. I've got eight hundred pages of reading before I do that catalog in Texas Saturday."

"I've got a lot of work myself. We're shooting in North Carolina this weekend."

When the doorman buzzed, I wasn't sure if it was her or Indian food (her favorite). But as soon as I kissed her I felt she sucked out my insides and left an ugly cave.

"Austin, you've been sort of scaring me this month."

"I'm pretty romantic."

"Your love letters are spectacular, but—"

"Hey, listen, it's not just you. I fall in love easily."

"Gee, thanks."

"You know what I mean."

"I told you last week. I think you're in this deeper than I am . . . and I think I want to see other people."

"Donnel."

"Whoever."

Then the food arrived, but I couldn't bring the curry to my lips.

"You're so quiet."

"I'm not very happy."

"I'm sorry. . . . He fractured his wrist. I'm going to check in on him in Houston after the Neiman-Marcus job in Dallas."

"I figured."

"Don't be so glum. You're so pessimistic. The glass is either half-empty or half-full depending on how you look at it."

"You mean we can either just be friends or I can time-share."

"Austin, don't . . ."

"Yes."

"What does that mean?"

"It means I don't want to lose you."

She stood up, I stood up, and we held each other.

"You're pretty lucky. Two big black guys . . . you'd probably like us both at the same time."

And something in the back of her blue eyes flashed.

We kissed a bit, but she still wouldn't stay the night. I didn't feel like trundling out half-baked philosophies and half nelsons to coerce her stay.

I need to date other women right away. I love her, but I do fall in love easily. Let me see if I can sleep.

4:13 A. M.

The real bitch of it is, I'm not so hung up on beauty anymore. She's not nearly as pretty as Monica or Didi. Maybe this is a step in the right direction.

Enough. Now I mean it. Get some rest.

4:41 A. M.

I've been trying to rub my heart through my sternum with the edge of my hand for hours. I'm second to him and her work! She went home tonight to finish all her reading to be with him! I've got to find somebody else during the week she's fucking him. Continuing to see her is a bad idea. Remember Kierkegaard's essay on Abraham and Isaac?

The only way Abram could muster the strength to obey God and kill his son was to convince himself that he didn't love his son anymore. Then when God said, "April Fool! Just kill a goat. Here's a quarter, go buy your son some ice cream," Abram (now Abraham) was left with a son he no longer loved. To make it through these days I'll have to convince myself that I don't love her. But if she does come back to me after realizing Donnel's a creep, will I be too turned off to care? No, my only choice is to see other women. 1. It's insurance against further heartbreak, and 2. it just might make her jealous. You never win anything from a position of weakness. As long as I chase after her, she can chase after him. Good night. I feel better.

October 31, 1987

Joanna

She called me.
"Morning!"
"Hi, Joanna."

"Are you having second thoughts about our arrangement?"

"Yes. But I'm going to date other people, too, and we'll just play it all by ear."

"Exactly. And when we're together it will be just like it always was."

"Which was pretty fucking great."

"Exactly. . . . You know, your problem is you think too much."

"Oh, thank you."

"I've got to go shop for this trip. Can you believe that panties at Victoria's Secret cost twenty-five bucks?"

"You're buying new lingerie for *him?*"

That night, when I picked her up at her house, she turned a bit (I think) so we just kissed on the cheek. Don't be paranoid, and don't whine, I cautioned myself. Later, at dinner we talked a lot about nothing.

"It's funny how paranoid I can get. Like when we kissed hello, I panicked that you had tried to turn your cheek."

She looked down at her plate and popped into her mouth so much hijiki seaweed that it sprouted out between her lips.

After dinner she took my arm, and in the cab she took my hand, but in front of her house she did not invite me up. She kissed me on my cheek and left. As my cab pulled away I screamed, *"You fuck!! You hurt me so fucking much!!"*

The cabbie didn't swerve, didn't slow. But his sneer was framed in the rounded rectangle of his rearview mirror.

She said she'd give us a chance, but she's not. Now here at home I ache to call her but know I'll just beg. My whole body leans to the phone. I'm tired of living. I want to sleep forever, but I dread the bed.

5:04 A. M.

I woke up crying. *Joanna, what about your letter, what about our first night when you seduced me? Are you cold because you don't want to hurt me? Or because you changed your mind. The*

. . . .

fourth-string jocks and Cuban gangsters of this world don't deserve to win.

I only owned three *Playboys* but stuffed them to the bottom of my tall kitchen trash can. My cable TV sex tape was only twenty-five minutes long, but I taped over everything with Shannon, the call-in psychic.

5:15 A. M.

We talked more profoundly on our first date than our last. If we are going to make a fair try of it, then let's lie down together, clothed if you need that, and let's tell each other our dreams.

I still can't sleep, and more words, more rehearsals, come to me, but I'm not going to write them all down. They're pretty much more of what you've already got.

I can accept the half-full glass, but now it's only a quarter full. Tell me the truth and let me go, that will hurt me the least. I don't blame myself. I think I've been kind to you.

She's so fucking weak. I know that if we slept together again, she'd come around. She's bad news.

Without these pages tonight I don't think I'd have made it. At least while I'm actually writing I don't need to massage my chest.

We barely know each other, but what we do know so far we like. So why chop down a flower that has yet to bloom?

I told everyone she's my girlfriend. I can't tell them now that I've failed again.

I'm the guy you told your dad about. I'm the guy of the lucky fourteenth date. I'm the guy whose hands you imagined on your body. I'm the guy you talk with better than with anybody else. Don't be weak. Ours could be the kind of romance they write about.

I've got a plan. We're both leaving town tomorrow, but I promised her I'd call before her flight. Now I won't. She will imagine a strength in me. Maybe it will even ruin her days with Donnel. Maybe she won't be able to come. Let her miss me. Only the strong are liked.

Yet on my eyelids I still see this image of her beauty: her hands steady her hips, and her belly is round like a moon, tight with my child.

Here comes the sun.

November 2, 1987

Joanna

> *Unrequited love's a bore,*
> *And I've got it pretty bad,*
> *But when you're with someone you adore,*
> *It's a pleasure to be sad.*

I dug out this old Billie Holiday tune and played it all morning long. Of course I barely made the plane. I'm reading the script as we fly down to Winston-Salem, North Carolina, for three days. We're doing a special episode on how to renovate a barn. I don't know why anybody doesn't just stand up and pronounce me a New York pseudointellectual phony. I don't know shit about barns. She leaves for Texas tonight.

I used to think she was perfect for me, tailor-made (except her color). Actually, we had great sex and her body is fantastic and she's politically correct. I still want more out of life. Still, the good days of my infatuation were great. I was blissful accompanied by her abstraction. Maybe imaginary love is the only kind that's good. You are young and single, strong, rich, handsome, smart, funny, famous (even though for a stupid reason), and sexy. You make love very well. A high-fashion model once called herself your saxo-phone. I'm letting her go. The heartache stops at 35,000 feet. *Let the healing begin now.*

Winston-Salem is not the South anymore. It looks exactly like the shopping malls of Hamden. We're not shooting until tomor-row, so I have the whole day off. Here, in the Holiday Inn, the tears came back. I've got to realize that I'm still too young to have wanted what I wanted from her. Success came too young. I'm coasting now. . . . *Stop it.* . . . I just cried again. I don't even know her, not really.

I just called her.
"Hi."
"You made it."
"Yep . . . listen, I've been thinking, and I think it's better if we not see each other anymore at all." Did I hear her begin to choke on a cry?
"Oh . . . that's a surprise. I was just thinking that it was all just bad timing. I'm not the ogre you think I am."
"Oh! Well, then what do you want to do?"
"What do you want to do?"
"I don't know. . . . Maybe we shouldn't decide anything until you come back from Texas."
"That's good."

Stupid! Stupid! Stupid! Stupid!

November 4, 1987

Aunt Alva

She lives in nearby Greensboro. I'd only met her once, at Grand-pa's funeral a decade ago, but I always remembered her eyes. She was even then as old a person as I'd ever known, and half her face was even then slack from a stroke. But she never missed my show and often wrote me fan mail. I went over after work.

"You're coming over? That would be just swell. I'm in the route 44 cloverleaf, 339 Dwight Street."

She really does live inside the cloverleaf. The city barreled the highway bypass right through her once lively and optimistic black neighborhood. The on-ramp curves so close to her house that it cuts off a corner of her yard. She was one of four black women at U Penn back in 1924. She came down here from Philadelphia café au lait society because it's the only place they'd place a black French and Latin teacher.

She must have been waving from her stoop long before I saw her. She didn't look any older to me than she did ten years ago.

"Welcome to my castle, Mr. Movie Star."

She fried me a steak and fixed sweet potatoes, green beans, root beer, and white bread with margarine. She wasn't hungry, so I assembled just one dented, tin TV tray and noisily worked it through the back door, then the screen door. The trees were already naked and sad, and the light already wintered, low and gentle and distant. Still, the sun let us sit outside on the back stoop, for most probably the last time of the year. The tractor-trailers, UPS trucks, and van conversions noisily encircling her tiny two-bedroom almost sounded like waves on the beach.

"You say you came to success too soon, that it just fell upon you without work. And you say that now you're coasting and that this little girl represented your dream of married life before you were ready for it, though when you were with her you thought you were ready for it."

"Exactly."

"You're crazy."

"Ma'am?"

"You've probably got seventy years more of living to do, but here you are talking older than me. At this rate you'll have your heart broken dozens of times before you rest. You're a romantic. Your uncle was a romantic. It runs in the family."

"You know I was adopted."

"But are you loved?"

"Uh . . . I guess so. Though I haven't talked with my parents in a while."

"You should. Marquita and Fletcher know why you changed your name to Jones, of course. You hurt them."

"I'm sorry."

"You're telling the wrong relative."

"I'm sort of messed up."

"Maybe you should seek professional help. Your great-uncle Hannibal, he was crazy as Crazy Cat but wouldn't talk to anybody about it until he turned the shotgun on himself."

"Wow. I never knew that."

"You shoulda come down sooner."

"I haven't wanted to kill myself since high school."

"That's good."

"Maybe it will all work itself out. She used to like me a lot."

"So you really think you can share her? Can men share women? I know that some women can share men, but I've never heard of it the other way around. But I guess it depends on how you look at the glass, half-empty or half-full."

I smiled. "She said the same thing."

"Then she's a sharp little girl."

November 20, 1987

Joanna

She's been back a few days but just now called. She's on her way over. I found a long piece of hair on my head from a waitress or somebody. I pulled it off, then put it back on in a more obvious place. It's freezing in the apartment and my lips are cold. I collected hot tap water in my palm, dipped in my lips to warm them for her. I'm trying to steady my breathing.

It wasn't so bad. Kiss on the cheek at first, then later in the cab we were making out. We were soon joking like old times. In front of my door I asked her:

"Would you like to come up?"

"Not tonight, but maybe soon."

November 28, 1987

Joanna

"No-o!"

"I'm sorry."

"For God's sake, Austin, don't apologize."

"We used to kiss . . . I don't know."

"Look, it's not you. It's me— Well . . ."

"Well, what?"

"So . . . you were a nerd in high school. Who wasn't? And now you sort of look like an athlete, and most of your pimples went away, fine. But how long is that going to be an excuse?"

"What do you mean?"

"I don't know . . . nothing. . . . I'm sure you were, uh, you are so proud to be dating these little model girls and you thought that would change your insides, but it didn't. There are a million miserable ex-nerds out there collecting model trophies."

"I don't think of you as a trophy."

"I'm not saying that, but, but maybe you've done *too* good a job at convincing yourself that you're sexy. I mean, you know you have a pretty body and hands, but ultimately, big deal."

"I know I'm sort of arrogant sometimes, but—"

"That's just it. You're not *really* arrogant. But you try so hard to be, which is worse, and such an easy bubble to burst."

"Thank you, Herr Dr. Tobin."

"I hate these kinds of conversations."

"Then let's stop."

"It's just that all the massages, all the 'You can sleep in my guest bedroom, my dears,' they're all as phony as saying 'trick of the trade' all day long, which you admit is bullshit and not good enough for someone as smart as you."

"At least you give me that."

"Oh, I don't like how you're making me feel. I don't know. I'm just a big girl. You're what, six feet?"

"Six two."

"Really? Well, in heels I'm at least that, and my other boyfriends have all been, bigger."

"Bigger?"

"Uh, yeah . . . bigger."

Oh, my God, I'm not big enough! I never thought that words I'd said to myself so many times would, when said by another about me, carry such weight. How big can his schlong really be? I mean, it was relatively easy to enter her, not like with some girls who need to be well lubricated beforehand, but I thought I fit Joanna fine, didn't rattle around like the last pencil in a blind man's cup.

My poor little wiener schnitzel. I'm back. I'm back in the pit. I liked myself when I was arrogant. A semi-well-known "stickman" in the tristate area. Suddenly I can't remember a single erection.

December 3, 1987

Joanna

She's over right now. Her toes are under my butt. She's come over to study geopolitical theory. While I am writing this she thinks I am doodling notes for my lawyer for our upcoming contract renegotiation. (We found out Bob Vila pulls down $230 grand, not including endorsements!) It was zero degrees outside, so she showed up in three pairs of sweat pants and two jackets. Now she's just wearing tight black leggings. I keep forgetting about her body, what fun it had with mine. I want her. Yet she's already told me she's going home tonight. I'm freezing here in my tank top, but I'm trying to turn her on. I force myself not to kiss her, not to touch her, though I ache to. I sense that somewhere in this night is the possibility of our making love. Then everything will fall into place as before. Remember, once she said you had a beautiful cock. Forget that bigger crap. It ain't the meat, it's the motion. Keep repeating that. She hasn't had sex in weeks. This is in your favor.

I just fixed us tea, delivered it to the coffee table.
"What service, Austin. I should marry you."

She sees my profile. My profile's not good. I lick my lips and pout them a bit, furrow my brow to look smart. She could just peep over my arm and read all about herself. Maybe that would be good. It worked for Jewelle years back. Sometimes I wish I weren't crazy. I dangled my fingers that she had once compli-mented right in front of her face, then I laid my hand on the couch right behind her. I just pulled it back to write about doing same.

She just reached up and kissed my hand!! The warmth from her lips buzzed straight to my heart. I wanted to write about it right away, but I didn't want to tip her off. Instead I counted to three hundred and am just now reporting the event.

Later she got up, came back, and curled in my lap. I gave her a back massage on the rug, then started kissing her neck. Her beautiful butt, amazingly full for a six-foot-tall white girl, got to rising. She massaged me, then had to go. I'm the Old Man in the Sea. And I'm reeling her in.

....

D e c e m b e r 5, 1 9 8 7

J o a n n a

She invited me up. We kissed and cuddled, then I said this to her:
"I better be going home now."
I'm very proud of me.

D e c e m b e r 6, 1 9 8 7

J o a n n a

I called in for my messages and heard this:
"Ciao, caro. Vieni a cena a casa mia stasera alle otto." ("Hi,
sweetie. Come over for dinner at my house at eight.")
"I love you!" I yelled at the phone. She's learning Italian so
fast. But she leaves tomorrow for the holidays.
I bought her a collection of Zora Neale Hurston's short stories,
signed it, "Maybe something wondrous will come. I feel something
stirring. Merry Christmas, Love, Austin." And I bought her a
stocking at Woolworth's and ironed on her name. I was going to
stuff it with candies she could take with her to Nebraska.

L a t e r ...

**O v e r a n d
D o n e W i t h ...**

We kissed and hugged at the beginning of the meal. The risotto
was delicious. At the end she said this:
"Senti. Non posso mai essere la tua ragazza." ("Listen. I can't
ever be your girlfriend.")
"I know. You think of me like a reserve parachute because you
know Donnel is going to hurt you again."

"You're probably right."

She kissed my cheek, then kissed my hands. I had to push past her to leave.

The phone's ringing right this moment. It's twelve thirty-three. It must be her. I'm going to let the machine pick it up.

"I just called to see if you got in okay. . . . I'm sorry."

I just put the book I'd ruined with a dedication into my own bookshelf. Then I pulled it out again, slowly dragged the ruined page clear out of the paperback's glue binding.

I shouldn't have worn those fucking silk boxers.

December 8, 1987

Fired

I don't fucking believe it! Sure my agent asked for a big raise, but I gave the stupid show the best years of my life. I'm "the Fix-It Kid," for chrissakes.

"Austin, it's not you, you understand. It's not even the money, because we go way back and we could have ironed this thing out. It's just that this show is getting so darned expensive to produce, it was killing us. We had no choice but to think up a new format. Gosh, we're all so sorry over here, but you'll land on your feet. Hell, you're a celebrity now. You could make a nice living off of 'Win, Lose or Draw' and 'The New Hollywood Squares.' "

Next season the idiots aren't going to have a host at all, just real homeowners getting pointers from real contractors. Michelle cried when she found out. Then she quit.

My agent is pretty sure Fox will bankroll a new show around me. But I don't know. I need to ask Joanna about graduate programs. I want to hear Joanna's sounds.

....

December 27, 1987

Marquita, Fletcher, and Lauren

Marquita had to deliver a baby on Christmas morning, so we didn't open presents until six. Last night I heard my own kid sister doing it with her kraut fiancé in her pink canopy bed. I'd learned to turn a water glass to the wall in college. It never would have occurred to me that somebody as uptight as Lauren could be so multiply orgasmic. I did get a little bit of a hard-on. I mean, *genetically* there would be no problem. And she is not unattractive. And since I'm pretty sure she still doesn't know that we're not really related, I am sometimes tempted, especially after she's refused to let me watch whatever it was I wanted to watch on the TV room's television, to freak her out by shoving my tongue down her throat.

Marquita and Fletcher leave for Barbados tomorrow morning, so we had to take down the tree today. Sweeping up needles, I was, when they caught up with me.

"Son. I know this getting fired has knocked you for a loop, but it might be just the perfect thing for you right now."

"Listen, Fletcher—"

"Could you please call me 'Dad' again? The seventies have *been* over."

"And can I be 'Mom' again, baby?"

"Sure, but I don't want to get into it right now. This is not a good time in my life, and I will not become a better person because of any of this."

"But, son. . . ."

"What, Mom?"

"Do you think that maybe you'll change your name back to your old name now?"

"I never changed my driver's license or anything. I just put 'AKA Austin Jones' on my checks."

∙∙∙

"If you want to find her, we could maybe help."

Lauren was out showing Adolph the sights.

"I don't want to get into this right now."

"Well, son, when can we talk? You hardly ever come back home anymore."

"Your father and I love you so much. We're so proud of the man you've grown up to be. And if you want to try and track down Shawniqua Jones, as I said, maybe we could help you."

"Mom. This isn't a made-for-TV movie. That doesn't matter to me anymore. Really. It wouldn't help. You're my only parents. I'm my only me. I do love you both, and I know no strange woman can fix me."

"I've told you before that we know a lot of good therapists."

"Dad, I'm trying to get better. I'm trying to work things out. And . . . well . . . I've been wondering . . . is it too late to apply to the Afro-Am doctoral programs at Duke and Cornell?"

"Yahoo! It's never too late. Hell, you know I trained both their department heads."

So school starts in September. I'll have to be up in Ithaca in August to find a place to live. I just wonder if I can pay the FBI to change my face, my hair, and my name and shorten my vocal cords like they do in the witness relocation program. Because the first smelly, bearded TA that says, "Too bad 'the Fix-It Kid' can't fix his oral examinations" gets a two-fingered poke to the throat.

Between now and then I'm going to move to a little beachside shack in Brazil's El Salvador de Bahia. I'm going to pack just two T-shirts, two pairs of shorts, and a steamer trunk filled with books. I want the little children/thieves in the surrounding *favela* to chase after me shouting "*Bom dia, U Professor!*" every time I ride my forty-year-old motorcycle into town. I'll fill the sidecar with plantains and powdered milk, then rumble back home. One day a girl, the village beauty, will eye me as I enter the general store. The rains that season will be warm, violent, and loud. As I start to drive off I will have to brake suddenly, skid dangerously, for she will now be standing in the rainy twilight in the middle of the road, barefoot, black, and wet. The first lesson in my Portuguese book will have already taught me *"Quantos anos você tem?"* ("How old are you?"), but I will know better than to ask. . . .

Stop!! Stop right there. You're going to Brazil, but you're not going to touch anyone, ever. Six months of monastic solitude. No condoms, no *Playboys*. Do this and you will return strong and new. When you return, no more taping cable soft-core, or CNN's "Style with Elsa Klench." (It's turned into your own twisted "Home Shopping Club" for models.) From now on, if a woman's *ever* been paid for her beauty, she's off limits.

I'm going clean.

January 11, 1988

Austin

I feel like a happy, holy monk. I'm staying in my parents' cottage on the Vineyard until my flight to Bahia. Only the back of the house has radiator heat, so I spend at least an hour a day splitting a jagged mountain of firewood in the backyard. There's just enough of a frosting of snow to cover the sand on the beach. The dead dune grasses, now dried and brown, rise out of the white and gesticulate in the wind. The wind never stops and is heavy, wet, and slow because it is full of the sea. Often the scalloped lines on the sand of that day's tides are etched on the shore in fragile ice, frozen ocean, full of holes. The jazzy oboe melancholy of a summer resort emptied, fastened down, and boarded up for winter is how I've felt nearly all of my life (except those brief periods in which I was in love). So when the freezing rain rattles my windows it rattles me, too—pleasantly.

I wake up at six-thirty and listen to Portuguese language tapes until lunchtime. I feel so delicious anticipating my flight from here, to New York, to São Paulo, to Salvador de Bahia February 16! I'm proud of myself for changing my life.

After lunch I read. First it was Ellison's *Invisible Man* (again), and all of Toni Morrison (again). Now I'm working my way through the Russians. Last week was *Crime and Punishment,* and this week is *Anna Karenina. Don Quixote* and *Moby Dick* await. I feel myself getting smart again with every turn of the page.

I cook and I whistle.

January 20, 1988

You

Besides that time I let Jewelle read the entries about her, I've never gone back and read you. *Anna Karenina* was actually pretty boring, and you were just lying there on this coffee table an artist neighbor made for us out of grayed driftwood and glass.

The stuff when I was a little kid at Andover is now pretty funny. Jewelle and Liz seem like a lifetime ago. Evil Shirley, however, I could cheerfully stuff in a microwave. But I trembled when I read Didi's and Joanna's entries. My words made me remember heartbeat for heartbeat what I used to feel. Twice I pitched you at the fireplace but each time missed. Naked, I howled and danced on the rug.

As a sixteen-year-old I once wrote, "In History 35 last week we learned that the Puritans kept diaries and would read them only after many years, hoping to notice the hand of God shaping the long run of their lives. Maybe I too will notice a pattern and stop screwing up." So now I notice a pattern, but it's one of realizing the mistake, analyzing it, writing about it—then going out and doing it again anyway, time after time. But what did I expect? Everyone knows that a heart and a dick can't read.

I think I might go home early. I'd like to see my folks and friends before I take off for South America.

....

February 11, 1988

A Call

"Mr. Jones?"

"Uh, sort of."

"Please hold for Mr. Wright. . . ."

"Austin Jones! Sorry to disturb ya. Your agent gave me your home phone number. My name's Brad Wright, general manager of the Playboy Channel. We were wondering if you'd be interested in helping us develop a home repairs show?"

"Ha. Ha. Ha. Good one. You're a friend of Michelle's, right? No. Wait. You're her boyfriend. Nice to finally meet you even if it is only on the telephone. Could you put her on?"

"Um . . . you don't understand. We're looking to expand into early evening programming."

"Anything you say, *Brad.*"

"Have I caught you at a bad time?"

"No, it was funny. And I can use a good laugh these days."

"Oh, God, I hate when this happens. Listen. Call Los Angeles information and get the number for Playboy Enterprises."

"Good afternoon. Is Mr. Wright in?"

"Austin . . . can I call you Austin?"

"I'm so embarrassed. Sorry about that, Mr. Wright."

"Call me Brad and don't worry about it. You should see what I have to go through every time I use the company credit card. But listen. We'd like to fly you out here to meet with everybody and kick around some ideas for a new show."

"Uh . . . I leave in five days for vacation, and around August or September I have a commitment."

"Damn. But we're looking to tape the whole season in seven weeks. You'd be done by mid-April. If you fly out next week, you can even come to our 'Midsummer Night's Dream Pajama Party' at Hef's mansion. He's a big fan of yours."

"You're kidding."

"Otherwise I wouldn't try to pry you away from your vacation. I told your agent what Hef told me, that you can name your price."

"Listen, bud, are you deaf? I said no, thank you. I am cured. I will take no part in your reindeer games. Sure, if I were dying of brain cancer and had a week to live, visiting the mansion would be my request of the 'Make a Wish Foundation,' but I'm not, and I'm not the crazy little jerk I once was. So just forget it!"

Okay. Now do you want the truth? I think I babbled something ending with, "God bless you. God bless you." I mean, what man in the world would pass up such an evening? He said they'd even pay the penalty for changing my Brazil ticket. And I'd make enough money in a seven-week shoot to really see Bahia in style, and buy a nice car for Cornell. It's times like these that I'm glad I don't have an analyst. I'm sure he'd forbid me from visiting the mansion. I know I would.

February 16, 1988

Misses March, February, & November

I wanted to turn around. I knew I should. I dreaded tempting my fragile and newfound sanity. What if one of the "Girls of the Big Ten" smiled at me? I'd dedicate months of my life to getting her to kiss me. I'd spend hundreds of dollars on pretty food. I'd give her rides to her old boyfriend, the famous NASCAR race-car champ's house, and wait hours and hours outside in the car because "they have to work some things out." I'd work up the courage to reach for her waist, but she'd twist away. Just when I'd had enough, somebody I barely knew would say, "Wow! Who was that beautiful girl I saw you with?" and I'd put up with it for months more. I swear to God I almost didn't leave the hotel.

But driving through Holmby Hills, Hef's Beverly Hills neighborhood, I had to open my mouth wide to breathe right. I was as excited as I was back in high school trying to slow dance with Joie. I had to round corners slowly because I slid dangerously on the rent-a-car's vinyl seat in my new silk pajamas. Brad Wright told me where to buy them. The saleswoman said, "Hef's pajama party, right? I just sold Paul Anka the same top and bottom, but in red."

At the gate, two weight lifters dressed as cops leaned over my rent-a-car, poked their flashlight beams around my backseat before finally waving me forward.

The lawn before the Tudor mansion was a conference of cars, administered by red-vested Mexican men.

Two women in lingerie cradled clipboards in the doorway.

Inside, so many people. So many men. Professional athletes and wrestlers, Vegas comedians I'd last seen on black-and-white sitcom reruns, the Six-Million-Dollar Man himself. No guy looked at another, everyone leaned, dodged, and craned his neck around the males in his way to catch a Playmate with a gaggle of suitors numbering less than a half dozen. On every dark-colored baronial wall dangled a portrait of a woman, nude. From the trays navigated by workers through the crowds I slid canapes into my palm, three at a time.

High heels and garters, pastel-colored push-up bras, the women looked more like marzipan candies than flesh. I recognized many of them even though they weren't sloppily washing cars, topless, or fiddling with a lasso, naked, save chaps and a cowboy hat. Eerie it was to see them so large, unfolded, and animated. Jalissa Edwin, AKA Miss February (Black History Month) 1987, was surrounded by two dozen suitors, all white and thinning of hair. Most of the Los Angeles Lakers encircled Miss November 1986, a blonde with a black woman's butt. Miss March 1986's line wasn't too bad, so I finally pushed to join her circle. I remembered that one of her turn-ons was *Lolita*. The only people I recognized in her fan club were comedian Slappy White and the World Wrestling Federation's Sergeant Slaughter.

A middle-aged man flopped his arm over her shoulder, then tried to cop a feel. Miss March jabbed him in the side, then turned right toward me.

. . . .

"It just behooves me the riffraff they let slip in here."

"You are so right. I think Nabokov said it best—"

"Austin! You made it. Now don't stay out too late tonight. Remember, our meeting is tomorrow at ten. We're all big fans of yours around here. Here, let me introduce you to Kathi Rae Walker. We're thinking of her as your co-host. You two could wear matching plaid shirts, only hers would be unbuttoned and, you know, just tied over her navel."

Brad Wright pulled me, elbow first, between Bubba Smith and I think the head coach of the Raiders.

"Kathi! I'd like you to meet someone."

Another push-up bra, more stiletto high heels, yet her blond hair was an elegant halo. I didn't remember the name, but I remembered the amyl nitrate and how it had made her centerfold come alive. I also remember the sore she gave me afterward.

"Austin, may I present Kathi Rae. Kathi's old Hollywood. Her mother was one of the sisters bathing in the train depot water tank at the beginning of every episode of 'Petticoat Junction.' "

"I really thought you should have been Playmate of the Year."

"Thanks, but shhhh! She is right behind you. But I'm really impressed with the work you've already done, and I'm really looking forward to working with you!" Then she giggled and covered her mouth.

"You two could be the Bryant Gumbel and Jane Pauley of the home fix-it world."

"Outrageous!"

"Kathi, could you show our guest the grotto? I've got to find Hef."

Silent she was, till Brad was swallowed again by the noisy house of men.

"Do you really want to see the grotto?" Her voice suddenly fell many octaves. "My husband says there are cultures growing in the waters of that cave that medical science has yet to identify. . . . What's wrong? Oh, Brad didn't tell you that I was married? If you don't want to talk to me or work with me anymore, I'll understand. I get it all the time. And if you're hoping to get lucky tonight, here's a tip: Stay away from months with Rs in them."

. . . .

"No. Don't walk away. It's just that you sound a lot different away from Brad, like Oscar Wilde trapped in the body of a Playmate."

She breathed deeply and looked away. "I should have a card printed up with my life story. But here goes: I was prelaw at the University of Colorado when a boyfriend I had just dumped took a picture of me skinny-dipping, Xeroxed it, and stuck it all over campus. I couldn't finish school there anymore, so I came back to L.A. I sent that same Xerox to *Playboy* the day the landlord padlocked my apartment for three months' back rent."

It was very cool but much quieter on the back lawn. A peacock and a flamingo stepped so carefully around us. The monkeys in the monkey house slept on each other. And no one, it seemed, was rutting in the bushes.

"Isn't your husband going to miss you?"

"He's on call tonight. He's a physician."

"Listen, please don't tell Brad, but I'm not sure whether I'll do the show or not. I was thinking of spending the summer in Brazil, and in the fall I'm going back to grad school."

"*Jura, nem fala! Te amo Brasil. Morei em São Paulo* my junior year." ("No kidding! I love Brazil. I lived in São Paulo my junior year.")

"*Incrível! Você fala muito bem!*" ("Wow! You speak so well.") And I meant it. "I've just been listening to some tapes since Christmas."

"Fuck the show, then. You'll have a blast down there."

"Well, I could use the money and we'd be done taping by April, so I could still spend the summer in Bahia."

"I guess. But be careful. You seem the type to get addicted to this life-style. You're young and good-looking yourself, for now, but it's easy to end up like these old fat guys pinching butts and coughing on themselves. . . . See that old man over there?" She pointed to a short, hairless man in his fifties helping a very young woman adjust her garter.

"At least he's enjoying himself."

"He's my father. He divorced my mom when I was three. They met on this very lawn. I was probably conceived in the grotto."

Kathi's father led the young woman toward the monkey cage.

"Kathi, could I ask how old you are?"

"Twenty-five."

"I know Boulder is huge, but the first girl I ever loved, Jenny Sheffington, should have been in your same class."

"Oh, my God! Jenny is a friend of yours? You seem so low-key. Everybody on campus knew about her, especially after that affair with the vice-provost."

"What? She never told me."

"You know she's living in Los Angeles now."

"Last time I talked to her she was in New Orleans."

"Well, I heard she's single again. Maybe we could all go out sometime? If you decide to do the show."

"I will. I think I will. You're not what I expected. We might be able to do something a little interesting."

"Brad just wants me to lean over a lot and test out the hot tub decking."

"I'll talk to him."

"Thanks. But could I ask you a question?"

"Shoot."

"It's sort of weird, but . . . I . . . I just have to ask. . . . Have you ever, you know, masturbated about me?"

"Uh."

"It's this thing I have. You wouldn't understand unless a naked picture of you cuddling a garden hose was glued to the wall of every frat house, garage, and fire station in the country. It's sort of this crazy tally I'm keeping."

I turned left and right, but no one was near enough to give me an excuse of silence. I only then noticed how the cold in the night had tightened this brilliant woman's nipples to tiny knobs.

"I don't know. Maybe once in your month. I really don't re-member. . . . Uh, probably."

"Look, I'm sorry, but it's the only way I can come close to equal footing when I'm talking to a guy. Sorry I asked."

There was so much silence between us, I thought she'd make up some excuse to leave.

"Look, a friend gave me an amyl nitrate to try, all right? For an instant your image turned into a living little three-D sexual leprechaun."

"Really?"

"I got a sore, I did it so much."

"Poor baby."

"Don't worry about it."

"Now are you . . . ?"

"Right as rain."

"That's good. It's just that if we're going to work together, I had to know. Now, would you like me to introduce you to any of my colleagues?"

"You told me I'd become an addict."

"For a guy that got an open wound from whacking off so much, I see that it's a little too late—"

"Shut up!"

"And almost all the girls would rather go out with black guys anyway. Except Jalissa, oddly enough."

"Promise you'll keep me away from these women. That's the only way I'll take the job. Bar me from the parties, bar them from the set."

"Deal." We shook on it.

"I like you, Kathi Rae."

"You *should* like me. You shared a transcendental moment with a full-color reproduction of my image."

"I was just kidding! I've never seen you before in my life, I swear."

"There you two are. Austin, I'd like to introduce you to our humble host."

I smelled his pipe before I made out his smoking jacket in the dark.

"Austin Jones. I'm a big fan of your show, big fan. I think you'll enjoy working for the 'family,' that's what we call everyone here at Playboy Enterprises, a family."

"Then can I call you Dad, Mr. Hefner?"

February 28, 1988

Michelle

Okay, okay, what comes first? I got her aboard as our producer. She arrived today. I met her here at the office. That was just fifteen minutes ago. I'm in the bathroom now, writing it all down word for word before my memory and imagination wreck it. And after this entry I hope you never hear from me again.

I didn't recognize her through the thick makeup. She teetered on high heels, couldn't look me in the eye after our long hug.

"Michelle! What happened?"

"One word and I swear I'll deck you."

"It's just that you're all dressed up and . . . and wearing makeup."

"I'm a full producer now. I've got to dress the part."

"I see."

"So . . . what do you think?"

"I've always said you probably had nice legs under all those pairs of overalls."

"Austin! Come on!"

"It looks nice. Did you get your makeup done a one of those makeover counters at Bloomingdale's?"

"Fuck you."

She turned to leave, but I grabbed her, pulled clump of tissues from a nearby box.

"All this crud isn't you. You know that."

I dabbed, then scrubbed at the cakes of powder and goop on her face. She closed her eyes and hung limp like a child when she lets her mother clean her face with a thumb and spit. Finally clean, she opened her eyes. She just opened her eyes and looked at me. Her eyes are black and infinite, and they refocused on just me after having been closed. I found myself rubbing at my heart through my chest.

"Austin? What? What's the matter ith you?"

· ·

"Can I take you . . . I don't know. Can we have dinner tonight?"

"Why are you asking like that? What? Like on a date?"

"Um . . . yeah."

"Why?"

"I don't know. I just . . . um . . . I just felt it."

"That's not funny. Stop it."

"I can't. I just felt this thing here, inside me. And I know what it means."

"Like with Didi? Joanna? Jewelle? God knows who else?"

"No one else. That's it."

She turned around and tried to leave but just circled my office, finally coming back to me. She was mad.

"I'd have to be crazy."

"Or crazy about me."

"You conceited bastard."

"No, Michelle. Just listen to who you're talking to. I wrote the book on unrequited love. You put up with years and years of listening to them whine about their girlfriends and boyfriends, you're there for them whenever they need someone to talk to, but when they need someone to kiss they always pass you by. You know I know. It almost never works. They almost never come around."

"So what are you saying . . . exactly?"

"That I came around."

For Erika,

My true love, now and forever.

About the Author

Trey Ellis, the author of *Platitudes*, lives in Venice, California.